Touching the Moon

Lisa M. Airey

Aakenbaaken & Kent　　　New York

Touching the Moon

Aakenbaaken & Kent   akeditor@inbox.com
www.aakenbaaken.com

This is a work of fiction. Names, characters, places and incidents are either the product of the author's imagination or are used fictitiously. Any resemblance of the fictional characters to actual persons living or dead is entirely coincidental.

ISBN: 978-1-938436-05-5

Dedication

To my family with love

Acknowledgements

Special thanks go to Samantha Reiter and Julie Shoemark for all their encouraging words. They read the book chapter by chapter as I wrote it and urged me on to the finish line. Thanks go to the editing team: Theresa Airey, Caroline Cassard, and Samantha Reiter and to veterinarian Jacqueline Zelepsky who assisted with the technical bits of animal surgery and animal husbandry. I am also sincerely grateful for the expert guidance and tutelage of Mike Orenduff who saw the potential in a rough draft and helped me to trim it down and dress it up! The path to publication was a long one... so nice not to have to go it alone.

Julie saw the wolf out of the corner of her eye. It trotted into the zoo enclosure with the pure unadulterated confidence of the consummate alpha male. His fur was a beautiful black-tipped gray and he moved on feet the size of horse's hoofs. From the ankle down he could have been a Clydesdale with claws.

The zoo community had affectionately named him Big Foot in tribute to the size of his paws, but the zookeepers were more mindful of his teeth. The animal had a mouthful of lethal incisors, and he loved curling his lips back to expose them.

The rest of the pack loped playfully behind him, nipping at each other's flanks or herding one another into the retaining wall that separated their living quarters from zoo patrons. They hopped over each other's backs like dolphins in the surf. They yelped and grunted and barked with delight. They had been removed for medical examinations earlier in the morning and were happy to be back into the 'man-made wild'.

She saw the lead wolf catch her scent just as she heard a small child point her out.

"Mommy, there's a lady down there with the wolves."

The pack had not been scheduled to return to the enclosure until 3 p.m. She glanced down at her watch. It read 1:35 p.m. She swallowed hard. It had read 1:35 p.m. last time she had checked too.

Safety protocol demanded an enclosure check before animals were returned to their habitat. There had been no safety check.

There were anxious voices above her, but the cacophony paled to the exploding pulse she heard in her ears. She stood rooted to the spot, her eyes wide as the lead wolf pivoted his head in her direction, nostrils flared.

Her eyes locked upon the hungry fire that burned within his dark pupils. There was silent communion between them. He was hunter. She was prey. Both of them acknowledged that she was dead meat.

The animal cut in her direction without so much as breaking stride, the rest of the pack in tow. His lips curled back as he approached her, a low, menacing growl rising from deep within his chest like the first portentous rumblings of an active volcano. The pack fanned to the left and right, flanking him, encircling her.

She didn't want to die like this. She didn't want to be ripped to shreds in front of an audience of pre-schoolers and soccer moms.

Big Foot stretched his neck out toward her, sniffing loudly, sniffing deeply. The other wolves did the same. In an instant, little tremors wracked her petite frame. She was doing her very best to remain immobile, but she was shaking visibly now.

The alpha wolf watched her intently, then did something totally unexpected. His lips rounded into a perfect 'O', and he howled softly and sadly into the circle.

There was a moment of complete silence when he finished. Even the shrieking children had quieted. Above her, she heard truck doors slamming and the quick scuffing of heavy feet across concrete.

"Tranquilizer darts," someone commanded. She heard a rifle load. Two. Three.

Big Foot howled again. Then, one by one, the other wolves joined the lament. She dropped her sampling tools and hugged herself as a series of small popping sounds were followed by surprised yelps.

"Reload."

Three animals sank to their haunches. More popping sounds, then another three sank slowly to the ground, their voices silenced mid-howl. Big Foot bolted forward, stopped a few feet in front of her then ambled slowly in her direction.

He turned toward his right hindquarters when the tranquilizer dart struck, but he whipped his head back around immediately, his eyes on Julie.

She heard a pistol click. Real bullets now.

"Don't hurt him," she shouted as a cold nose touched the back of her hand. The animal whined softly, his breath hot and moist upon her. He wrapped a pink tongue around her thumb then released it.

Several zookeepers were in the enclosure now, racing toward her, their pistols armed and at the ready.

Slowly, the animal collapsed at her feet. Slowly, Julie sank to her knees. Everything was going dark.

She looked up. The sun was like a full moon in the night sky.

She drew a shallow breath then plummeted to the earth like a meteor.

When you got right down to it, a busted lip wasn't all that bad as a graduation present. Julie had been delivered far worse in the twenty years since her mother re-married. Her only regret was that her stepfather had ruined what should have been a happy day.

She had a right to be happy, she thought with defiance. She had graduated from veterinary school with highest honors and survived an extraordinary confrontation with a pack of timber wolves as she wrapped up her internship at the zoo.

She played with the cut on her lip and tried to will the swelling down. Her mother's second husband had been a constant shadow in her formative years. And even now, damn him, he still found a way to loom large. Guess the cap and gown was too much for him to endure.

She merged onto the interstate stuffing down her hurt and anger. A light rain started to fall and she set the windshield wipers to intermittent. It had been six years since he'd raised a hand to her... ever since she turned eighteen... ever since she had moved out of the house.

She shook her head to stop what she referred to as the downward spiral, the negative thinking, the wrongful thinking. She had spent so many years blaming herself for her bruises and broken bones. But she was not to blame. She had believed that if she were perfect, everything would be all right at home. But perfect was never good enough, not when someone maliciously wanted to find fault. She gave herself a mental nudge.

She didn't deserve what happened today. Not the verbal abuse. Not the swift backhand slap. None of it. Not today. Not ever.

She pulled off the highway and into the parking lot of a Silver Diner. She took a stool at the counter and ordered up a short stack with some sausage patties and a side of hash browns. The coffee was poured without asking.

The waitress glanced at her lip, then looked up at her sharply. "Cut myself shaving," Julie said in response to the silent question. That earned her a smile.

"You traveling far?" asked the waitress.

"Oh yeah," she said meaningfully.

"Good," said the waitress. "Good for you, honey." She slipped the meal ticket through the pass-through to the kitchen and nodded at Julie before moving down the counter to refill a trucker's coffee cup.

Julie watched her for a moment then opened her road map to the ugly phosphorescent glare of the overhead lights and squinted.

Her route took her from her home state of Virginia through Maryland, Pennsylvania, Ohio, Indiana, Illinois, Wisconsin, Minnesota and on into South Dakota. Although she could probably make the journey in three to four days, her car could not. She would need to stop her travels each day when the temperature gauge started to needle upwards.

She ate her meal with purpose, eating both the orange slice and parsley sprig garnish. When the waitress brought the check, she handed Julie a to-go bag.

"What's this?" Julie asked in total confusion.

"A little roadside assistance," said the waitress warmly. "You go, girl. You hear me? You go, and don't you dare go back."

By the time she crossed the border into South Dakota, her past felt like a dust speck on the rearview.

She pulled over at the South Dakota state welcome center and scanned the horizon. Farmland, low hills. The air was sweet.

There was a map of the state mounted within a glass case and she oriented herself by the compass rose. State sport: Rodeo. State bird: Ring-necked Pheasant. State tree: White Spruce. This was home to Wild Bill Hickok, Calamity Jane, Sitting Bull, and Mount Rushmore. *Dances with Wolves* was filmed here.

She looked at the southwest quadrant of the state and the landscape photos that gave drama to her final destination. She was headed for a more rugged part of the territory, an area with deep canyons, rolling plains, pine-covered mountains and flat-topped hills called buttes.

Her heartbeat quickened.

Her little town was too small to be given a dot on the map, but she found Rapid City easily enough. She was headed about an hour's drive south of that city to the Black Hills. Although she'd never set foot in Fallston, she already considered it home.

Julie leaned against the hood of her red Corolla and polished off a bottle of water. Her car engine ticked and popped in the heat of a summer sun. She tossed her empty water bottle onto the floor of the backseat and resumed watching a herd of buffalo grazing lazily in the distance.

The used car salesman who sold her the car had promised it would easily turn 200,000 miles. She was testing his veracity every day.

She glanced helplessly at the yellow orb above her. It was darn near impossible for an engine to cool down with such hellish ambient heat. Her head pivoted as a squad car pulled up behind her, and she watched as two tall gentlemen in uniform stepped from the car and approached her.

"Howdy," one officer said by way of greeting. "Car trouble?"

"It was running a bit hot, so I'm letting it cool."

"Where are ya headed?" asked the other, glancing down at her out-of-state plates.

"Fallston," she replied. "I've accepted a position there as veterinarian."

"Really, now," the first officer said. "In Fallston? You have family there?"

"No," she replied, surprised by his surprise, "Why do you ask?"

"Uh, it's just that most young folk leave town unless they've got reason to stay. I can't imagine we're on anybody's list of must-see destinations."

"Oh," she said, her face falling. She'd driven halfway across the country to work in a place that people were ashamed to call home? "Is it that bad?"

"No! No!" the first officer said quickly, trying to erase the frown lines that he had put on her forehead.

"It's a great town, a great little town… not a whole lot to do."

"Well, I've got a new job to keep me busy, officer. I don't think I'll be lacking for things to do."

"Of course not. I wasn't inplying any such thing," he said back-pedaling. "I'm Dan Keating, by the way. This is my trainee, Elliott Rand."

"Julie Hastings", she replied, shaking his hand. She shook Elliott's too. "Thanks for stopping."

"It's our job," he said and smiled.

She smiled back. She'd never met anyone who looked so wholesome or felt so genuine. "How far out am I?"

"Oh, just another couple of miles. We'll follow you in to make sure you make it without a hitch."

"Thanks. But, I should be okay."

"Just in case," he countered.

"Appreciate it," she said, capitulating.

She got in her car and turned the key. The temperature gauge read almost normal. She gave a sigh of relief as she slipped into gear and merged onto the roadway. She was unsure of how to interpret the welcome. Either they are mighty suspicious or mighty helpful in Fallston. She checked her rearview and found Officer Keating a few car lengths behind. She wondered if he was running her tags.

She had hoped to make town before the veterinary office closed. She looked at the clock on the dashboard, then glanced quickly back to the road. Right on Seminary, left on Elm, left on Lewis.

Officer Keating had made her apprehensive without cause. The town was a picture postcard. Trees lined the streets. Kids screamed and shouted as they raced their bikes. Dogs barked. Cats darted across the roadway.

She pulled into the veterinary parking lot with butterflies in her stomach. Officer Keating cruised on past her with a wave.

She waved back then climbed out of the car, trying to erase almost two thousand miles of travel from her weary frame. She rubbed her hands together roughly to warm them. Her anxiety had turned them ice cold despite the heat.

As she entered the office, an old-fashioned door-bell jingled above her. Then, she stood frozen for a brief moment as her lungs went into vapor-lock. The office reeked. It smelled of cleaner and bleach and an underlying sickness that no amount of chemical treatment could erase.

"We're closing," said an older woman, rounding the counter with a vivaciousness that belied her age.

"I just wanted to introduce myself," Julie said quickly. "I'm your new vet."

"Ah, Miss Hastings. I'm Rose," she said warmly, positively sprinting toward her in welcome.

Julie shook her hand and assessed her new colleague. She was pencil thin, gray-haired and spry with an energy level that could fuel all of Manhattan.

"I'm afraid everyone has gone for the day. On Fridays, we try and close a little early." She patted an errant curl back into place.

"No worries. I just wanted to connect, if I could, before my first 'official' day in residence." Julie's eyes darted from the sacks of seed corn in the corner to huge bags of dog and cat food arranged in orderly piles along an ancient wall of shelving.

"I understand," said Rose. "We'll all be here Monday morning at 7 a.m. sharp. Unfortunately, I've got choir practice and am in a bit of a hurry."

"Fair enough," Julie said as she was gently ushered to the door.

"I do look forward to hearing all about your pretty self on Monday though. And I do apologize for the abruptness of my welcome. I'm a woman with a mission today. You might say... I'm on a mission from God."

"Gotcha," said Julie, wondering if Rose had ever seen *The Blues Brothers*. Julie climbed back into her car and tried to blow the overpowering stench of antiseptic and bleach out of her nose. The chemical miasma seemed to cling to her even outside the building. "Woof," she said softly to herself. Time to order baking soda by the tractor-trailer load.

She grabbed the directions to her rental property. She had found a small cottage. As she pulled into the driveway, she was relieved to see that the photos had been accurate. Self-consciously, she grabbed the manila envelope that held the keys and approached the entrance.

The kitchen was doll-house white-on-white and quite pristine. A small ice cream parlor table and four chairs were set off in a sun-soaked corner. The living room was papered in an old English rose pattern. The furniture was stuffed and the end tables boasted big lamps with beaded fringe-work.

She climbed the stairs and peeked into the bedroom. A queen-sized bed filled one-half of the room, its French country headboard and footboard in faux green patina. The room was all earth tones and soft greens. It felt like a spring forest.

The bathroom was butter yellow with daisies stenciled along the walls near the ceiling. A small window looked out over the back yard. She cracked it open then went back into each room and opened all the windows.

She unloaded two suitcases from the car then carted in her laptop and books. Not much to her worldly goods, but at least they were hers.

A little note card was pegged to the refrigerator with a ladybug magnet. "Make yourself at home," it read. The realtor had signed her name. Julie smiled. *That won't be too hard to do*, she mused. *I'm living in a fairy tale.*

She dressed professionally for her first day at work. Black skirt. White blouse. Lab coat. She bound her chestnut curls into a small bun. Although she arrived well before seven, the other veterinarian was in and waiting for her.

He was a senior gentleman, lean and lanky with dark hair that was silver-shot. His face looked both patient and kind.

"Cole Peters. I figured you'd be here early. Got a pot of coffee brewing for you in welcome."

Julie shook his hand. Although warm, his skin was papery and fragile. He was older than he looked.

"Very nice of you to truck all the way out to Fallston to take this position, Ms. Hastings," he said, pouring coffee into two mugs. "Cream? Sugar?"

"Both please. Thank you."

He doctored up her brew then passed it to her. "So tell me about yourself."

"What would you like to know?"

"Oh, just about everything and anything you'd care to share. Why veterinary school? Why Fallston? How do you like the mother-in-law house? You've got the old Sweeting place, right? Do you have family in South Dakota? Are you afraid of lions, and tigers and bears?"

Julie chuckled. "I like taking care of animals because they love so easily, so unconditionally. Fallston needed a vet, so here I am. The Sweeting place is a doll-house. I'm living right out of the pages of the Brothers Grimm. I have no family here, and I'm not afraid of lions, tigers or bears provided that there is a solid safety barrier between us."

"I do believe you addressed every burning issue I had," he said with a grin.

"I aim to please."

"I can see that." He took a sip of coffee and eyed her speculatively. "How do you handle pressure?"

"I like to think that I've got a good head on my shoulders."

"How do you handle sexism?"

She looked up at him in surprise.

"This is the Wild West, Ms. Hastings. When a cowboy comes to town looking for help with a breech birth, he might not count you as viable assistance."

"Why did you hire me then?"

"I didn't," Cole responded in a level, matter-of-fact tone. "That Kyle Johnson, newly retired to sunny Florida, did."

"I see," she said, her stomach flipping. Suddenly, her hands were quite clammy and cold.

He studied her carefully. "I'm thinking that you've got enough spunk in you to turn around popular opinion about your competency among the cattle folk. Just make sure you don't make a mistake. Not one."

"Talk about pressure."

"You seem to have a good head on your shoulders," he countered, sending her own words back at her. "Have you worked with large animals before?"

"Yes."

"Do you have a healthy respect for things with teeth?"

"Absolutely. Regardless of size."

"We have a lot of wild animals out here. You should always be on guard both inside and outside the office."

"Outside?"

"If you hike, wear a bell on your belt. Keeps the bears away. Unfortunately, some say the damn thing attracts wolves."

"You've got to be kidding," she said, her face incredulous.

"No. Unfortunately, I'm not. One rancher put bells on all of his sheep. So, as I'm told, now the chimes kind of work like a dinner bell."

"Oh!" Julie exclaimed, her hand flying to her throat.

"And wear boots that cover your ankles if you do opt to hike. They protect against snakebite and sprains."

"Anything else?"

"Watch out for elk. They might be standing in your driveway when you come home at night. My cousin is your realtor. The Sweeting place borders the woods. You don't want to hit one, and you certainly don't want one to trample you in a frightened rage."

Julie nodded, thinking of her bell-less hike over the weekend. Then she did a mental shift as she registered the lack of privacy so typical of small towns. His cousin, the realtor?

"Danger is greatest at twilight, especially when driving a car. The animals are moving and they cross the roadways as they get ready to bed down for the night. They also move right before a rain or snowfall. A lot of animals on the roadways are a sure sign of weather moving in."

The door jingled and Rose waltzed in carrying a tray of spice cupcakes. "Good morning," she enthused. "I brought us a treat for your first day. Sorry about Friday."

Julie looked to Cole and explained her brief fly-by upon her arrival in town.

"Well, shall we give you the grand tour first?" Cole asked, refilling her coffee mug.

"Sure," Julie said, mentally trying to digest the list of warnings, cautions, and snippets of sage advice. She was a vet and not ignorant of the animal kingdom, but South Dakota sounded like a different kind of world.

"Let's get you acclimated."

Somehow, Julie thought, getting acclimated might take a little more time and effort than anticipated.

The first few months were a blur. She gave all the appropriate booster shots for rabies and distemper, prescribed pregnancy vitamins, gave tick baths and extracted a mini-Frisbee from the stomach of a pygmy goat.

Cole was still handling most of the big-animal house calls while she learned the ropes. She genuinely enjoyed his company. Rose's too. The three of them worked well together and they worked hard. There were a lot of animals in Fallston.

It had taken her over two weeks to get rid of the chemical miasma that had greeted her upon her first visit. She changed their cleaning products, purchased Bad Air sponges and single-handedly gifted Arm & Hammer baking soda their annual sales numbers within a fortnight.

It was tough for her furry friends to heal in a "sick" building, and tough for her to work in such an environment as well. As she entered the office, she took a sniff and smiled secretly.

Cole hadn't said anything about the change in the atmosphere, though she did see him heft a Bad Air sponge on the first day of her stench campaign. He had pursed his lips thoughtfully, set the sponge down, and gone about his routine.

He watched her as she worked, but was never obtrusive about it. He gave her a lot of space and she filled that space gratefully. She was polite with their customers. She was competent and dependable. She worked hard for him and even harder to win his approval.

She had made big points when she had been entrusted with kennel duty one weekend. It had been her turn to take care of the boarders, but while she fed the four-legged ones Saturday and Sunday, she took care of the kennel too. Cole had been thinking of replacing the linoleum, but what greeted him

Monday morning was so brilliantly white and pristine that he opted to order new furniture for the reception area instead.

He had commented on the kennel cleaning then handed her a few office furniture catalogues over coffee mid-week saying something about her being a breath of fresh air. She had blushed at his choice of words, but was inwardly pleased. She dog-eared certain preferred selections and handed the catalogues back to him the next day.

He had ordered what she had suggested, much to her delight. As she got a pot of coffee brewing, she surveyed the reception room, picturing in her mind's eye how it would look in a few months' time.

The front door jingled. It was early yet, and she frowned at the intrusion. Two Native Americans struggled with the door as they lugged a stretcher through. She set her coffee down and raced to assist.

A wolf lay unconscious on the gurney, blood dripping freely onto the reception floor.

"This way," she instructed, ushering them into examination room #1. She slipped on a pair of gloves.

"Gunshot wound," said the elder man.

The animal's breathing was fast and shallow. She slipped a muzzle onto the unconscious animal and hooked up an I.V. with saline, then shot a sedative into the catheter. Her actions were automatic as her professional training kicked in.

"Is he someone's pet?"

"Feral."

She quickly checked the wolf's body from snout to tail looking for injuries other than the huge, gaping holes in its abdomen. The bullet had passed all the way through. There were both entrance and exit wounds.

"Why was he shot?" she asked, aligning her surgical equipment on a tray.

"Ranchers and wolves don't peacefully coexist."

Julie grunted and nodded her head in understanding. "The nurse isn't here yet," she said. "Can you help me? He's losing a lot of blood."

The elder man nodded. "I'm Ben Half Moon."

"Julie Hastings."

"Whoever did this used a powerful rifle," she said, exploring the wound. "With a very big bullet." She'd seen her share of bullet wounds in the dogs that had developed a taste for chicken back in Virginia. Live chickens. Farmers didn't take kindly to four-legged predators, domesticated or not.

"Ben, slip on a pair of gloves. I'm going to need you to unwrap some packets of gauze and place them on my tray as I ask for them. The gauze is on the far counter."

She gestured with her chin. "Grab some suture packets while you're at it."

"Sure."

It was the last time she looked up. She staunched the bleeding by cauterizing the severed blood vessels, siphoned out the gastric juices from the abdominal cavity in order to avoid corrosion then injected a saline wash to prevent infection. In the interim, Ben did whatever was asked of him. The other Native American was clearly uncomfortable with the surgery and excused himself to the waiting room.

"You ought to have considered a medical career," she teased, dropping a wad of blood-soaked gauze into the pail at her feet.

"I don't do well with the injured. Suffering upsets me greatly."

"More gauze."

He placed another wad on her tray.

"You are looking at this backwards," she chided. "The wolf isn't suffering. He is being healed."

"How old are you?" Ben asked quietly.

She glanced up at him with a tight smile.

"Old. Don't let my looks fool you."

Julie discarded another blood-soaked gauze.

"I am fooled by very little," he said.

She gave him a hard look. "Then you know that your wolf is getting better every minute. Suture packet, please."

"I'm here," said Rose, swinging through the door of the examination room.

"Can you ready a comfy kennel for me, one with a foam floor? I'll need a big space, but don't give him too much room to move around. This big boy is going to need to lie very still for a while."

"I'm on it," chirped Rose.

"Will he make it?" asked Ben.

"The bullet just nicked the duodenum, but the rest of his intestines are intact," she said, as she sewed the wounds closed. "But, it's a gut wound and the wound is serious. It is definitely life-threatening."

"Will he make it?"

"I won't know for sure until tomorrow, Ben."

The Sioux nodded. "You will save him. I know you will."

Julie looked up at him in surprise.

"You are more than a doctor. You are a healer. I feel better and I'm not even the patient."

4

Ben's words were all she could think about.

After the operation, the wolf was moved into the kennel. Although it proved problematic and inconvenient, Julie managed to move all the boarders in that room to other areas of the building so that the wolf would have true peace and quiet.

She placed a few extra Bad Air sponges near his kennel and opened a window to give him some ventilation to make sure his senses weren't overly offended. A feral wolf had sensibilities a hospital environment would diametrically oppose. She monitored him carefully. He was well-sedated for the first day or two. Protocol mandated a soft, bland diet, but the wolf turned his nose up at the canned food she offered him. He was despondent and she worried.

After two days of not eating, Julie made him a savory broth from roasted veal and beef bones. It was full of marrow and sage, pureed carrots, turnips and onion. His nose flared the moment she placed the bowl in front of him.

"Come on, Big Boy," she soothed. "Eat for me."

He did.

Always harboring a healthy fear of "teeth", as Cole put it, she passed his food bowl beneath the grill and stepped back, her voice soft and melodic. He watched her as he ate. And she watched him. In fact, he wouldn't eat without her. So she spent considerable time on the kennel floor.

She fed him well and gradually nursed him back to health. As the days passed, she sat closer and closer to the cage. He didn't shy away. In fact, if she came in for a social visit to deliver a stick of beef jerky, he seemed genuinely happy to see her.

It saddened her more than she cared to admit when Ben Half Moon came to claim him, but she was happy for his release.

Lions and tigers and bears! Oh, my!

On Saturday, she went for a hike in the state park. It was a warm day and the heat made the air fill with the heady scent of resin. She sported a nice pair of over-the-ankle leather boots, backpack, and a bell that jingled on her belt.

There would be no bears with the noise she was making as she climbed a vertical trail of rock and scree. She took an ancillary path off of the main track and followed it through the forest of Ponderosa pine and spruce. The woods grew deep and very, very hush. Unconsciously, she altered her footfall so that it made less noise.

There was a deep green pool fed by both stream and waterfall at path's end. She spread a blanket and stretched out in the warmth of the sun's rays. She ate her picnic lunch and drank the contents of her water bottle. And her eyelids grew heavy as the sun warmed her. The breeze buffeted her body in soft percussion. Woods. Warmth. It was such sweet surrender.

She awoke with a start.

The sunlight was golden and mellow through the leaf canopy above her. She must have dozed for an hour or two. Her head swiveled quickly to scope her surroundings and jolted back in shock when she found an enormous wolf watching her serenely from a rock outcrop above.

She scrambled to her feet, her heart hammering. The wolf trotted down off of the rock escarpment and entered the clearing where she had napped. He approached her tentatively then sat on his haunches as if asking silent permission.

Her mouth went dry.

The wolf inched toward her, crawling on his belly, and she tried to quell her panic, but her fear was a tangible thing. She broke out into a sheen of acrid sweat. She was trembling so hard her knees knocked together.

She stood frozen to the spot as the animal drew closer. And as he drew closer, he hugged the ground. He licked her foot then rolled over exposing his underbelly.

"Big Boy?" Her voice was corn-husk dry. She didn't know what to think. He wiggled his body, his tongue lolling, mouth open, four legs pawing upward.

She knelt down slowly and rubbed him. This was a feral wolf? He grunted with satisfaction as she massaged his legs and loved upon his ears and neck. She checked his underbelly. The wound was scabbed over and whole.

"Good to see you, Big Boy. Thank you for remembering me!" she cooed.

He sat up abruptly, and suddenly, they were face-to-face and eye-to-eye.

She looked down immediately, knowing that such close eye contact would be interpreted as a challenge. He moved closer to her, and with dawning awareness, she realized just how vulnerable she was, her naked throat but a foot from a wild animal with very large teeth.

She stood slowly and the animal watched her. She packed up her things, eyeballing him surreptitiously. When she started back down the trail, he shadowed her. But, with each step, she grew more comfortable. He walked close to her… always touching her leg.

"Jeesh," she exclaimed after a piece. "You are a tactile animal aren't you? Needy, needy, needy."

When she got close to the end of the trail, she stopped and tentatively stroked his back and flanks. He grunted in satisfaction. Her hands moved hesitantly to his chest and he pressed himself into her, voicing his pleasure. She scratched his ears and he groaned.

"Damn!" she said. "You are a most expressive beast!"

Then, without warning, he opened his mouth a fraction. All the fangs were there at the ready. She froze. In fact, she stopped breathing. Into the stillness, a pink tongue escaped to lick her hand. She collapsed on her knees in a pool of jitters. The wolf, sensing her anxiety, laid his head on her shoulder. This did nothing to quell her fear.

The both of them were locked, not sure as to how to move, when suddenly, in the distance, they heard a hiker's belt bell. It jingled, a high- pitched, melodic chime. Big Boy lifted his head and bolted into the underbrush. Her chest heaved in release and she power-walked to the parking lot in search of an *I Love Lucy* episode and a refreshing glass of Provence rosé.

The next Saturday, she hiked to her wading pool and waited on her wolf. He posted almost immediately. In fact, they were only twenty feet apart when he emerged from the underbrush. Once again, her heart started to pound, but his quiet manner reassured her.

She reached into her backpack, opened the Ziploc bag she carried and emptied some scraps of tenderloin onto a paper plate. With care, she slowly set the food out between herself and the wolf, then withdrew to sit upon her haunches.

The wolf kicked his head upwards… once… twice… sniffing. Then he inched forward slowly. Hesitantly, he took a piece of steak. His eyes never left Julie and she never moved at all. He ate everything, then sat down and looked up at her expectantly.

They sat staring at each other.

"Come here, Big Boy," she whispered. And he slunk toward her, ears perky and playful, his belly hugging the ground. He was close enough to touch, and she did so.

Very hesitantly, she stroked his fur, then she reached into the backpack and grabbed a cookie. She flattened her palm as if feeding a horse and offered her hand forward. The wolf sniffed carefully and extended his tongue to pick up the offering, ant-eater-style.

"See?" she said. "So very easy." And she put another cookie on her palm. The wolf drew closer and took that morsel from her hand as well, licking her palm for good measure.

"Don't hike alone," said the locals, but she was never alone. The wolf was her companion, and he always growled a warning when another hiker approached.

Although he usually let the interloper pass by with nothing more than a cautious and watchful eye, the wolf never let anyone get too close... to him or to her. One particularly chatty man from out-of-state almost lost his hand when he went to introduce himself to her with a formal handshake. She figured that she had about a ten-foot safety bubble around her up on that mountain, and that the perimeter was vigilantly guarded.

There were days when she re-visited the swimming hole to swim and then dry in the sun with his furry head flat upon her abdomen in complete repose. There were days when she'd find a warm patch of sunlight and curl up and take a nap, a hand lightly resting on his flank or shoulder. She feared for nothing.

He found her Saturday, after Saturday, after Saturday.

5

September opened under a cloud.

A group of high school kids hit a dog while cruising, and Julie couldn't save it. She was called out to help with a late-season breech birth, but the cow had died before she got there. She had saved the calf, barely, but needed to butcher the mother to do so.

By Saturday, she didn't even know if she had the strength or stamina to go for her weekly hike. She debated long and hard, but eventually hit the trail, although much later than usual.

No wolf.

Her disappointment was a bitter thing and she wallowed in self-pity as she hiked. She entered the clearing by the waterfall and scanned the tree line.

Still no wolf.

"Big Boy," she called. Silence.

She dropped her gear and laid out her blanket, then opted to go poke around the rocks and boulders by the waterfall.

"Hello," said a masculine voice behind her.

She was so startled that she fell. Badly. Not only did she end up in the water, but she managed to wedge her ankle tightly between two very stalwart rocks. She screamed in pain as the momentum of her fall tried to separate her foot from the rest of her. She lay there, wet, bruised and immobile, the cold water soaking her clothes and chilling her to the core.

"Are you okay?"

She tried to focus on the voice. It came from above.

She shook her head from side to side and tried to get up. A firm hand held her in place. "Not so fast. Let's make sure that you can actually get up before you do so."

She found herself looking into the jet black eyes of a giant Dakota Sioux. He was frowning at her, his lips pressed into a thin, hard line. "Did you hit your head?"

"No. Just everything else," she said, her voice strained as she grappled with the pain.

"What hurts?"

"My ankle."

The Native American worked at the stones and freed her ankle, then helped her up off of the rocks. "That your blanket?"

"Yes."

"I'm just going to pick you up and carry you to it, okay?"

"Let me walk," she said, her eyes glancing up at him then dropping down swiftly. The man looked as if he were chiseled out of stone and was just as cold and unforgiving.

"You should test your feet on flat ground, not here."

She stared at him with uncertainty.

"With your permission?" he asked, and without waiting for a response, he scooped her up and carted her back to her blanket. He set her feet down gently.

"Does the ankle bear weight?"

Julie shook her head to the negative.

"I am very sorry to have frightened you so badly. I was surprised to see someone else in what I thought was my super-secret fishing hole."

Julie sat down and unlaced her hiking boot. "I don't think that it's broken. Thank goodness I purchased the ankle support boots. But..." She scanned the tree line. Where was her wolf?

"Why don't we put your ankle in water? The chill will keep the swelling down. I'll carry you."

She looked up at him. He was a full foot taller than she and absolutely massive. She swallowed. "Let me try to walk."

She took two painful steps and paused, wiping a sheen of sweat from her forehead. The pain was excruciating. She scanned the tree line.

"I would help you if you would allow it," he said softly.

She looked back at him while she wrestled internally with the sharp stabs of pain. She really didn't have much of a choice. She took a ragged breath and nodded mutely. He stepped toward her and lifted her up into his arms as if she were weightless.

"Let's get you back to water."

"Thank you," she said.

He just nodded.

"I don't know your name."

"Gray Walker."

"I'm Julie Hastings."

He set her down by the stream and deepened a little pool by scooping out some silt and sand and gently placed her foot into the icy water. She gasped, gritted her teeth, then turned away from him, her face contorted in agony.

"You need to… power through."

She pulled her foot from the stream. "I can't. It hurts too much."

He placed his hand on her knee and ran the length of her shin with increasing pressure until her ankle and foot were in the water again.

"Trust me."

She shook her head to the negative, and scanned the tree line. "What are you looking for, Julie Hastings?"

She looked up at him in confusion.

"Are you expecting someone?"

"My wolf."

"Your wolf?"

"He's a ferocious beast," she said, her jaws still locked as she tried to control her pain. "Very protective. He'd tear you apart in less than a nanosecond if you hurt me."

"I am forewarned."

"He's big, feral, with a huge head and massive jaws."

"I get the picture."

"He won't let anyone come within ten feet of me…" her voice trailed off, ever conscious of Gray's hand upon her ankle. "Unless…"

"Unless?" he said helpfully.

"Unless… he knew I wouldn't be harmed."

"Well, we seem to have a very perceptive and intuitive wolf. He is not making an attempt on my life. He knows you are safe."

She nodded stiffly.

"How about if I catch us a couple of trout and cook them up for lunch?"

He released her ankle and stood. She shivered and released a pent up breath.

"Does the water chill you?"

"It's the pain," she lied.

He held her eyes for just a second too long, long enough to make her uncomfortable with her untruth, then switched the subject. "How did you befriend your wolf?"

"I'm a vet. He was brought to me injured. I nursed him back to health."

"He's tame?"

"Well, he was wild when I met him, but he's domesticated now."

"Women have that affect on men, I'm told."

She almost smiled. "He found me hiking one day after he had healed. In fact, he always finds me when I'm in the woods. It's odd not to see him."

Gray cast his line and was rewarded with a strike. He reeled in the fish in a furious spray of water. "Do you always hike at the same day and time?"

"More or less, but today, I'm a little later than usual." She test-wiggled her ankle and was rewarded with a shooting stab of pain. She grunted softly. "Perhaps he thought I wouldn't hike today."

Gray dropped the trout into his fish basket and cast the line again. Strike.

"Either you are an extraordinarily talented fisherman or there are some mighty hungry trout in this stream." She paused. "Perhaps I really should remove my foot."

Gray turned and gave her a smile. His eyes twinkled bright and happy. "Your foot is safe. I've caught the two great whites that were circling."

She watched as he collected dry twigs and deadfall and kindled a small fire. When he had it burning steadily, he gutted the fish and skewered the two trout on two thin, pliant sticks and cantilevered them over the open flame.

"Are you allowed to do that in a state park?" she asked.

"No."

"I didn't think so. Aren't you worried about rangers?"

"Absolutely not. This is my state, my state park, my fish."

"What logic!" she said with a snort. So what do you do professionally... outside of blatantly skirting the law by syllogism?"

"I'm a youth counselor over at the Sioux reservation."

"Teach by example, do you?" This earned her an ear to ear grin. "Do you like what you do?" she asked, frowning at him in return.

"I do, when I'm successful in steering someone in the right direction. Do you like your veterinary work?"

"Most days," she said. "I feel great when I save an animal, horrible when I lose one."

He nodded in understanding.

"This week was a rough one," she said in a tone that ended that line of conversation.

"You're not from around here." It was a statement of fact.

"No. Are you?"

"I've lived here all my life."

That explains his fearlessness with regard to park rules. He probably knows the rangers, went to school with them and buys them beers on Saturday night.

He tested the fish with a small penknife then transferred them from the sticks onto a flat piece of wood pulled from his backpack. Opening them up to expose the white flesh, he removed the bones. "I have forks," he said. "But it honestly tastes better if we use our fingers."

She scooped up a morsel and popped it into her mouth. She couldn't help herself. She moaned. "My God, this is fantastic."

Gray nodded and took a bite himself. "How's the ankle?"

"Numb," she replied, focused on the fish in front of her.

"I'll have to carry you down the mountain."

"You can't carry me down the mountain. I'm heavy. Besides, as soon as I get feeling back in my foot, I think I'll be able to walk."

"If you walk today, you'll limp tomorrow," he replied, snagging another piece of flaky trout. "I'll carry you."

His face was fierce, darkly so. She had to work at keeping her voice modulated when she answered. "No. And thank you. Really."

Her eyes lifted to scan the tree line.

"Tell me about this wolf of yours. Your eyes hunt for him constantly."

"Oh," she said, heat rising to her cheeks. "He's quite special. More human than animal, really."

She stopped speaking abruptly and they locked eyes.

Gray looked amused. "I'm not offended by such thinking, Ms. Hastings. I'm Sioux."

A soft breeze wafted over her skin and she closed her eyes, chastising herself for her stupidity. When she opened them, Gray was staring at her. The earnestness of his gaze unnerved her.

"Sorry," she said. "I'm just out of sorts today."

He nodded, then packed up his gear, rested it by a tree and returned to her. "I would like to help you. First, let's pack up your things, then, let's talk about whether you are up to a hike… or not."

As he folded her blanket and re-stuffed her knapsack, she pulled her foot from the water, dried it on her right pants leg and put it gingerly back into her hiking boot. She stood and took a tentative step. The ankle ached, but the stabbing pains were gone. She took another step. She was mobile, but the idea of walking a few miles downhill was out of the question.

"Can you walk?"

She shook her head.

"I didn't think so." He slid both packs onto his shoulders then lifted her up effortlessly into his arms. "You are in safe hands, Julie." He squeezed her lightly. "Look around. There is no wolf tearing at my throat."

Her breathing quieted. "Thank you, Gray."

For a few moments, they were silent. He fell into an easy rhythm as he trudged downhill. He was sure-footed and soft on his feet despite the fact that he carried her in his arms and all their gear on his back.

"Julie?"

"Yes?"

"Why are you so afraid?"

The question was so caring and spoken so tenderly that she decided to answer it.

"My stepfather beat me badly," she said, "All through my growing-up years, I was his personal punching bag. He was a big man. You are a big man. Big men scare me."

He could hear the frightened child in her very words. "Not every man is a beast."

"I know that. I'm grappling with that. Unfortunately, this is not something that I can... get over... quickly."

"Why didn't your mother protect you?"

"I don't know," she said. "And I don't know why she stays with him. I left home as soon as I could, and I left the state at the first opportunity."

"You don't keep in contact?"

"No."

"Other family members?"

"Um... could we talk about something else?" She squirmed in his arms, physically expressing her emotional discomfort.

"Of course," he said. "I'm sorry."

"I try not to think about the past too much," she explained. "That's all. It's not a place I want to be."

It took almost an hour to reach the parking area, so he filled the awkward silence with tales of his childhood... his first pony, his first stint as a cowboy, his first rodeo. The stories were fascinating and he had an interesting way to tell them. He'd make a statement then qualify it. But the qualification was always expressed as a question that she had to answer. He made her an active part of the story.

"On my tenth birthday I got a four-legged present," he said. "You know what every ten-year-old boy wants for a pet, don't you?"

"A puppy?"

"That's very East Coast, Ms. Hastings."

"A mountain lion?"

"Tsk. Tsk."

"A horse?"

"Ah, third time lucky. And of course you can imagine the terribly original name for said beast?"

"Lightening?"

"Very good!"

His voice was deep and comforting, but she was stiff in his arms. Tightly wound.

"Did you drive over?" he asked, stepping onto asphalt. He searched the lot and eyed a police cruiser making the rounds.

"No, I walked."

"Then, I'll carry you home."

Dan Keating pulled up beside them and powered down his window. "Everything okay here?"

"No, actually," said Julie, "I've sprained my ankle. Mr. Walker was kind enough to cart my clumsy self down half the mountain."

Gray set her lightly to her feet and she wobbled slightly, all her weight on one leg.

"Would you like for me to take you home?" Dan asked.

"Could you?" she asked, relief washing over her. "I've imposed on this gentleman more than enough for today." She turned to Gray and offered her hand. He took it. "Thank you. Thank you for everything."

"My pleasure," he said with a nod.

Gray helped her into the squad car and handed her her pack. "Keep it iced. Keep it up."

"Will do," she replied brightly, trying very hard to mask her pent up anxiety with politeness.

Dan pulled away and she shivered violently.

"You all right?" he asked, his eyes sliding in her direction.

"No," she said, "Yes, he's just... Gray is... just a little scary, that's all."

Dan nodded. "He didn't do or say anything to upset you, did he?"

"No," she swallowed. "Not at all. He was great. It's just, well, I don't know him. And I was alone. And he's BIG and he's scary." She swallowed again. "I'm just glad he's such a good guy. He is a good guy, right? He wouldn't have hurt me, right?"

She was babbling.

"Hey." Dan pulled to the curb.

She turned to face him, her face pale, and her eyes large.

"I'm going to stop by Jake's BBQ and get us some nice beef brisket and a side of beans. Rib-sticking stuff. You can wash it all down with a nice little pilsner. Then I'll take you home."

She opened her mouth to protest.

"Don't make me use the handcuffs."

She shook her head.

"Gray is rather on the monster-side of mean as far as looks go," he said, throwing the car into gear. "And I can see where you'd be terrified."

She nodded vigorously.

"I can't imagine meeting that man in a dark alley on a moonless night." She shivered. "He had me in vapor-lock in the bright light of late afternoon."

"We'll just order you up a very large little pilsner. You'll be fine. I've never had any trouble out of that man, despite his appearance."

He pulled into Jake's and helped her inside. She wasn't particularly hungry, but she tucked into her beef and beans, grateful for the chatter of voices around her. She drank her beer as if she had just walked out of the Sahara.

"He really had you spooked, didn't he?" Dan asked.

"Oh! No," she said, becoming aware of her body language. She was hugging herself. She released her own arms and took a more moderate sip of beer.

Dan was watching her carefully.

"Really!" she said, "Hey, and the food is terrific."

He nodded.

"He was nothing but a gentleman. And you didn't have to do this." She gestured to the food on the table.

"I've been wanting to ask you out," he said carefully, "And trying to figure out a way to get you to go." When she didn't respond to that, he continued. "Word has it you don't date."

"Well, I'm just trying to get settled in. I'm taking things slow."

He nodded and sat back against the cushion of the booth, surveying her. "Perhaps in the new year?"

"Perhaps." She gave him a small smile. He was ruggedly handsome and his eyes were so blue. He had a sassy bit of curl to his locks too. Marlboro Man. He was a Marlboro Man in a police uniform.

"Come on, I'll take you home."

He wrapped his arm around her waist when she stood and helped her back to the squad car. He also had her by the waist when he deposited her on her front door step.

"Thank you kindly," she said.

"It was my personal pleasure, Ms. Hastings." He kissed her hand.

Her heart stuttered, and for the second time in one day, she forgot to breathe.

Julie baked Dan a tin of gingersnaps and dropped them off at the station that Monday. He was out on patrol, but she put a post-it note on the tin at the reception desk. The dispatcher/receptionist was friendly and polite and overly helpful. She introduced herself as Barbara Rand and was taking total delight in the fact that Dan was getting a cookie delivery.

Elliott, the young cadet who had been accompanying Dan the day she first drove into Fallston, was just getting off duty. He looked exhausted and spent, yet when she caught his eye, he smiled at her in recognition.

"You look a little down," said Julie, as they stepped outside.

"That obvious, huh?" he responded, looking at his feet.

"Did you lose someone, Elliott? Is there anything I can do?"

"Yeah, I lost someone, Julie." He rubbed his forehead. "My girl decided that she wanted to move to New Orleans. She got a big break as a lead singer in a jazz band there and took it."

"Hey. Long distance relationships can work. Don't you worry." She looked at his sandy brown hair as it tossed in the wind. His eyes were dark. Looked like he hadn't been getting much sleep.

He glanced up at her with a pained expression. "She doesn't want to come back."

"Okay," she said slowly. "Would you consider moving to New Orleans, then?"

"No," he said, his voice heavy with regret. "That city would kill me as much as this back-country kills her."

Julie sighed deeply. "Then, Elliott, its best that you both found this out before you were married with kids."

His head shot up sharply.

"Forgive me for being blunt. You two weren't right for each other. Perhaps you were good for each other for a time, but now you both have to move on."

He frowned.

"You know what? I think we all live our lives in little compartments like separate and distinct TV shows… childhood, adolescence, relationship one, relationship two, etc. We are single and wild, married and settled, widowed and lonely or divorced and fancy-free. Some of the shows last longer than others, that's all. But every television series comes to an end. And next season, well, there's a whole new list of offerings."

He laughed despite his pain.

"Compartmentalizing 'things' helps me move on."

"And where are you in the TV guide, Julie?"

"Right now, I'm the featured attraction of the Discovery channel, Elliott. Maybe you should try that out tonight."

He grinned. "The Discovery channel?"

"Yeah." She shrugged then grew serious. "With the two of you pulling towards such opposite poles, did you ever feel that you compromised more than you should have?"

"She said so."

"Why?"

"Well, her love is jazz. I like country and pop. She was the lead singer in my band."

"You have a band?"

"The Copper Pigs."

"The Copper Pigs?"

"We're all cops. So, we took the Brit slang word for policeman and the American slang word for policeman and put them together to come up with our name."

"What's your passion? Music or police work?"

He frowned again, and took a deep breath. "It's hard to explain really. I love being part of a team. I love the force, that sense of community. It makes me very happy. But there's a part of me that needs to come out from behind the badge and make some noise."

"I hear you."

Dan Keating pulled up in his squad car. They both watched him approach, but Julie wanted to finish the conversation.

"Elliott, there is no reason you can't do both. I bet any nightclub would be very happy with a band that's all cops. Imagine! They'd have their own security squad right up there on stage."

His jaw dropped. "I never looked at it that way."

"Market it that way," she said, giving him a slow and significant nod.

Dan stepped up to the two of them, his eyes darting back and forth between their faces. It was obvious that something significant had transpired. Elliott hadn't smiled in weeks.

"Hello, Officer Keating."

"Hello, Ms. Hastings. What brings you to my world?"

"You, good sir. I dropped off a tin of gingersnaps at the front desk for you, as a thank you for Saturday."

"A thank you wasn't necessary, but I'm very grateful for the cookies. Where are you headed, Elliott?" Dan asked.

Elliott wasn't headed anywhere, but he got the hint.

"Home."

"Good day?" Dan asked.

"Yes," said Elliott cryptically, receiving all kinds of silent signals in man-speak that he was to vacate ASAP.

"See you tomorrow."

"Yeah, tomorrow," said Elliott. He smiled at Julie and nodded to Dan then headed off.

"Can you visit for a while?" Dan asked.

"No, actually, I can't. I had a small break in my day, which is why I stopped by, but I need to head back to the office."

"I see." He didn't hide his disappointment well. "Thank you for the cookies."

"Enjoy."

Both of their heads turned as Elliott drove by with a honk to the horn.

"Did you know about his break-up?" asked Julie.

Dan grimaced. "It was for the best. She was no good for him."

"Did you tell him that?"

"On multiple occasions."

"I see." She paused. "Well, good for him then that he's escaped whatever would have dragged him down."

"He's too young to see the agony he's been spared, but he will."

"Relationships are messy, aren't they?" she said softly. "And there is no happily ever after. Good that he has you for a touchstone."

He looked at her quizzically.

"Have a good week, Dan."

6

Gray Walker stopped by the office a few days after the hiking accident to check on her ankle. She wiggled it for him and thanked him again, handing him a tin of homemade cookies in gratitude for the lift down-mountain. He was not only surprised by the gift, but genuinely pleased.

"I baked them for you," she said by way of explanation, "But then I had no idea how to get them to you. I'm so glad you stopped by."

"Me too."

Dan Keating stopped by that week to check on her also. He gave Rose quite a scare by waltzing into the waiting room wearing his police uniform, but she recovered as soon as she realized that it was a social call and that he had no intentions of taking one of their more thirsty bloodhounds to the pound for raiding the local goose farm. For the fifth time.

He had wanted to chat, but Julie was pulled into an emergency surgery with a very sick feline.

That day it snowed, and that first snowfall descended as a permanent base for subsequent storms. Julie's days were an endless battle against Mother Nature. She chipped ice off of her car, shoveled her driveway, and salted every surface in sight. Again, and again and again.

Her world consisted of her home and the veterinary office and the connecting distance between the two. She spent Thanksgiving with Cole and his large circle of friends. She shared Christmas with Rose. But she was going to celebrate New Year's Eve alone, by choice.

The last day of December ushered in yet another layer of snow. They closed up the veterinary office at noon and she drove home in good spirits despite the weather.

To her surprise, a very anxious wolf was waiting on her doorstep. His forelegs pounded the ground like pistons in excitement at her arrival. She hadn't seen him in weeks and was nonplussed to find him standing in front of her.

She glanced around. The streets were deserted. Nobody was out in this weather, but she wondered how he had found her and why he had dared to venture so far into town.

"Well, now, if you aren't a welcome sight!" She opened her front door.

"I'm going to watch old movies and camp out in front of the fireplace all day and all night." He chased his tail. "Sound good to you, too? We'll make a party of it. Do you want to come in?"The wolf sniffed in the doorway, then stepped inside and slowly walked his way through the entire house. She stripped off her winter gear and followed him as he made the rounds.

When he returned to the living room and sat down, she shut the door and locked up.

She scratched his neck as she made toward the kitchen. "Hungry?"

He yipped.

She warmed up some beef stew and served his lukewarm in a bowl on the floor. She ate hers standing up. After cookies, she started a fire, kicked off her shoes, popped in a movie, and settled into a thick blanket on the floor, her back to the sofa. The wolf lay down beside her, quiet and content.

They snacked, they snoozed, and they snuggled… his big wolf head in her lap, her hands stroking his thick fur. He grumbled in displeasure when she got up for any reason and nudged her arm if she stopped loving on him.

"You know that you are incredibly demanding," she complained.

The doorbell rang.

Big Boy was on his feet in an instant. Julie hushed his hostile growl as she made her way to the door. When she saw that it was Officer Keating, she opened it.

"Hey! What brings you by?" she asked, stepping back to allow him to enter. A gust of frigid air stepped with him across the threshold. His face was ruddy from the cold and his eyes seemed all the more blue by stark contrast. As he stepped close to her, the wolf growled again, deep and low.

"Holy hell!" Dan yelled, reaching for his gun.

"No, no," she said, crossing over to the wolf and placing her hand on his massive shoulder. When standing, he reached her waist. "This is my wolf."

Dan just stared at her. "You've brought a wild animal into your home?" He was incredulous.

"He showed up on my doorstep today."

Dan frowned. She could see him processing the threat… to her, to the community.

"I don't like this," he said, his voice official.

The wolf growled again, his lips curled back, exposing large canines.

"He must have been in the woods behind the house and smelled me."

Dan's frown deepened. "Do you have any idea of the danger you're in?"

"None at all," she said, pinching the wolf's muzzle together with her hand. He stopped growling immediately. When she released his snout, he licked her hand.

"Can you control him?"

"Yes. He's being protective, that's all."

"Protective?"

"Yeah, he's quite the body guard. Once on the trail, a hiker approached me. The guy was quite friendly, totally non-threatening. But, Big Boy," she faltered, opting to give the story a more generic ending. "Big Boy didn't like him."

Dan looked at the wolf. "If I approached you, what would he do?"

"How about if I approach you instead?" she said, stepping toward Dan and placing her hand atop his... the hand that was still resting on his gun.

She stood in front of him, soft and warm. Her chestnut hair fell in soft curls down her back and her green eyes looked up at him expectantly. He forgot about the wolf.

"You are so beautiful," he said quietly.

"Thank you," she said with a blush. "But you didn't stop by to tell me that."

"No, it just kind of popped out."

"So, what can I do for you, Officer Keating?"

"Today, well, at midnight, we start a whole new year."

She nodded.

"You're settled in."

She nodded again, her eyes wary.

He moved toward her and a menacing growl filled the air. With a grimace, he pulled her outside on the front step and pulled the glass storm door shut behind them. She shivered in the cold and he stepped closer to block the wind.

"I was hoping you'd consider another meal at Jake's."

"Oh." She turned to see Big Boy's snout flat against the glass, his growl a ferocious rumble.

"I'll settle for a maybe."

He watched the emotion play across her face.

"Maybe." Her voice was a whisper.

"Okay!" he said, clearly considering this a major victory. "Happy New Year, Julie." And he lifted her chin and kissed her gently on the lips.

Big Boy tried to tear the door off its hinges.

"You need to go, Dan," she said, looking back at the wolf.

"You need to get rid of that wolf," he said, backing toward his squad car. He watched her step back into the living room, the wolf calm and sedate by her side. As she reached up to tuck a Christmas light back into position, the wolf glared at Dan and bared his teeth again. When Julie looked down, the wolf erased his mal intent. He was all smiles and pink tongue.

7

Officer Keating dropped by her house the first Saturday in January and officially requested two hours of Julie's time. He put chains on her tires then took her out to an empty parking lot to show her how to drive in the snow and how to pull out of a skid.

She didn't want to go, but he had insisted, telling her that the excursion was part of his official duties in keeping the roadways safe. She had raised an eyebrow at that one, but the look he gave her was no-nonsense, and she had acquiesced.

As it turned out, she actually responded instinctively behind the wheel, spinning her tires in the opposite direction of the skid to pull herself out of rotation. Dan was pleased. He instructed her in the art of downshifting to climb snow-covered inclines. They practiced braking on ice. She had so much adrenaline in her by the end of the lesson that she was positively quivering.

She followed him to Jake's, expertly navigating the treacherous roadways then whooped like an Indian when she emerged from the car healthy and hale. They both settled next to Jake's roaring fireplace with a hot mug of Irish coffee.

"You did well," he said, clinking his mug to hers.

"You are a good teacher."

He stared at her, his blue eyes twinkling. She took a sip of her hot spiked drink and hummed. "Thank you for taking me under your wing."

"I'd rather do that then have you wrap yourself and your vehicle around a telephone pole."

"I'm actually a very good driver," she said defensively.

"That's obvious. But unless you grew up surviving our winters, you need some Special Driver's Ed."

"Do you offer this service to all new residents?"

"You're the first new resident we've had in a while, and the first new resident that's needed a winter driving lesson."

"Do you know everybody in town, Dan?" She slid her eyes to the stone fireplace and the stack of burning logs within it. They glowed orange hot and emitted a heat that rendered her boneless. Or was that the Irish whiskey?

"Most," he said. "The British have a special theory regarding crime prevention. Instead of just outfitting their police force with firepower, they increased the number of cops on the beat. The town and city cops walk their area of coverage, get to know the residents, get to know their daily routines. That way if something seems off or doesn't quite fit the usual patterns, they know immediately. And because of their presence, their constant and watchful presence, thieves and thugs are less likely to try anything."

"Interesting." She took another sip of her drink.

"You know, in the USA, the statistics say that there is very little small town crime. But it's not that the people that live in rural areas are any more virtuous, it's just that the police force knows the town folk. They recognize something immediately when it's out of place, so do the neighbors, and they're not afraid of speaking up. It's a good type of Big Brother-ing."

He watched her grow solemn and thoughtful. "Earth to Julie."

She turned to him and smiled.

"What were you thinking?"

She shrugged, but the seriousness was back in her eyes. "Just that it must have been very nice growing up here." She looked to him for confirmation.

"It was," he said carefully. "But routines can get tedious, even if they are safe."

She nodded and looked back to the fire. "Still," she said quietly, "It must have been very nice."

Elliott walked in with a couple of friends, spotted them and headed in their direction. His brown hair stood straight up with static electricity when he removed his skull cap. After removing his gloves, he tried to tame it, but only succeeded in making it worse. Dan ribbed him a bit as he stood to shake Elliott's hand then greeted each of the men in turn. Julie stood also and was quite surprised when Dan tugged her in front of him, placed a hand on her hip and introduced her to each of the men. They were all policemen, and according to Elliott, all members of his band.

Robert, whom they called Ro-bear, was the drummer. He was tall and lanky with blonde hair, a square jaw, crooked nose and chocolate brown eyes. He took her warm hand into his and shook it firmly.

Petey played bass guitar. He was shorter than the rest of them, but that wasn't saying much. He still stood about 5' 9" and wore an impish grin that reached all the way to his sparkling blue eyes.

"I can see that you are trouble, Petey," she said as she shook his hand. The other men roared and did a lot of back slapping and upper arm punches. She must have accurately pinned his personality.

"'Trouble' is his middle name," said Dan with a chuckle. "We're really not all too sure that he's on our side."

Petey didn't look the least bit offended by the comment, but she gave him a look of friendly warning for good measure then turned to meet George.

"I play the harmonica and fiddle," George said, breaking into an ear-to-ear grin. "I'm no trouble at all."

"That's not what your wife says," quipped Petey. There was another round of raucous laughter. Suddenly, all the men were pulling up chairs, studiously ignoring Dan and his ferocious frown, and delving into some of the wildest, funniest banter she'd ever heard. Dan, unfortunately, was on the receiving end of most of the jokes and he groused at them in displeasure, but that only served to goad them on.

Elliott had plopped down right next to her. He leaned into her, nudging her gently when he delivered private commentary on the dialogue at hand. He had outrageous one-liners to deliver about everything and everybody, like a comedic commentator at a sports event. He was so "little boy"– playful, high energy, exuberant and totally immune to her personal space. He invaded it constantly, so much so, that she ended up nudging him back across her invisible comfort line, elbowing him in the ribs on multiple occasions. He seemed to enjoy the contact and made it a sport.

Two trays of chicken fingers, four baskets of French fries and two pitchers of beer later, Julie stood.

"I need to swing by the veterinary office, gentlemen. It's been a lovely afternoon." She shook hands all way round.

Dan rose with her and laid a few bills on the table, nodding at the men as he took his leave.

"I'll walk with you, Julie," he said, taking her elbow.

"Thanks, Dan." They moved toward the exit door. "You don't want to stay?"

"No," he said. "It was a good time, but I've got some work to do also." When they reached her car, he brushed off a light dusting of snow.

"You're a good man, Charlie Brown. Thank you for today."

"A peck on the cheek, here." He lowered his head to receive payment.

She kissed him, then said, "Give me the other side." She kissed him there too.

"Two kisses. Well, well, Ms. Hastings. You give me hope!" His eyes narrowed. "How is that wolf of yours?"

"Oh, he comes and goes. And don't worry. He's not cutting through town. I watched him the other day. He moves about through the forest in back of me."

Don nodded thoughtfully.

"I don't leave him in the house alone."

"There's something not quite right about him. I can't put my finger on it." Dan scanned the sky. "It's the eyes, I think. They are… very knowing."

She shivered. "I know that he was a little aggressive with you, but he's very gentle with me."

Dan scowled at her, then spoke firmly and not with a little heat, "A little aggressive with me? I want you to be careful, Julie. I really do. I don't think you should be letting him inside at all. This is Officer Keating addressing you now."

"All right," she said, a sternness coming into her voice as well. "I will take your counsel under advisement." Her posture grew rigid and there was a firm and stubborn set to her jaw also.

"Hey," he said soothingly, "I'm just concerned about you." He smiled at her, but his eyes were troubled. He reached for her and tugged her arm as she turned. "Julie, I'm not trying to boss you around. I'm just trying to keep you safe. It's my job. It's my nature."

8

Cole Peterson greeted her at the veterinary office door the next morning with a hot cup of coffee in a go-cup and a medical kit.

"I'm due up at the Double Bar Ranch this morning," he said, his face frowning. "But my arthritis is acting up. I'd like for you to cover for me."

"Of course!"

"Tim Whiting is afraid that one of his best bulls has infectious kerato conjunctivitis, and he doesn't want to contaminate the herd."

"Does he have the animal in isolation?"

"Yes."

"Any words of wisdom?"

"Whiting is an ex-Vietnam vet. The only thing tender on that farm is the beef."

She smiled. "Roger that, Chief. I can be tough."

"I know. That's why you're still here."

As it turned out, Whiting had been just a tad bit paranoid. The bull had an infected tear duct which was easily remedied. She treated the animal with an antibacterial eye-wash and gave instructions on how to repeat the application in her absence.

"I've taken a blood sample just to make sure that we're not dealing with a systemic infection," she told him. "Why don't you wait until the results confirm my diagnosis before returning the bull to the herd?" He nodded at her words. "But I think you're going to be all right."

He nodded again, but there was genuine fear in his eyes. As an ex- Vietnam vet, she was sure that he wasn't comfortable with any abnormal bodily fluids. Tropical diseases were ruthlessly quick and debilitatingly effective in ushering you to a watery grave, and most of that water was your own.

She cleaned herself up then headed back to the office, handling her vehicle like a practiced snow driver.

"No drifting, no drifting," she whispered to her Corolla as she rounded a sharp s-curve.

She took her foot off of the accelerator immediately, her jaw falling slack in surprise. A squad car was off to the side of the road with its door open and lights flashing. A red sedan pulled out full-speed just as she slowed. Her eyes caught the tag – BDR 421 – then the policeman, lying in a pool of red in the snow.

In her panic, she slammed on the brakes and spun 360-degrees before she skidded to a stop in the middle of the road. She felt as if she were in slow motion as she put the car in park and pulled the emergency brake. She left the engine running and the car door open as she bolted in total panic to take care of… Elliott!

He was on his back with a gunshot wound and bleeding out. She opened his jacket to examine the wound. The bullet had nicked an artery. A thin jet of red blood pulsed from his chest like a geyser with every heartbeat. He was still breathing, but his breathing was labored.

"Elliott? Can you hear me?"

He didn't respond.

She raced to the squad car, grabbed the radio and froze. Elliott Rand, cop. Barbara Rand, police receptionist and dispatcher. It clicked in a nano-second. Her voice was pure stainless steel when she squeezed the toggle.

"This is Julie Hastings. There is an officer down by the red barn with the hex sign. Gunshot wound. We need a Medivac with blood on board. Issuing an APB for a red car, Bad Dog Running 421. Plates with a setting sun."

She heard Elliott's mother respond. "Roger that. All units. All units. Officer down on Bluemount Road."

Julie raced for her medical kit and the spare blankets she kept in the trunk and wrapped Elliott as warmly as she could, then ran back to the squad car.

"Barbara," she said, breathing hard. "I need your permission to clamp an artery. I'm not a people doctor. I'm a vet, but I don't think the Medivac is going to get here in time. He's losing too much blood. Will you allow me to do what I can to save your son?"

It was a brutal way to tell Barbara the bad news, but Julie had no time for polite protocol.

"Yes," came the quivering reply. "Oh, God. Please. Please save him, Julie."

Julie released the radio and raced back to Elliott, donned surgical gloves and staunched the bleeding. She had to take a deep breath to steady her hands. "It's just a little pig," she chanted over and over as her fingers slid inside his chest cavity. "Just a little pig."

By the time the helicopter had arrived, she had stopped the bleeding, but that didn't change the fact that Elliott had lost too much blood.

The helicopter blades never stopped turning as the paramedics strapped Elliott to a stretcher and loaded him on board. She climbed in with them and watched as they cut the sodden clothes off of his body, wrapped him in heat blankets and heat pads then hooked him up. They delivered an I.V. in one arm and administered blood in another.

And it wasn't going to be enough.

She watched Elliott's blood pressure fall in disbelief. She had tried so hard. She squeezed her eyes shut in frustration, then slapped the inside of her elbow. "My blood type makes me a universal donor and I'm clean. Let's get a transfusion going right now into another part of him."

"How much do you weigh?" asked the paramedic.

"I'm 130 pounds."

The paramedic just looked at her. He wasn't buying.

"I'm a medical doctor," she countered. "I know the risks. I'm telling you that my weight is 130. Stick me. He's got a family. People who love him."

"And you don't?" the man countered.

"And I don't," she said. She wasn't bitter. She wasn't sad. He could see the naked truth in her eyes.

"Please," Julie said, "Let's save this young man."

Person-to-person transfusions were uncommon, but not disallowed if the situation was desperate enough. It was desperate enough. There was risk on both sides. The recipient ran the risk of contracting disease. The donor ran the risk of donating beyond the safety limit. There was no way to monitor the transfusion amount.

Julie showed her credentials and rolled up her sleeve.

The pilot radioed in, "Command, this is Chopper One. We've got a situation. I'm going to need two stretchers and two immediate blood transfusions upon arrival."

The men at the police station, who were monitoring the emergency channel, frowned in confusion. Dan, traveling with his siren wailing and his lights flashing en route to Rapid City Hospital just clenched his jaw. He knew exactly what was going on.

If Julie died, he was going to kill her.

Dan entered the hospital room smelling of stale coffee and nervous sweat. Julie was hooked up to numerous monitors and was receiving a pint of blood. She was milk white and fighting little tremors.

"Dan!" Her relief was written all over her face. "I need a blanket or two or ten."

"I'm on it."

She closed her eyes and heard an enormous amount of shouting, then felt nothing but warmth. Dan pulled up a chair and sat beside her, holding her hand.

He swallowed, taking in the antiseptic white walls, white bed, and the gunmetal gray machines surrounding it. "Julie?"

"Yes?" she whispered, eyes closed.

"How much do you weigh?"

"Enough. Enough to save a life. Sometimes, Dan, breaking the law is the right thing to do." She paused. "Has he slipped into a coma?"

"No. They cleaned him up, removed a bullet, sewed him back together and gave him more blood. He's going to be just fine."

"I was hoping so."

"You saved him."

"Yeah. Only because I am a vet, and I was working on a Copper Pig." Her tongue was sticky inside her mouth. She had to swallow, before she continued. "Funny, huh?"

"Very funny, Julie." He rubbed his thumb back and forth on the back of her hand. "We caught them. Bad Dogs Running. We caught them."

Her smile was fleeting. "I'm so glad."

"How do you feel?"

"Fine."

He smiled. As a cop, he could smell an untruth a million miles away. "You don't lie very well."

"I'll have to practice up."

He squeezed her hand. "What can I do for you, Julie?"

She was suddenly very focused. "I left my car in the middle of the road."

"Shhhh," he soothed. "We took care of that already. It's sitting in your driveway. The keys are at the station."

"I had a blood sample for the lab."

"We figured that out too," he said. "One of the men delivered it to Cole Peters. Cole said it was still sound. Don't worry."

"Okay. Okay. Thank you, Dan. Thank you so much."

"Anything else I can do for you, Julie?"

"When I wake up, can I get a hot cup of coffee and a Krispy Kreme?"

"You're easy, Ms. Hastings."

"That's what they all say."

The next day, Dan delivered. There was a hot tray of Krispy Kremes and a café latte from a gourmet coffee shop at perfect sipping temperature. She inhaled everything.

The hospital released her and she traveled back to Fallston in Dan's squad car. She slept most of the way. He didn't want her leaning against the car door so she leaned against his shoulder instead, wrapped within his right arm. He smelled of man and metal and gunflint.

He deposited her on her doorstep with a furrowed brow. "I'm going to get some carry-out and come back," he said.

"I'll be okay."

"Yes. Yes, you will. As soon as I feed you some dinner."

Dan opened her kitchen door and escorted her into her house, flipping on lights in the process. "Do you have any special cravings?"

She looked at him. "I should pack protein."

"Huh?"

"Beef. I need red meat."

"Got it. Brisket. Beans. Rolls."

"Coleslaw?"

"I swear. Women do love their vegetables. I've never quite understood the attraction."

He left to fetch something to eat while she snipped off her hospital bracelet and took a shower. Her body felt sluggish and slow. It wasn't fair. She wasn't the one with the bullet wound. She could only imagine how Elliott was feeling right now, but then he was probably on some serious pain meds.

She examined the dark purple bruising on her left inner elbow. Tough to hit a vein clean while racing through turbulence. Her right inner elbow wasn't nearly as bad, but was twice as sore.

She sported a baggy pair of old sweats upon Dan's return. He took one look at her and grinned. She looked like a freshly scrubbed waif in swaddling clothes. She was sitting at the kitchen table drinking orange juice. He kissed her on the forehead and kept her sitting while he set the table and refilled her glass.

"Eat," he commanded. She was ravenous. "Drink," he ordered.

She downed half a glass. He refilled it.

"When will Elliott be released?" she asked.

"Not for a few more days."

"Please tell him that my thoughts are with him and that he is as pretty on the inside as he is on the outside."

Dan grinned. "I'll tell him and his mother both."

Julie shut the door, locked it and slowly made her way upstairs. She looked at herself in the mirror. She had dark circles under her eyes. She let out a pent up breath. Small price to pay for saving a life.

She was about to crawl into bed when she heard the soft and lonely howl of a wolf by her window. She made her way downstairs and found Big Boy sitting patiently on her kitchen stoop. She opened the door for him slowly and he entered with care and caution.

"You know that I'm not well, don't you, Boy?" she asked softly, giving his neck a loving scratch.

She moved slowly back up the stairs and he dogged her ploddingly. When she slipped beneath the sheets, he put a paw upon her bed.

She patted his big foot gently. Next thing she knew, there were two paws upon the bed. She rolled toward him only to find him inching himself slowly up upon the mattress.

She pushed feebly at his chest. "Down, Big Boy."

He just kept climbing, nudging her over, nuzzling her neck. She didn't have the strength to fight him, so she fell asleep wrapped around him like a stuffed toy. He took up half her mattress.

9

Although Julie was back to work within two days, Elliott was out for three weeks. On his first day back at the station, the force and their spouses threw a little welcome home party for him. Naturally, Julie was invited. Little did she know that the party was for her too.

Dan stood up after everyone had greeted one another and shared with the group Julie's comments about Elliott being as pretty on the inside as he was on the outside. Elliott's mother was a river of tears, her teardrops catching in the corners of her smile.

Then Dan grew serious and told the group how Julie had convinced the paramedics to take her blood and save Elliott. "She told them that it was worth the risk to her person to save Elliott because he had people who loved him. She, on the other hand, had no one."

Julie hung her head and tried to swallow the large lump in her throat. Leave it to Dan to ferret out what happened in the Medivac. She looked up at him, her face stricken.

"I would like for you all to show her just how wrong she is," Dan said.

The rest of the morning was a blur. A sea of faces swam in front of her. She was hugged, cried upon, kissed and squeezed. By the time everyone broke for coffee and cake, she was a bundle of nerves.

Elliott approached her, sat down next to her, and nudged his thigh against hers. "Everyone's so thankful, Julie, but no one more than me."

Dan stood behind her, placed two warm hands on her shoulders and kneaded gently, trying to soften the muscles that were knotted in tension. Julie looked up at Dan with troubled eyes. She wasn't happy with him. He pursed his lips at her frown and squinted his eyes.

"Don't you dare go giving me any trouble, Ms. Hastings," Dan murmured. "I will lock you up for disturbing the peace."

On Valentine's Day, Gray stopped by to see her with a litter of puppies that needed shots. He stood there like a gigantic and silent pillar in black. Black boots, black jeans, black belt, black shirt, black eyes, black hair.

She glanced up at Gray as she worked. He was staring at her intently, a pensive expression on his face.

"Mr. Walker?"

"I forgot to return your cookie tin."

She sighed, releasing a breath she wasn't aware that she had held. "You can return it anytime. There isn't any hurry."

When she finished with the puppies, Julie escorted Gray to the reception area and shook his hand good-bye. His hand swallowed hers in a rocky cavern of muscle and callus. The raw strength behind his gentle touch was enough to snap her eyes upward.

At that moment, Dan Keating rose from one of the plastic chairs in the waiting area and captured her attention. "Officer Keating," she said in surprise. He also toted a carton.

"Another box? Gray had puppies in his, what's in yours?"

"Posies," he said, pulling out some purple African violets in a green ceramic bowl. "The office could use a little color."

"Oh!" She was nonplussed. "They are lovely. Let's put them right here on the end of the counter."

He set them where instructed.

"Lookin' good," he said, nodding in her direction. Her blouse dipped low. The skirt was tight. Her hair had slipped from the loose band at the nape of her neck and her curls framed her face softly.

"They do," she said, looking back at the flowers in order to hide her blush. It was not what he meant and they both knew it.

Dan glanced awkwardly at Gray, then turned to Julie. "May I speak to you officially for a moment?" He was using his cop voice.

She frowned in confusion and ushered him into examination room #3, waving good-bye to Gray in the process. Her nose sniffed the air automatically, hoping for freshness. It smelled faintly of antiseptic and cold metal. A hospital smell, but not unpleasant.

"What's up?" she asked when they were alone.

"How often do you run into Gray Walker?" he asked. He neatened his uniform as he stood before her.

She shrugged and shook her head, "Fairly often, I guess. Every now and again."

"I want you to think on this."

She searched his eyes then concentrated on the question. She grabbed a squirt bottle and disinfected the examination table, her movements slow and thoughtful. Come to think of it, she was seeing a lot of Gray Walker. Seemed like every time she turned around, he was there. But then, so was Dan.

"I don't run into him with any more frequency than I run into you."

"Julie, I go out of my way to run into you," he said with a grin.

She looked out the window and watched Gray unlock his car door. He was looking right at her. She nodded and he nodded back.

"Maybe he does too." She shrugged. "Is something wrong?"

"No, not that I know of. But I just want you to be aware. I've never seen him in town so often. And when I see him, you are usually somewhere in the vicinity."

"I don't see the problem."

"I'm not saying that there is a problem. Just be aware, okay?"

"I thought you said he was a good guy?"

"I said I never had any trouble out of him," he said somberly. "I don't want that to change."

"You think he's stalking me?"

"I know I am," he said with a grin.

"Stop!" she admonished.

"How about if I take you out to dinner?"

"How about if I bake you a tin of cookies?"

"Can I come over to your place and eat them? Watch a movie?"

She swallowed and wrestled with her indecision.

"Just a movie and cookies?"

"Absolutely. I'm talking about a totally G-rated evening." He placed his hand over his heart. "This Saturday, okay?"

"Sure. Seven-ish?"

"It's a date."

He watched the color drain from her face.

"Or was that a fig?" he said, trying for a save.

"Definitely a fig, Dan Keating," she said sternly. "I don't date."

The following week, Gray Walker was back for another veterinary visit. "Mr. Walker," she said formally, "what brings you in today?"

He nodded to her in response to her greeting. He was standing in the middle of the room with an old dog in his arms. It looked part Beagle, part Collie and all-round mutt.

"I have a patient."

"Here, please," she said, patting the examination table.

She touched the dog gently. The animal was nervous, quivering. "You're a good ole boy, aren't you?" she asked rhetorically. She touched him tenderly, nuzzling his ears, rubbing his chest. "Oooooh," she cooed, "How many prairie dogs did you catch in your prime, I wonder?" Her hands moved over him knowingly.

She looked up at the Sioux. His face was expressionless.

"Gray Walker, this dog doesn't have a whole lot of time left. My professional opinion is that his kidneys are failing. I could try to sell you on a guilt trip of expensive dialysis but I don't believe in that, not for animals that don't choose it and don't understand what is being done to them. Most animals fear the vet visit enough as it is. Where is his owner?"

"Too old to make the visit."

"Is he well?"

"No."

"Are they close?"

"Yes."

"Then, you call me when the shaking gets worse. You'll know when the end is near. I'll come visit and this old boy can go to sleep where he is most comfortable and secure, in his own dog bed by the fire. He doesn't want, need or deserve a hospital visit at the end."

Gray nodded. "Thank you."

She looked him in the eye. "You're very welcome."

"If you walk with me to the car, Julie, I'll return your cookie tin."

"All right," she said, unbuttoning her lab coat. "Cookie tins are always at a premium mid-winter."

He smiled. A fleeting thing. "I liked the oatmeal raisin cookies very much," he said, leading the way. He gently laid the dog at the back of the SUV and tucked him in midst pillows and blankets. Julie was silenced by the tender care he took. He walked around to the driver's door, opened it, and retrieved the tin from the passenger seat.

"Might this magical vessel come with a refill?" he asked. He held the tin as if it was something sacred.

She grinned. "That could be arranged."

10

Dan was at her door on Saturday at seven sharp sporting a new pair of blue jeans, tan leather boots and a crisp white shirt rolled up at the sleeves. He had two bottles of wine, microwave popcorn and five DVDs.

She took a look at him and laughed. "You must have been a boy scout! I've never seen such pre-planning!" He stood in her doorway awkwardly, his arms full. She ushered him in, pecked him on the cheek and relieved him of the movies.

"Do you like red or white?" he asked. "I didn't know, so I brought one of each."

"White would be nice tonight. And for the record, I like both. The corkscrew is in the drawer to the left of the sink. I'll fetch glasses. What movies did you bring?"

"All the classics – *The Good, the Bad and the Ugly, Patton, Animal House, Indiana Jones* and *Star Wars*."

"Into action are we?"

"Of course. I'm a cop."

"Let's watch *Animal House*," she said as she set the stemware on the counter. "That movie is so funny."

"*Animal House* it is." He handed her a glass of Sauvignon Blanc and clinked his glass to hers.

"Catch any bad guys today?" she asked, taking a sip.

"Nah, although I did pass out a few speeding tickets to some out-of-towners as they recklessly trundled down the mountain in their mobile homes."

"There ought to be a law."

"There is."

"What made you decide to be a cop?" she asked, motioning for him to move to the living room.

"An old TV series called *Starsky and Hutch*. It was a cop show about two good guys who always managed to save the day in the span of thirty minutes. I liked that."

She smiled. "You're not an adrenaline junkie?"

He sat on the couch and set his wineglass on the coffee table. "We have to import adrenaline to Fallston," he said flatly. "It isn't produced here naturally."

She took a chair next to him. "Nothing exciting ever happens in Fallston? What about Elliott getting shot?"

He huffed in acknowledgement. "That will go down in the record books as the crime of the century. And your Bad Dogs Running were not from around here. They weren't even from South Dakota."

He toasted to that, clinking his wine glass to hers.

"For the most part, I deal with bar fights, DWIs, a little vandalism, and some breaking and entering. In each instance, it's usually just people trying to find something to do to break the routine. Without something constructive... well, as they say, idle hands make mischief."

"Why haven't you moved somewhere else, Dan?"

"I don't know. I guess I like the quiet." He paused. "Why are you here? Why are you still here?"

She smiled. "I like the quiet too."

She popped the Jiffy Pop and they sat on the floor companionably with their backs to the sofa, the popcorn between them. There was a running repeat of dialogue between them, "This is one of my favorite parts" and "Mine too."

Their hands kept touching in the popcorn bowl. After the fourth or fifth mid-bowl collision, she turned to him accusingly. "You're doing that on purpose."

"I am," he said. "Sooner or later, I'm hoping that our fingers will link up and stay stuck for a while."

"That may take some time."

"I'm a patient man."

On Monday morning, Rose asked Julie if she would like to join the church choir for karaoke night at Jake's.

"But I'm not a member of the choir," said Julie.

"Doesn't matter," came the curt reply.

"You sure I won't feel like a third wheel?"

"If I invited you to a church function and you ended up feeling like a third wheel, well, shame on us!" said Rose, hotly.

"All right. I'll try to come. What time?"

"Well, we all eat first, around six-ish. We eat at Jake's, naturally, then we take turns singing until about ten."

She hesitated. "I'll be in work clothes."

"You look nice," said Rose, surveying the conservative blouse, skirt and no-nonsense pumps. "It's a church group."

"I might smell like kennel."

"Jesus was born in a manger."

Julie sighed. "All right, Rose. You win. I'll be there. Thank you very much for inviting me."

She ended up arriving late, as there were two emergencies at the close of business, but she waded through the bar easily enough and headed toward the back room where the choir group convened. She could hear some off-pitch warbling from the entranceway.

She scanned the room as she removed her coat and hat. Looked like most of the police force was in the bar celebrating someone's retirement. Dan and Elliott both caught her eye as she made her way to the back. She crossed herself then tossed her head towards the church group by way of explanation. They both broke into ear-to-ear grins.

As she resumed her course, she slowed her pace, registering the warmth that had suddenly wrapped around her heart. For the very first time in her life, she felt that she was a part of something, many somethings. And they were all good.

She stopped, turned back around and locked eyes with Dan. She was overcome with emotion. He sensed it and crossed the room quickly, hesitating when he stood before her.

"You are a wonderful man," she said, simply. "And, I'm so happy to be in Fallston, to be a part of something so wholesome and so good."

When she closed her eyes, a hot tear ran down her cheek. He cupped her face and wiped the tear away with a calloused thumb. "I think you are pretty wonderful yourself, Julie. And Fallston is glad to have you."

He bent to her slowly and kissed her softly on the lips. When he pulled back, she stepped toward him and hugged him tightly. He didn't let go until she did, and she hugged him a good long time.

"Gotta go," she said, stepping back. "The Holy Rollers are expecting me."

He grinned. "Do they know you call them that?" There was a twinkle in his eye.

"Hell no!" said Julie

"I'll keep it confidential."

"You do that, officer." She tossed him a saucy grin. "You are sworn to protect and serve." She straightened his badge, gave him a nod then walked to the back room.

Rose had saved her a seat and gave her a grand introduction. Julie blushed but thoroughly enjoyed the warm welcome. She listened to each singer, nursing her glass of Pinot Noir, finally admitting to herself that the congregation sang better together than they did separately. But there was one older gentleman who could have sung opera. He was a rich and powerful tenor even though he was in his seventies.

"It's your turn, Julie," said Rose, after everyone had had his or her moment in the limelight.

"Me? Oh, no. No."

"This is a sharing thing," said Rose. "Everybody sings, for better or for worse... as you've heard." She had whispered the last bit.

She would have protested in earnest, but Rose just arched her eyebrows in silent command. Julie knew from working with the woman that once she took a position on something, her word was law. Rose was a 5'2" walking, talking holy commandment.

Julie did the big swallow and walked to the small stage. She was only dimly aware of the cheerful banter surrounding her as she perused the song list. She selected an Andrea Bocelli duet, *Let This Be Our Prayer*, then tapped the elderly tenor on the shoulder. He was surprised and delighted both by her request and by her choice of music.

The whole audience quieted when the soft music started, and she watched their lips part in pleasure and surprise. They recognized the piece. Julie gave Rose a nod, then turned to her singing partner as he began the slow and sad lament that served as intro. They didn't need to read the words. Both of them knew the lyrics by heart. They sang to each other in perfect sync to the music, their voices rising and falling, hitting every note pure, sweet and true.

Julie could sing, really sing. So could he. As the song built to its crescendo, they silenced all of Jake's. Patrons crowded into the karaoke room and jammed the doorway just to get goose bumps.

Rose beamed at her as the song ended. There was a moment of stunned silence and then the crowd was on their feet clapping and whistling. Everyone tried to recruit her afterwards to join the choir.

"Hey!"

Elliott was at her elbow. "Need an emergency exit?"

"Where's Dan?"

"He was only here for dinner. He's on-call tonight and had to go. That's why he was in uniform."

She hesitated.

"I'm just doing the knight-in-shining-armor thing, Julie. The whole bar knows how you feel about Dan."

She felt her cheeks color.

"Yep. Dan is a tall man, to be sure, but he was a whole foot taller when he walked out that door tonight. It could have been a movie scene. It *should* have been a movie scene." He looked up. "Rose! I promised to take Julie home." He wrestled Julie out of the throng with all the abrupt tactlessness of the young.

"I owe you, Elliott," she said when he had maneuvered them clear.

He chuckled. "Do you, now?" The slow drawl in his voice captured her full attention, and she pivoted her head in his direction.

"I need a lead singer for the Copper Pigs."

"Oh, that's very underhanded."

"Not at all. I'm being straightforward. We've been hosting auditions for weeks and no one fits the bill. You do."

"I'm not a singer."

"Yes, you are. Listen, the Copper Pigs entered into a competition several months ago and paid a hefty fee to enter. First place takes home $5,000. That would be $1,000 for each of us, you included. The boys and I are musicians. At best, we sing back up. Would you help us through the competition? Just get us through the competition. Please."

"I don't know."

"Why don't you just come over Tuesday after work and sing a few songs? You know, test the waters. Julie, we're desperate."

She looked into his earnest face and took a deep breath. "Where do you live? And what time on Tuesday?"

11

Gray called the veterinary office on Monday and asked if Julie would be available to visit the reservation later in the day. The old dog needed to be put to sleep. She had offered to provide this act of kindness, and he was taking her up on that offer. She phoned Dan on her lunch break and told him what she was up to. He cut right through what she had thought was casual conversation.

"Are you telling me this because you are worried about being with Gray?"

"No," she said, "Yes. I don't know. You told me to be aware. Well, I'm aware."

"Are you still running into Gray every time you turn around?"

"Yes. He is always courteous and polite, but it is uncanny how often I run into him. I checked the database at work." Dan could hear the switch in her tone. "In all the record-keeping history, Gray has visited our office once. I see him at least once a month now, sometimes twice."

"I see."

"Maybe he's got new responsibilities at work and pet care is one of them."

Dan didn't comment.

"Maybe he feels responsible for me after having hauled me down the mountain the day I twisted my ankle."

Again, no comment.

"Maybe…" she faltered. "Maybe he just likes me. You told me that you go out of your way to see me. Maybe he does too."

"Maybe you should give me a call when he returns you to the office?" he prompted.

"Okay."

And so they were off. Gray's car was as big and wide as he was, and she felt dwarfed by its cavernous interior. She needed help climbing into the vehicle and she struggled with the seatbelt. In the end, he had to reach across her and buckle her in like a child.

"Although you certainly would never know it, I'm really rather competent," she said, smoothing her skirt and settling into the front seat.

"Of course you are."

"The seatbelt is tricky."

"It catches if you pull it at the wrong angle."

She nodded. "And the cab is high."

"Especially when wearing a skirt. It restricts your movement."

She looked at him suspiciously, not sure as to whether he was making fun of her or not.

"I personally don't wear skirts for that very reason," he explained, turning to her with a smile.

"You're logic is flawless."

They drove for a full hour, and he spoke to her about his people and the battles they were waging against New Age charlatans who stole the rites of Sioux spirituality and marketed them for personal gain. It was an issue that was unfamiliar to her, and she listened with rapt attention.

"There are people out there who try to out-shaman the shaman," Gray explained. "They are so-called holistic healers, tarot card readers, psychic mediums. You can't imagine how many poach our ancient symbolism and rituals. They misinterpret. They misinform."

"There are 70,000 Sioux in the Dakotas, Nebraska and Minnesota," he continued. "Less than half still speak the language. We're doing our best to preserve our culture, but this is very hard to do when it is stolen, bastardized and popularized."

Gray pulled into the driveway of a modest wooden home. He took a deep, cleansing breath.

"Thanks for doing this," he said.

"Who belongs to Bud?" she asked, knowing the dog, but not the human to whom it belonged.

"Finch."

Gray knocked once on the front door and they entered, Gray softly announcing their arrival. The elderly man was sitting on the sofa, his pet resting on a blanket beside him. The two were so still, a heavy weight of pain and suffering surrounding them both.

"Finch," Gray said. He addressed the elder with solemn reverence and he continued on in his native tongue. Julie waited patiently while they spoke. Although she never took her eyes off the two men, she noted the hand-carved wooden furniture, the woven rugs, and the tallow candles. A log fire burned hot behind her in the hearth. The room was Spartan and clean.

The dog was not even remotely disturbed by strangers in the house. His eyes had opened briefly then closed again. He nuzzled his head into Finch's lap with a weary groan.

Gray motioned Julie forward and she explained what she was going to do while gently stroking the dog and holding on to the elderly man's hand. Gray had already dug a grave, so when it was over, the three of them buried the animal in the pale blue light of late afternoon.

Finch seemed to fade into even deeper silence when it was over, his mind numb and disconnected. Gray heated a can of soup and made sure that Finch ate it before they left.

"You are a caring vet," he said, as they headed back to town.

"I know how tightly people can bond with their animals, especially if they live alone or have personal traumas. It's so much easier to deal with pain if you've got the quiet understanding of a silent friend, a friend who loves you anyway, despite everything."

His eyes cut to her as they pulled into the veterinary parking lot. "I appreciate everything you did today, Julie."

She nodded. "I have cookies for you," she said, fetching them from her car.

He took the tin gratefully.

"Pecan tassies," she said by way of explanation. "Like miniature southern pecan pies, but better."

"I don't believe that I've ever had such a cookie before."

"Then you are in for a treat." She was about to drive home, when an odd thought struck her. "Gray?"

He turned.

"How on earth did you dig out that grave? The ground is frozen solid."

"Wheaties," he said, his face carefully neutral. "Breakfast of champions."

She grinned at him and let it go. When she got home, she called Dan Keating.

He answered on the first ring. "Alive and well," she chirped.

"Very glad to hear it," he said, his voice deep and low. "No problems?"

"None," she said. "I feel so silly for worrying about him. He's a very nice man, genuine and deep. I shouldn't have called you this afternoon."

"You call me anytime you have a worry," he said. "Number one, it's my job. Number two, I like hearing your voice."

She chuckled. "Thanks, but I guess what I'm saying is that perhaps your concerns are misplaced too. He's a good guy."

12

On Tuesday after work, she drove to Elliott's home. Elliott greeted her at the door and wrapped her in a big bear hug. Petey, Ro-Bear and George squeezed her in turn. They all sported beers. Elliott pushed one into her hand before she even set her purse down.

"Pizza-time," said George. "Elliott made us wait until your arrival."

Elliott sent George a warning look.

"Which is only right and fair," added George quickly. "But we're starving."

George did not look like he was starving. George looked as if he were a major shareholder in the local Krispy Kreme franchise. Julie removed her coat and took a swallow of beer. "Don't let me hold you up, men. Dig in."

"No, no," said Elliott, lifting the first of three large pizza boxes. "Ladies first. What would you like, Julie? We've got pepperoni thin crust, pepperoni thick crust and pepperoni double cheese?"

"Choices, choices," she said as if mentally debating the question. "Pepperoni thin crust, please."

Petey pulled out a chair for her at the table. Ro-bear handed her a wad of napkins, the extra hots and Parmesan cheese.

"Guys!" she said, uncomfortable with all the attention.

"We need you, Julie," said Elliott. They all nodded vigorously.

"Please eat, guys. Then I'll sing a few songs, and we'll see if y'all still feel the same way."

They dug in as if they hadn't eaten in a week. She wondered if they even chewed the pizza. Then, as quick as dinner started, it was over. The pizza boxes were force-fed into the trashcan. They popped the tops on fresh beers and grabbed their instruments.

Julie examined a play list while they warmed up. Then they played music all evening, and Julie sang until her voice grew rough.

"Well," she croaked. "What's the verdict?"

"She's a keeper," said Petey.

"Lock and load," said George.

"Done deal," said Ro-Bear.

"Welcome to the band," said Elliott.

Julie took a weekend and headed into Rapid City to buy clothes for the contest. The Copper Pigs had been vague when she questioned them about the look they wanted. On her way back to Fallston, she called Elliott and told him of her purchases. He invited her for a fashion show/dress selection party, promising to have pizza and beer at the ready.

The men were in the living room watching football when she arrived. Elliott helped her into the house with her packages and set her up in the kitchen which would serve as changing room. As he explained, this arrangement would be most convenient as she could easily bring in the next round of beers with each outfit she modeled.

"You are a sexist pig," she said without heat.

"I'm a Copper Pig," said Elliott. "Give me a beer, woman."

She was sporting a casual denim outfit and struggling to pin a toy police badge to the 'v' of her halter-top when someone knocked at the kitchen door.

Both parties were taken by surprise when she opened the door. "Hello, Dan!" she said, stepping back to allow him entrance.

He frowned at her in confusion, waves of emotion washing over his face. She stepped into him and pecked him on the cheek.

"What are you doing here, Julie?"

"Elliott hasn't told you?" It was her turn to be confused.

"Told me what?" His voice was hard.

"He asked me to step in as lead singer for his band after his girl went to New Orleans. It's just for this one gig, the band competition."

"He didn't tell me."

"Well, I know he's been keeping it somewhat quiet because his girl will actually be in town for the event and will attend the show. He doesn't want to tip his hand. But, I thought he'd have told you at least. Elliott feels that she is coming back to watch him fall on his face. He, naturally, envisions a different scenario."

He watched her fumbling with the badge. "Do you need some help with that?"

"Thanks," she said, handing him the badge. "Pin me, please."

He affixed the badge to her top, his warm fingers playing softly across her exposed skin. "You look nice," he said.

"Thanks. I have three outfits to try on for the guys. This is the first. They didn't give me a whole lot of instruction as to what they were looking for with regard to look or image, so I was shopping blind."

"I think they'll like this one."

"You haven't seen the other two."

"Do I get to?"

"Sure! The men are in the living room drinking beer and watching football. I'm going to give them a little fashion show."

He went to the refrigerator and grabbed a cold one. "I'm very glad I stopped by."

She smiled and he stepped up to her and kissed her softly on the lips. His eyes twinkled as he touched the cold beer to her exposed belly. She squealed.

Wait until he got a hold of Elliott.

She thought the men liked the jeans and halter-top. Their eyes darted between her and the big screen while she modeled the outfit.

"You look great," Dan said, his eyes full upon her.

"Ohhhh," she retorted. "I think you just like me. You'd probably say that I looked great if I wore nothing at all."

His eyes grew wide. "I'm sure I would," he enthused. "When do I get that fashion show?"

Elliott cut in. "Next outfit, please. Who needs beer?"

Two hands went into the air. She pivoted on her heel and changed.

They were definitely under-whelmed by an artsy skirt and vest outfit. They were more interested in the commercials than what she wore. She went back and changed into a copper cocktail dress.

"All right," she said, emerging. "This is kind of Vogue-meets-Victoria's Secret." She moved under a ceiling light. "And look, it really catches the light. This one has the stage presence the last outfit lacked, I think."

No one said a word, so her head snapped up in the silence. Their faces were slack with shock, and she had their undivided attention.

"What? Y'all don't like this one either?" She swallowed and shrugged, wrapping her arm across her waist self-consciously. "No problem." She turned and headed back to the kitchen.

"Julie!"

It was Elliott. She pivoted on her heels and looked at him. It was his turn to swallow.

"If I may speak for the band," he said then stopped, looking from face to face. They all nodded vigorously. "That dress is…" He fumbled. "We just were so surprised that we… It's perfect."

"Really?" she said, a tentative smile on her lips.

"Really," Elliott parroted. "Right, men?"

"Absolutely."

"For sure."

"Damn straight."

Her head pivoted to Dan, waiting for his approval.

"If you are going to wear that outfit in Fallston, Julie, you will need police protection," said Dan.

She blushed. "I definitely have that, don't I, men?"

"Most definitely."

"Yes."

"Absolutely."

"Don't you worry about a thing."

She beamed at Dan. "See! It's a wrap."

She performed a corkscrew wiggle that started at her hips, transitioned to her bust and finished with her neck and head.

Dan's eyes nearly popped out of his head. "What was that?"

"Happy dance. I only let loose when I feel safe. I'm totally safe, right guys?"

"Like Fort Knox."

"The Pentagon."

"The White House."

"Camp David."

"Great," she said. "Then I'll wear this sparkly little number and hope to sing on key."

She didn't expect a case of the nerves, but there were at least a thousand people in the music hall, and her gut was in an uproar. The bands had all drawn straws and the Copper Pigs were dead last.

Although Elliott had told the troupe that last was very good, the minutes passed slowly backstage and her tension and worry continued to build.

"Relax, woman," Elliott admonished.

"Easy for you to say," she countered.

He took a deep breath and nodded. Ten minutes later, he approached her with a cup of tea and said, "Drink this."

"What is it?" she asked, inhaling a rich, earthy, peaty note. "Lapsang Souchong?"

"Nope," he said. "It's Lipton laced with Gentleman Jack."

"What's Gentleman Jack?"

"An attitude adjuster. Drink it, Julie. You'll be right as rain."

She did. And she was.

The stage fright completely dissipated and her body was infused with a heady warmth. When the spotlight hit her on stage, she was already hot, her previously stiff muscles liquid and relaxed.

Although there had been an endless string of practices the week prior to the competition, the band watched her make moves they'd never seen before. And the audience loved her. They ate her up, especially the right quadrant of the hall. Nothing but policemen and their families there.

She hit every note with strength and with passion. Despite her stage fright, she was high-tensile strength upon delivery. Her notes sang true.

Eight competitors were eliminated to three. They made the cut! When the finalists were brought on stage, the Copper Pigs took first place.

Midst the high-fives and the macho, manly hugs of champions, Julie calculated what one thousand dollars would do for her and smiled.

"Elliott," she said, tugging on his arm when the curtain went down. "Thank you for this opportunity. If you need me again, I would like to help out."

He grinned. "Really, Julie?"

"Yeah," she said. "I'm up to my eyeballs in debt from veterinary school. This could help me."

"Done. The guys will be most pleased."

"By the way, did you see your ex out there in the audience?"

Elliot's smile spread even wider. "Victory never tasted so sweet."

They caravanned to Jake's to celebrate with a good portion of the audience in tow. There were so many people crowding into the small establishment that the party ended up spilling into the parking lot. There was an open-container law in effect outside the confines of the little restaurant, but the officers turned a blind eye that evening much to the owner's relief. The juke box wailed at full volume and the voices were even louder.

Julie found herself wedged tightly in a corner surrounded by Copper Pigs and Dan Keating. He had his arm around her waist possessively and his fingers toyed with her copper tassels in a slow tease.

She tried to ignore his touch, but failed. She turned to him, her awkwardness written all over her face.

He smiled at her good-naturedly. "You feel good, woman. I've never touched anything that felt so nice."

She blushed. She had intended to ask him to stop, but she took a long sip of her drink instead. She was working on a Perrier and lime. The raging noise around her was deafening. She retreated into the silence of her mind and relaxed against Dan. He nuzzled her neck and she let him, then she turned and found his ear.

"I'm going to run to the ladies room."

He released her reluctantly and watched as she threaded her way through the crowd, her copper dress swaying provocatively. He noticed more than one man turn in her direction. His eyes caught Elliott's then swung back to find Julie again. He didn't see her. He stood and went to find her. All kidding aside, the woman was going to need a little police protection tonight.

He was waylaid by many bar patrons as he pushed through the crowd. The going was slow. His feet tingled with the thrumming bass beat of the juke box. The floor pulsed beneath him.

He looked up as the throng parted. Julie was crossing the dance floor. Then, in less than a heartbeat, pandemonium erupted. Dan saw the mirrored ceiling panel move above her. By the time he realized what was happening, the dance floor was covered in broken glass as one mirror after another fell onto the hardwood. Bar patrons pushed to escape the flying shards of glass and ran rough shod for the exits, almost trampling each other in their fear.

Dan could hear the police taking charge behind him, quelling the panic and restoring order, but the quiet that ensued was eerie and unnerving. Only one form remained on the dance floor – Gray Walker. The hulking Native American was bent in half. Something delicate and copper-sheathed was wrapped in his powerful arms. Julie dangled like a rag doll beneath his chest.

"Julie," said Gray. "I'm going to straighten up and flip you into my arms. Don't wiggle. I don't want to lose my footing."

"I'm all wiggled out, trust me."

His chest rumbled in what was pained laughter. "You wiggle quite nicely, Ms. Hastings," he said, standing erect, shifting his hold on her so that she nested snug in his arms. "I was in the audience tonight."

She turned to look at him, but his eyes were closed. Then, her eyes lighted upon the blood streaming down the side of his head. Her eyes took in the devastation around her and fixed on Dan. He was making his way toward her very slowly, the wood slippery with broken glass.

"You're hurt, Gray," Dan said, as he approached. "Give Julie to me."

"No," Gray said, tightening his grip on her. "I'll walk her clear."

Julie turned a frightened face toward Dan as Gray squeezed the air out of her, then she focused upon the Native American that held her.

"Look at me, Gray."

His eyes were closed. He seemed to open them reluctantly and with great effort. His irises startled her. They didn't look human. She blinked, swallowing hard to clear her head, then looked again. Gray's dark chocolate eyes regarded her carefully.

"I think you have a concussion," she said, searching his face and her mind for an explanation of what she thought she had seen. "You might get a dizzy spell and drop me."

"I won't."

"Why don't you give me to Dan?"

"Be still, Julie." He moved slowly through the broken glass, his feet sliding like icebreakers through the shattered crystal.

"Get me a first aid kit, please," Julie called out to anyone and everyone within earshot.

When she was on her feet, she tugged Gray over to a quiet corner and sat him in a chair then pulled up a seat directly opposite. They regarded each other silently, her eyes professionally assessing his. She swallowed. His pupils were not dilated. In fact, his eyes looked quite normal. She shuddered, dispelling the unease she had experienced on the dance floor.

"Bend down, Gray," she said softly. "Let me see your head."

He did as he was told. She touched him gently, moving his hair so that she could find the cut. "It's not deep," she told him quietly. "But head wounds tend to bleed extensively."

Dan returned to her with a first aid kit and she went to work. "I would have thought that you'd need stitches, but I don't think you will. You must have an inordinately hard head." He lifted his head to look at her. She was smiling. "Thank you, Gray." She paused. "If any of those panels had struck me directly, I think I'd be in the hospital right now. Or the morgue."

"I know," he said quietly.

She faltered. "I am sorry that you are hurt."

"Just a scratch, Julie. Don't fret."

Someone had called for the paramedics, and she glanced up as they trundled into Jake's, their footfalls heavy and hurried. Although Dan had wrapped a steady arm around her waist, she kept her hand on Gray's shoulder until the ministrations of the emergency personnel forced her to step back completely.

Gray's head turned in her direction when she broke contact. There it was again. She swallowed. His eyes had grown very black.

Concussion, she thought. Definitely a concussion.

13

March came in like a lamb. It was calving season.

The snow had melted, but the locals all warned her that winter was far from over. She found that hard to believe. The flowers were up! The sun was warm! And the skies had been blue and cloudless for the better part of a week.

In fact, the weather had been so mild that one of the town residents opted to do a little yard work and inadvertently dropped a tree limb onto the main power line running through town causing a wholesale power outage. With an unexpected half-day at the office, Julie drove home to change, don her boots and take to the trails.

She opted to tackle a new trail and hiked for hours up-mountain enjoying the change in scenery. When she gauged her energy level to be halfway spent, she turned around and headed back down.

The air was turning colder. She glanced skyward and frowned at the leaden sky. She hadn't noticed the clouds moving in. But then, she had spent a good bit of time watching where she put her feet on the unfamiliar path.

She came to a fork in the trail and was surprised by her confusion. Left or right? She couldn't remember. She went left. The trail dipped and she was encouraged. She was heading down. But, after a short while, the path led upward again.

She buttoned her coat, wishing that she had brought her hat and gloves. Another fork.

She went right. Parts of the scenery looked familiar, and the trail spiraled downward but then turned up-mountain once more.

The first tendrils of fear started to curl into her stomach. She looked at a sun that was well past its zenith, a pale brightness behind thickening clouds. The first snowflake fell from the sky and touched her on the cheek, then another, then another. The woods were unusually quiet.

She started forward once more, moving quickly in an effort to quell her panic. Just up ahead, she thought, surely there will be another fork. But she hiked for another hour to no avail. There were a few inches of snow on the ground now. She debated retracing her steps and whimpered softly in her confusion.

She stuffed her hands in her pockets, rotating where she stood, staring out into a wall of white. She was absolutely and completely lost.

He appeared out of nowhere, a massive, dark, tree-trunk of a man, stepping out of a frenetic swirl of icy snowflakes. Her scream was long and piercing.

"Julie," he said frowning. "It's me, Gray."

Her heart skidded in her chest. What were the coincidental odds of running into this man in the middle of the wilderness in a blizzard? Absolutely none. She took a slippery step backward.

"I need to get back to town," she said, her voice tight and strained.

He was silent a minute and she took that opportunity to spin on her heel and head back in the direction from where she had come. He was by her side in an instant.

"You will never make it."

"I will."

"This storm will get worse and quickly too. You'll lose visibility. You'll wander aimlessly in the woods." When she didn't stop, he tugged on her arm and spun her to face him. "You'll die, Julie."

"I'll take my chances."

"I have a hunting cabin not far from here. Come weather out the storm there. This..." he gestured hopelessly, "This is suicide."

She stared into his ink black-brown eyes and took another step backwards. He was stalking her. Had to be. Where on earth did he come from?

"I know that I frighten you," he said. In fact, he could feel her fear. It was colder than the air around them. "I can't help the way I look, but I mean you no harm."

She wanted to believe him, but her mind couldn't focus on much. She was cold. She was tired. And now, she was terrified.

"I helped you when you hurt your ankle, didn't I?"

She nodded mutely.

"I saved you when the ceiling panels fell at Jake's, didn't I?"

She nodded again.

"Let me help you now," he said. When she didn't respond, he continued, "Julie, I know what you see when you look at me, but that's not who I am."

That hurt. Mostly because it was true. He was monstrous in size and mean in appearance. She swallowed hard, staring into his eyes for something reassuring. He held her gaze, willing her to trust. She tried to focus on his face, but her eyes were full of tears.

"Please, Julie. I can't leave you here wandering around in a blizzard. I don't want anything to happen to you. Let me take you someplace safe."

Choice. She looked down at her feet. The snow was getting deeper.

"Please," he said, and held out a hand. It was massive. She looked up at him, the indecision written on her face.

He nodded encouragement. "Take my hand, Julie."

She reached toward him hesitantly and Gray sighed audibly with relief.

"Good," he said, "Good, good. This way."

His voice turned her around. The snow fell in thick waves that were carried on a frigid wind. The snowflakes stung and burned, their crystalline edges biting like miniature knives into her unprotected skin. Gray ripped off his gloves and jammed them onto Julie's naked hands.

"We need to move faster."

She picked up her pace.

They walked upward for a good while then he took a fork through the forest and emerged into a large clearing. The winds were more intense out in the open and he paused, waiting for the white whirlwinds to pool and eddy in hopes of catching the faint glimpse of the kerosene lamp he had left burning in the window.

They were approaching a full white-out. He sniffed the air carefully, trying to pick up the scent of his cabin. He had left a fire burning in the hearth and he tried to ferret out the smell of smoke, but the winds were shifting so quickly that the information was fleeting.

He tugged her into a hobbling jog while trying to get a bead on his cabin as visibility dwindled to next to nothing. They stopped for breath. Then he took a step, unexpectedly stumbling over his front porch.

Bent at the waist, he felt for the stairs. They were already buried in snow. They crawled up the four risers, moving like zombies. When he found the door handle, he pulled them both inside, tumbling out of the blinding white of the storm and into the light.

"Get out of your wet clothes," he said. He raced to a scarred cedar chest and pulled out an old pair of sweats. "Change into these."

He helped her out of her parka, gloves and shoes. "I won't look," he said, turning back to the fireplace, adding logs and stoking the embers. "Hurry."

Her fingers were numb and uncooperative and she fumbled miserably while removing her sodden clothing. Once dressed, she stumbled toward the fire.

"Rub your hands and stomp your feet," he insisted. "I need to change too." Back again he went to the cedar chest, rummaging deep within its confines. He grabbed a thick flannel shirt and another pair of sweats.

The hunting cabin was a one-room affair. Bed, kitchen, table and chairs. Hearth. Over in one corner of the kitchen was a hand-pump, for water, she assumed. No electricity. The two-burner stove top was high-quality camping gear and ran on propane. Kerosene lamps. Candles. Rustic.

He joined her by the fire.

"My hands and feet sting," she said.

"Frost-bite," he said, stating the obvious. "Let me look." He examined her, relief washing over his face when he saw that her skin was red and not blue or black. "You'll sting for a while, but you won't lose a digit or an appendage."

She knew that too, but it didn't stop the discomfort. Her hands and ears burned as if she'd been doused in boiling water.

"I'm sorry," she said contritely. "I'm very sorry… for my fear."

"Me too," he replied, moving to the shelves in the kitchen to select a can of soup. He prepared it while she warmed. When it was hot, he gestured for her to sit.

"This will warm you up from the inside," he said, adding a shot of sherry into each bowl. "Take the edge off."

They devoured the meal in silence, their spoons scraping loudly against the cheap dime-store china.

"You can take the bed and the quilt. I'll take the buffalo pelt and sleep on the floor."

It was hardly an equitable deal after all they had been through, but she was both too ashamed and too relieved to comment. She got into bed stiffly and did not move one inch once she pulled the covers up to her chin. Despite his words, despite his deeds, she did not let down her guard. She listened hard. She listened to his breathing and his movements as he settled down for the night. She listened for something stealthy, something furtive. H fear was as cold and numbing as the winter storm had been. Once more, her being turned to ice.

Morning was a welcome thing, but her arms and legs refused to bend with ease. At first she thought she was dead and that *rigor mortis* had settled in, but no, the stress and strain of the forced march through the snow and the tense state of her nerves had put her muscles into lock-down. Every movement brought a wave of agony as she sat herself up in bed.

Gray silently set a steaming cup of coffee by her bed. She preferred cream and sugar, but this black, bitter brew was the perfect complement to her dark self-recriminations.

"I owe you an apology," she said

"Apology accepted."

"What can I do to make this right?"

"Trust me a little."

She looked out the window. Day had dawned and it was still snowing. All she could see was a wall of white.

"I think we have to prepare for a prolonged stay," he said after breakfast. He had found a box of blueberry Pop Tarts. They were a little old and crumbly, but they ate them gratefully. "The storm is far from tapering. If anything, it's only getting stronger. I'll need to move some wood from the woodpile and stack it under the protection of the front porch overhang. Get it out of the weather."

"How can I help?"

"How good are you with a shovel?"

She shrugged.

"You clear off the front porch and I'll stack the wood." He looked out the window and frowned. "I'm going to tie ropes to both of our waists that will orient us to the front of the cabin. We'll work until we chill, come in to warm, then go back out again."

And so they did, all day long. They had soup for lunch and soup for dinner. And that was a good thing. Julie was too tired to chew. When darkness descended, she fell into bed and slept like a rock. Gray, on the other hand, lay sleepless. His aching muscles screamed all the louder for lying on the hard, unforgiving floorboards, and as the fireplace burned down to embers, a cold draft stole across the cabin to chill him.

Despite his discomfort, he was not displeased with his day. He turned to watch Julie's sleeping form. *Let it snow,* he chanted silently. *Let it snow. Let it snow.*

Julie awoke to the smell of coffee.

"Gray," she said, snapping awake and surveying a window of white. He walked over to her with a mug and placed it on the small table near the bed. "Please," she said, gesturing for him to sit. His weight sagged the mattress and her body slid slightly in his direction. "What are we going to do today?"

"The hard work is done. You can rest. On my end, on days like this, I carve little symbolic beads that the women of my tribe string into necklaces. I thought I might make a few today. You could watch."

She nodded and he looked up at her hair. It was a mass of morning tangles. She followed his eyes.

"I should wash it."

"If you intend to wash it, you should do it early, so that it can dry completely before evening falls. It gets drafty in here at night."

"I know."

She didn't want to admit that she was cold at night. The quilt was no match for the winter chill. Then she thought of him on the floor and wondered if he was warm enough in the buffalo robe, but she didn't ask.

They ate the rest of the Pop Tarts for breakfast, and he gave her soap, towel and a bowl of hot water for washing.

"I'm going to step outside for a little bit," he said, graciously giving her some privacy. He bundled up and walked out into the storm. "There's more water warming in the kettle over the fire."

She made short order of her toilet then she re-filled the kettle with water and swung it over the open flame in case Gray wanted to wash up too.

Then she took stock of the pantry. The odds and ends stored there didn't bode for inspiring meals, but at least they wouldn't go hungry.

She fixed lunch and did the dishes. It helped to keep busy. She peeked over her shoulder at him as he set out little bits of bone and some small knives. He was completely focused on the task. She smiled inwardly and joined him at the table. He glanced up at her, pleased that she sat close to him.

He set out a row of small carved animals in front of her. As she watched, his big fingers deftly handled the objects he had fashioned.

"Every creature is admired for certain traits," he said by way of explanation. "Take the wolf."

She picked up the first bone carving.

"The wolf is a teacher. He shares knowledge and leads people through the forest, the forest being allegorical for whatever difficulties surround the wearer at the moment. You have a wolf."

She nodded.

"A good thing to have, Ms. Hastings."

"Yes," she murmured, lost in thought. "He is wonderful. We've got a good friendship going."

"Ah," he said. "This brings me to the porcupine." She looked down and picked up the next figure. "Porcupine speaks to the importance of faith and trust in our lives, the innate belief that people are good and that all things will turn out as they should."

She looked up at him, listening hard to his words, but he studied the table. "The deer," he continued, gesturing to the next piece, "represents the power and strength found in gentleness."

Julie swallowed. She knew he was communicating to her on more than one level. She, too, looked down now. She couldn't meet his eyes.

"The butterfly, as you can imagine, symbolizes transformation." He pointed to the next piece of bone. "But more importantly, it represents the ability to know or change your mind. It's a special kind of consciousness, like when you choose something cognitively and with purpose. This type of choice represents a tough decision because it usually requires leaving the past to embrace a very new and different future. From what you've told me, from what I understand, you embodied the butterfly, Julie, when you moved to South Dakota."

She didn't comment. Instead, she ran her hands across the tiny off-white carvings, picking up a few to examine them more closely. The work was intricate and Gray was a skilled carver.

"What is that?" she asked, pointing to an ear of corn that bore a face midst its kernels.

"This is a corn maiden," he said reverently. He passed the figure to her. "She cares and provides for her people by giving of herself. She gifts them her flesh and this sustains them."

Her eyes scanned the table. "It's the only figure that is a plant. All the rest are animals."

"Very observant," he said, beaming. "The corn maiden is very special. But let's keep to the animal kingdom for now. Certain animals, in addition to their inherent meanings, symbolize the four cardinal directions. There is even an animal for above and below. And colors are significant. They are linked with those six points too."

"How so?"

"Due north is symbolized by a yellow mountain lion. Northeast is depicted by a white mountain lion."

"Ah! Mountain lion is north."

"Correct."

"And the color confirms the cardinal direction or pulls the compass needle off of the mark."

"Very good."

"I'm from the south east, so I'd be a white something."

"A white badger. The badger is the symbol for south."

"Got it," she enthused. "This is fascinating. What is your favorite animal, Gray?" she asked, glancing down at the tiny figurines.

"I am a wolf man myself," he said softly.

"Yes. That fits you." She rubbed the round face midst the corn kernels. "I like the corn maiden."

He sat back in his chair and looked at her.

"Is that wrong?"

"No, not at all."

"Do you think there is another symbol that would suit me better?"

He shook his head. "No, I think the corn maiden is perfect for you."

For dinner, they ate the leftovers from lunch. When they lost light, they turned in for the evening. Gray banked the fire and locked the door.

"Have you heard of Iktomi?" he asked, settling into his buffalo robe.

"The Sioux trickster?" she said, climbing into bed.

"I'm impressed."

She rolled to the edge of the mattress and looked down at him. "I went to the library and got a few books after our visit to Finch."

They were both quiet a moment out of respect. "Do you know the legend of the dream catcher?"

She shook her head in the darkness.

"Iktomi is a trickster, but he is also a great teacher. If he were a fetish, what would he be?"

"A wolf," she answered with confidence.

"Very good. He is an Indian that can take wolf form. He can also take the form of a spider. The wolf is a pathfinder. The spider weaves the paths."

"I see."

"Long ago, a Lakota shaman hiked up a mountain in search of a vision. He carried a willow's hoop loaded with offerings. These offerings would be in exchange for the dream message he hoped to receive. Iktomi, the teacher, saw him and assumed his spider form. He spoke to the spiritual leader about life and how the decisions we make become the forces that shape our lives. And while Iktomi spoke, he took the shaman's willow hoop and began to weave a web within it. Iktomi explained that certain influences are best ignored as we travel on our life's path, while other influences will do us good if we pay attention to them. The trick is to know which is which. The spider spun his silk in an intricate pattern mirroring the complexity we find in life."

Julie nodded in the darkness.

"As he finished, Iktomi left a small hole in the center of the weave explaining that this hole would allow the negative influences in our life to pass through and to escape our notice. The web, on the other hand, would serve to catch all the good dreams, hopes and inspirations that would help us keep to the correct life journey."

He was silent a moment.

"That is the legend of the first dream catcher," he finished. "There is one tacked to the wall behind your head."

They were both quiet a moment. "Are you on the right path, Gray?"

"For certain."

"I think I might be on the right path too."

"I'm sure you are, Julie. You're here."

She smiled at that. "South Dakota has been good for me."

It wasn't exactly what he meant, but he didn't correct her.

"Gray?" she called, "Where are you? Give me your hand."

He reached out for her in the darkness, and she reached for him, their hands contacting halfway between them. She gave his hand a squeeze then released it. "Thanks for sharing. You share so much."

She rolled over to drift off to sleep. Then her eyes flew open. His hand was ice cold. She slid out of the bed and dropped her feet to the floor. With the fire nothing but a mass of gentle coals, the wooden flooring was frigid and drafty and riddled with slippery currents of arctic air.

She looked at the large dark form nestled within the buffalo robe at her feet and queried softly into the night, "Gray?"

He turned.

"It's too cold for the floor."

"I'm fine," he replied, rotating back onto his side. She reached down and touched him lightly on the arm. His flannel shirt was chill to the touch.

"I had no idea," she said, regret coloring her words. "I had no idea that you were sleeping like this! Oh, I feel horrible. Come sleep with me in the bed."

He sat up slowly and turned to face her. Her teeth chattered briefly as a chill wracked her. "Can't we just hold each other and keep each other warm? I don't bite. And after these past days in your company, I don't believe you do, either."

He rose quietly, his massive torso towering over her slender frame. He grabbed his buffalo robe and covered her thin quilt with it. He looked at her and nodded, his eyes searching, then peeled both coverings back and climbed into the bed. He took up more than half of the mattress.

She stood there stiffly, suddenly quite aware of just how closely they'd be sandwiched together. He reached for her hand and tugged her toward the bed.

"Come."

"Is there room?" she whispered.

"There is. We'll just be close, that's all."

He continued to tug on her gently until she climbed in beside him. She moved into his arms tentatively and laid her head on his shoulder. She didn't know what to do with the rest of herself.

Sensing her awkwardness, he reached over and grabbed her left hand and stretched it across his chest. She let it rest where he positioned it. Then, he reached down and grabbed her left leg behind the knee and pulled it up and over his left leg so that their two bodies were tightly intertwined.

"Okay?" he asked.

She nodded silently, petrified to move and mortified by his touch.

"Go to sleep now."

She could scarcely draw in a breath. Although he was cool to the touch when he crawled between the blankets, within minutes his body heat toasted up the bedcovers. She relaxed immediately and hummed as she snuggled closer, pulling herself more deeply into the warmth of his embrace.

She didn't see his smile even though it dazzled the darkness.

The next morning, she found herself on her side completely spooned by Gray's massive arms and legs. He had her pulled tightly into his chest, his face nestled into the nape of her neck. His deep breathing tickled her. She felt like a kitten swamped within the huge frame of a St. Bernard. Slowly she tried to disentangle herself, but her movements woke him and his arms tightened to hold her in place.

"I like sleeping with you," he said. "It's nice."

They stared at each other briefly – eye to eye – his twinkling while hers flashed in the first signs of panic. He flipped her onto her back, rubbed his nose to hers then sprang onto the floor in one lithe, graceful leap.

"Breakfast," he announced. "I'll cook. You set the table."

It took her a moment to adjust. She went from some fairly uncomfortable personal contact to work detail in three heartbeats. She shook her head in an effort to assess the moment. His no-nonsense, all-business attitude had her nonplussed.

"Box pancakes is the best I can do, but I have real maple syrup."

"Not a bad consolation prize," she said, recovering.

He gave her a smug little grin and fired up the grill. He cooked. They ate. They discussed the storm. The endless snowfall had finally abated.

"When do you think we can make it into town?"

Gray got up and stared out of the window.

"There's four feet of snow out there, Julie." He turned to her. "I don't think we'll be going anywhere anytime soon."

He watched the emotion wash over her face and added, "Of course a March snowfall is usually followed by a heavy spring rain. This will cause a quicker melt. I don't imagine you have winters like these in Virginia?" he said, unrolling his carving tools from their leather wrap.

"No. For sure not. And I'm not used to the isolation."

"You should get out and socialize. I coach a boy's baseball team each spring. Sioux boys. We call ourselves the 'Braves'."

"Fitting."

"We practice on the ball field opposite the veterinary office. You should stop by after work for practice and games. I could use some help."

She assessed his words.

"Seriously. Think about it. You'd have some fun and get out a little more." Julie turned abruptly to face the window. She was overcome by shame.

Gray Walker was a good man. A very good man.

She jumped when he touched her elbow. He handed her a buffing cloth and she dabbed her eyes. He handed her a newly carved bead.

"It's to polish, Julie," he said softly.

"Oh."

She looked at the cloth stupidly.

"But salt is good for buffing," he murmured. "It cleanses as it polishes."

When night settled, she asked Gray for a t-shirt. "I need something fresh for tonight," she explained. "I just can't stand wearing the same clothes for days and nights on end."

He handed her an extra-large t-shirt and moved to the sink. "Will you be warm enough?"

"Warm enough? You're a blast furnace. No problem there."

She gargled with mouthwash. It was the best she could do without a toothbrush, then climbed into bed. He joined her there, pulling her head onto his left shoulder, her arm across his chest and her leg atop his leg. He wriggled contentedly as he settled her into him.

She glanced up at him. "You are a happy camper, aren't you?"

"Yes, I am. Right now, I consider myself the luckiest man on planet earth." He looked at her in the darkness, his eyes burning brightly. He gave her a squeeze. "Good night, Julie."

He held her in his arms and listened to her breathing as it grew deep and slow in slumber. He nuzzled her hair, breathing in the scent of her, and tried to slow his racing heart.

After a long time, he too relaxed, but he couldn't fall asleep. He slowly stroked her shoulder and caressed her back, staring at the ceiling, his mind lost in thought and totally focused on the sleeping form within his embrace.

She awoke the next morning once again wedged against his chest, his arms wrapped around her indiscriminately, his face nuzzling her neck. She tried to slip out of bed, but his arms tightened as soon as he felt her move.

"Let me up," she whispered.

He pulled her close and rubbed noses. "Eskimo kiss."

"Nose-rubbing is kissing?"

"Uh huh." He smiled. "With respect and tender affection. I like you, Julie Hastings."

"I like you too, Gray Walker."

"May I see you after the snow storm?"

She nodded slowly.

"Promise?"

"I'll come to your baseball games."

He tucked a curl back behind her left ear, his eyes drinking her in.

"Okay," he said quietly.

"You have a wonderful touch."

"You're not afraid?"

"No. Not anymore."

"That's good to know," he said, his eyes twinkling.

They ate breakfast, drank coffee, made beads, fixed lunch, drank tea, told jokes, debated world politics, ate dinner and discussed the local gossip. But she felt as if she only had half of his attention.

"Gray," she said. "Why do you keep looking out the window? You've done it all day long."

"I'm tracking the sun."

"Why?"

He pivoted his head slowly in her direction and fixed his liquid eyes upon her. A corner of his mouth quirked upwards.

"Oh."

"I know you've been hurt," he said quietly. "I'm very grateful that you trust me enough to let me hold you." He rose and handed her a t-shirt. "I won't betray that trust."

It started to rain that night. And it rained hard. The wind whipped and tore around the cabin ferociously. He held her tightly.

"It's a brutal storm," she whispered.

"Uh huh."

"Will it wash away the snow?"

He stilled. "Probably."

"Might we make it into town?"

He squeezed her tightly. "I don't know."

"I've been missing for a while now. I'm sure they are wondering why I haven't posted at work."

"Where is your car?"

"In the parking area of the state park. I drove the day I hiked, just in case I needed to get back to the office."

He rolled her onto her back and kissed her neck. She giggled and pushed him away.

"They will start looking tomorrow," he said.

"For what?"

"For you."

He kissed her lips lightly. She didn't pull back. In fact, she nestled in closer to him.

"The rain will make a search possible. They'll run your tags when they realize your car has been there for the duration of the storm. Keating or one of his team does a daily cruise through the state park parking area, weather permitting. Your car would have been on the logbooks the day the storm started. They will be most distressed that it is still there almost a week later. They'll initiate a search."

He found her earlobe and tugged upon it with his teeth. He couldn't help himself. She was so inviting. She squealed and wriggled free, settling on her side, her head on his shoulder.

He pulled back and looked at her for a moment deciding. Then he pushed her onto her back and pinned her. He found her lips and gently parted them, kissing her tenderly. He felt her body stiffen then slowly relax as she opened to the experience, and he was careful to do nothing that would cause her alarm. He kissed her slowly, deeply, hypnotically as the moon rose, large and luminous midst the storm clouds. He tasted her lips, caressed her back, ran his fingers lightly along the curves of her body. Her neck was warm, soft, delectable. He breathed deeply, squeezing her tightly, pressing his body against hers.

"Gray," she said, suddenly quite focused. He pulled back instantly, her scent warm within him. "I…"

He put a finger to her lips.

She listened to his heart hammer in his chest as he rested upon her and wondered if he could feel hers beating in syncopated rhythm. He kissed her once more, soft and chaste, then, he flipped her over like a rag-doll and spooned her, his arm encircling her waist protectively.

"I know, Julie."

The next day was a day of melt. The snow had turned to thick slush and water sluiced away, trickling downhill in little rivulets. They stood out on the front porch of the cabin and surveyed the landscape. Thick chunks of snow were breaking free of Gray's SUV exposing paint and glass to the sun. The snow, which had reached the car's door panel, was compacted down around the tires.

"One more day," he said, pulling her to him. "If I'm lucky, two." He crushed her to him in a strong hug and didn't release her. She was tightly cocooned, his massive arms encircling her completely. Her face and arms lay flat against his chest, and she relaxed within the granite walls of his embrace. She felt like he was made of steel and stone, not flesh and bone. The thought sent a shiver down her spine.

"Come back inside," he said, tugging her back across the threshold and out of the wet. "I've made a potato-beef jerky hash."

"You know what?" she said, sitting down and spearing a spud. "I don't want to eat potatoes ever again. And I don't want to see a can of soup once more in this lifetime either."

He watched her, his dark eyes glinting like diamonds in the failing light. She huffed into his silence and finished her meal.

"You think I'm spoiled," she stated quietly.

"No." He paused. "Your comments come from a completely different place." When she didn't say anything, he continued. "Your words tell me that you've had very little of what you wanted or what you needed growing up. All I hear is your frustration. You work too hard and give too much for anyone to ever think you were spoiled."

She felt like he was inside her soul. "Gray," she hesitated. "I've got this friendship with Dan Keating."

He nodded. "I know, but that doesn't mean you can't be part of a ball team." She lifted her head to look at him, the corner of her mouth quirking upward. He handed her a t-shirt.

When he finished the dishes, he slipped into bed beside her. "Having you beside me like this has been wonderful," he whispered, "I don't want there to be distance between us when I return you to town."

He kissed her softly then kissed her again, his touch exquisite in its tenderness. She thought of Dan and guilt squeezed a hot tear from the corner of her eye. He captured it with his lips.

"Don't deny me, Julie," he said softly. "We're good together. We're good for each other." And he held her into the dawn.

14

The rain pounded the snow into wet slush and the landscape was ugly and bleak. As they descended the mountain in Gray's four-wheel drive, a growing sense of unease washed over them both but for different reasons. Julie fidgeted nervously in her seat and he glanced over at him.

"Everything okay?" he asked.

"Yes, I'm just a little unsure of things," she replied, turning her face toward the window.

"No need for that." He found her hand and gave it a squeeze, but ended up needing both hands on the wheel. He released her with regret. "What are you thinking?"

She took a while to answer him. "I'm confused."

"How so?"

"Well, we've never even been out socially together and I've already slept with you – well, shared a bed."

"Ah."

"Doesn't that bother you?"

"Not in the slightest," he said and gave her a grin. "I am perfectly content with the way things worked out."

"I'm—"

"Julie," he interrupted. "Don't over-think this. We were caught in a blizzard. There was some forced intimacy that turned out to be a wonderful opportunity for us to get to know each other." He paused. "Through it all, I hope I've earned your trust."

"You have."

"The blizzard was a good thing. I got an assistant baseball coach out of the deal."

"Now, wait just a minute, Gray Walker. I never committed to that. That's a huge responsibility."

"Perhaps what you said got lost in translation because what I heard was a firm commitment to socialize, with me primarily and thirteen ancillary chaperones on a very regular basis."

"When did you hear this?"

"Last night, in bed. I whispered the suggestion softly into your ear just as you were dozing off. You nuzzled your 'yes' right into the hollow of my neck."

"Hey, Gray," she said softly, and glanced out the window. A very pregnant silence stretched between them as he waited for her words. "I would like to know. How did you find me on the mountain? During the blizzard?"

She heard him take a deep breath, then exhale.

"I have an answer," he said. "But the telling will take some time, and now is not the right time. But, I will answer your question Julie, if you'll just believe in me a little bit."

"Is it something… bad?"

"No," he said firmly. "This just needs a lot of explaining. Some things are like that. But, for the record though, I wasn't stalking you. I know that it must have appeared that way, but it wasn't the case."

There were a lot of official-looking vehicles in the parking lot of the state park, too many squad cars, a search and rescue team, police dogs and an ambulance. She and Gray stood on the fringes of the yellow tape, ankle-deep in wet slush.

"My car is within the perimeter they've established," she said, pointing to the red Toyota Corolla in the far corner. "And someone has removed the snow. That's good."

Grey watched the activity, a worried frown on his brow while Julie jingled her car keys anxiously, not sure of how to reclaim her property. She saw Dan Keating and waved.

"Julie!" Dan shouted. He was shocked, relieved, overjoyed. "Oh, God!" He raced across the lot and wrapped her in a big bear hug.

She squeezed him back enthusiastically.

"We feared the worst."

"No worries," she blushed. "Gray pulled me through."

He looked at her for just a second too long, then he glanced up at the Sioux and assessed him with a critical eye. "What happened?" he asked, his voice all cop.

Julie answered. "I had taken a new trail and gotten lost. Gray found me in the forest, in the snow." Dan cocked his head to one side. Gray didn't say a word. "I weathered out the storm in his cabin."

Dan's eyes lifted to Gray's once again as he chewed on that bit of information, then dropped back to study Julie's face.

"You doing okay?"

"Of course! But I'm positively dying for a real meal. We've been living off of canned soup." She gently slammed her body into Gray's. "Chicken and stars, chicken noodle, chicken and rice, tomato and rice, cream of mushroom, cream of broccoli—"

"All right," he said, and looked at Gray again. The Sioux's face was inscrutable. "I'll take you home." Dan reached for her hand, but she pulled away.

"No," she said, uncomfortably. "I appreciate the offer, but I will drive my own self home. My car is here." She turned to Gray. His face was stoic and closed, lips pressed together tightly. She frowned. He looked frightening in the thin blue light of morning. He was quite another person in the moonlight.

"Let's make sure your car starts, Julie." It was Gray who had spoken. At last. She nodded silently, and both men escorted her to her vehicle. The tension was as weighted as the muck beneath her feet. The Corolla fired to life and she beamed back at them, letting it idle.

"Did anyone else get caught on the mountain when the snow fell?" she asked.

Dan nodded slowly. "Another woman," he said. Julie could tell from the way he spoke that it wasn't good. "Looks like she was attacked by an animal."

Gray stiffened.

"She's..." Julie let the question hang.

"She's dead," said Dan.

"Is she local?" asked Julie.

"Yes," said Dan. "But, I don't think you know her. She was a nurse over in Rapid City."

He turned to Gray. "Susan Featherweight."

Julie watched Gray's face go white.

"Does the family know?" Gray asked.

"Yes," said Dan heavily.

"I will stop by their home," Gray said quietly. He locked eyes with Julie. "I'll swing by when I'm finished."

Julie nodded and he turned to go. There was a moment of uneasy silence as she and Dan watched Gray slosh through the melting ice and snow, then Dan spoke in hushed tones.

"Julie?" She looked up at him expectantly. "Are you okay?"

"Yes." She smiled at him reassuringly. "I am totally fine."

Dan nodded slowly. "I'm uncomfortable with this."

"It's all good. I just need to go home."

"Why are you so unsettled?"

"Because I'm ashamed of myself, Dan." She stared hard at the dashboard, unwilling to meet his eyes, her voice tight with emotion. "Gray has rescued me three times now, and I have given him nothing less than fear and distrust each and every time. I'm disgusted that I could make such a tender, caring soul feel so low. It amazes me that he still seeks my company. I do not deserve his care or his kindness."

Dan watched her carefully, weighing the situation. "All right," he said slowly, squeezing her shoulder. "But don't beat yourself up too much. Your fear is natural. He's a very big man and you are just a little thing. I'll swing by the veterinary office tomorrow."

She nodded stiffly.

"Julie?"

"Yeah?"

"Are you sure you I can't take you home? I'd like to do that."

"No. I'm good." She sighed. "Really." She rubbed her cheek against the hand still resting on her shoulder. "I'll bake you some cookies. You go do your cop thing."

Trust. He asked for trust, and she was going to give it to him. Julie pulled into her driveway with a sigh of relief. She had picked up some kitchen essentials at the supermarket and purchased a bottle of wine. Tonight, she was going to fix a real meal. She entered and tossed her keys on the counter.

First things first. She picked up the phone and called Cole Peters, then she dialed Rose. With her professional life back in the saddle, she trotted upstairs and took a long hot shower then dressed and made dinner.

Sara McLaughlin was playing on the stereo when Gray tapped lightly at the door.

"You look lovely," he said, his eyes sweeping the length of her in obvious approval.

"I'm making us a fabulous feast. Could you open the wine?"

She clinked her glass to his then took a sip. "Hard to believe we were stuck up in the mountains this very morning with just a fireplace and some tins of soup, huh?"

He nodded.

"It all seems so... other."

Gray nodded slowly, his eyes watchful.

"You visited the woman's family?"

"Yes. Not good. The community is distraught. Her parents are ghostlike in their grief."

"Do they know how she died? Was it the storm or the animal attack?"

"It was not the weather." Gray turned and looked out the window. "Something got to her first."

"Where was she found?"

"Not far from where I found you," he said flatly.

She just looked at him in shock. "Oh my God."

"I don't think you should venture onto the trails alone for a while."

"Was it a bear?"

He looked at her sharply. He'd rather she hear it from him. "It was a wolf."

"It wasn't my wolf! Gray, I assure you with every fiber of my being, it wasn't my wolf! My wolf is kind and tender and loving."

"I thought he was fierce, ferocious and mean," he said. The corner of his mouth quirked upward slightly.

"Not my wolf."

"Well, don't be surprised if Officer Keating comes calling," he continued. There was an edge to his voice. "He knows your wolf travels with you in the woods. He knows your wolf visits you here in the house. He's going to have a few questions, I'm sure."

"And you know this… how?"

"Because you live in Smalltown, USA."

She nodded, acknowledging both his words and the seriousness of the situation. "Please sit. I'm so sorry about Susan. Can you eat?"

He took a sip of wine. "Despite it all," he said sadly, "I'm very, very hungry."

"Stress," she replied. "And a liquid diet. Please eat."

He took a bite of beef and moaned in satisfaction. Deep. Long. Loud. She laughed, brightening the atmosphere, scattering their troubles like cold water droplets on a hot skillet.

"Gray Walker, you are an expressive man."

He leaned back in his chair and patted his belly.

"I like your smiles," she added. "You should smile more often."

There were bowls of Bananas Foster for dessert, and when Gray was finished, he licked the spoon. He looked hopefully back towards the empty sauté pan and pursed his lips in disappointment.

"You're great for my ego," she murmured, clearing the table.

"Thank you for dinner," he said, rising. "I will miss you tonight."

He placed a hesitant hand on her waist, and when she didn't step away from his touch, he tugged her to him gently. His eyes roved across her face, drinking in the sight of her. Then he bent down and kissed her lips. She hesitated for a moment, unsure of herself and her feelings. The snowstorm was over. Her life was back to normal. And yet, here was Gray, touching her in a way she would have never allowed under normal circumstances. She wasn't sure that she wanted her life to change this much. She wasn't sure of anything.

He pulled back, his face clouded. "You are very far away," he said quietly. He tugged on a curl. "Come back to me, Julie."

Her eyes focused upon his. She regarded him silently for a moment, then she leaned forward, wrapped her arms around him and hugged him tight.

15

There was a lot of explaining to do at the office the next day. Cole and Rose had been deeply worried. Then Dan stopped by carting a topographical map of the mountain. The hiking trails had been super-imposed and he asked her to track her route. She did so, getting just as confused as she had gotten on the mountain.

They went over the trek repeatedly. When he was sure that she had pinpointed her route with some accuracy, he laid a transparency overtop the topographical map showing the site where Susan had been attacked. It was, as Gray had mentioned, very close to her lost and random wanderings.

"Did you hear anything?" he asked.

"Not a thing," she said. "The woods were so quiet. Spooky, actually. When Gray found me I was already rather frightened."

"By what?"

"I was lost, cold." She shivered inadvertently.

"Julie, Susan was raped before she was attacked by the wolf."

She stiffened in surprise.

"How was Gray when he found you? Normal? Agitated? Disheveled?"

She frowned, uncomfortable with the insinuations. "He was calm and very concerned for my well-being."

"Why was he there, Julie? Why was he there – where you were – in the forest?"

Well, now. That was the $64,000 question, wasn't it?

She drew a breath. "I don't know," she said thoughtfully. She remembered that moment. Then her thoughts flashed to the nights in the cabin, "But, I don't care."

"You should."

"Why?" she asked heatedly. "Gray had plenty of opportunity to do me harm. He didn't. He saved me, Dan. I would have died out there, too."

"Don't you find it odd that his path crossed yours on that mountain?"

She fell silent. Of course, she did, but Gray Walker was a good man and she said so.

"Okay, so, let me get this straight, Gray appears out of nowhere in the middle of a blizzard, and you just follow him to his cabin? No second thoughts?"

"Don't be insulting." She was getting irritated now. "I was frightened, and it took Gray a lot of verbal coercing to make me see that heading back to my car down-mountain in a blizzard was suicide. He was inordinately patient and waited for me to agree to a wiser rescue option. My hesitation almost cost us both our lives."

"Anything happen in that cabin that I should know about?"

"He carved beads out of bone, fed the fire, fed me. I was with him in a one-room cabin for a week. I think I would have seen signs had he been the one to hurt Susan. When I wanted to wash, he left the cabin in its entirety for far longer than he needed to. He never got closer to me than I was comfortable with, and as you know, I have a very wide comfort bubble."

"Julie," he said somberly. "We're going to get a DNA sample from Gray."

She swallowed. "Do me a favor," her voice came out as a husky rasp. "Do it quietly, please. He's a youth counselor on the reservation. The inquiry could destroy him and his reputation. He loves his job."

"I can do this quietly."

"Dan, he's not the one."

"Maybe. Maybe not. We'll know soon enough," he paused. "You see that wolf of yours up there while you hiked?"

"No." She went to say more, but he held up a hand.

"Don't you dare tell me your wolf wouldn't attack a hiker. Your wolf damn near tore a house down trying to get to me."

She was quiet for a moment. She studied her hands. She could feel him watching her. It made her uncomfortable.

"Did Gray stop by your house last night?"

"He did. He had visited Susan's family. He told me about it. He stayed for dinner."

"I'd like you to avoid Gray until I get the test results back."

She looked up at him, her eyes large and luminous.

"I don't think you ought to go hiking on your own either."

She nodded stiffly.

"And I want you to call me if you remember anything unusual about that day on the mountain. Anything unusual at all."

Gray stopped by the veterinary office later that week with the spring baseball schedule and an invitation to the coaches' meeting at the local high school. He dropped off a team roster, sample score sheet, a small booklet on baseball rules plus a local list of in-field protocols.

She hefted the manila envelope with grave seriousness. "I do believe that I've bit off more than I can chew," she said cautiously.

"No welching," he said, his face grave. He nodded at her to reaffirm his words then left.

He never mentioned the DNA testing. She didn't mention it either. He was not a match and Dan told her so. Those were tense days, but they were behind her now.

Her thoughts wandered often to that day in the snow-covered woods and how he had found her. It was a thought that detonated softly within her consciousness when things got quiet and still. Surely, Dan would have asked Gray that question, but obviously, whatever explanation had been given was a satisfactory one. Nothing had come of it. Like the DNA. So, she silenced her mind.

Dan asked her to dinner twice after the snowstorm. Twice she declined. He wasn't happy about the distance between them. His feelings manifested themselves in how often he questioned her "officially" about her hike on the mountain. She gave him the same answers to the same questions. Then he asked a new one.

"Why won't you go out with me?"

She didn't know what to say. She couldn't tell him that she thought about Gray Walker every quiet moment, that somehow her world had shifted on its axis during that snowstorm. She was on edge. Dan put her on edge. Because something had indeed happened in that cabin, but for the life of her, she couldn't say what.

In the band, she found release. Elliott monopolized her Saturday afternoons and Sunday mornings. She and the band practiced hard and played hard. They constructed strong sets and staged them well. A bad girl routine had her in a prison uniform that was cropped inordinately short singing Lee Ann Rimes' *Idle Hands*, Jo Dee Messina's *My Givadamn's Busted*, Maroon Five's *Wake Up Call* and Carrie Underwood's *Before He Cheats*.

She adapted a few Johnny Cash songs into the bad girl repertoire and finished the set with the sad and lonely ballad from *Pulp Fiction – If Love is a Red*

Dress. Elliott played the guitar solo and whistled the accompaniment. It brought down the house every time she sang it.

16

Julie glanced at her watch and walked across the parking lot quickly. Work had run late, so she was a tad tardy arriving to ball practice. Gray had the team sitting on the bleachers going over some formalities. She stood off to one side near the front of the tiny assembly.

"This is Miss Julie, your assistant coach," he said, gesturing to her and acknowledging her arrival. She raised a hand in greeting. "She is late, but we'll let it slide this once. From here on out, all offenders will drop a dollar into the pizza fund. Miss Julie will drop two.

What cheek, she thought, unbuttoning her lab coat.

Underneath, she sported a skin-tight pair of blue jeans and a scoop neck turquoise shirt that fit her snuggly. First one young man, then another turned her way. By the time she had reached the third button, the entire team was watching her with undivided attention. Gray glanced over, took in the curves and the cleavage and smiled.

He cleared his throat, corralling their focus. "We don't have a long practice season, men," he stated. "I'll need you to work hard over the next two weeks. Where are my pitchers?" Four hands went into the air. "Throw to each other. The rest of you, run the bases until I say stop."

"What am I going to do?" Julie asked when the boys were into their work detail.

"Your work really won't start until the official games begin," Gray explained. "During the season, you'll be the first base coach."

"What does first base coach do?"

"Stands there and cheers the boys on as they run to first."

"That sounds easy enough."

"That's why you are also official scorekeeper. I know you can multi-task." She narrowed her eyes at him and tried to look threatening. That was tough to do to someone three times her size, but she did her best.

On all counts.

When a boy got a hit, she screamed with excitement and jumped around ecstatically. The boys watched her and smiled, their eyes wide with delight.

Gray Walker never saw so many line drives in his entire baseball career. Hoo-hah.

As practice ended, Gray sidled up close and made a polite inquiry. "I've burned at least three pounds off of you this evening. May I invite you to pizza and beer to replace a debt owed?"

She looked up at him and they locked eyes. "I tried to come up with a colorful pick-up line all practice," he admitted. "How did I do?"

The honesty made her smile. "The colorful pickup line is pure Gray," she admitted, tongue in cheek.

"I'm a pepperoni kind of guy, but completely flexible."

"Well, it just so happens that I'm a pepperoni kind of girl."

He placed a hand over his mouth and spoke into it as if talking to command central. "Houston! We have launch."

Gray rang her up at the office two days later.

"Listen," he said, "There's a ballgame on television Friday night. All the coaches and scorekeepers are meeting over at Jake's for some barbeque and a few beers. The scorekeepers have to track the game. I'll pick you up at five, okay?"

She frowned into the receiver but said, "Sure."

"Wear what you wore at practice."

"What?" she asked, not quite sure that she'd heard correctly.

"Don't you know anything about baseball?" he chided gently. "You never change your luck. You wear the same clothes. You do the same things. You say the same phrases, you chant the same cheers."

"I don't follow you, Gray."

"We had the best practice ever this week. Those kids never had so much fun or tried so hard. Do you know that they didn't win a single game last season?"

"You've got to be kidding!"

"Nope. I was assistant coach last year. I know their track record."

"All right," she said slowly, "But, this isn't a game day. Why would the don't-change-your-luck rules apply?"

"The baseball is an 'O', Julie Hastings, and like the ball, everything about the game is stitched together tightly."

"Got it, Confucius. Jeans and the turquoise top. Pick me up at five."

"You'll need your scorebook and a few sharp pencils with erasers."

"I'm on it."

He hung up the phone with a mischievous self-satisfied grin. She was a total knockout in that outfit, and he couldn't wait to see her in it again, and again, and again.

She wore her game clothes and her game face when he picked her up at the veterinary office. Her scorebook was gripped tightly in one hand. She had six sharpened pencils in the other.

Gray looked her over appraisingly. "You follow instructions," he said with a smile.

"Of course I do," she groused.

"I have something for you," he said. "Just a token."

She cocked her head.

"I know you like wolves."

He handed her a box.

Her eyes flashed to his with excitement. "Did you make me something?"

"Open the box."

Inside was a pair of earrings. The studs were turquoise and from them dangled bone-carved wolves, their faces lifted upwards as if howling at a turquoise moon. They were exquisite. She pulled out her silver hoops and made the substitution.

"That is now the official uniform," he said in all seriousness.

"Got it, Coach."

Jake's was packed. They found the baseball crowd and she slid into a chair next to a beautiful Sioux woman who also carried scorebook and pencils. Gray sat to the right of Julie and placed his hand on her knee. Julie locked eyes with the young woman and smiled, very conscious of the heat burning a hole through her blue jeans. She pulled her knee away ever so gently.

She was introduced to three couples, all from the reservation. There was a lot of playful banter and Gray was the brunt of most of it. Everyone couldn't wait to tell some embarrassing anecdote about him. She watched his cheeks flush then redden.

There were stories of Gray showing up in a neighbor's backyard buck naked in the middle of winter, of some wild surf-side joy ride in a four-wheeler during his college days at Washington State, full moon rising. When he was little, he claimed to talk to animals. At frat parties, he could identify any woman in the room by scent, blindfolded.

She was captivated by their tales. Gray was not. When the ball game started, he rapped across her score sheet with his knuckles insisting that she focus and not listen to a bunch of tall tales. She squeezed his hand, laughing softly, trying to mitigate his mortification. His hand found her knee and she let it stay.

She paid attention to the game. Scorekeeping wasn't hard. Track the hits. Track the runs. She blackened her diamonds and tallied the pitches.

"No," said Gray, looking at her work. "The batter struck out 'looking'. He gets a backward 'K'. He gets a forward 'K' if he strikes out swinging."

"Oh," she said, erasing her mark. "I thought a strike out was a strike out." Julie glanced over at the score sheet of the woman sitting next to her. Ruby was her name, like the Kenny Rogers song. She had penciled in a backward 'K'.

"How did you know about that?" she asked indignantly.

"I'm in my second season," Ruby whispered back.

"Damn!" said Julie. And they laughed, clinking beers.

It was a terrific evening. Gray dropped her off on her doorstep under the light of a full moon. They both paused to look at the ivory orb so dominant in the night sky. A soft wind played upon them and shushed through the trees. Gray gave her a chaste kiss good night, his hands lifting her shirt to contact the warmth of the small of her back. He rested his hands on her hips, his thumbs playing along her lower ribs. She was very mindful of the skin contact. Odd, really, but the touch didn't feel as sexual as it was communicative.

"Thanks for tonight," he said.

"Good fun," she said. "You will do well this season on the ball field."

He shrugged softly. "Great expectations considering the team's track record."

"I do have great expectations," she said. "Your stars have changed, Gray Walker."

He walked back to his car silently. She was wrong. Since she had arrived, his whole universe had changed.

Elliott was obviously solicited to bridge the widening gap between Dan and Julie. Every time the band got together, Elliott asked about the two of them and how they were doing.

Julie just hung her head and shook it to the negative. "It's not working out."

"Why not?"

"Because."

"Because?"

"Because, because."

"You're seeing Gray?"

"I assistant coach for Gray. I'm not seeing him either, except for game days. You and the band get most of my attention."

He grinned. "I like that. I like that a lot."

She gave him a grim smile. "Oh, Elliott. I feel like I'm in high school. I know nothing about…" She froze and gave him a deer-in-the-headlights look.

"You can talk to me, Julie. Dan is my friend, but so are you. You can speak freely."

"You're just going to run back and report to Dan."

"No. I won't."

"Yes. You will."

"No. I won't," he lied, and very convincingly too. "Can't you tell me what's going on?"

She paused, struggling for words. "I'm in way over my head."

"How?"

"I've never been in any kind of a relationship before and I'm bad at it."

"Talk to me. I know all about bad relationships."

Julie smiled and elbowed him good-naturedly, then grew quite serious. She stared at her feet. "Something happened," she whispered. "Ever since the snow storm, Gray has… he has a pull on me. I can't explain it."

"You are attracted to him?"

"No. Yes. No. I'm very confused."

"You said that something happened? What happened?"

She remained silent and stared at her feet. She had a scuff on her right toe that needed polishing. She made a mental note.

"Julie?"

"Oh, it was nothing, Elliott." The fact that she wouldn't look him in the eye told him otherwise.

"What kind of nothing?"

She leaned into him and put her forehead on his chest. "Tell me," he said.

"It was cold in the cabin. Gray slept on the floor. He gave me the bed. It wasn't until the third night when I realized how cold it was on the floor."

"And?"

"I told him to join me in the bed."

"You had sex?"

"No."

"No?"

"No. But, we slept together."

Elliott did a mental nod. Points to Gray. He wasn't sure he could maintain such control if he had Julie in bed.

"And I feel a little strange about it," Julie continued. "Gray calls it a 'forced intimacy' because of the cold. He says that he was very happy to hold me and that I shouldn't fret."

"He said that?"

"Yes."

"So why do you?"

"Why do I what?"

"Fret?" He gentled her word back at her.

"Because I feel different. I feel that everything in my whole world shifted because of the time spent in that cabin."

"How? In what way?"

"I don't want to sound girly."

"I speak Girly. It's my second language. I majored in it at college."

Julie gave him an I-bet-you-did glance.

"In all seriousness, Jules, I'd just like to listen to what you have to say."

She shrugged.

"Come on," he coaxed.

"I don't know, Elliott. I'm all mixed up inside. As I told you, there wasn't sex, but we slept together. So, when I'm around Gray, I have a sense of physical intimacy that goes beyond my emotional ties. It messes me up." She sighed. "I guess I understand, now."

"Understand what?"

Julie shrugged again. "The old adage about never forgetting your first time. I can't imagine how I'd feel if we'd actually... I mean... I'm a train wreck and all we did was keep warm. And Dan. Dan keeps pushing. Part of it is official. Part of it is just personal."

"And Gray? How is he handling things?"

"He's so neutral, he could be Switzerland. He asked nothing of me in that cabin. He asks nothing of me now. You know, Dan suspected Gray as Susan's murderer and rapist. I knew that there was no way."

"Because you shared a bed platonically?"

"Yes. And because I know Gray is attracted to me. And he did nothing whatsoever to take advantage of the situation. He was so very proper... is so very proper."

"I could tell Dan to take it easy, if you like?"

"No, Elliott. I don't want to have this conversation with Dan. I think it will get very awkward."

"Dan needs to know this information."

Julie cringed.

"I think both of you are letting your personal relationship get in the way of the truthfulness of this investigation," he continued.

"No. Elliott. Gray is already exonerated. Me adding more credence to the DNA testing serves no purpose. I told Dan that Gray was not the one. I told Dan this before the DNA testing."

"You were so sure?"

"Absolutely. You can't share close quarters like that and not get some kind of bead on a person."

"Julie?"

She looked up at him innocently and waited for his question.

"You slept in the same bed with Gray and the man never even attempted to kiss you?"

She blushed deeply and stumbled verbally. "He did kiss me. In the end."

"And?"

"When I asked him to stop, he did."

"Just like that?"

"Just like that."

Elliott paused. "You do know that the DNA results were inconclusive, right?"

Julie frowned. "Dan said that there was no match."

"There wasn't an exact match."

"Meaning?"

"Certain sequences matched, but not others."

"Meaning?"

"Meaning we don't know."

"Elliott, you are talking nonsense. Either there is an exact match or there isn't."

"Well, in this particular case, there seems to be a bit of a gray zone."

When Dan showed up on the lunch break the next day, Julie's stomach flipped. She turned cherry red, certain that Elliott had betrayed her confidence. She stood rooted to the spot trying to finagle her way around a public or private encounter.

"Hello," said Dan. He gave her an award-winning smile and his blue eyes sparkled brilliantly.

She smiled despite herself. Then, sobering, shook her head no.

"Will you allow me to apologize?"

She frowned at him in confusion. "For what?"

"For acting like a Neanderthal. I like you very much, Julie. And I worry about you. And the cop in me, well, I think I've told you before. I'm genetically engineered to protect. I didn't mean to be so hard on you about the snowstorm."

She was going to kill Elliott. "Arrest me now," she said, her voice low and deep.

His jaw dropped. "What for?"

"For the murder that I'm about to commit."

"Elliott did what any good cop would do."

"You are all just one big happy family, aren't you?"

"We do look after our own."

Julie was distraught.

"You are part of the family too," Dan said quietly.

She was at a total loss for words.

"You could have told me, you know."

She shrugged and looked away.

"Julie?"

She found his eyes. "You scare me, Dan Keating."

He frowned in confusion. "Me?"

"It's your pursuit of me."

Dan was quiet for a moment. "Sweetheart, if Gray Walker doesn't scare you, I shouldn't either. And I don't scare off lightly."

"Meaning?"

"Meaning that I'm still here. I just won't be so obvious about it."

She gave him a half-smile.

"And I listen well," Dan said, his voice firm. "You should try me sometime."

17

On the day of the first game, Julie was dressed for victory – blue jeans, turquoise top, wolf earrings, smile. She had baked some peanut butter cookies for the boys and tossed them into the cooler with a few bags of fresh orange slices. When Gray picked her up, she had already negotiated everything onto the outside patio and hefted a few cases of vitamin drinks to set alongside her duffle bag.

Gray was disapproving. "I do the heavy lifting, Julie."

"I was just trying to expedite," she countered.

"No," he said firmly. "So long as I'm the boss, scorekeepers lift nothing but pencils." She gave him her gruffest of attitudinal huffs, but he ignored her as he loaded his SUV. When he returned to her, she had her hands on her hips.

"Now it's time for the valuable cargo," he said, bending swiftly to snatch her up into his arms. She squealed in surprise as he carried her to the SUV and deposited her in the passenger seat.

"I am fully capable of climbing up into your car when I'm not wearing a skirt, Gray," she said petulantly.

"I know," he replied, lifting his head to look at her. "I just wanted to have you in my arms for a minute, Julie. It's been a few months since the snowstorm. I miss the feel of you."

She fell silent in surprise and the corner of his mouth quirked upwards as he buckled her in, leaning close so that he nuzzled her neck before he shut the car door.

"Scorebook?" he asked, as he climbed behind the wheel.

"In my duffle bag," she replied, her neck still tingling from his touch.

"Pencils?"

"Also in the duffle," she said. Her voice had dropped an octave and Gray checked his side view mirror to hide his smile.

"What's in the cooler?"

"Homemade cookies and orange slices."

"Yummm," he said, stretching out the word like a piece of molten taffy.

She looked over at him in his baseball uniform.

"You look like the biggest, baddest ballplayer I've ever met," she said playfully. "I don't think you'll have to worry about losing this season, Gray. You'll win all your games by default. The opposition won't take the field with you on it."

He lifted his chin a notch. "Think so?"

She nodded vigorously.

"Hope so. My boys could use a feel-good season. They have very low self-esteem, Julie. They lack purpose and direction, but more than that, they lack confidence. I swear that insecurity is the root of all evil."

Her thoughts turned to her stepfather.

Gray glanced her way as if sensing her mood. "None of that, Julie. Let the bad things pass through your dream-catcher. Hold on to the good things only."

He reached for her hand and she squeezed it tight.

When they arrived at the field, Julie was approached by a tall, slender woman in ponytail and ball cap. She introduced herself as Karin Swenson, scorekeeper for the White Sox.

"My son is #11," she added, handing Julie her roster so that Julie could copy down the opposing team's line up onto her game grid. "I'm also Dan Keating's sister."

"Well, you've got a wonderful brother," Julie said, glancing up from her work.

"Yes," Karin agreed. "He's a super guy. You should get to know him better."

Julie blushed.

"Your first game?" asked Karin.

"Yes."

"It's my seventh season."

"Whoa," Julie said.

"Yeah." Karin looked up at Gray and her voice changed. "Like anything else in life, once you get sucked in, you're pretty much a goner."

Julie gave her a tight smile, not sure how to interpret her words.

"He's scary big," Karin murmured.

"Yep, and the kids adore him."

"And you?"

"Oh, I think the kids like me too," she said, deliberately misinterpreting the question.

Gray motioned for Julie to join the team huddle and she hurried over to listen in on the pep talk. When they broke with a cheer, Julie stepped toward Gray and kissed him on the cheek. He cocked his head in question.

"For good luck," she said.

She went to move away, but he caught her hand. "I hope you understand that if we win, you'll need to do that every game."

"Then, I guess you could say that the ball is in your court. Right, coach?" Julie watched his dark eyes flare and she chuckled as she took her place at first base.

Kenneth Running Deer, one of her favorite boys, hit a line drive every time he came to bat, and there were usually at least one or two men on base when he did so. He brought in so many runs that the team started to chant "Ken-do, Ken-do!" each time he approached the plate. It was a chant that she had initiated.

Brian Rain Cloud almost pitched a no-hitter. His fastball was so fast that all the boys would "hiss" like a summer rain when he did the wind up and the pitch.

The young men fed off of each other's adrenaline, and Julie periodically served cookies and oranges to keep their energy levels up. As it turned out, however, Gray was her most voracious eater. He even called a time-out just to get another fist-full of snacks.

They trounced the other team and their victory cries were pure testosterone.

"Let's celebrate," said Gray to Julie as they packed up the gear. "We've won a game. This is one game more than we won all of last year."

She beamed at him. "What do you have in mind?"

"A cold Corona with lime to wash away the infield dust and a hot pizza to keep the hunger at bay. You do know that it's traditional to re-cap the game over a meal, don't you?"

"No. I didn't know that."

"A hard and fast baseball rule. Keep your evenings clear on game days."

They had won their tenth win when Julie suggested that they celebrate with dinner at her house. Gray's surprise was expressed in quiet study. He gazed at her thoughtfully.

"What are you fixing, Julie?"

"Beef stroganoff over homemade spätzle, a side salad with warm bacon/mushroom dressing, and apple dumplings with toffee ice cream… unless you'd rather have pizza and beer?"

A slow smile spread across his face and he shook his head to the negative.

"Then, let me head on home. You come when you've wrapped up. I'll need a minute or two or twenty to get things together."

By the time he walked through her kitchen door, she had chips and dip on the table and wine poured into two glasses. They re-lived the game as they feasted, laughing at the team's antics and reveling in the pivotal points that loaded the bases or scored a significant run.

Julie set dessert on the table.

"What was with Keith today?" she asked. "He seemed rather out of sorts."

Gray gave her a sharp and significant glance.

"He's usually so playful," she commented. "And he seemed so down today. Are there problems at school? At home?"

"At home," said Gray softly.

"What kind of problems?"

Gray took a deep breath and looked at her solidly. "I think he's being physically abused by his father."

Julie grew quite still, almost as if her soul had left the room or her fiery spirit has reduced itself to one insignificant cold, blue flame. Gray reached out to touch her hands. They were ice.

"I've been working with juvenile services. All the paperwork has been filed, Julie. It's a matter for the courts now."

That statement seemed to bring her back from a great distance. "I haven't seen any bruises," she said. Her voice was a whisper.

"I think his father hits him in places that won't be seen, for the most part. Keith has a lot of broken bones for a boy who plays no contact sports."

"Is that what made you suspect?"

"No," Gray said quietly.

"What, then?"

"His eyes."

Julie looked up.

"His eyes can be quite haunted at times."

"How bad is it?"

"I think it's very bad, Julie."

"Then Keith could be dead by the time the courts process the paperwork."

"I know this." Gray's big shoulders sagged. "We're doing the best that we can."

"Have you spoken to Keith?"

"I'm trying. Right now, he's a bit uncooperative."

Julie nodded in understanding and they were both momentarily quiet. "I never talked about my injuries either," she said softly, breaking the silence. "And trust me, a lot of people asked. I lied to everyone, even my friends. I was so ashamed. In the end, I just withdrew from social contact altogether."

Gray listened intently.

"It was easier to be invisible to everyone. A non-entity. That way there were no painful questions to be answered, no lies and no excuses to cook up on the spot." She looked up at him. "You know, there was this guidance counselor once. In high school." She stopped talking and looked out the window. The pain in her eyes was so sharp it could have etched a diamond. Gray massaged her cold hands gently, but firmly, willing them to warm, waiting for her to speak again. "Mr. Thompson." She swallowed. "He was very nice, and he tried to help, but I was so broken on the inside, I couldn't see, and didn't see, all his care and concern. When I finally recognized it, I ran from it. Tenderness was such a foreign emotion. It hurt."

"He came to visit me in the hospital after my stepfather almost beat me to death. I told him that I had fallen down the stairs." A single tear ran down her cheek and she brushed it away quickly. "I guess the good news is I don't remember much of it, the actual beating. He knocked me out three or four punches in. I weighed even less then than I do now. It didn't take much effort to do me harm." She paused to draw a quiet breath. "Help had finally arrived in the form of this guidance counselor, and I bolted in the other direction. Doesn't make much sense, does it?"

She looked up at him.

Gray looked as if he were about to engage in a savage hell-fight. She sat back in her chair and swallowed. "I'm sorry," she apologized. "You are so angry."

"Don't you dare apologize, Julie," he said, his voice thick with emotion. "I'm not angry with you. I'm just angry. Only bottom feeders prey upon the defenseless."

She sighed and gave him a weak smile. "Actually, Gray, I think I'm the tougher one. I ended up having more mental muscle. As they say, what doesn't kill us only makes us stronger. I'm not without scars, but I'm all concrete and reinforced steel on the inside. I'm Fort Knox."

Gray was quiet a moment.

"Yes, yes you are." He looked at her. "But even Fort Knox opens its doors on a regular basis to admit its trusted caretakers. Julie, I would like to be your trusted caretaker."

She remained silent.

"It's what I want," said Gray simply. "I've never wanted anything more in my whole life."

18

At Tuesday's game, she brought four dozen double-chocolate cupcakes with liquid fudge centers. They couldn't find all of the balls that they had knocked out of the park during the pre-game warm up.

A parent from the opposing team pulled Gray aside. "What are you feeding them?" he asked.

"Julie."

Although the team was in top form, Keith couldn't run the bases before coin-toss because of a "stitch in his side." Julie gave Gray a stricken look. Gray benched him to keep him from further injury. He didn't seem to mind. He ate cupcakes and joined Julie in cheering on his teammates to another victory.

When Keith's father pulled up in his cobalt blue James Bond BMW after the game, Julie approached the car.

"I see Keith is favoring his right side," she said with all the neutrality of an atomic bomb.

"He fell down the stairs," the man said cavalierly as he glanced at his Rolex.

She looked at his smug face and expensive clothes. Douglas Hawthorn descended from a long line of Hawthorns. They were gold magnates and had made money steadily off of Black Hills gold until the vein tapped out.

"Are you going to fix those stairs?" she asked.

"The kid's clumsy."

"That's what I told my teachers and coaches when I was too young to know better."

He looked at her.

"I suggest that you stop and desist before you end up behind bars." She walked away.

"Come back here. You can't threaten me."

She turned back to him and said, "I did no such thing. Consider our talk an infomercial."

Elliott picked Julie up after work on Friday night en route to a gig they had near Rapid City. She was distracted and quiet as she sat in the passenger seat, and Elliott was hard pressed to pull her out of her dark funk.

"What's going on, Julie?"

"Baseball stuff."

"Baseball stuff?"

"Yeah."

"Did the Braves lose?"

"Of course not."

"Would you like to talk about it?"

"No, not really."

"Anything I can do?"

"I don't think so."

"Try me."

Julie was quiet for a moment, weighing her thoughts. She took a deep breath and exhaled her stress and frustration. "One of the boys is being abused by his father."

"Gray working on this?"

"Yes."

"Who is being abused?"

"I don't know if I'm supposed to tell."

"Gray told you, as first base coach, didn't he?"

"Yeah."

"Well, I'm a cop. I patrol the whole baseball field."

She turned to him and gave him a weak smile. "Keith Hawthorn."

"The golden child?"

"Gray says that Keith is more black and blue. He's filed a court order to put the boy in protective custody."

Elliott whistled low and long. "Gray is mighty big, Julie, but then, he'd have to be to take on Douglas Hawthorn. Will Keith testify against his father?"

"Don't know."

"Julie?"

"Yeah?"

"You know how you told me that life is like a series of TV shows?"

"Yep."

"Let's do a little Emeril tonight, and put this on the back burner, okay?"

She turned to look at Elliott, giving him her full attention.

"My grandma always told me that worry was an insult to God." He glanced over and watched her face fracture in pain. "Gray's set things in motion. Let's let it go for tonight. Is there anything you can do right this evening to protect Keith?"

She shook her head to the negative.

"Then let's sing. Pick yourself up. Pump yourself up. You are no good to anyone like this."

She nodded. "Okay."

Somehow, she powered through. Her smile was bright, her stage presence magnetic, kinetic, and fresh. She hit every note and packed more energy into her delivery than usual.

When they left the stage, Elliott pulled her to him and gave her a squeeze. "You are ever the professional, Julie Hastings. An amazing performance. No one would know how much you were hurting on the inside."

Julie's throat convulsed in a dry swallow. She nodded at him silently and swallowed again. He had no idea just how much she was hurting on the inside.

They entered the baseball semifinals undefeated. The boys strutted around like roosters, their backs straight, their shoulders square. They knocked their fists gently together as they walked past one another in silent salute.

Keith sported a massive black eye that day. Julie touched his face gently, making sure that no facial bones were broken.

"Skateboarding accident," he replied, in response to her silent question.

"Must have hurt."

"Yup," Keith responded. "I'm a bit of a daredevil."

"You know, I had a lot of bruises too, growing up. I also had a lot of broken bones. I told everyone I was clumsy. Saved a lot of explaining."

He gave her a sharp glance and not one more word the entire game.

And the game was a close one. Both teams were playing well, but Kenneth Running Deer ran like his namesake and caught a pop fly to end the game with the Braves on top.

Julie did a bunch of high-fives with some pretty keyed up 16-year olds as they grunted out their "hoh-hoh-hoh-hoh" testosterone-rich chant. Even Keith was smiling. She sighed. At least his father couldn't rob him of this little victory.

As they packed up, Gray raided the ice chests.

"Any more goodies?"

"What are you looking for?"

"The brownies with the fudge bottoms and fudge topping."

She handed him the last one.

"Hey Gray," she said. Her tone captured his immediate attention. "I have to travel to Pierre this week. There's a three-day veterinary conference Cole would like for me to attend."

"When?"

"Tomorrow. It's a Wednesday, Thursday, Friday thing. I think I'll drive home Friday night after the closing dinner so that I don't miss the game on Saturday morning."

He frowned. "No, I don't think that's a good idea. Driving that late at night is too risky. You could hit an animal, have a car problem, get into trouble. Drive home the next morning."

"I'd have to get up before dawn to get here in time. The sky is just as dark then, and I'd have the truckers to contend with on the road. Coming home that evening is the best course of action."

She held up a hand when he went to speak again. "Gray Walker, somehow I have managed to keep myself whole for 24 years. And God knows I've been challenged on that score. I can take care of myself."

"I don't think your decision is a wise one."

"Do you or don't you want me there for the game?"

"Not if it puts you at risk."

"I appreciate your concern. Truly. I do," she said. "But, I'll get back by Saturday morning."

She squeezed his little finger then released it, giving him an affirmative nod. The news had not put him into a good mood.

"All right," he said grudgingly. "Then let me take you to dinner."

"Oh, I can't tonight," she said, her face falling. "I'm sorry. Truly, I am. But Dan asked me to help the guys down at the station to stuff envelopes. It's their local fund-raising drive."

He was visibly displeased.

"I'm working a fundraiser for the community," she said slowly, a tad angry at herself for feeling compelled to explain her actions.

He nodded. "When will you be back at your place?"

"I don't know. Ten?"

He tugged on a loose curl then tilted her head up to kiss her on the lips. The kiss was long, deep and compelling. She was surprised by both the public display of affection and the power of his possession. She could hear her boys whistling at them from the bench.

"Go do your good deed," he said and brushed her lips once more to seal the kiss.

She arrived at the station, brushing the infield dust off of her jeans. There wasn't time to change and she felt badly about that. When she greeted Dan, she apologized for her appearance.

"Sorry about my baseball uniform. Tommy Red Fox slid into first and caked me in a cloud of dust."

"Your uniform?"

"Yeah, I wore this to the first practice and the boys played well, so Gray said I had to wear it every time they have a game. We all have to play by that superstitious 'don't-change-a-thing' baseball luck thing."

Dan chuckled. She looked good enough to eat in that outfit. Gray was playing it all right.

"Meet the force and all of our forceful supporters," he said then more loudly, "Most of you know Julie, a gifted veterinarian who specializes in Copper Pigs." A dozen men and women waved and greeted her enthusiastically. They were amidst a sea of solicitation letters, donation forms and envelopes. He held out a chair for her.

"Coffee and doughnuts?"

She grinned. "What is it with you guys and doughnuts anyway?"

"They should change their motto from 'Protect and Serve' to 'Eat Dessert First'," quipped a dashing redhead at the front table.

Dan brought coffee and munchables and motioned her to an empty workstation. He showed her how the mailing was pieced together and turned what would have been a mundane exercise in "Post Office 101" into a standup comic act. By the time Elliott and the band joined them, she was wiping away tears. She had laughed that hard.

Naturally, the conversation automatically switched to music and singing gigs. Elliott filled her in on the latest bookings and was effusive in his praise of her vocal talent.

Petey added, "Yeah, but you should see Slinky move."

"Slinky who?" asked Julie.

"Slinky you," said Petey.

"Knock, knock," said George. And the table roared. She missed the joke.

"Good thing I am so expert in public relations."

The men snickered.

"Public relations?" asked Julie. More snickers. "What do you mean?"

"Oh," said Ro-Bear. "It's like this. If some member of the public wants relations with you, George reads them their rights."

"Their rights?" asked Julie.

"Yeah," said George. "I give them the right to get gone, the right to leave in peace—"

"The right to leave in one piece is more like it," quipped Petey.

"Knock, knock," said Ro-Bear, hammering the table with his fist. The table roared again.

"Knock, knock?" asked Julie.

"Knocking heads!" said Ro-Bear.

"How often have you had to exercise your role in public relations, George?" she asked in shocked disbelief.

"I do believe my job is a permanent position. I've even required an assistant from time to time."

"No!"

"Last week, there was a persistently persuasive young man who insisted on meeting you," said George.

"Same Sioux?" asked Ro-Bear, stuffing an envelope.

"Yeah."

"Band groupie?" asked Julie.

"Something like that," said George, giving Dan a significant look. "The fans are why Elliott started driving you to our gigs."

"Whaaaat?" Julie wheeled on Elliott. "You told me your carpool idea was to conserve energy and protect the environment."

"I didn't lie," said Elliott. "I'm saving myself the energy I'd have to spend busting somebody's nose." George thumped the desk again for emphasis. "And as for protecting the environment, well, you're part of the environment. Like a natural resource, right men?"

"Right as rain."

"Roger that."

"Damn straight."

A boisterous gaggle of women joined the table wiggling themselves in between the men. Brenda belonged to George. She was a full-figured woman and matched his width and girth. Becka was Ro-Bear's wife and just as tall and lanky. Cynthia, a Marilyn Monroe look-alike, had Petey's ring on her finger.

Her sultry eyes and come-hither smile served as a perfect foil to Petey's ornery, impish grin.

The ladies blew into the room like a gale force wind and completely dominated all conversation from that point on. They were curious about her and the evening began to take on an interrogatory edge.

Yes. She liked South Dakota. No. The winters weren't so bad. No. Even the blizzard was a good experience – she ended up as an assistant baseball coach as a result. Yes. She missed Virginia, specifically the beach and the peanuts, in that order. She attended Virginia Tech. She liked singing. She'd knocked $10,000 off her student loans since she'd been moonlighting with the Copper Pigs. Yes, she thought Dan was a handsome, wonderful guy. And clever. And thoughtful. And funny. No, she wasn't afraid of Gray Walker. Not anymore. Yes, she really did keep a pet wolf. No, she wasn't afraid of him either. No, her family wasn't upset about her moving out west. No, they wouldn't be visiting. They weren't close. No, she had no intentions of moving back east.

By the time they had stuffed the last envelope, Julie was a little shell-shocked from the polite yet friendly rollercoaster of an inquisition. After she had said her good-byes, Dan escorted her out to her car.

"Oh," she said turning abruptly and feinting a return into the building. "I forgot to tell the ladies my shoe size!"

Dan chuckled. "If there was a question they didn't ask, it was because they already knew the answer," he said good-naturedly. "They just wanted to get to know you."

"Yikes!" said Julie. "Get to know me! All that was missing was the bare room with the light bulb!"

"Well, here's a question for you. The last one."

"Shoot."

"What's up with you and Gray?"

"We're friends."

"Good friends?"

"Tracking in that direction."

She drove home distractedly. In fact, her driving was so sloppy that she had to mentally rein in her thoughts and focus on the road. She had almost sideswiped a trashcan and taken out a traffic cone. It had been such a long day that she almost ran over the wolf that was waiting for her in her driveway.

"Holy cow," she said, leaping from the car. "Big Boy!"

He bounded over to her, sniffing her intently. "What is it?" she asked, "You crazy beast."

But he was all over her, smelling her intently.

"Oh," she said, trying to put two and two together. "I'm not upset." She pushed against his massive chest. "I laughed until I cried tonight. You are smelling happy tears."

He touched his nose to hers and stared her in the eyes. She pulled back uneasily. "You smell Gray on me, don't you? Well, remember the scent." She wrapped her hand around his snout and applied a little pressure. "You are not to harm a hair on his body," she said, looking directly into his eyes. "You may growl all you want at others, but not at Gray."

When she released him, he sat before her with what she swore was a grin. She sighed, assessing him critically. "So, do you want to spend the night?"

Yep. That wolf could grin. She was sure of it.

19

The drive home from Pierre was a long, but not so long that Julie couldn't tackle it after the closing dinner festivities. She had dialed into the classic country station on her radio and was absently humming along as she cruised down the black expanse of roadway.

It was a moonless night and the skies were dark. Gray was right about driving under such conditions. Her eyes scanned the roadsides for deer, fox, bear, and elk. She didn't want to hit anything.

In fact, she was so busy scoping for critters that she didn't see the nail-studded piece of plywood lying in the middle of road. She was on top of it before she could react. There was no way to avoid it. Construction cones flanked the right shoulder and an on-coming truck made it impossible to swerve left.

Two tires blew completely. She gripped the wheel tightly, fighting for control and rode the adrenaline rush as she pulled to the side of the road. Too fast. She'd been driving too fast.

She slowed the car as she passed the construction site, then sidled off to the shoulder, her mouth cotton. She took a shaky breath and fumbled her cell phone, dropping it on the floor by her feet. She fished for it for what felt like an eternity, finally finding it underneath her accelerator.

Irritation compounded her fright, and she took a deep breath in an attempt to mentally adjust her attitude. There was no hurry home.

She dialed AAA on her cell and waited for the tow truck in the silent dark, watching the stars wink out. Clouds were moving in and she fidgeted uncomfortably. A stiff wind was picking up and she worried about rain. On the plains, when it fell, it fell hard. It fell in buckets.

A couple of hundred feet up the road was a rather seedy biker bar. The neon sign flashed XYZ. She watched the rough crowd come and go, catching a cacophony of karaoke on the wind each time the door opened.

She sat in the dark and thought about calling Gray, but he had a Sioux Council meeting that evening. She didn't want to interrupt him to get an "I-told-you-so." She hung her head while gripping the steering wheel and wondered if Gray was an "I-told-you-so" kind of guy, but then she was too ashamed to find out.

By nine o'clock, road rescue had wrenched her car up onto the flatbed. Normally, she'd have ridden shotgun with the tow-truck driver, but the young man disturbed her. When he introduced himself as Luke Skywalker, she had smiled, but she didn't like the way the man averted his face or looked down when he spoke to her. His eyes always stopped at her chest. Her outfit wasn't overtly sexy, but it was overtly feminine. The skirt, although a ¾-length strait-line, was slit to mid-thigh. And the blouse, although long-sleeved, was tailored and dipped a little low. A discrete lace camisole covered her skin, but it didn't hide her curves. She felt naked under the man's scrutiny.

With a sick feeling of unease, she popped the trunk and removed her leather duffle bag. "I've got a friend en route to pick me up," she lied. "I'll pick up my car tomorrow at the garage."

"You gonna stand on the roadside in the dark?" he asked.

"No," she replied, tossing her head at the neon. A large group of people poured out of the front door and she waved to them. In their drunken stupor, they waved back. "I'm going to get myself a beer at that bar and wait for his arrival. Should be any minute now."

Actually, she had done no such thing, but she put as much conviction and confidence in her voice as she could. The tow truck driver's reaction was hostile and belligerent. He looked at the crowd of drunken bar patrons, then climbed up into the truck and peeled out recklessly, spewing gravel in his wake.

She stood for a moment in silence and wondered what to do. She was midway between Cottonwood and Wasta and a significant distance from home. On a quick and decisive huff of air, she dialed Elliott Rand. He was on the line quickly.

"Julie!"

She hesitated. "Hey, I'm in a bit of trouble, Elliott. I was in Pierre for a veterinary conference today and was driving home. I ran over some nails and blew out two tires. I've got AAA, and they sent a tow truck. Unfortunately, I think that if I had gotten into the cab with the driver, I'd be six feet under tomorrow."

"What?" His voice was flat.

"Call it intuition, call it paranoia. I opted out. So I'm about a couple of hundred yards from a biker bar on Route 14, suitcase in hand. With what I'm wearing, I'm going to get into trouble if I go into the bar, and I'm going to get wet or get eaten by a bear or a mountain lion if I don't. I don't know what to do. Can you come get me?"

"Hang tight. Just give me a minute."

He put her on hold and was back on the line in short order. "Go to the bar. I've called Dan. Dan has called a cop-friend in that county who is heading over to pick you up. Dan's unfortunately in the middle of a very messy homicide."

"What?"

"I know. Contrary to outward appearances, it's not always pot luck dinners and church socials around here."

She paused. "Thanks, Elliott. But you should not have troubled Dan. If I wanted to trouble Dan, I would have troubled him myself."

"He's troubled enough by you, Julie. Trust me. I did what I should have done. Dan's plan is sound. Be safe. Be careful."

"No worries. It's a public place, right? What harm can come?"

She walked to the garishly lit building and stepped inside. It smelled of stale beer, rancid fry-oil and cigarettes. She closed her eyes briefly and moved toward the bar as inconspicuously as possible. Right. How to be inconspicuous moving through a biker bar in business attire with a suitcase in tow?

She felt the eyes turn upon her, but she ignored them and grabbed an empty bar stool. The barkeeper was Sioux, and he turned his dark eyes upon her in question.

"Could I have a vodka tonic with lots of lime?"

He nodded silently.

Wine wasn't going to get her through the next half hour. "Is there place for my bag behind the bar?"

He nodded again and took her luggage from her as if it weighed nothing. He must be related to Gray, she mused. She had about a three-minute interval of silence before the first man approached her. She took a deep pull on her drink.

"I'm waiting for someone," she said.

He didn't buy it. Neither did the others.

For the next twenty minutes, she fielded questions and deflected full-disclosure. No last name. No occupation. She was in the health field. Traveling. Flat tire. Too many rough and tumble cowboys were closing in on her personal space. Some were gently touching her. It was fleeting contact, like little gnats you can't see or catch.

She was beginning to get properly panicked when another Sioux pushed his way into her space and introduced himself. She opened her mouth to speak, but he spoke first.

"I'm Officer Running Deer. Is your name Julie?"

She frowned in confusion. She knew this man. He was her short-stop's father. Why was he acting like they were strangers?

He showed a badge because he was in plain clothes. "I'm to take you into protective custody. May I have your full cooperation?"

"Absolutely," she said slowly. She slid off of her barstool and turned to take care of her tab. The barkeep shook his head and handed her her suitcase.

"No monies owed," he said quietly. She smiled at him and stuffed ten dollars in the tip jar. Her male admirers went silent and gave The Law a wide berth. She gave the more aggressive man in the bunch a lethal look. "I told you that I was waiting for someone."

He paled and his eyebrows shot skyward. "We were just making nice with the lady," he said to Officer Running Deer.

"No more," said Running Deer. He ushered Julie out of the bar and into his squad car.

She took a deep breath after she was buckled in and released her pent-up nervousness in a shaky sigh. "Tom?"

"Yes?"

"Why did you act like you didn't know me in there?"

"Because those white boys would not have let an Indian leave with the likes of you unless it was official."

Julie groaned.

"Just FYI, Julie Hastings, you were not in the most enlightened spot on planet earth tonight."

"Yeah," she said softly. "Thank you for saving me. I needed saving."

He grunted and picked up his radio. "Barbara, patch me through to Officer Keating, please." There was some dead, crackly air time, then Dan came on the line. Tom powered on the windshield wipers. It was beginning to rain.

"Dan," said Tom Running Deer, "I've got one Julie Hastings in protective custody. Good call, that. Very good call. I'm off shift and on my way home. I'll transport her back. Take care of that homicide. No worries here."

"Thanks, Tom. I owe you," came the response. She could hear Dan's stress and strain over the air waves. He sounded rough.

Tom signed off, then turned to Julie. He was accusatory. "Why didn't you call Gray?"

"Excuse me?"

"Why didn't you call Gray?"

"I would have, but Friday is his counsel night."

"Julie, you are more important to him than counsel night."

She was caught off guard. "I was trying to be respectful of his obligations." But there was more to it than that. He had warned her. She hadn't listened and, in the end, her pride wouldn't knuckle under to her need.

"So you called Dan?" He was trying to be neutral, but failing in the attempt.

"No," she said, her feathers ruffled. "I called Officer Elliott Rand. I was hoping to call in a favor. He owes me one. I was hoping he'd come fetch me. Instead, he called Dan who obviously called you. So here I am."

"Julie," he said. "I have to be honest with you. I'm not taking you home tonight." She pivoted in her seat and stared at him as directly as her seatbelt would allow. "I am taking you to Gray."

"Why?"

"Because you have some damage control to do tonight," he stated simply.

"Tom," she said, trying to control her anger. "I need you to explain."

"I'm sure that by now, Gray has heard all about your flat tires and your adventures at the XYZ bar."

"I didn't have any adventures at the XYZ bar. I had a vodka and tonic."

"The bartender is Sioux. I'm sure he called Gray to tell him what was up with one very well-dressed Julie-on-her-own, especially since he knows that this particular Julie belongs to one Gray Walker."

"I do not belong to Gray Walker," she said hotly.

"Gray thinks that you do."

"He does? And why is that?"

"Because you've slept with him."

Julie froze. "What?" Her mouth was cotton-dry.

"Julie. Gray is Sioux. True Sioux. It doesn't matter if you slept together platonically or not."

"It was a blizzard and it was cold. And how do you know about this?"

"All of Fallston knows about you and Gray and the hunting cabin. What you need to understand is that there was a time when the simple act of sharing a buffalo robe was a matrimonial act, sex or not."

"A buffalo robe?"

"Uh-huh."

She shook slightly as she remembered Gray's dark eyes searching hers in quiet question as he laid the buffalo robe atop the bed.

"I didn't realize that what I was doing was anything more significant than trying to keep us both warm." Her voice was a whisper.

"I know, Julie," said Tom. "Except—"

"Except what?"

"Except that Gray has considered you his woman since the blizzard. Please listen to me."

She did her best, but her ears were ringing.

"He will be very hurt by the fact that when you were in trouble, you called Dan and not him."

"But I didn't! I called Elliott!"

"Dan or Elliott, I'm just telling you how it's going to go down."

She tried to quiet her breathing.

"I can tell you right now that he's going to be even more upset when he hears about that slick biker boy with his hand on your thigh."

"The touch was not welcomed."

"I know. I was there. Changes nothing."

"This is ridiculous."

"He's going to be upset. Just talk to him. Explain it to him."

Within a heartbeat, Tom's cell phone chimed and he spoke softly into the receiver. "I take it that your meeting is over," he said. There was a moment of silence. "Pull over on Manor Road. I'll find you there." Julie watched him terminate communication. The rain was falling heavily. It was more of a solid sheet of water than drops.

"You know, Gray is one of my best friends," Tom announced. "I'm happy that he's found you."

Julie turned and looked out the window, seeing nothing.

"I know you're probably sitting there wondering why on earth you ever got involved with that big, silent, protective Sioux in the first place."

Julie grunted softly.

"Well, if you opt out now, Julie, you'll be ruining the chance for a lot of happiness for the both of you. That man worships the ground you walk on. He'd do anything to please you. That kind of emotion is something you just don't find often. In fact, some people never find it. Never know it. Not ever."

Tom hit the blinker and pulled off to the side of the road behind Gray's SUV. The rain was hammering the car. The noise was deafening.

Gray popped out of his automobile and opened the passenger door then trotted to the passenger door of the squad car as Julie unbuckled her seatbelt. He scooped her up and raced back to the car, depositing her gently on the seat.

Tom met Gray at the rear bumper and handed him Julie's overnight bag.

"She's upset," he said cryptically.

Gray nodded. "Thanks, Tom."

Gray hopped back into the SUV and eyed Julie carefully. "Sorry about the rain," he said.

"Not your fault, Gray," her voice was tight and she closed her eyes in an effort to consciously relax.

"Sorry about the flat tires."

"Not your fault either."

"Sorry about the XYZ bar."

Julie groaned and closed her eyes. He reached for her hand and gave it a squeeze.

"You're upset."

"And scared and angry and wet and tired and cold," she added. Her stomach growled fiercely.

"And hungry," said Gray.

"Yeah."

She watched him out of the corner of her eye. He didn't look agitated or jealous or obsessively possessive. She shook her head. Either Tom blew this incident all out of proportion or Gray was a very good actor.

"Julie?" He spoke so softly that she could barely hear him over the frenetic slapping of the windshield wipers. "This is very bad driving. I'm going to take you to my home tonight, not yours. It's closer." He paused. "Is that okay?"

Her heart began to pound.

"Please say 'yes'".

She was quiet a moment. "Yes."

"I'll fix you something to eat."

"Okay." She paused. "Could I take a shower? I smell like cigarette smoke."

He smiled. "Of course. And, after dinner, if the storm lets up, and if you want, I'll take you back to your place. Naturally, I would hope to hold you tonight, but that will be your choice. Rain storms and snow storms don't carry the same sort of isolationism, but one could always hope that you'd see it that way."

"I see."

"Or perhaps you might just choose to stay because you enjoy being held snug and safe in my arms? Do you remember?"

"You should sell cars, Gray Walker."

His smile widened.

"No pressure. You choose."

"Okay."

"Now, tell me what happened tonight."

She did. He wasn't pleased with most of what she had to say. She could see his jaw was rigidly set and his hands gripped the wheel far too tightly.

By the time Gray pulled into his apartment complex, Julie was talked out for the most part. He ushered her into his apartment in silence.

The apartment was Spartan and neat. All was in earth tones, warm, rich and friendly. While she picked up his personal momentos to examine them, he fetched her a clean towel and washcloth. "Here ya go," he said, tugging on her earlobe. "Please, be comfortable."

"Thank you."

She took her shower and slipped into a soft cotton t-shirt and cotton pants. She walked barefoot into the kitchen, her towel-dried hair curling softly.

"Sit, Julie. I've made you some pasta." She ate, thanking him for the meal, and told him about her conference.

He listened.

While she sipped a cup of hot tea, he asked her about the AAA driver again. The conversation was repeatedly interrupted by a crack of lightening, a roll of thunder or a particularly heavy barrage of raindrops.

"Stay," he said softly.

"Okay," she responded, her eyes gazing out the window, drinking in the night. It had been months since the snowstorm. She inhaled slowly. This time, she was choosing to spend the night. She turned to Gray and acknowledged him. "I see you Gray Walker, and I like what I see."

She changed in the bathroom. She had packed a nightgown in her duffle. It was a soft peach satin shell that flounced softly mid-thigh. When she entered the bedroom, he hummed in appreciation.

"Gray Walker, you hum like that when good food is set upon the table."

He smiled, eyes flashing, and held out a hand. "Come here to me, woman," he said softly, and tugged her toward the bed. He waited until they were tucked in before he spoke again. "So, Julie," he sighed. "Now that I've got you warm and safely snug in my arms, I want you to tell me what really upset you this evening."

He felt her muscles tighten. "I told you already."

"You didn't tell me all of it."

He waited. And waited. Then, he crushed her to him gently. "Speak, woman. You were afraid of me tonight. That hasn't been the case since before the blizzard."

"Tom and I had a conversation."

It was Gray's turn to stiffen.

"He said that you consider me your woman because we shared a buffalo robe." Gray laughed softly. His chest rumbled deep, rich and easy. "Do you consider me your woman?" she asked.

"Well," he sighed. "That is a loaded question. If I say yes, you'll consider me an anachronism and a male chauvinist. If I say no, you'll think that I don't care about you enough, that I'm not sincere in my pursuit of your affections." He rubbed her shoulder with his chin. "Julie, I think a more appropriate question is this – Do you consider me your man? In this day and age, it's the woman who chooses, you know."

She was silent.

"So, are you going to answer the question?"

"You didn't answer mine," she said, tucking her hand underneath his t-shirt and burrowing her face into the hollow of his neck. "I'm not going to answer yours."

"Fair enough," said Gray, trying to keep the smile out of his voice. He placed his right hand on top of hers, the t-shirt between them. He didn't need an answer. Not a verbal one anyway. She'd already told him what he needed to know, even if she didn't acknowledge it herself.

20

After breakfast, Gray drove her back to her home so that she could change into her baseball uniform. Fortunately, she had made a double batch of snicker doodles, Rice Krispy treats, and Chex mix in advance of her trip to Pierre. The boys wouldn't starve. She glanced at Gray loading the SUV – neither would the team's biggest boy.

She called the garage and inquired about her car. The manager on duty told her that he had not received a red Toyota Corolla the evening prior. She called AAA and spoke to a representative, explaining her situation.

She was on hold when Gray appeared in her doorway and tapped his watch. She gave AAA her cell number, locked up the house and dialed Elliott on her mobile. She left a message asking if he could pull any strings to track down her missing vehicle.

The ballgame was a total adrenaline rush as usual. The boys played so well. She was a little surprised to see a police cruiser enter the parking area with its lights flashing and more than a little surprised when a second car pulled in behind the first.

Dan got out of the first car, Elliott the second. Both of them strode toward the ball diamond with grim faces and downcast eyes.

The referee called a time out in the last inning and a hushed murmur rose from the crowd. Both coaches and the referee approached the police officers and stood in quiet huddle. Then Gray pivoted in Julie's direction and waved her over, his face dark.

She was genuinely confused as she approached the men. Her first thought had been of Keith, but Keith stood resolutely on first base, alive and well. She searched each face as she approached the group, looking for a clue. Her eyes found Dan's and she waited.

"Julie, we need to ask you some questions about the AAA driver that responded to your call last night."

She cocked her head, her mind moving swiftly. "He wasn't an AAA driver, was he? That's why my car isn't in the garage, isn't it?"

"Could you come back with us? Now?" said Dan. "We need to ask you a few questions."

Julie just looked at him.

"Julie?" he said, all cop.

Her breathing was short and shallow. "He was going to kill me, wasn't he? I knew it!" She pivoted to Elliott. "I knew it. That's why I didn't get into the truck!"

"Come back with us to the station," said Elliott.

She shook her head to the negative and heads popped up all way round.

"Julie."

It was Gray.

"Wh-what?"

"You need to go with Dan and answer some questions."

She looked at Gray for a moment, willing him to understand her dilemma. For all the world, she did not want to hurt Dan Keating. She had spent the night in Gray's arms. She hoped she'd be able to keep that to herself.

After the game, Gray drove to the police station and waited an hour for Julie to be released. Dan was none-too-pleased to see him in the waiting room.

"Someone needs to take Julie home," said Gray. "Unless you've recovered her car?"

"Not yet," said Dan with a frown. The two men stared at each other.

"Did we win?" asked Julie, rounding Dan and crossing the room to Gray.

"By a run."

"What happened to our big lead?"

"It left when you left the infield," he said. He looked up at Dan. "What's the word?"

Dan frowned. "The man who responded to Julie's call for roadside assistance was not the real tow truck driver. The real tow truck driver was found mauled to death near Rock Creek."

"Mauled to death?"

"Yeah."

"Did you check the AAA call record, the call before Julie's?"

"Way ahead of you."

"Any leads?"

Dan shrugged, giving up nothing. Gray cocked his head and held the silence. "Can I take Julie home?"

Dan nodded, disgruntled and displeased. Julie had been very uncomfortable during questioning, but then, he imagined he would have been also had he come that close to... To what? The man who had responded to her call had obviously stolen the truck, and now, her car. But that didn't necessarily link him to the dead man. Perhaps he was nothing more than an opportunist who had inadvertently stumbled upon the parked tow truck.

The dead man had been found at a rest stop near a scenic overlook. Dan took a deep and uneasy breath. He had been mauled like the woman who had been trapped in the blizzard on the mountain.

Dan watched Julie and Gray walk across the parking lot to Gray's SUV, pleased by the large amount of open space between them as they made their way. He didn't reach for her and she didn't reach for him, but they stopped every now and again to face each other and talk. Gray reached inside his jacket pocket and removed his car keys. Dan stiffened. Car keys! How did the false tow truck driver get the keys to the truck? The real driver would have certainly had them on his person when he was attacked by whatever animal had attacked him.

Dan was standing in silence, lost in thought when Elliott entered the waiting room.

"We've found the tow truck," he said.

"Where?"

"Abandoned on the outskirts of town," reported Elliot. "Good news is, Julie's car is still on the flatbed."

Dan scowled. That was not good news. That was not good news at all. If theft wasn't the motive behind the misappropriation of the tow truck and Julie's car, what was?

21

Julie started off her workweek with three terribly injured pets. A border collie rounding up a herd was gored by an irate steer and required almost 100 stitches to keep its intestines inside its body. A black lab had gotten its hind leg caught in an illegal wolf trap and required an amputation below the shattered bone. A German Shepherd chased a rabbit and managed to snare himself into a tangle of barbed wire. The animal had to be sedated before he could be cut free, and it took Julie all afternoon to disinfect and stitch up the multiple cuts that crisscrossed his body.

She was never more grateful to administer simple vitamin supplements and booster shots to the rest of the town's household pets. No matter what Dan Keating said, sometimes the standard routine was just what the doctor ordered.

The new furniture arrived for the waiting room. It had been on special order and had taken the better part of a year to make it to South Dakota. The result was a very safari-esque appearance. The veterinary office now looked as good as it smelled. She surveyed the room with a smile on her face then grabbed her purse and headed for the door.

Dan called her cell before she had even turned the keys in the ignition. "Are you on your way home?" he asked.

"I am," she said.

"Can I come over?"

"Have you eaten?"

"No."

"Would you like some dinner?"

"Very much."

"I'll be home in ten minutes," she informed him.

She pulled some homemade meatloaf out of the freezer and started warming it up. Although Dan was not big on vegetables, she warmed a fresh green pea puree and set out some frizzled onions and bacon bits to serve as toppings. Then she took out some refrigerator dough and made rolls. By the time Dan walked through the kitchen door, the house smelled like food.

He helped himself to some crackers and cheese, opened the wine and poured them each a glass. He wrapped an arm around her waist from behind and gave her a gentle squeeze as he deposited her wineglass on the counter. She was busy shaping the dough into fantails.

"I haven't seen much of you," he husked.

"Work, the Copper Pigs, baseball. The only free time I have left is eating and sleeping."

"I'd be happy to join you in either activity."

She chuckled and shook her head as she slid the rolls into the oven. A quick bark pulled her attention to the kitchen door. Dan was on his feet immediately, his face a mixture of anger and alarm. She crossed the room, removing her apron, and gave his arm as squeeze as she passed.

"Trust me, Dan," she said. She opened the door a crack and no more. Big Boy barreled into it, then sat back on his haunches in dazed confusion. "I have company," she said to the wolf. "A dinner guest. You may come in and join us if you can behave yourself. No growling tonight. I'm very tired and don't have the energy to offset your *über* alpha protectionist policy."

The wolf's head dipped, so she opened the door. Big Boy walked in, looked in Dan's direction, then took a spot on the kitchen floor near the table. She fixed the animal a cracker with cheese and hand-fed him. He was the poster dog for obedience school training.

"Wow," said Dan. "Is this the same wolf?"

"Uh huh," she murmured, handing the wolf another cracker-cheese combo. The animal took the food ever so gently, licking Julie's fingers and eyeballing Dan in the process.

She shrugged when she saw Dan's expression. "He likes this combination. In fact, he likes everything I cook, don't you Big Boy?" She laughed. "I know why my wolf visits. What brings you to my door tonight, Dan?"

"I have been thinking."

She cocked her head and waited.

"Julie, do you remember the night of the police fundraiser?"

"Sure," she said, trying not to frown. "What about it?"

"I know there was a lot of teasing and joking, but do you remember George speaking of a young Sioux who was anxious to meet you backstage?"

"Yes," she said, her brow knit in concentration.

"Well, wasn't it a young Sioux that was driving the tow truck that night?"

Julie fell quiet.

"I'm not sure where you are going with this. There are a lot of Sioux men in South Dakota, Dan."

Julie stood up, pulled the meatloaf out of the oven and set it on the table. The rolls came next then the peas. She loaded on the bacon bits and onions. Big Boy started to prance. She fetched a large plastic tray that read "Fido" and fixed the wolf a plate. "Do start," she said to Dan. "If I don't feed him straight away, he gets rather ill-mannered."

Dan watched as she placed a scoop of pea puree onto the plastic dish.

"You've got to be kidding," he said with a snort. "A feral wolf will never eat something like that. I won't eat something like that. It's green."

She loaded up another spoon and dumped it onto Dan's plate.

"Try it. Just one bite. If you don't like it, you don't have to eat it."

Dan growled in protest which brought Big Boy's head swinging up fast in his direction.

"If the wolf can't growl, neither can you, Dan." She buttered two rolls and cut up two slices of meatloaf then set the tray on the floor. The wolf waited patiently for her to fix her own plate.

"He's waiting for you to start?" asked Dan incredulously.

"Uh huh," she said, taking a forkful of meatloaf. She winked at the wolf who tucked into his meal like the beast that he was.

Dan grunted. "The peas are really good."

Julie grinned. "Wait until you try the meatloaf."

There was a quiet pause while Dan attacked his food. He was a speed-eater, but after the second forkful he slowed down, tasting everything, savoring everything.

"I asked George if he could work with a police artist to come up with a sketch."

"A sketch of the young Sioux who wanted to meet me after the singing gig?"

"Yes."

"Did he?"

"His memory is fogged on that score. It was weeks ago. How about you? Do you think you could give us a sketch of your tow truck driver?"

She frowned and shook her head. "I never saw the man's face. He wore a ball cap. It was dark and he never looked at me."

He swore softly.

"Dan," she said, "Honestly now, what are the odds of the same Sioux band groupie being the man who falsely answered my call for roadside assistance?"

"What are the odds of Gray Walker finding you by chance in the middle of nowhere on an unfamiliar walking trail in the middle of a blizzard?"

She was stunned speechless. "You don't give up, do you?"

"Not when it matters," said Dan. He got to his feet. "And you matter very much to me, Julie."

He went to take a step toward her, to kiss her goodnight, but the wolf ambled between them, sat on his haunches and gave him direct eye contact. Dan eyed the wolf, then looked back at Julie.

"He's very protective," Dan murmured.

She nodded.

"So am I." But his comments were directed at the very sentient being that sat like a sphinx between them.

22

Baseball finals were a blur. Gray seemed more keyed up than the boys, and it took all she could do to keep his ferocious appetite in check. Game day rations had tripled since the start of season, but then Gray ate more than the 13 boys put together and even more if he was stressed.

When he handed her the starting line-up on a cafeteria napkin, she raised an eyebrow and raised the lid to her tin of peanut brittle. He snagged a fist-full.

She made the rounds and administered her sugar high to the rest of team then copied the starting line-up into the scorebook. Keith was batting first, but he hadn't arrived yet. As the minutes passed, she grew more anxious.

It wasn't until coin-toss that Keith plopped himself down on the bench next to her. She turned to greet him and froze. It wasn't the purple bruise on his perfect 'outside' face but the devastated countenance on his 'inside' face that made her snap.

She flew to the bat bag, grabbed a Louisville Slugger and trailed after Keith's father as he made his way back to his designer sports car. He hadn't even turned the key in the ignition before she blew out a headlight.

"What the hell?" he shrieked, climbing from the driver's seat. She shattered the windshield.

The whole team was galvanized. The umpire dialed 911 on his cell phone. She knocked out the passenger door window and took out a taillight. She stared at him maliciously as she circled and destroyed the glass of his James Bond BMW. Gray was racing toward her from across the field when she took her first swing at his person. Keith's father was screaming like a girl and she hadn't even hit him yet. She swung again, but he escaped the blow.

In the next instant, Gray had her tackled to the ground. She fought him like one possessed. "He deserves to die, Gray," she shrieked. "Let me kill him! Please! Let me kill him!"

"No, Julie. No. You can't go to jail. He deserves to go to jail, not you."

"I don't care!" she screamed. Gray wrested the bat from her hands.

"Julie!" Gray squeezed her hard enough to silence her. "Be smart." He bent his head to her ear. "Do you want to save this boy? If so, be sane. Be cool."

His words chilled her. She stilled beneath him and stood stiffly when he released her. She looked at Keith's father and locked eyes. "Gray Walker is the only reason you are still breathing air," she said. She shuddered in disgust. "If you press charges, so will I."

"What?" he stammered. "The boy fell down the steps."

She took a step toward him, but Gray restrained her. "You better fix those steps then," she said, low and lethal.

Elliott arrived with his squad car screaming. It was Gray who held the baseball bat so Elliott addressed the big Sioux. "Could I ask you to drop the bat, Mr. Walker?"

"Elliott," said Julie, wrenching the bat from Gray. "It was me that destroyed the BMW." She was disheveled and breathing heavily.

"You?"

"Mr. Hawthorn asked me to."

"He what?" Elliott looked at Douglas Hawthorn who just stood there and nodded.

"Why don't you get the ball game started?" Julie said to Gray. "I'll wrap up here then join you."

Gray squeezed her tightly, kissed her on the forehead and returned to the bench. The boys were waiting for him expectantly. He looked into their pie-sized eyes and took a deep breath.

"You all know that Keith fell down the steps. Well, Ms. Julie has been after his father to fix those steps for a while now. Today, she decided to... er... hammer home her point."

Everyone looked at Keith. Their faces were a muddle of confusion, upset, horror, and pity. Keith's face was a mask, but his eyes were staring at Julie.

"Is Ms. Julie going to go to jail?" asked one of the boys.

"No," said Gray, watching as Elliott pulled from the parking lot and a tow truck sidled up to the wrecked BMW.

"Why not?" asked one of the guys.

"Because the Great Spirit walks by her side," said Gray. "She's a mighty fine addition to the team, don't you think men?"

"Hoh-hoh-hoh," they chanted.

As they broke from the huddle, Gray handed Keith the Louisville Slugger that Julie had used to destroy his father's BMW. "This is yours now, and yours alone," Gray whispered. "It's packed with powerful good juju. You keep it and you use it every time you come to the plate. You make it sing your name."

"Yes, sir," said Keith.

"Keith?"

"Sir?"

"The Great Spirit walks by your side, too."

Julie was not surprised to see Dan Keating leaning against the hood of his squad car in the parking lot at the end of the game. She turned to Gray and excused herself.

"Hello, Slugger," said Dan by way of greeting.

"Hello, Dan."

"You and I need to take a little ride," he said amicably.

"Don't arrest me in front of the boys, please."

"I'm not. I'm not going to arrest you at all. But I'd like to have your full cooperation."

"Absolutely."

She waved to Gray and slipped into the front seat of the squad car.

"There is some paperwork in that folder," Dan said, gesturing to the side-door pocket. "I'm going to ask that you fill that out."

"Okay," said Julie. She removed the folder and glanced through the pages. It was an incident report. Her eyes scanned the questions as Dan maneuvered the car through town. When the car stopped, she was surprised to find them in front of a duplex. She looked at Dan in silent question.

"I have your full cooperation, remember?" he said with a smile. "This is my home. Come in. I'll fix us something to eat while you take care of the forms."

Julie frowned.

"I didn't want to do this at the station, Julie. Did you?"

"No," she said softly.

He escorted her inside. The house was neat and clean. From the inside, it looked like a mountain lodge. There was lots of heavy wood furniture and all the colors were autumnal. It even smelled like fireplace.

He poured her a glass of red wine and handed her a pen. She finished her report just as a bell chimed in the kitchen.

"I'm rather hungry," she said, handing him the pile of papers. "Demolition burns up a lot of calories."

"I can't wait to hear all about it."

"You know why I did what I did?"

"Elliott filled me in. But I don't approve. The whole thing could have escalated dangerously. There were other ways to handle the situation."

"I wasn't thinking too clearly at the time."

He placed the lasagna on the table and shoveled a piece onto her plate. "That I believe. How did Douglas handle you wrecking his precious toy?"

"I think I upset him tremendously, but what really sent him over the edge was when…" she faltered. He looked up.

"Yessssss?"

"Oh, nothing."

"Nothing, my eye," said Dan, looking at her carefully. "What did you do when you finished with the car? Did you take a swing at Douglas?"

She chewed her pasta, quietly studying her plate. "This is very good. What brand is it?"

"Damn it, Julie. He could have locked you away for assault."

"I didn't hit him."

"You missed?"

"Yes, then Gray tackled me and took my weapon. I do declare that for a big man, Gray sure moves like stealth itself. I never saw it coming."

"Bruises?"

"On me? No. He cushioned me from the fall, but I think I gave Gray a few. I didn't exactly go down willing."

Dan sighed. "How many witnesses?"

"Both ball teams, plus the umpire, and a few parents."

"How's Keith? How did he take all this?"

"I have a friend for life."

Dan chuckled.

"I'm glad you came and got me," said Julie. "I was dreading the post-game wrap up. Gray will probably ask me to step down as assistant coach now." She looked out the window trying to control her emotions. "Which is a pity, because I really like the boys. And I was starting to feel a part of this community. But, I set a very bad example today."

"Hey," he said, inching his chair next to hers. "None of that. What you did was wrong, yes. No doubt about it. But Douglas isn't pressing charges. And I think he'll think twice before he lays a hand on his son again."

"Dan." She looked him straight in the eye. "I threatened that man's life today. Publicly."

Dan took a deep breath and exhaled. "I figured as much."

"You did?"

"Uh huh. That's why you're here doing paperwork, Julie. Things need to be documented in case there's another incident."

"I won't attack his car again."

"No, but he might go home and think of ways to get even with you in some form or fashion. You took him down a few pegs in front of his son and all his friends."

"Yeah."

"A man with anger issues and low self-esteem processes things a little differently than the rest of us. You were emotional today. He might be emotional tomorrow."

"Yeah."

"Be on your toes for the next couple of whiles."

"Couple of whiles?"

"Uh huh. I think I'll swing by your place in the evenings sporadically and make sure you're okay."

She narrowed her eyes at him. "All in the line of duty?"

"Yes, ma'am." He took their plates and put them in the sink. "Now, official business aside, what's going on with you and Gray?"

"Meaning?"

"Do you two have a platonic relationship or is it more?"

Although she resented the question, she answered it. "It's platonic. He has kissed me on occasion and he has held me, but he doesn't ask for anything more."

Dan digested that, wrestled with it. "I want more, Julie."

"I know. But, I don't think that I can deliver. I don't think that I can provide what you need. This hurts me very much because I like you so."

"You are giving me a very mixed message."

"I'm sorry. I don't even know how to begin to explain things to you. It's all very… complicated."

"When I tell a story, I usually start at the beginning," he prodded. "That makes the telling a little simpler."

She looked up at him. Her eyes were troubled. "I was abused too, Dan. I went to school with bruises all the time, just like Keith."

He swallowed.

"Keith was so hurt, and I'm not just talking physical wounds. Your body gets used to punishment. It's the mental damage that wreaks the most havoc. It was a very wounded young man that sat on that bench today. I couldn't take it."

"I understand."

"No," she said, with a little more heat than she intended. "Gray said the same thing. There is no way either of you can possibly understand. You haven't lived it."

"When did you tell Gray?" he asked, trying to sound casual. "During the snowstorm?"

"No." She took a deep breath. "Remember when I sprained my ankle on the mountain?"

"Uh-huh."

"Gray had to carry me down the mountain. I was terrified of him and he asked me why. So, I told him."

They were both silent for a minute.

"You know, you never told me how you sprained your ankle." He watched her stiffen. "Julie?"

"I slipped on some wet rocks in the stream and fell. I wedged my ankle between them." Dan knew that there was more to the story, he could tell from her body language.

"Were you stuck?"

"Gray got my ankle free."

"So. Gray was with you. Were you hiking together?"

"No. I was alone. Or, I thought I was alone. I was standing on the rocks when Gray said 'hello.' I was so startled that I slipped and fell."

"I know you hike every Saturday," he said. "Do you hike the same trail? Frequent the same spots?"

"Usually, why?"

"Have you ever run into Gray before that Saturday on the trails?"

"No. Never. And I almost always go to that little grove. It's my picnic spot. That's why I was so startled. I didn't expect to find anyone else there. Well, any person there. I've always considered it my own. That's where I always meet my wolf."

It was Dan's turn to stiffen.

"I know you don't like him, Dan, but I saved his life and he has protected me on numerous occasions. That wolf is the only reason I feel safe hiking alone."

Dan pressed his lips together and looked her in the eye. "I know that you don't want to hear it, Julie, but in my professional opinion, I don't think that you are safe with that wolf at all." When she didn't say anything, he spoke again. "Come on. I'll walk you home."

It was dinner time and the gentle scraping of silverware could be heard from the open windows they passed. The streets were quiet.

"Are you making any headway on the real AAA driver's death?" she asked.

He shook his head. "He was mauled by a wolf," said Dan, letting the statement fall as it would, like a coin hitting the floor of a silent church.

"Was he alive when he was mauled?"

"Yes."

Julie closed her eyes to try and block out the visual. "Are wolf attacks normal around here?"

"Not normal, no."

"Is the animal rabid?"

"No."

"You've checked?"

"Of course."

"It doesn't make sense," Julie said softly. Dan just looked at her. "Was Susan alive when she was attacked?"

Dan nodded.

"And she'd been raped first. So, she'd have been hit, maybe bleeding? And the tow truck driver, perhaps he had been mugged first. Had he been hit? Was he bleeding? Is the wolf attracted to the wounded?"

"You think well."

She shrugged and held his gaze. Dan was so perfect, so good, so strong. She felt nicked and chipped around him, unworthy of the praise, unworthy of him.

"Julie?" He stopped walking. "If you had never been on that mountain in the blizzard, would you be seeing Gray?"

"No," she said flatly. "But that's because I would have never gotten to know him. I wouldn't have allowed myself to get to know him. It's his size, his looks. It's intimidating." She paused. "We were in pretty tight quarters for a week. We learned to work with each other and to work around each other." She shook her head. "I told him I'd come to a few of his baseball games. Next thing I knew, he had me registered as assistant coach. Now, I swear, he's like an old shoe."

Dan placed his hands on her shoulders and slid them down her arms to her elbows. "I wish I had been the one to find you on that mountain," he said. He reached down and grabbed a hand and lifted it to his lips. He kissed her knuckles softly.

She pulled free gently. "You are a great guy, Dan, and a good friend."

They walked the rest of the way in silence, each lost in their own thoughts. When they reached her door, he touched her chin and coaxed her face toward him, bending low to kiss her on the lips. "I can be an old shoe too, Julie. You just need to walk with me for a while."

23

Julie knew the road as soon as Gray turned onto it. "You are taking me to your cabin?"

"Uh huh."

"I thought we were going to discuss the state finals over breakfast."

"At the cabin."

"Stale Pop Tarts?"

"No. As a matter of fact I have a fruit salad, scrambled eggs, bacon, and mimosas."

"At the cabin? How?"

"I packed a cooler with ice."

"Clever man."

"With so many items on the menu though, you'll have to help cook."

"Not a worry. I can cook."

"Yes, you can."

She stepped inside and stood, sweeping the room with her eyes. The cabin hadn't changed, but she had. She turned to look at Gray, but he had his back to her, rummaging around in the cooler, ferreting out the eggs and bacon. She joined him at the propane cook-top and helped prepare their meal.

He bumped against her gently as they worked, teasing playfully, his hands ever reaching for her hip, her waist, a shoulder, a ticklish rib.

"Watch those hands," she groused.

"The better to feel you with, my dear."

She took a wooden spoon to his knuckles. "Focus."

"I *am*."

"On *breakfast*."

After they had eaten and cleared the table, Gray fixed them both another mimosa and unfurled a thick wad of blueprints across the tabletop.

"I have some news," he said. "I'm going to build a house, a very large log cabin complete with running water, electricity, and heat. It will be a real home and I am going to build it very close to where we are now."

"What brought this on?"

He shrugged. "I need a nicer place to take you."

Julie was thunderstruck. "Gray, you have an apartment in town."

"It doesn't feel right." He closed his eyes. "When I think of you, Julie, I think of this mountain and the snow, the smell of wood smoke on your skin, your hand on my chest and your head on my shoulder."

Julie swallowed.

"I held your body and your trust."

"Gray, I'm sorry I can't give you more… of me."

He gave her a tender smile. "What we share is enough."

"Are you sure?"

He nodded. "Sex isn't everything, you know."

"Have you ever…" She let the question drop.

"No," he said, his expression pained. "I haven't."

"Do you want to?" she asked.

He smiled, laughter in his eyes. "I am a man, Julie Hastings. I'd be lying if I told you I didn't. I'd be lying through my teeth if I told you that I didn't want to make love to you. But, when you're ready, Julie. And not until."

"There's been no one before me?"

He shook his head uncomfortably. "There was a girl once, someone I liked very much, but her parents didn't approve."

"Why not?" she asked.

"They didn't trust me with her," he said softly. He lifted his eyes to meet hers. "I frighten many people, Julie. It's my size, my strength, my looks. Plus…"

"Plus?"

"Well, my father didn't treat my mother very well."

"I see," she said, her voice was a whisper.

"I guess they thought, like father, like son," he said. "I can't blame them."

"They were wrong."

"Thank you for saying so."

He stared at her, his eyes soft. She swallowed. "Where are you going to build your house?"

"Just beyond the ridge line. Our tribe does not have dwelling rights within the state park."

"But this dwelling is within the state park, isn't it?"

"It's just a hunting cabin."

"A hunting cabin? Within a state park?"

He shrugged. "My state—"

"I know, I know," she finished for him, "I know exactly how you think. Your state, your state park, your Julie."

A slow smile spread across his face and he nodded. "Mind reader."

Julie walked to work on Monday. The morning was warm and dry, so she used the opportunity to get some exercise. On the way home, she rounded the corner of her driveway just as the sun was setting. She took a last deep lungful of air and froze mid-breath. The smell took her to her knees and she retched pitifully onto the sidewalk. She wiped her face with her hand, her eyes fixed upon her doorstep, then fished for her cell phone and dialed 911. Ro-bear fielded the call. By the time he arrived, Julie was so pale, she looked blue. He put a hand to her forehead. She was both cold and clammy to the touch. He got her inside and wrapped her in blankets.

"She's in shock," Ro-bear said as Dan pulled into her driveway. "Someone left her a present on her doorstep."

Dan stilled. "What?"

"A small dog. Someone doused it in gasoline or kerosene and put a match to it."

"Burned it to death?"

"No. Just burned it."

"For the love of Christ."

"Julie?"

It was Dan. She looked up to find him standing in her living room. "How are you feeling?"

A tear slid down her cheek. He reached for her hand and held it tightly.

"We have a witness," he said. His eyes had lost their sparkle. In the half-light of the living room, they looked slate gray. "Your neighbor, Mrs. Reilly, saw a blue sports car in your driveway an hour before you came home. She watched a man put something at your door."

Another tear slid down her cheek. He wiped it away.

"She got a good enough look that she's certain she'd be able to identify the man in a line-up. We're going to put him away."

"This is all my fault. The car, the dog—"

"No."

"Yes. Yes, it is, Dan."

"If you hadn't confronted Douglas Hawthorn, maybe Keith would have been the burn victim," said Dan. He gripped her hand gently and the silence stretched between them. "You've taken this pretty hard."

She looked up at him and her eyes spoke volumes.

"What's going on, Julie? You've treated some animals with gruesome injuries. Knowing what I know about human nature, I can't imagine that all of those injuries have been accidents either. What upset you so?"

She didn't respond.

"Julie?"

"My stepfather."

"Yes?"

"He was beating me. Freebie just tried to make him stop."

"Your dog defended you?"

"To his death." She looked up at Dan with haunted eyes. "I knew that smell. I knew that smell the moment I turned into the driveway."

24

Cole and Rose gave her big hugs when she returned to work. Often, during the course of her workday, one of them would pat her gently on the shoulder or hand her a hot cup of tea. The choir sent flowers, as did the Copper Pigs.

Dan made a point of stopping by her house each evening. Even if he were on-duty, he'd take a fifteen-minute coffee break at her kitchen table. Gray called during the day, sometimes stopping by to bring her lunch. Even her wolf visited. In fact, he posted every night and demanded mattress space when she slipped between the covers of her bed.

Gradually, she put the incident behind her. Gray was working with social services and spending a lot of time in court. Keith was in the custody of his maternal grandmother. Douglas Hawthorn was behind bars.

Gray stopped by on Friday afternoon with a necklace he'd crafted out of bone. All corn maidens and wolves. A gift.

"My house is all staked out. I'd like for you to come see it."

She nodded.

"Tonight. Please."

He reached out and gently ran his fingertips down her arm. The look he gave her made her chest tighten.

After work, Julie swung by the supermarket to pick up some dinner supplies. A single bag of groceries sat in the passenger seat, yet she had to continuously downshift as she started up the mountain. Her Toyota was struggling with the grade. At least the roadway was dry. She'd never make it in the mud.

Gray had obviously been waiting for her, or perhaps he could simply hear the tortured groan of her engine from a mile away. He stepped out of the cabin as soon as she pulled up next to his SUV.

"Dinner," she said.

"I see that," he murmured, looking at the paper bag. "But, I'm more interested in dessert." He pulled her into his arms and kissed her softly.

"Dinner first," she said, breaking free.

"That implies that dessert is second," he said, carrying the bag into the cabin. He set it down and grabbed her again. "I've missed you."

She pushed him away with a squeal. "The wine is cold and the chicken is hot. Set the table."

He obeyed then pulled her into another firm embrace. She wiggled her way free and gestured to the table. He nodded, tucking into the offerings she had brought. But his eyes were full upon her. She stilled and returned his stare. His pupils were incandescent fire.

"Don't you look at me like that, Gray Walker," she admonished

"Like what?" he asked innocently.

"Like I'm some kind of chew-toy. I am armed and quite dangerous." She lifted up her knife and fork and wiggled them for good measure. "Be afraid."

He stood up and lit a fire, polishing off the last of the chicken fingers by the hearth.

"I bought you a present," he said.

"A present? What kind of present?"

"It's a toothbrush."

"A toothbrush? That's a little odd for a pres…" Her voice trailed off. "I see."

"It's in the toothpaste cup by the sink. Next to mine." She looked over and saw it there, still wrapped in its plastic packaging. Her eyes slid back to Gray's.

"There is mischief in your eyes tonight, Mr. Walker."

"Not too much mischief."

"Mischief nonetheless," she repeated. "What's gotten into you?"

"Full moon," he said nonchalantly and walked over to the cedar chest to pull out a t-shirt. She swallowed hard and got to her feet. His eyes danced as he approached her. "I ache to hold you, Julie Hastings."

He pulled her into bed, then pulled her on top of him and kissed her. He flipped her onto her back and kissed her. He wrestled her into his favorite sleeping position.

"You move me like a sack of potatoes," she groused. "And you are touching me. All over." His hand cupped a breast.

"My potatoes," he retorted.

"Says who?"

"You."

"Excuse me?"

She expected an explanation, but how could he deliver to her a physiology that she consciously denied? She was attracted to him. He knew it, but he remained silent. His stillness stilled her also.

"Gray?"

"Yes?"

"Why do you say that I am your potatoes?"

"Your body tells me so."

She took a couple of shallow breaths, her back tucked tightly against his chest.

"Your body also tells me, not yet."

25

On Friday, Julie drove out to the Circle C Ranch. It was a routine call. Jess Harrington raised a magnificent herd of black Angus and he liked to keep it that way. The visit always proved challenging because Jess and his cowboys expected her to mount up and ride out to the herd to do her doctoring. Although she didn't bounce around in the saddle anymore, she still ended up a tad tender and stiff the day after.

They gave her an old, dappled gray brood mare called Starlight to ride, an animal that doggedly followed the other horses, was too old to gallop, and too insensate to mind her inexpert ridership.

Every time she visited, she would promise herself to sign up for riding lessons so that she'd be more polished in the saddle next time. Then next time would come around and she'd have the same conversation with herself all over again.

A pack of eager and energetic border collies corralled the herd and she dismounted, touching the cows, examining their eyes, ears and noses. The animals looked healthy. She looked up and found Jess watching her. She gave a thumbs-up and he tipped his hat, ambling off to speak to his foreman.

When she was finished, she saddled up and headed back to the ranch. The air was cool, the sun warm. The wind teased her skin into goose bumps.

"What puts such a smile on your face, Ms. Hastings?" asked Jess, sidling up next to her.

"Everything," she answered. "The squeaky leather, the solid sound of the horse's hoofs as they touch the earth, the smell of horsehair and dust." She shrugged. "I like it."

He nodded in understanding. "You should learn to ride."

"I've been thinking the very same thing."

"Next time you visit, give me the whole day. I'll teach you."

"Really?"

"Yes," he said, giving her a sidelong glance. "My horse will live longer that way."

Her lips parted in surprise and he laughed low and deep at her expense.

"Thanks," she said. "My apologies to Starlight."

He gave her a pound of t-bone steaks neatly wrapped in butcher paper when they got to the ranch and she drove back to the office in the fading light of day. The windows were down, the radio up. It was a glorious sunset. The clouds expressed the oncoming night in pink, coral, purple and dusty lavender. She rounded a curve, her eye on the sky and struck an elk full-on in the chest. The sound of the impact was the last thing she remembered.

Dan paced nervously outside the curtains in the emergency area. This was his second visit to the hospital checking up on one Ms. Julie Hastings inside one calendar year. He paced in anxious frustration.

"I want to see her," he groused to the head nurse.

"After she's been seen," came the calm reply. "You're not family, Dan. She needs privacy in there."

He scowled. It's not like Julie had privacy anyway. He could hear every snippet of dialogue.

"Can you give me something for the pain?" Julie asked. He could hear the agony in her voice.

"Not until we x-ray you. We need to make sure that you don't need surgery."

"What I need is morphine."

"None of that, Sweetie."

"How about some Percoset?"

"No."

"Percodan?"

"No."

"Valium?"

"Nuh uh."

She whimpered. "Who found me?"

"Jess Harrington, but Officer Keating responded to the emergency call."

"Where's Officer Keating now?"

He spoke right up. "Here." He parted the curtain and stuck his head inside.

"Dan, have you made any good drug busts lately?"

"And you need to know because?"

"Because I need some of the good stuff and I need it straight away. I'll take anything. Anything." She grimaced as another wave of pain wracked her chest.

He snuck in and held her hand.

"I don't think that's a good idea."

"Well, if you won't sedate me at least you can try to outlaw those damn airbags."

"That damn airbag probably saved your life."

"The jury is still out on that one," she said. "I feel like death."

"I need to ask you a few questions," said the nurse, her eyes sliding to Dan.

"He can stay," said Julie.

He squeezed her hand in solidarity.

"Now, when was the date of your last period?"

"I swear," she turned to Dan in total mortification. "You're lucky that you are a man. Do you know I could be here in cardiac arrest and they'd ask me that question? They'd ask me this if I was in here for stitches."

"Can you give me a date, Miss Julie?"

"No." Julie grimaced in pain.

"We're trying to rule out pregnancy."

"Rule it out."

"I need a date."

"Pick one and while you're at it pick out a few pain killers too."

"Can you be sure that you're not pregnant?"

"Gloria." Julie was suffering too much to be patient. "You have to have sex first to run the risk of pregnancy. Trust me. I'm not pregnant."

"When were you last sexually active?"

Julie gave a long, suffering sigh. Her voice, when she spoke, was flat.

"Gloria, I've never been sexually active in my life."

"Oh," she said, meekly. "Got it." She excused herself. "Let me get the radiologist."

Julie was afraid to open her eyes. "You still there?" she asked Dan.

"I'm holding your hand," he said, smiling. The news gave him hope. He had thought that, despite her words, she and Gray had crossed that bridge. "Hey… and the color is back in your cheeks."

"I'm sure."

"Julie?"

"Yeah?"

"It's only me."

"Dan, I'm blushing because it *is* you. I was expecting her to ask me whether I had cataracts or warts or hemorrhoids or dandruff…" She trailed off.

"It's not a crime, you know."

"Obviously you've never read *Cosmo*."

He snorted. "Around here, we've got another set of standards." He watched her writhe in pain. "Hey," he said, "You've got to focus on something else beside the pain or the pain will consume you."

"Like what?" she asked.

"Focus on me," he said.

She turned toward him and gave him her full attention. "How come you haven't married, Dan?" she asked bluntly. "You are warm, funny, handsome, caring, good-hearted—"

He held up a hand. "Keep going and you can add fat-headed to your list."

"You are not like that at all!"

He gave her a tight smile and she was immediately sorry that she'd asked the question.

"I had a girl I was quite serious about."

"What happened?"

"She went away to San Francisco as part of a work-study program and never came back. She was seduced by the city, so to speak."

"You didn't want to go to her?"

"I wasn't given that option."

"Oh," she said. "Definitely, her loss."

He smiled. "I'm long over it. Besides, I've got my eye on someone else these days." He lifted her hand and kissed it.

"Ah," she said, her voice breaking, "I'm absolutely no good for you, Dan."

"Why do you say that?"

"Because you are perfect and I am damaged goods."

"Explain this, if you don't mind."

"You need someone whole, Dan Keating. If there is a scorecard in the sky tallying up life's battle-weary, I walk among the wounded."

He frowned at her words, "Julie, you're not being fair to yourself or to me."

"Oh, I'm trying to be extraordinarily fair. I like you very much, Dan Keating. I can't give you what you need. I know that and I don't want to hurt you."

Dan would have protested, but their conversation was interrupted by a visit to radiology. When the x-rays were over, Julie waited for the doctor in a small visitation room and focused on her breathing, every inhalation sent sharp pains through her chest and abdominal cavity. She tried to ride the waves of agony like an adult and muffle her pathetic whimpering.

Dr. Joel Peterson entered her room and moved with a briskness that indicated a stressed and frenetic work schedule. She followed him with her eyes since every muscle movement resulted in another radiating wave of pain.

"I see that you've cracked a few ribs before," he said by way of intro.

"Ah, are you insinuating that I've cracked some new ones today?" she responded.

"Two," he replied, "but they are fresh fractures on old breaks. Were you in a car accident prior to this one, Ms. Hastings?"

"No."

"Play any contact sports?"

"No. Can I get some painkillers now?"

"Yes, but I'd like to take a few more x-rays."

"Of my ribs?"

"Of the rest of you," he answered.

"Why do you want to take more x-rays?" she asked. "Nothing else hurts."

"I'm obligated to contact social services if I see signs of abuse."

She just stared at him. "That's not necessary."

"Fortunately or unfortunately," he said. "It's the law. You are not obligated to talk to them, but I am."

"I'd rather you didn't."

"I don't have a choice." He paused. "At this point, you've got an opportunity here to let me do some x-rays courtesy of the state. They might serve you well down the road. You never know. It's good to have a documented record, even if you do nothing with it."

"Okay."

"May I ask who did this to you?"

"My stepfather."

"I see." He was quiet for a moment. "Where is your stepfather now?"

"Half a country away."

"Good." He sat down and looked at her speculatively. "You've got two very anxious men waiting for word in the emergency room."

Gray had arrived.

"You might want to, um, put them in separate rooms," she whispered, "They don't play nice together."

"You are going to have to help me here," he continued. "One is carrying a weapon and cuffs. The other looks like he could kill me with a glance. What do I tell them?"

Her smile turned into a grimace of pain. The doctor stuck his head out the door, flagged a nurse, ordered up some pain meds then rotated his head back in her direction. "Well?"

"They both know of my past. You won't be spilling any secrets."

"Be good to yourself, Julie. Make sure others are too," he said, then left the room.

The battery of x-rays was damning. Joel Peterson called both men into radiology while the nurses wrapped Julie's ribs and started her discharge papers.

"I don't think there is a bone in her body that hasn't been broken at least once," said Joel Peterson. "Normally, when we see such colossal damage, it's because of an accident, one incidental, catastrophic occurrence. This is not the case, gentlemen." He put a few x-rays up on the mounted light boxes on the wall. "The re-growth patterns on her skeleton show very disparate break and healing times. This woman has been abused and broken from early childhood on. Physically, she's a train wreck. Her internal scars are massive."

"How is she now?" asked Gray, his face neutral, his body still.

"Well, that's the good news," said the doctor, taking a breath. "Only two fractured ribs and they are re-breaks along poorly healed fracture lines. She's going to be in a good bit of pain. Someone will need to take care of her upon release."

He wrote out a prescription for Percoset and proffered it to the neutral space between the two of them. They both snatched for the paper aggressively, but Gray won.

"Can we see her?" Gray asked.

The doctor nodded. "She's still a tad fragile, gentlemen. We've had some frank conversation. I would venture to say she's a bit emotional. We've given her something for the pain, but I don't think it has kicked in yet."

When the two men entered her treatment room, she greeted them with a weak, "Hey." She took a ragged breath. "The gang's all here."

Gray stepped up and took a hand. Dan walked around the bed and took the other one.

"How is my car?" she asked.

"A little humpty dumpty," said Dan matter-of-factly. In response to the confusion on her face, he finished the rhyme. "All the king's horses and all the king's men, couldn't put—"

"Got it," she said, her voice full of pain.

"Julie," said Gray. She followed his voice with hollow eyes. "You need a four-wheel drive vehicle here. There is nothing to mourn."

"Can I go home?" she asked. "I really, really want to go home."

"Let me see what I can do," said Dan, and he exited, giving Gray a weighted look. He didn't like them alone together, but this was about Julie. He'd use his pull to expedite her discharge papers.

She had been right when she had spoken of her abuse. He hadn't understood and couldn't understand. He hadn't lived it. He'd been accused of many things in his life, but never perfection and never would he have thought perfection so damning.

Gray took her home and stayed with her while she mended. It took her a month to feel back to normal and he tended to her every need. He cooked. He cleaned. He did her grocery shopping. When she was strong enough, he drove her to work each day, and he picked her up and drove her home each evening. He kept fresh flowers by her bedside.

He rubbed arnica on her bruises and wrapped her ribs after she showered. He helped to dress her each morning and he helped to undress her each night, placing a soft kiss on her lips before descending to the couch to turn in.

Dan checked in on her religiously and volunteered to help her with her transportation shortfall. The annual police auction was fast approaching. She had a good chance of finding a nice, confiscated vehicle that sold for a song.

In the end, she ended up with a green car that both men agreed upon. It was either a four-wheel or all-wheel drive. She didn't care which, and she got it for a pittance.

26

After they won the baseball divisional finals, Julie displayed their championship trophy at the veterinary office and placed a donation bucket beside it. The players' families had scrambled to come up with hotel fees in Butte. State finals would be even more costly. Rose typed up a flyer that solicited support, and Julie smiled often during the course of her day as she heard Rose wheedle and cajole dollar bills out of every customer that stopped by her desk.

Nobody could stop Rose when she took up a cause. She coerced her choir group to sing a fundraising performance after mass one Sunday and she placed donation cans on the counters of all the local merchants. She single-handedly bankrolled their trip to state finals and even enabled the team to sponsor a few parents along for the ride.

Gray called a team meeting the Wednesday before their Friday departure for the competition. "Men," he said, as they sat midst their parents on the bleachers. "Friday night is the welcome dinner. We will sit together as a team and I expect you all to behave like professional ballplayers. Dress code is jacket and tie."

"Whaaat?" The outcry was unanimous.

"Jacket and tie," said Gray. "And a dress for the first base coach." He gave Julie a nod and she nodded back.

A parent spoke up. "I've refereed state finals, Gray. I've attended that welcome dinner. The dress code has always been casual."

"This is my dress code, Stan," he said, looking back to the boys. "If you want to win, you've got to look like winners. Jacket and tie, or you don't go." The grumbling was plaintive. "And I want you sporting dress shoes," said Gray. "With socks. No sneakers at the dinner."

Again, he turned to Julie, "Heels for you please, first base coach." It was all she could do to keep a straight face.

"Rose Campbell over at the veterinary office has amassed enough money during her fundraising campaign to pay for your hotel rooms and meals. Every single one of you is to write a thank-you letter and bring it with you Friday morning. The bus will be making a very loud and rowdy visit to the veterinary office before leaving town. I want you each to hand her your letter personally and say something nice. Your letter should be legible. It should be sincere. It should be in an envelope. If you forget your letter, you will not board the bus."

Gray had their rapt attention."First base coach will have a bouquet of flowers for Rose."

Julie gave him another nod.

"Any questions?" he asked.

There were none. He looked to Julie and stepped aside, "Assistant Coach?"

"Men," she said, stepping forward. She watched their spines stiffen as they acknowledged the compliment she gave them. "We'll be decorating the bus early Friday morning before departure. Anyone who'd like to help needs to be here an hour ahead of time."

"I'll be looking for your A-game," said Gray. "Bring it to me Friday."

Julie dumped three empty doughnut flats into the trash can near the ball park. Brian came behind her with the empty juice boxes. The bus was a riot of colorful slogans, most of them incorporating #1. Everyone had showed up. Even parents had stayed to help decorate. Devon's father, who worked for an automobile dealership, brought nylon streamers. The boys attached them to the side view mirrors, back bumper and emergency exit door. The bus was going to turn some heads.

Gray pulled up to the veterinary office with a caravan of parental cars all honking their horns loudly. Julie hadn't told anyone at the office about their surprise visit, so Rose looked stricken when she opened the front door. She was clearly frightened by all the commotion.

Her jaw dropped in surprise as Julie handed her a bunch of red roses. Then, the boys filed out of the bus and marched across the street shouting "Rose! Rose! Rose!" each of them handing her their personal thank you card.

Rose cried. The dogs in the waiting room barked loudly. Horns blared. Traffic stopped. And Cole stood watching the organized display of gratitude with a wide, disbelieving grin.

"Win," Rose shouted, clutching her thank you cards. "Win! Win! Win!"

Julie rode shotgun and called out the directions as Gray navigated the roadways en route to the state finals. They were the last team to arrive for the welcome dinner, their reserved tables noticeably empty midst the packed university cafeteria.

As they walked to their seats, past the kids in cut-offs and flip flops, t- shirts and camouflage pants, the room grew silent. Julie reached for Gray's hand and he held it snuggly. The boys were aware of their stunning entrance. They looked good. They felt good and they walked a little taller as they continued across the room.

Gray watched the boys' confidence build as they ate. He watched their eyes scan the room with a superiority they had not felt until this night. When their team was announced, the boys stood in unison and grunted out their manly chant.

They were the only team to declare themselves vocally. The room was intimidated and Gray was quite pleased. He leaned over and kissed Julie on the lips. It was a chaste kiss, but the boys saw it and demanded another. They picked up their silverware and tapped upon their glassware until Gray leaned over and kissed Julie again at which point the boys erupted into their macho chant once again.

Julie blushed deeply and Gray grinned. When the welcoming ceremony was over, the Braves strutted toward their bus with a jaunty spring to their steps while all the other teams just mulled about trying to keep track of each other midst the throng.

"Silence, until we clear the parking lot, men," Gray ordered. They obeyed him. Barely. He had no sooner finished the turn onto the main roadway when they broke into cheers and shouts.

"Did you see how they all looked at us, Coach?" Keith shouted.

"They were afraid of us," said Brian.

"Terrified of us," said Devon.

"We looked so good," said Peter.

"You looked like winners," said Gray, shouting to be heard above their voices. "The first battle is already won, troops. Your opponents are afraid of you. They think that you are better than they are. And they are right."

The noise was deafening.

"I will have your solemn promises that you will sleep tonight and be at your best for our games tomorrow. No playing in the hallways. No carrying on. It's a single elimination tournament, so we cannot make one mistake, starting with tonight."

When he was assured they were all safely tucked in for the night, he knocked upon the door that separated his room from Julie's. He'd asked for adjoining rooms and was delighted to be so accommodated.

"Gray?" she whispered.

"Little pig, little pig, let me come in." He laughed low and mischievously as she swung open the door.

"Little pig?" she said, her hand on her hip. He was still chuckling when he pulled her into his arms and dipped her backwards for a Hollywood-style kiss.

"Pig?" she repeated, shrieking in surprise.

"Listen to you squeal!" he said delightedly, and he captured her mouth with his own.

They won the first round of competition without breaking a sweat, but the second game caught them feeling cocky and playing slip-shod. They battled back in extra innings to carry the day.

Gray sent them to their rooms after a firm reprimand then visited Julie in hers. He was quiet when he slipped into bed beside her, his hands reaching for her possessively, his touch tender and warm.

"I love you, Julie Hastings," he said softly, but she was already asleep in his arms.

The next day they played like the champions they were. They beat the first team 7-0 and the second team 5-1. Julie screamed and cheered until her voice was hoarse. She was dust-covered and exhausted again by day's end. They ate chicken fingers and French fries on the bench for lunch and pizza from the box on the bench for dinner.

She joined Gray during the room-check/body-count, tossing bags of Pepperidge Farm cookies into each room after everyone was accounted for. They had long devoured all her home-baked goods.

She collapsed into bed barely conscious of Gray's embrace. He spooned her, nuzzling her neck, holding her close. "You are an incredible man, Gray Walker," she murmured. He answered her with a soft snore.

She awoke to the alarm. Gray was already up, dressed and in the hallway rousing the team. They hit the pancake house then hit the ball field with coolers and gear and the highest of high hopes.

Their cheering section had grown significantly overnight. Many families had driven into Sioux Falls for the final game and this pleased the boys immensely. Julie spied Rose and Cole in the bleachers and beamed.

A reporter for the local paper was also on hand. One of the player's moms had snapped pictures of the veterinary fly-by as they had headed out of town, and Rose had made front-page news. For this week's sequel, the reporter was hoping for a trophy and a trophy shot of Rose with her team.

Gray pulled the boys into a tight huddle. "You've got your number one benefactor in the audience," said Gray. "You've got your families too. Plus a reporter who would like to make you front-page news. Are you front-page news?" he asked them. Silence. "Are you front-page news?" he shouted.

"Front-page news!" they repeated "Hoh-hoh-hoh!"

With each line drive, with each base hit, Julie slapped the runner with a high-five and chanted, "Front-page news!" As each man rounded third, Gray called out, "Front-page news." As each man slid into home, the bleachers exploded with "Front-page news!"

By the end of the ninth inning, they were, indeed, front-page news. The reporter captured the players lifting their trophy high, Rose beaming proudly to one side, Gray with his arm wrapped around Julie's shoulders on the other, her neck tucked into the crook of his elbow as he wrestled her close.

27

Gray showed up unexpectedly at Julie's door the weekend after the big win. He awakened her with his persistent knocking, and she opened the kitchen door for him in her pajamas, her hair all tousled by sleep. He toted a bag of groceries.

"I thought I'd make you breakfast," he said.

She smiled, her eyes fuzzy and unfocused. "I'm not awake yet."

"Go wake up. Then I'd like to deliver a very special invitation."

When she returned, freshly scrubbed, she sat at the table and eyeballed him expectantly.

"I'd like for you to come with me to the reservation," he said. "Next weekend is a Making Relatives ceremony. I want you to attend." He placed some scrambled eggs and bacon onto her plate and filled her coffee mug.

"What is a Making Relatives ceremony?"

"It's a ritual that honors our relationship to the Great Spirit. It also acknowledges our relationship to our fellow man, in this case, you, in particular. I'd like to make you a relative of the Sioux."

She frowned. "You can unilaterally do that? Just make me a Sioux?"

"Not I, no. The council must approve those nominated."

"You nominated me?"

"Me and Tom Running Deer, and a few others."

She had lifted her mug to take a sip of coffee, but only got halfway. "Why?" She set her mug back down.

Gray smiled at the look of genuine confusion on her face. "Julie, do you have any idea how your care has impacted the boys on the team?"

She shook her head to the negative.

Gray took a sip of coffee, and nodded toward her plate, waiting for her to pick up her fork before he continued. "Most of those boys were marginal students at best. Every single one of those boys had significant increases in their grade point average during the last half of their school year."

"Increases? With all the time spent on the field during ball season?"

Gray nodded. "Their grades improved. The confidence they built for themselves on the field filtered through to the rest of their lives."

"Well, they were certainly walking tall after the welcome dinner at the state finals." She was quiet a moment. "But that was your doing, not mine."

"Julie. These young men are Sioux like me. I'm their youth counselor and their coach. I'm supposed to believe in them. You were an outsider. The fact that you believed in them so unconditionally boosted their opinion of themselves tremendously. You committed yourself to the team and they felt that commitment. You never missed a game. And there were some parents who never attended one. You fed them, doctored them, encouraged them and cared for them. With that kind of support, they had to perform. And now that they have tasted what it is like to be winners, well… there's no going back."

"Do you know how many college scouts were in the bleachers during divisionals and state finals?" he continued. Julie just looked at him. "Six of our young men are currently being courted by various colleges and universities. We're talking scholarships, woman!"

Julie broke into a smile. "That's fantastic! Please, please tell me that Keith is among those being courted?"

Gray nodded, smiling back. "He's got three universities sending him mugs, knapsacks, and t-shirts with their logos on them."

She sat back, closed her eyes, and let the joy wash over her. He reached for her hand and locked fingers with hers. "The boys are like mini-celebrities at the reservation and my phone is ringing off the hook with parents calling to sign up their sons for next season."

She looked at him and beamed.

"Please eat," he commanded. She huffed at him, but sat forward and speared a forkful of eggs. "But I need to be clear, here," said Gray. "No one is inviting you to join the Sioux Nation because you helped cheer on a team to victory. You are being asked to join because you gave where you saw a need. That's what this ceremony is all about – taking care of one another, lending a helping hand, making a difference."

"I'm very flattered, Gray. Thank you," she said quietly. "I'm truly honored. But help me to better understand. What is expected of me if I accept this invitation? Are there duties and obligations?"

"In this ceremony, we are committing to you, not the other way around. As part of the Sioux Nation, you will have 'human resources'. If you ever have a need, we will do our best to answer the shortfall."

She nodded. "What happens at the ceremony?"

"I will give you a gift. It would be appropriate for you to give me one in return."

"What are you giving me?" she asked.

"A pair of moccasins." He looked at her naked feet under the table. "You pad around here without footwear all the time."

"What would be an appropriate gift for me to give you?"

"The Sioux abide by a steadfast rule. We feed the hungry, clothe the naked and shelter the homeless. Any gift that is symbolic of that spirit would be appropriate."

"It's like Christmas?"

"Yes," he continued. "But, there is more to this than gift giving. As your sponsor, I will feed you a piece of buffalo meat from my hand. You will also feed me. It's a symbolic gesture of care and protection."

"Like the cake ritual at a wedding?"

"Yes. Afterwards, there is feasting, tremendous feasting. Everyone will try to stuff you full."

"Like Thanksgiving?"

He nodded. "Like Thanksgiving."

Julie laughed and her laughter was low and easy and relaxed. He smiled with her.

"Will you accept?"

Julie took a deep breath then nodded.

"Good," he said. "I'll pick you up Saturday morning and bring you back Monday evening."

"How long is this ceremony?"

"I will need you for three days and two nights."

"Where will we stay?"

"In my tipi."

"That's a very public statement." Her voice was heavy and concerned. "Everyone is going to scream 'buffalo robe!'"

He chuckled low and deep.

"You laugh! How can you laugh?"

"I like the idea."

On Tuesday, Julie requested a formal meeting with Cole. She had a lot of guilt riding on all of her missed time at work. There had been baseball finals and two stints in the hospital. Now she needed a three-day weekend to become a member of the Sioux Nation. She didn't even know how to format the request without embarrassing herself professionally.

Cole entered the conference room and assessed her quiet agitation. Before she told him what was on her mind, he opted to diffuse the tension first.

"Coffee?" he asked.

"No thanks," she replied, her voice tight and quiet.

He filled two mugs, added sugar and a little cream to hers and handed her the hot beverage, locking eyes as he did so. She pursed her lips, but accepted the mug, wrapping her cold hands around its warmth.

Cole drank his cowboy style, black with no adornments, but when he took a sip, he grimaced. "Tastes like I'm licking a three-day-old ashtray."

"Mine's delicious too," she answered absently.

He raised an eyebrow and took another sip. "That was a really nice thing that you and the team did for Rose."

"That was entirely Gray's idea," Julie said. "Right down to the rowdy hand-delivering of the thank-you notes."

"Really?"

"Really. And he hand-carved those raccoon earrings that you've seen Rose wear every day. In fetish-speak, raccoons are resourceful creatures. She funded the trip to the state finals, as you know."

"Gray did all of this? No prodding?"

"All on his own," she avowed. "No prodding."

"He sounds like a good man, Julie," he said slowly.

"He is. He just looks meaner than hell."

Cole laughed. "He does indeed. With his build, I wonder why he ever chose to get into youth counseling. Surely, he must know how intimidating he looks, especially to a young person."

"You'd be surprised," said Julie. "He commands respect, first out of pure unadulterated fear, then out of blind devotion, deference and admiration. The kids love him. Personally, I have a theory—"

"Oh yeah? What's that?"

"Have you ever feared something so much that you wanted to be that thing that you fear just so that you wouldn't need to be afraid anymore?" The question stumped him, so she phrased it differently. "If the deadliest thing in the jungle was a tiger and you were in the jungle, wouldn't you rather be the tiger?"

"I see where you are going with this."

"Have you read *The Life of Pi*?"

He nodded.

"I'm sure that the kids fear him at first, but then, they want to be just like him. And he leads by good example."

Cole smiled. "You like him?"

"I like him very much." She paused. "He's asked me to become a member of the Sioux Nation."

Cole lifted both eyebrows this time. "That's not a small gesture."

"I didn't think so, but Gray was rather vague about it all."

"This is not something that you want to consider lightly."

"I'm aware."

"You'd be going from no family to a nation of relatives within 72 hours. Relatives are a lot of work."

"The police force adopted me months ago," she countered. "I haven't felt overly pressed. In fact, it's been wonderful."

Cole nodded. "You need a day or two off for the ceremony?"

"Yes," she said. "And I feel guilty about asking. I've lost so much time this year."

Cole took a deep breath and released the air slowly. "This year has been hard on you physically, and you've missed some time, but you put in long hours, more than your share. I don't have any problem with you taking a day or two for pleasure. It's well deserved."

Julie purchased a copper bracelet for Gray for the Making Relatives ceremony. It was about an inch thick, flat and hand-beaten. It looked as rugged as he was. The only need it fulfilled was a deep ache Gray felt in his left wrist when rain threatened, but she thought that enough to make the purchase.

She passed Gray a go-cup of coffee when he knocked on her door Saturday morning and handed him her duffle. She was a bundle of nerves. "Tell me what to expect."

"Well, today," said Gray ushering her into his car, "we will burn some sage as part of a purification ritual. This pulls all Sioux and their guests together in spirit."

"Okay."

"Then sage and tobacco will be placed into a buffalo bladder." He watched her face fall.

"Bear with me, now." She nodded. "The bladder will be sealed, tied and wrapped in buckskin," he continued. "This object represents both the Great Spirit and the force of his spirit on earth, for all peoples, in all directions."

She nodded again.

"The next day, at dawn, all of the Sioux and their guests will smoke the peace pipe. The bag will be passed to everyone who must kiss it to acknowledge their willingness to live together in peace."

"I have to kiss a buffalo bladder?" she said, trying to keep her face neutral.

"You do," said Gray firmly. "Then, to show our willingness to come together as one people, the Sioux and their guests exchange gifts."

"Christmas in July," she teased. "I'm looking forward to that."

"On the last day, we enter a special tipi, again burning sage. Our faces are painted."

"In war paint?" Julie asked, her jaw dropping.

"Peace paint, Julie," he scolded. "Dried buffalo meat is purified over the burning sage and I will place a bit of this meat into your mouth and you will place a bit into mine. After we do this, we will smoke the pipe again acknowledging you as a relative of the Sioux Nation."

"All right."

"Then," he continued, "After we smoke the peace pipe, there is chanting and feasting. I hope that you have packed your appetite."

Julie patted her belly. "Always," she said. "Feed me, love me, keep me."

"That's the idea."

When they arrived, Gray took their gear and tossed it into a tipi. Julie fingered the brightly painted animal skin stretched tight against its wooden supports and stepped inside.

The interior was brighter than she expected. She looked up and found the source of illumination. There was a small opening at the apex of the structure.

"Smoke hole," said Gray following her gaze. He unrolled a soft and pliable camping mat, then unzipped a heavily padded sleeping bag and spread it out on top. He took another sleeping bag, unzipped it and laid it atop the first.

Julie watched his body move, his muscles bunching beneath his shirt. "Gray?" He stopped and looked up. "Could I have a hug here?"

He stood immediately and went to embrace her. "Everything okay?" he asked.

"Yeah," she said, nuzzling into him.

"What are you thinking about?"

"Having your arms around me tonight," she said. "I'm looking forward to it. You are just winning me over. Completely."

"Goody," he breathed, nipping her neck. He pulled her from the tipi, his arm around her waist. She let herself be led, wrapping an arm around his hips, her fingers locking onto a belt loop. They bumped into each other a few times as they synchronized their stride then made off to the common area. A sea of tipis stretched across the meadow.

"How did you know which tipi was ours?" she asked, surveying the grounds.

"Because I constructed it," he said with a smile. "I also painted it. The design is mine."

"But they all look so similar."

"Think 'Dalmatian', Julie. They all have spots, but each dog sports an individual pattern."

She harrumphed at him, swinging her attention back to the conical dwellings. Then her eyes shifted to a young man who stood in front of them watching them approach. He was slender, but strongly built, like a long-distance runner. His whole stance conveyed challenge and confrontation. His aggression was palpable.

"Who's that?" she asked. He looked vaguely familiar to her, but she couldn't place him.

Gray followed her eyes. "That is Lync Swiftwater. Stay clear of that one. He's bad news."

"Why is he watching us with such ferocity?"

"He doesn't have a guest for the ceremony," he said. "I do."

"This bothers him?"

"Very much."

"But I thought that this ceremony was all about building relationships and peace among all peoples."

"It is," Gray said slowly. "Have you never gone to church and fought your way out of the parking lot?" She looked at him blankly. "Same rules apply. People of all nations talk peace. Not all live it. Come on," he said, pulling her to the left. "Let me introduce you to some nice people."

He moved her off toward a group of women who were loading up tables with casserole dishes and trays of food. As he did so, he glanced back over his shoulder and gave Lync a hard look.

Julie chatted with the 'lunch ladies' then bumped into Ben Half Moon later that afternoon. He pulled her aside good-naturedly.

"We are very happy to welcome you, Julie. And it's good to see Gray with a guest."

"He's a wonderful man."

"To be sure." He paused. "I understand that he is building a house."

Julie nodded.

"That is a big statement."

"How so?"

"Well, a man must prove that he is able to provide before he can earn a wife. He is working very hard to prove himself worthy."

Julie's mouth fell open.

"And we've all been working very hard at fostering your relationship," he continued.

"Excuse me?"

"When we found out that Gray was sweet on the new veterinarian," he nodded at her, "we started asking him to take our pets into town so he would have an excuse to see you more often."

Julie shook her head in shock. "Gray orchestrated all those visits just to see me?"

"No. We orchestrated all those visits. The Sioux community."

"Did Gray know what you were doing?"

"Nothing was ever said," explained Ben with a shrug. "Nor was there a need for words. Julie, you are here to become part of the Sioux Nation. What you must understand are the many ways in which we take care of each other. Gray had a need. We recognized it and did our part to help him on his path. I guess you could say our actions embodied what this ceremony is all about."

Julie was stunned. "I see."

"When we see you two together, we feel a part of the union."

"Is that why so many watch us?"

She saw a cloud pass across his face. "That is part of it."

"What is the other part?"

"Gray is a very special man, Julie. They are curious to find out more about how you and he relate to each other."

"Is this because of our different backgrounds?"

"Yes… and also because of something that happened almost twenty years ago."

Julie waited.

"Gray had his eye on someone once, when he was younger, in his teens. Her family didn't approve."

"Gray told me about this."

"Did he now?"

Julie nodded. "Who was the young lady? Have I met her? Did she marry?"

Ben shifted his weight uncomfortably. "She did not marry." He looked away. "You have not met her, but you do know of her. She was the woman who was attacked and killed the day of the blizzard."

Julie's stomach turned. In her mind's eye, she replayed the scene in the state park parking lot when Gray was informed of the victim's name. She had thought that his shock stemmed only from the fact that she was one of his own.

"He was still in love with her, wasn't he?" she asked, her heart fracturing into tiny shards of hurt.

"No, Julie. He had moved on. I know this. And I know that what he feels for you is quite different from what he felt for Susan."

She looked doubtful.

"Gray didn't fight for Susan. He conceded to her family's wishes, but he fights for you, Julie."

She nodded mutely.

He tossed his head across the throng of people milling about in front of the ceremonial tipi. "Gray is getting anxious. You best go to him now. Certain things are important to him and you are one among them. He knows that we've had a serious talk. Go stand beside him, he'll feel better."

Ben Half Moon was right. When she moved up next to Gray, he clasped her hand firmly and smiled as if all was right with the world.

Over the next days, Julie stood beside Gray in the ceremonial tipi listening to the melodic cant of the sacred words. The air was thick with the rich and heady smoke of burning sage.

Julie tried to focus on the ceremonial proceedings, tried to fully participate in the spirit of the ritual, but Lync did much to fragment her concentration. His envy was a palpable thing. Too often, she caught him staring at her with hostile interest. She called Gray's attention to their silent watchdog. Gray was not pleased.

On the last night, Julie listened to the rise and fall of all the voices as they joined together in song. She and Gray were sitting together on the ground,

Indian-style. Without thinking, she placed her palm on his thigh. He turned to her, his eyes fire-bright, and placed his palm on her knee.

When the singing was finished, the feasting began. Julie was hugged by many who welcomed her into their community. Everyone fed her. Everyone over-fed her. Although separated from Gray by the crush of well-wishers, she found his eyes upon her every time she searched for him.

The Sioux danced under the stars as if pulled by the same celestial forces. Round and round they went under an ink black sky.

She found Gray at her elbow. "Let me fix you something to eat, Julie. I, too, am pledged to care for you."

"No more food," she begged.

"Then what else can I give you?"

She fell silent and placed a hand on his chest. His heart beat warm and steady beneath her palm. He laid a hand atop hers then lifted her chin and gazed into her emerald eyes. "I've given you that already, Julie Hastings," he whispered. "Many, many moons ago."

They walked back to their tipi arm-in-arm at the close of the ceremony. "You spoke with Ben Half Moon," he said into the quiet.

"Yes," said Julie.

When she didn't elaborate, Gray grunted. "Anything you would like to share?"

"No," said Julie with a smug, little grin.

He grunted again. She thought that he was responding to her sass, but he had stepped in front of her like a linebacker, shouldering her behind him in one swift, very physical move. It happened so fast, Julie didn't have time to react. They were walking along, then suddenly Gray was face to face with Lync. The disturbing young man would have collided with Julie had Gray not managed to pull her out of the way in time.

Julie gripped the back of Gray's shirt with one hand and rested the other on the flat plane of his back. She was suddenly surrounded by sound. It was a growl, deep, low and ferociously primal. She felt the vibration of it in the palm of her hand and it moved up her arm in the form of little goose bumps.

Julie released Gray as if he were hot to the touch and stepped back in alarm. It was an animal sound, but it was coming from Gray. Lync gave her the briefest ghost of a smile, then stepped away into the dark.

She was rooted to the spot. Gray turned to her with a frown. "Come, Julie." He had to practically tug her into motion as they made their way back to the tipi.

"You growled at him!" she exclaimed. He wrapped an arm tightly around her waist.

"He's a nuisance," said Gray. "I spoke to him in a language I hope he understands."

"You growled at him!" she exclaimed once more.

He ushered her into their tipi and pulled her onto their bedroll.

"You growled at him!" She repeated for the third time. And he growled again, more softly this time and with different intent.

28

Elliott picked Julie up after work on Friday. They had a gig near Wasta and a bit of a drive to get there.

"*How* was your weekend?" he asked.

"Very nice. How was yours?"

"I didn't do much. Band practice. Ball game. Stopped by my parents' house for Sunday dinner. *How* did you spend your time?"

He obviously knew exactly *how* she had spent her weekend. "I visited the Sioux reservation, kissed a buffalo bladder, smoked some questionable tobacco, and had my face painted."

"That Gray sure knows how to show a girl a good time."

She chuckled. "How did you hear about my weekend?"

"Smoke signal."

"Elliott!"

"That's *Kemo Sabe* to you, Sioux."

Elliott and Julie were the last to arrive at the bar. The band had already set up the stage and were clustered around a pizza box in the back room.

"Howdy, guys!" Julie chirped as she dropped her gear.

They rounded on her in one swift and choreographed movement, their cheeks bearing bright streaks of red lipstick. "*How!*" they replied, their palms raised in salute.

Julie groaned.

"*How* did you like sleeping in a wigwam?" asked George.

"It was like camping, but more... organic. So kind of you to ask."

"*How* do you like your new relatives? All 70,000 of them?" asked Petey.

"The more the merrier," said Julie.

"*How* did you like kissing a buffalo bladder?" queried Ro-Bear.

She held up a hand, "*How* would y'all like to shut the hell up? My tomahawk is getting thirsty for pig and at the rate y'all are goin', I'm going to feed it!"

"Damn! Seventy-two hours with the Sioux and she's already gone savage on us," said George.

"All right guys, enough," said Elliott. "Tonto here has to change into her buckskins."

Julie couldn't think of a sassy rejoinder, so she just spun on her heel and grabbed her garment bag.

"You know, Elliott," said Petey, "I've been thinking."

"That's new and different, isn't it boys?" said Julie to no one. She heard a few snickers.

Petey ignored her. "Perhaps we ought to incorporate a little Cher into our song list. I've always liked *Half-breed* and *Jesse James*."

"How about Tim MacGraw's *Indian Outlaw*? I've always been partial to that one," added George.

She left them to their teasing and found the ladies room. She was going to have her little victory tonight. She had a new outfit. It was a short little golden sheath with red beads sewn onto the fabric and it finished in a soft golden fringe that fell mid-thigh. There was only one shoulder strap, the other shoulder was bare. Her high heels were lethal weapons. She stepped back from the mirror with a small smile.

She put gold tassel earrings into her ears, tucked a large gold cloisonné hairpiece midst her curls then added gold bangles to her right wrist.

She re-entered the back room to stunned silence and slack jaws. "What?" she asked coyly. "Have you never seen a squaw in a beaded dress before?"

As they loaded up their cars with their instruments and amplifiers, Julie pulled George aside.

"Hey, I've got a question for you."

"Shoot."

"That young Sioux that was so anxious to meet me a while ago?"

"Yeah?"

"Did he seem nice like a fan? Or was he more threatening? You know, a bit of the dangerous sort?"

"Why do you ask?"

"Well, I ran into a guy at the reservation this past weekend and he watched me intently. But not in a good way. It's probably nothing. Gray said the man was just jealous because he did not have a guest of his own for the ceremony."

"What did he look like?"

"He was a little taller than me, muscular, but built like a runner or a swimmer. Brown eyes. High, flat cheekbones. His hair was shoulder-length with bangs that were cut diagonally so that one eye was often hidden behind his hair."

"Did Gray know him?"

"Yeah. Gray knows everybody."

"What did Gray say?"

"He told me to stay clear of the guy, that he was trouble."

"Sounds like good advice to me."

"Do you think it's the same guy?"

George shrugged. "Hard to say. Every Sioux I know has brown eyes and high cheekbones. The young man I dealt with had his hair in a long braid."

"Well then, it's obviously not the same guy."

George scratched his shoulder absently then ran a hand through his hair. The barber had taken it a little short today. The cut was almost army issue.

"Penny for your thoughts?"

He smiled. "I'm much more expensive than that, Julie."

"How about a nickel?"

"How about you let me puzzle this one through? He hasn't threatened you, right?"

"Not really," she said slowly.

He frowned. "Well, why don't you ride off into the sunset. I'll explore our options."

"Meaning?"

"Go home, get some rest. Don't worry."

29

Julie was hiking the mountain at a good clip, especially considering the extra weight she was carrying. She switched the picnic basket from her left arm to her right. A backpack would have been more practical, but she had opted for romantic. The picnic hamper had been an expensive whimsy.

Her Saturday hike was taking her straight through the state park en route to Gray's building site. She smiled softly thinking of wrap-around porches, big kitchens and her big Sioux.

She stopped abruptly frowning into the silence. The birds had stopped singing. She listened hard. Nothing. The lack of sound was disconcerting.

A cool breeze rustled the leaves softly. Rustle. Rustle.

She nearly jumped out of her skin. Something big was moving through the underbrush off to her left. She froze and listened hard. Nothing. Her chest tightened. With quiet footfall, she made her way forward. Just the wind. Just the wind. Maybe a squirrel. Goodness knows that a mouse can sound like an elephant if it scampers across dry leaves and bracken.

Rustle. Rustle.

Her heart skipped. Off to her left. Bigger than a squirrel. Definitely bigger than a squirrel. She glanced nervously into the foliage, but could see nothing. She stopped again and listened.

Silence.

She started forward once more. She could hear it, whatever it was. When she stopped, it stopped. It was pacing her. She reached into her pocket and pulled out her cell phone. With relief she saw that she had signal. She dialed Gray.

He answered on the first ring. "Gray?"

He could hear her panic and fear. "Are you on the trail?"

"Yes."

"I'm on my way."

She snapped her phone shut and with another nervous glance around her, she started back up the mountain. She walked much faster now and she held to the far right side of the path. The animal was also tracking faster. She could hear it moving swiftly through the woods. It came from behind, drew level to her, then raced forward, always out of sight. A four-legged something. Not a bear. The feet were swift and sure.

She drew a deep breath and tried to slow her pounding pulse. It had moved on and away from her. She hesitated now. It had moved off in the direction she needed to go.

She deliberated. *Stay? Go? Stay? Go?*

She stood stock still for a few minutes trying to make a decision, her ears straining to hear for more movement in the underbrush. She hugged herself. All she could hear was the fast hammering of her own heartbeat.

She looked down at her picnic hamper. Food in the woods. She'd never considered that a danger before. Perhaps she should re-think the wisdom of such a thing. She started up the path again. If the animal returned, she'd ditch the hamper and move on without it. She rounded the corner and stifled a scream.

"Did I scare you?" Lync said with a calm that irritated and angered her. He wore a white Izod shirt and jeans. You could tell from his *GQ* pose that he liked the way he looked in his clothes.

"You speak?" She cocked an eyebrow. "I thought you only stared and growled."

"That was your boy that growled, not me," he said with a smile. "You look like Little Red Riding Hood off for a visit to grandmother's house with that basket of yours."

She just glared at him.

"Aren't you afraid of meeting up with the Big Bad Wolf, little girl?"

"No," she said tersely. "I happen to like wolves." She started on her way again and he fell in step alongside her.

"No surprise there, seeing as you're dating one."

The comment took her by surprise and she stopped and stared at him. "Now, what the hell is that supposed to mean?" she asked, wondering if there was such a thing as 'dislike at first sight'.

He studied her face for a moment, lost in thought. Then his eyes grew wide and gleeful. "You don't know, do you?"

"Know what?"

"You don't know!"

"What are you talking about?" She was really getting irritated now.

"You're seeing Gray."

"Yes," she said, frowning at him. "We're a couple." He leaned in close and sniffed.

"I beg your pardon," she said, pushing him away from her.

"No, you're not," he said, a smooth smile spreading across his face.

She wanted to smack it off of him. "Not what?"

"A couple."

"The hell we're not."

"Oh, he's been marking his territory, all right." He sniffed again. "But he hasn't staked his claim." She went to push him away again, but he grabbed her wrist with a wicked chuckle and refused to release it.

She tried to free herself from his grasp, but his grip was unusually strong. In exasperation, she looked up at him ready to unleash a torrent of expletives, but the words died on her lips. He was very still, too still. His eyes were watchful and intent, like a hunter, like a predator. Her stomach turned.

"I want you." He said it quietly. A simple statement of fact.

"I am with Gray," she said, trying to be composed and confident, but her hands had already turned to ice.

"Not now, you're not."

In the silence, she heard a thundering. Her heart? The staccato was fast and furious. Then, as one, both of their heads turned in the same direction. Barreling down the trail was her wolf, teeth bared. He launched himself at Lync going directly for the jugular.

Julie screamed long and loud.

Suddenly, Lync was gone. She fell backwards as his hand released her and landed in the dirt, her scream shifting from one of terror to one of surprise as she fell flat on her back.

She scrambled to her feet in a panic, trying to put as much distance between herself and the snapping jaws as possible. Big Boy was viciously tearing into another wolf and both seemed to be ripping apart men's clothing. She scanned the clearing for Lync. The white Izod and blue jeans were in shreds. The man was nowhere to be seen. Her mind slowly began to wrap itself around what was happening.

A shoe got kicked to the tree line. She stared at it stupidly then looked back at the flying fur and flashing teeth. Lync was indeed in the clearing, he just wasn't Lync any longer.

"Oh. My. God." She said the words, but no sound escaped her lips. The two animals growled at each other in menacing challenge and ripped at each other's hides, their teeth searching for purchase. Her eyes searched for a weapon. She rushed into the tree line and found a thick stick, but her hands were shaking so badly, it took her three tries to pick it up.

The savagery of the fight was turning her stomach. The wolves' jaws clacked together loudly, forcefully when they contacted nothing but air. Worse was the sickening thud and wretched ripping as those jaws contacted flesh.

The two beasts broke apart, circling each other, their lips curled into hateful snarls. Suddenly Big Boy lunged. He sank his teeth deep into the throat of the smaller wolf and shook viciously, tossing the animal around like a rag doll. The smaller wolf twisted frantically, desperate in his effort to break free. Big Boy just locked his jaws and bore the smaller wolf to the ground.

There was only one wolf growling now and the growl was that of a victor. When the smaller wolf went limp, Big Boy released him.

That was a mistake.

With lightening speed, the smaller animal broke free, spun around and attacked her wolf head on. Julie shrieked as Big Boy took the bite on his shoulder, but instead of trying to wrest free, her wolf lunged again, this time catching the smaller wolf's right fore-leg between its jaws. He bit down and wrenched the appendage viciously. Julie heard the ball joint pop out of its socket as the foreleg dislocated from the shoulder.

There was a yelp of surprise and a broken whimper as the two animals separated once again. The smaller one was beaten and bloody. It swayed on its feet and limped off unsteadily into the forest. Big Boy stared after him twitching with adrenaline, his hackles raised. Then he pivoted slowly toward Julie.

She shuddered as his eyes found hers. 'Kill' was still written all over his savage face. He was covered in blood. As he walked toward her, she backed away. Big Boy stopped his advance, sat on his haunches and whimpered, then took another tentative step toward her.

She bolted backwards and slammed right into a tree. Before she had time to react, her wolf was by her side licking her hand.

She looked at his shoulder. It was bleeding from a vicious series of puncture wounds. She looked back at the tangle of clothing in the clearing and started to shake. It all happened so fast. There was Lync. Then, there was a wolf in Lync's clothing.

She trembled violently. *And where was Gray?*

Big Boy nuzzled her arm, commanding touch. She ignored him. He nuzzled her again.

She did not respond.

He touched her cheek with his cold nose then darted off into the woods.

A few minutes later, Gray crouched down beside her. He was naked. Julie looked at the blood streaming from a vicious series of puncture wounds on his left shoulder and they locked eyes.

"I don't understand," she said.

"I could…" He swallowed. "I could try to explain."

She looked at him, her eyes large and fearful. She nodded and he placed a tentative hand to her elbow. When she didn't pull away, he helped her up. He stared down at her, his face full of concern. Tenderly, he wiped away the tears that were cascading down her cheeks. She released a broken sob and closed her eyes.

"You're naked," she said stupidly.

"Shhhh," he said softly and pulled her into his arms. "It's going to be okay." He held her tightly while she cried.

"He was going to—"

"No," he stopped her. "No. Don't think about that." But Gray was thinking about that. Lync was no longer a nuisance. Lync was a problem.

"You… you… "she stammered. "Are you…" She didn't know how to form the question and she shuddered again violently.

"Let's talk about that a little later, okay?" Her body convulsed again, racked by emotion and he worried that she was slipping into shock.

"But you're a wolf," she said brokenly, and she started to sob again in earnest.

"Julie, listen to me," Gray said softly. "I need you to take a deep breath. Please. Deep breath. Can you do that for me?"

She tried.

"Come on."

She tried again. He led her over to a fallen log and leaned against it, pulling her into his arms again. He mussed her hair and nuzzled her neck and rubbed her back until she got control of her emotions. They were quiet for a long time.

The silence became a soft, cottony cushion that surrounded them both. She became aware of the breeze, faint and cool. She smelled the rich, mossy undergrowth and the sharp, clean scent of chlorophyll. Her tears had dried. In fact, she thought she might be salted to Gray's chest.

"I think I'm tear-dried to you," she mumbled. He lifted her face and searched it.

She was a wreck.

"I'm not like Lync," he said carefully.

She nodded.

"I won't hurt you."

She nodded again.

He stood her upright, crossed the clearing, rooted through the picnic basket and removed the tablecloth. He wrapped it around his waist.

"I apologize," he said softly then he picked up the picnic basket. He hefted it. "What's in this thing?" he asked, trying to re-introduce a little normalcy.

"Dinner and a bottle of wine."

"And you carted this all the way up here?"

She nodded. "It was starting to get a little heavy."

He switched the basket to his left hand and extended his right. She walked toward him automatically and placed her hand in his. They started up the trail in silence, Julie never more conscious of his touch. They were headed up the trail, not down the trail. They were headed up. He took the fork towards his hunting cabin. She swallowed. She wanted to go home. Home was down. There was ringing in her ears.

"I don't feel so good," she said, stopping. A wave of dizziness washed over her and she weaved. He held her again as a shudder wracked her slender frame. "I'm sorry."

"Don't apologize," he said, hugging her to him. She was stiff and unresponsive in his arms. He could feel her quaking and he held her until she stilled. When she was in control again, they trudged on. It felt like an eternity until his cabin came into view.

She was sweaty and edgy and still quite light-headed. All she could focus upon was her hand. She wanted him to release her. A few times, she had tried to wriggle free, but he just gave her a reassuring squeeze and held on tight. He wasn't paying attention. She wanted him to let go, not hold on. He tugged her to the cabin door and gently muscled her in.

He nudged her toward the bed, but she took a kitchen chair instead and put her head between her knees. He wet a washcloth and handed it to her.

"I'm a little thirsty," she said, holding the cold compress to her face. He was back quickly with a glass of water.

"You should lie down."

"I'm fine."

"Julie."

"I'm fine. Really."

"Would you like to wash?"

"Oh," she said. "Yes." She moved to the hand pump and he gave her a solid stream of water while she scrubbed her face, neck, arms and hands.

"Better?" he asked.

"Much."

"Please, lie down. I'll warm up some dinner."

She didn't want to lie down, but she honestly didn't feel like she had the strength to even keep herself upright in a chair. She let him guide her to his bed and remove her shoes. He tucked her in like a child.

"Rest, okay?"

She nodded, closed her eyes and fell into the welcoming arms of sleep.

She awoke to soft, golden lamplight. It took her a moment to remember where she was and why she was there. Then, everything came sharply back into focus and she took a shaky breath. Gray was busy lighting candles, but he turned at the sound.

"Sleeping Beauty awakens," he said brightly.

She looked at the stars through the picture window. "How long did I sleep?"

"Several hours." He paused. "Hungry?"

"No."

"Well, dinner is ready. You should try to eat something."

She had packed a tangy short rib mole, and its fragrance filled the small cabin. Wine was poured into two glasses on the table. She got out of bed and he helped her to her chair.

"You're still a little wobbly."

"I'm sorry."

He frowned. She'd been apologizing since Lync had accosted her. "There is nothing to be sorry about, Julie."

"Of course, I'm sorry." She took a sip of wine.

He scooped some beef onto her plate, served himself, then sat down.

"What did Lync say to you on the mountain?"

She took a forkful of food and looked out the window. *What had he said?*

Their dialogue played through her mind. Lync did not know that she didn't know that Gray was a…

Gray ate, waiting for her response. When none seemed forthcoming, he tried to re-capture her attention. "Julie?"

She turned to look at him questioningly. "Did he hurt you?"

She took a sip of wine and frowned. *Did he?* She couldn't remember. He had sniffed her. She shuddered. She took another bite of food. He had grabbed her wrist. She shuddered again.

Gray set his silverware down and folded his hands, resting his head upon them. She was very far away, in shock. Fear lodged cold and hard in his gut.

"Julie," he tried again. "Would you like to hear about the house?"

She looked back at him and nodded mutely.

"I'm breaking ground next week."

"That's good," she said. He was speaking, but she wasn't listening. His voice was like background noise. Elevator music. There, but not there. It was a buzzing in her ears. She ate her meal.

"I'd like to walk the site with you tomorrow. Finalize the plans."

She took another sip of wine and he refilled her glass. "I have to work tomorrow."

"Tomorrow is Sunday," he reminded her.

"I think I have kennel duty."

"Rose has kennel duty this weekend," he said quietly.

She swallowed another sip of wine. "There is something I have to do. I just can't remember what."

He finished his meal and removed his plate.

"Listen," she said, getting to her feet. "I would like to go home now. Would you take me home?"

"No," he said, turning to face her.

She stepped back as if she'd been struck. "No?" Her voice was a dry and dusty croak. She folded her arms to still the little tremors that were beginning to shake through her. "What do you mean, no?"

He crossed the room to stand beside her. "Julie, if I let you go tonight, your fear will grow a thousand-fold. I'll never get you back. I don't want to lose you. Not to fear."

She shuddered again and gripped herself even harder. "I need to go home, Gray."

She pivoted toward the door, but he reached it before her and blocked her way. He could smell the fear on her now and his nostrils flared.

"Please let me leave." She wouldn't look him in the eye.

"No, Julie, no. I don't want you to leave. Not like this. Not terrified of me."
She tried to move past him, but again, he moved between her and the door. She
looked at the muscular arm blocking her escape then looked up at his face.

"Please," he begged. His eyes were worried and fearful. "Please stay. You're
breaking my heart." He said it as a whisper. She closed her eyes and took a
ragged breath. "After everything, Julie, after everything, can't you give me just
one kernel of faith and trust?"

She lifted her head slowly and met his eyes. They stared at each other
silently for a moment then she nodded and sat back down.

"Like always," he said, ferreting a t-shirt out of the cedar chest and handing
it to her.

She took the garment with a shaking hand. He nodded encouragement. "I'm
going to do the dishes."

She undressed slowly, then slipped the t-shirt over her head and folded her
clothes neatly on top of the cedar chest. She moved mechanically, grabbing her
guest toothbrush while moving to the water pump.

She heard the deadbolt slide in the door and she jumped, hitting her hip on
the stone basin in the process. Lync. Lync was shocked to know that she didn't
know about Gray. She tried to rub the soreness out of her hip. *Why was that such
a surprise? No one in their right mind would admit to being a werewolf.* She rinsed
the toothpaste out of her mouth, dropped her toothbrush into a ceramic cup
and stood staring at it for a while, lost in thought.

"Julie?" She jumped again. "You will get cold."

She crossed the room slowly and sat on the edge of the bed. He opened his
arms for her and nodded. She slipped in and rested her head on his shoulder,
wrapping the rest of her around his warm frame, as if on automatic-pilot. He
gave her a little squeeze.

"Thank you," he said, his voice cracking with emotion.

She lay there for hours staring into the darkness. She listened to Gray's
breathing, deep and slow, then she focused on a strong but quiet, muffled
sound. His heartbeat.

He sounded human. She thought of him and the baseball team. So many
proud moments. She closed her eyes.

He's a werewolf.

She thought of the Sioux gathering and how he seemed to grow a foot taller
with her on his arm. She had never seen him smile so often as that weekend.

He's part beast.

Her heart squeezed. He had saved her today and she had repaid him with mistrust, wolf or no. She swallowed hard. Here she was, snuggled up to him as usual. As always. And she was safe. So very safe.

As ferocious as he had been on the trail, he'd never shown her anything but tenderness, patience and respect. There were men, men like her stepfather, that behaved far more beastly than Gray did.

"Gray," she whispered. He turned on his side to face her. "You're still awake?"

He nodded.

"I'm glad you kept me tonight. It was the right thing to do."

Suddenly, his dark eyes burned very bright and shiny. She found a hand and guided it to her ribcage. It was a show of trust and he knew it.

She leaned into him and kissed him gently on the lips. "You are going to explain all of this tomorrow, right?"

He nodded.

"All right, then," and she fell asleep, snuggled up in his arms.

When she opened her eyes, she found him staring at her. He was thoughtful and watchful. Julie gave him a tentative smile and his lips quirked upwards briefly.

"How long have you been watching me sleep?"

"A while," he murmured. He brushed her hair back with his fingers and traced the outline of her ear.

She glanced over at the window to see a brightness found only in late afternoon. "What time is it?"

"One," he said, tickling her nose with a strand of her own hair.

"One!" Her stomach grumbled.

She tried to roll out of bed, but he wrapped his arm around her waist and pulled her back. "Thank you for last night," he said somberly. "I know you were upset."

"I'm better now," she said quietly. He bent to kiss her and paused, silently asking permission. She closed her eyes and lifted her lips up to him to complete the kiss. When they separated, they looked at each other for a moment.

"I have a lot of questions," she said softly.

"Well, let me answer the most important one before you even ask it." He paused. "I'm human, Julie. I hurt. I suffer. I love. I feel. Although I can shape-shift into a wolf, I am not a beast. I'm a man."

She nodded.

"I need you to know that."

She nodded again.

"I am still Gray. But I am also Big Boy. The only thing that's changed is that now you know that we are one and the same."

"You are in wolf form often?"

"Yes. There is a female veterinarian in town that I guard on her Saturday hikes. She likes me *a lot* and she feels very safe when I am by her side."

Julie swallowed and looked toward the window.

"Hey, there is a man in the moon, right?"

Julie nodded, and turned back to face him.

"There is a man in your wolf. He's just hidden."

"Life is not that simple."

"Life is very simple, Julie. We're the ones that complicate it up with our disbelief. There were those who doubted that man could fly. And look at us now. We've already touched the moon."

She slid out of bed, reaching for her clothes. "I'm getting dressed now."

"And I'm cooking," he said, moving toward the kitchen area.

"I'm confused."

"I know you are. And there's a lot to tell you, but we should go slowly."

When she was dressed, she reached for dishes and silverware to set the table. "Yesterday, I watched a man change into a wolf." She held a plate cradled to her chest and leaned against the table watching his back as he prepared their breakfast. "How is that possible?"

"No one knows the mechanics of it," he replied carefully. "But, it's genetic. The ability to shape shift and the tales of those who possess the gift are ancient."

"This is a Native American thing?"

"No, but Native Americans are more accepting of those who can change form. They honor us for our dual natures." He mixed water into the boxed pancake mix and whipped up a batter.

"It's genetic, you said. Meaning hereditary?"

"Passed on from father to son."

"So, your father was a werewolf?"

He turned to face her. "Werewolves are fictitious creatures crafted in Hollywood. In reality, wolf-men are called lycanthropes."

"In reality?"

He nodded slowly.

"Gray, you can change form at will?"

"Yes."

"The full moon?"

"That does impact ourmoods, but no, I do not turn into a psychotic killer when the moon is full. Just the opposite. I ache to hold you at that time, Julie."

"But doesn't the full moon force you to shape shift?"

"Only on a movie set. In real life, we are not compelled."

Julie measured out coffee into the old-fashioned percolator and set the coffee pot on the free burner. Gray turned on the flame. A quiet silence stretched between them.

"Does it hurt to change?" she asked at last.

"No. It's just a little awkward."

Gray stacked the pancakes onto a serving plate then pulled the maple syrup down from the shelf above him.

"Do all lycanthropes possess your strength?"

"Yes. We are extraordinarily strong and we feel little pain." He watched her carefully as he spoke. "We can run for miles without breaking into a sweat. Our endurance is off the charts. Our vision is keen, so is our hearing and our sense of smell."

"You are always smelling me."

"That's because you smell good," he said, and gave her a smile. "The day of the blizzard, Julie?" His tone altered and her head snapped up in full attention. "I smelled you on the wind." He locked eyes with hers. "That's how I knew you were in the forest. That is how I found you that day."

"I've always wondered about that."

He extended a hand and she reached out to squeeze it. "I wasn't stalking you," he said. "But in the end, I did track you and find you. I couldn't tell you this at the time, because I didn't know how to tell you."

"I was so afraid."

"I know and I understand, but I don't want you to be afraid now. No fear, Julie." He pulled her to her feet, grabbed her around the waist and gave her a firm hug. "Don't be afraid of me."

She nodded stiffly and pulled away. Gray released her reluctantly then poured out another batch of pancakes on the griddle. He glanced back at her over his shoulder trying to gauge her feelings.

"How many lycanthropes are there?" she asked.

"In the world? I don't know. Not many. There are only two of us within my tribe."

"Yes," she shuddered involuntarily, her thoughts flying to Lync. She remembered the look Lync had given her in the forest. His eyes had terrified her. She fetched the coffee and poured.

"How can you be such a nice lycanthrope and Lync be such a horror?" She saw Gray flinch at her words, but was too numb to feel regret.

"Nature and nurture," he responded. "Just like with regular folk. What makes one man a serial killer and another a priest?"

She rubbed her hands over her eyes, pressing her palm against her forehead. "Did you grow up knowing you were different?"

"Yes. But I didn't know how different. My father told me when I was an adolescent. He did his best to explain things." Gray served her then took a stack of pancakes for himself. They began to eat. "By the way, you cannot change form until you reach adulthood. It's Nature's own safe-guard that we make it that far."

"What do you mean?"

"Imagine a bunch of adolescent muscle-heads with more muscle than maturity? We'd kill each other off."

"There is rivalry between you?"

"Absolutely," he said gravely. "There can only be one alpha male in the pack."

She was silent for moment and he let her digest things.

"Then Lync wasn't really interested in me. He was actually challenging your authority."

He hesitated, not wanting to overwhelm her with too much information at once. "He definitely meant you harm, Julie," he said slowly. "That's why I attacked."

"You were going to kill him."

He looked her directly in the eye. "I will do whatever needs doing to keep you from harm. I am not a killer, but if you were in danger, I would kill if I had to."

He looked down, frowning. "I need you to understand," he said, his voice heavy with the weight of his words. "My aggression was completely protective." He looked up at her, willing her to believe him.

She nodded her head.

"Can you tell me what happened yesterday, what he said to you?"

"He made an off-hand comment about me dating a wolf and then laughed at the confusion on my face. He was surprised, stunned really, that I didn't know you were a lycanthrope. I think he found that very funny, in a malicious kind of way. He kept saying, 'You don't know. You don't know' like I was some kind of idiot."

"You are not an idiot."

"Thanks. But, why would he assume that I knew?"

Gray shrugged.

"I mean why would he assume that? It's not something that just pops up in casual conversation. 'Oh, by the way, I'm a wolf-man'."

Gray was silent. She fell silent too. They looked at each other for a long moment.

"Were you ever going to tell me?"

"Not until I had to."

She was going to ask him why, but after her behavior yesterday, she knew the answer to that one already.

"Who else knows?"

"The tribal council and most of the elders."

She was thoughtful for a moment. "I thought they had treated you with deference when we were at the Making Relatives ceremony."

"A cautious respect is more like it," he said simply.

"Are you dangerous, Gray?"

"Have you ever felt threatened around me?"

She had been terrified of him in the beginning. But threatened? No. She paused. "I was a little overwhelmed last evening, especially when you wouldn't let me leave."

He looked her in the eye. "I would never harm you as man or wolf. I needed to show that to you. I was desperate to make you understand."

She heard the strength and truth in his words. She took a sip of coffee. She was silent again. "Are you sorry that you are a lycanthrope?"

"There are times when I view it more as a curse, like last night when I saw the terror in your eyes, but nothing has changed."

"Gray, everything has changed. It's going to take me a little time to adjust. Werewolves were make-believe for me until now."

"Werewolves *are* make-believe, Julie," he said forcefully. "Fictional monsters. I'm not a monster. I'm a lycanthrope."

"Okay," she said. "Okay." She looked up at him. "What are we going to do about Lync?"

Gray gave her a silent and steady stare. "I'm not sure."

"What about the police?"

"If you go to the police, how are you going to explain what happened on the mountain?" he asked softly.

She sighed heavily. "I could stick to the truth of the matter. I could tell them that Lync accosted me and that your efforts to protect me ended up in a fight. No one would need to know that you two fought as wolves."

Gray shook his head. "There is not a mark or bruise on my body to corroborate your story."

"What do you mean?

"I don't have any battle scars."

"Your chest?"

He unbuttoned his shirt to show a smooth, unmarred chest. "I healed overnight. Lync would have also."

"So what do we say?"

"We say that when I arrived, Lync stopped harassing you."

"Just like that?"

"Just like that. Think about it, Julie. What man in his right mind would want to tangle with me?"

"Lync."

"But, Lync is not in his right mind. The police will believe you."

Julie was silent for a while, replaying his words in her head. The logic of his evaluation of the situation was solid, but the problem was unsolved.

"But what about Lync?"

He frowned. "I will keep you safe, Julie." He pressed a key into her hand. "This is to my apartment in town. In case you just want to come over, in case you don't want to go home alone. I don't want you to worry."

But, of course she worried. This went beyond her comprehension and knowing. She was in an entirely new reality and it disturbed her greatly. He took her home after breakfast and she took a long, but fitful nap.

That evening, Gray showed up on her doorstep as a wolf. She let him in. "Ready for battle are you?"

Gray peeled back his lips and exposed his fangs.

"Got it."

She gave him some steak in a bowl, but she placed the bowl on the coffee table instead of the floor. She usually ran a chatty dialogue when her wolf visited. That evening, she was silent and thoughtful while moving throughout the house.

She sat on the floor to watch a movie and he snuggled close, like usual, his head in her lap. She scratched him absentmindedly. If she stopped, he nudged her, as always, urging her to continue her affections.

She showered, slipped into her nightgown and crawled into bed waiting for Big Boy. He had ducked momentarily out of her room, but when he returned, he walked on two legs, not four. She wasn't exactly surprised by this new honesty. In fact, she had almost expected it. She made room for him in the bed.

"When you are a wolf, do you understand my words? Remember what I say?"

"Yes, I'm me when I'm in wolf form."

"Your eyes? Do you remember what you see?"

"Of course," he said. "Why?"

"You've seen my naked body lots of times."

"That's true," he said softly. "And I love your body when I look at it with these eyes and with my others."

"Gray?"

He nuzzled her ear.

"Why is Lync so fixated on me?"

"Probably for the same reason I am?"

"Which is?"

"You pull me."

"Huh?"

"I've wanted you as my mate since the moment I first saw you."

"Love had nothing to do with it?"

"Oh, there are massive quantities of that now," he said, tugging on a curl, "but in the beginning, it was a fatal attraction."

"A fatal attraction?"

"I can't live without you, Julie."

The next morning, Gray awoke early and watched over her while she slept. She was pale. He touched her cheek and sighed guiltily at the charcoal smudges beneath her eyes. She awakened slowly as if pulling up from a very deep sleep.

"Good morning," he murmured. She smiled.

"What is it?" she asked. His face was somber, his jaw set.

"Your ordeal on the mountain is written all over your face, Julie. Even in your sleep you look exhausted and spent."

She shook her head in dismissal.

"How are you feeling about everything?"

"Okay," she said. "It took me a while to fall asleep last night. I've been doing a lot of thinking."

"If something starts to eat at you, you need to tell me right away. Don't worry about hurting my feelings. I need to know where your head is, where your heart is, all right?"

"All right."

"Promise?"

"I do."

While she dressed for work, Gray changed back into wolf form. She let him out as she walked to work, wrapping her arms around his massive chest to give him a powerful goodbye hug.

Cole looked up as she walked through the office door Monday morning and did a double take. Despite the rouge and the cover-up, Julie looked shattered and haunted.

"We've got a few minutes. Why don't we talk?" he said in an avuncular manner. Julie joined him wordlessly and took a seat. "What happened this weekend?" Cole asked, handing her a cup of coffee.

She looked up at him, trying desperately to keep control of her emotions. She didn't know what to say, so she spoke the truth. "Met that tiger in the jungle," she whispered.

"From the looks of it, the encounter didn't go so well," he said softly. She brushed away a tear.

"Have you been hurt, Julie?"

She shook her head no.

"You look very upset."

She looked at him with a ravaged soul. "I thought I was a tough cookie," she said, taking a deep and shaky breath.

"You *are* a tough cookie" They both fell silent, and Cole waited for her to collect herself.

"You know, they teach us that the sky is blue." She looked out the window. "All our lives we are told that the sky is blue. I see it with my own eyes. But it isn't really blue, is it? It's black. Space is black. Our atmosphere is just an illusion."

"Julie."

"I'm not handling this new reality very well."

"What can I do?"

She worked very hard at a smile. "Nothing, Cole, but thank you so much for asking." She took a ragged breath. "I've got some things I need to work out and I've got to figure this one out all by myself. I think that I'm over the worst of it. I hope that I'm over the worst of it." She wiped away another tear. "Right now I'm just trying to get myself back in the saddle, so to speak."

"Well, young lady, anytime you need a leg-up, you just holler. I'm here to listen too, if you need an ear."

"I appreciate that." She expected polite respect, but what she saw was complete understanding. She was rather confused by this. Their eyes met wordlessly.

"I'm right here Julie."

"Cole?"

"Yes?"

She was so fractured. "I don't know what to do."

He waited. "Can you give me a little more to go on?"

"I really like the tiger."

"Ah. Well, can you like the tiger from a distance? Would that work? You don't have to go into the jungle if you don't want to."

"I'm already in the jungle."

"Can you get out?"

"I'm not sure. And I'm not sure that I want to get out."

"What does your heart tell you, Julie?"

"It tells me to hang in there."

"Then hang in there, okay?"

She nodded.

"Hey," he said softly. "I happen to know a little bit about tigers. I've lived here all my life. You know, I've run into a few myself on occasion."

"I'm not sure that we're talking about the same thing," Julie said carefully. "I'm not really talking about tigers."

"Neither am I," said Cole meaningfully. "If I'm on the right page, Julie, and I think that I am, I don't think you need to be afraid of your tiger. You just need to get used to the fact that he's a tiger. Does that help?"

She nodded mutely.

"Are you afraid of tigers, Cole?"

"The first time I met one, I was terrified," he admitted. "Now, I have a healthy and cautious respect."

"I see."

The front door jingled.

"Why don't I let you handle surgeries today? Are you up to it?"

"Sure."

"I don't want you scaring the two-legged."

"That bad, huh?"

He put a hand on her shoulder as he walked by and gave her a small squeeze. "You sit here and finish that cup of coffee. I'm going to take all the morning appointments. If you're up to it, you can deal with people after lunch."

"You look better," said Cole, looking her over as he locked up. She brightened a little. "Get some rest tonight."

She nodded mutely then began her walk home. She usually walked at a fast clip, but not tonight. She didn't have the energy. She trudged slowly, staring mostly at her feet, lost in thought. She was only dimly aware of a car slowing down beside her.

"Hey beautiful!" She turned and saw Dan Keating's police cruiser creeping along beside her. He had the passenger window down and was talking to her as he drove. She gave him a little smile, but continued walking.

"You doing all right?"

"Yeah."

"Doesn't look like it."

"I'm just a bit out of sorts today."

"Can I tempt you with a visit to the station for some stale coffee and a couple of day-old doughnuts?"

"Officer Keating, you can't possibly be trying to pick me up in your police cruiser!"

"I am."

"With an offering of old coffee and stale pastry? Don't you think you'd have more luck offering a girl wine and roses?"

"Not in your case."

She laughed.

"Hop in this car, Julie Hastings."

She stopped walking, undecided, and stared at her feet.

"You know that you are craving a Krispy Kreme. Surrender, woman. Yield to your desire."

She walked over and got in the car.

"Wow," he said. "I'm going to revamp my entire pickup strategy."

"How are you doing, Dan?" She leaned over and kissed him on the cheek then hugged him tightly.

"Fair to middling, but better than you."

"Oh, I'm all right."

"Is it Gray?" he asked quietly.

She pulled back and looked out the window, "No."

He sighed. "Do you play poker, Julie?"

The question surprised her. "No, why?"

"Don't start. You'd be bankrupt in short order."

She kept her face averted as they drove, growing more uncomfortable by the minute. "Hey, Dan, perhaps you should just let me out here. I'll walk home."

"No. I don't think that's such a good idea."

"Why not?"

"George and I talked today."

"And?"

"And Gray and I talked today."

"And?"

"And you and I need to talk today."

Her heart started to pound. She could feel her face flush with adrenaline, so she shifted her body to stare more pointedly out the window. "The promise of old coffee and stale doughnuts was just a ruse then? Bad police officer!"

He chuckled.

"What did George say?"

"That you have a secret admirer, maybe two."

"What did Gray say?"

"That you met one of them on your hike on Saturday."

"You know, there is something to be said for the anonymity of a big city."

Dan parked the car, walked around and opened her door. "Not in a pig's eye."

Her eyes flashed to his as she registered the double entendre. "Come on in, Sweetheart. Welcome to my world."

When they were inside, he sat her in the cafeteria and pointed at the coffee machine and doughnut boxes. He hadn't been kidding. The coffee was old. She made fresh. The doughnuts were stale, so she zapped them in the microwave for a few seconds so that she didn't break a tooth. She hadn't realized how hungry she was. Dan returned with a fifth of Jack Daniels and spiked her coffee.

"I'd like for you to tell me what happened," he said.

"I'm really not much in a talking mood," she replied.

He uncapped the bottle and added more whiskey to her coffee. She pursed her lips, but didn't make a move to stop him. "Gentleman Jack has a way with the ladies," he said, wiggling the bottle and ushering her down the empty corridor and into his office. She sat down on his worn corduroy couch and rested her coffee mug on the low table before her.

"So," he said, taking a chair opposite.

She shrugged.

"I understand you had some unwanted attention at the reservation."

She nodded.

"Tell me."

She did.

Dan listened hard. She loved that about him. He had a way of hanging on her every word. That usually made her feel so good about herself, so confident. Tonight, it made her nervous. "I didn't think much of it," she lied, "Until I saw him on the mountain."

"I'd like to talk about what happened on the mountain."

She swallowed and immediately reached for her coffee. He watched her carefully, noticing the slight tremor in her hands when she set the mug back on the table. "I thought you and Gray spoke about that already."

"He only could tell me about the events after he arrived. I want to hear about what happened before he arrived."

"Oh," she said, and took another sip of coffee.

"Gray said you called him from the trail."

"Yeah," she said, and took another sip of coffee.

"He said you were spooked."

She nodded.

"Julie?"

She looked up.

"I don't want to play twenty questions."

She huffed and turned her head. "You are being very official."

"This is official."

"Then why did you spike my coffee?"

"It's also personal."

"I thought I had the right to be silent."

"Only if I arrest you. Since I haven't done that, silence isn't an option."

She frowned at him, went to open her mouth then shut it again.

"Julie, another woman was raped and mauled on that mountain on Saturday."

She stiffened in shock. The horror of it washed over her in a wave. *Lync?* She felt her stomach rebel. The coffee, Jack Daniels and stale doughnuts weren't sitting too well.

"I didn't know."

"I can see that."

"Was she local?"

"Yes."

"Was she Sioux?"

"Yes."

"Where did it happen?" She had to ask, but she didn't want to know.

"Before I tell you, I'd like for you to show me where you walked on Saturday." He unrolled a layout of the park. Its hiking trails were clearly detailed. He uncapped a highlighter and offered it to her.

She glanced up at him then took it. Although her hands were shaking, she was much more certain of her route this time versus last, but the last time she had been lost in the middle of a blizzard. When she finished marking her route, she capped the highlighter and waited.

He laid a transparency overtop the hiking trails. The body was found very close to her path. She closed her eyes. It made no sense. Lync would have had to have attacked the woman before he had attacked her because he had a dislocated shoulder afterwards. How could he have raped and murdered already that morning? He was perfectly composed and neat in dress when she met him.

"What happened on the mountain, Julie?" She couldn't help herself, she shuddered. "Can you talk about it?"

"Nothing makes any sense," she said slowly.

"Did you see this woman?" Dan held up a picture.

Julie stared at it a long moment before shaking her head no. "I didn't hear any sounds of a struggle. No screams."

"What did you hear?"

"The woods were abnormally quiet." She swallowed. "I got spooked and called Gray on my cell phone. I asked him to come get me."

"Where was Gray?"

"He's building a house above the ridgeline on the other side of the state park. A dump truck had just emptied a load of stone. I could hear all the noise."

"How long did it take Gray to find you?"

"I don't know. I'm very confused."

"Julie? Hear me now. Please. It's important that you focus because I'm starting to think that you are the real target and these others just happen to be consolation prizes."

She positively couldn't think a coherent thought. She tried to bolt for the door, but he grabbed her upper arm in a vice grip and pulled her back towards him. She wrestled with him briefly, but he just wrapped his arms around her and pulled her close.

"Talk to me Julie," he said fiercely, rocking her slowly in his arms.

She trembled silently while he held her and he murmured soft, unintelligible words against her curls. "Were you assaulted?"

"No."

He pulled back from her to look into her eyes. Finding truth, he nodded with relief.

"But you were threatened on the trail?"

She stilled as she thought about what to say and he watched her war with herself. He was accustomed to watching a suspect disassociate truth from the adjusted truth they cared to share. It was rare from a victim.

"Julie." He dropped his arms, his hands searching for hers. "I have three dead. Each and every one suffered before they died. Good people. Innocent people. They have suffered. I need you to talk to me. I need you to tell me everything, even if it doesn't make sense, especially if it doesn't make sense. I need to stop this."

She slowly dropped her head onto his shoulder. He could feel her soften physically with... release?...relief?

"Speak to me. Please."

"The forest got very quiet," she said. Her voice came out dry and deep. "It was silent. I can't begin to explain how eerie it was. The birds stopped singing. The insects. There was a total absence of sound. I was on edge even before I realized why." She paused, remembering. "Then, I became very aware, so aware I could hear my own blood circulate through my body. It was as if all my senses were heightened." She swallowed. "My skin tingled, my ears began to ring. I could smell a hundred different scents on the wind. I knew something was in the forest. I could feel it. It was hunting." She looked him straight in the eye. "It was hunting me."

"There was no sound?"

"Not at that moment," she said. "I stood frozen in place for... I don't know how long. When I finally took a step and started to move back on up the trail, I heard something off in the bushes to my left."

"What did you hear?" he reached for her hands and held them firmly.

She shuddered. "An animal. It was furtive and four-legged. But big. And it was tracking me." She shuddered again.

"Did you see it?"

"No, not even a shadow. Not even a glimpse. I couldn't figure out what it was. It was heavy, but quick. I couldn't make sense of it."

"Your wolf wasn't with you that day?"

"No. Every now and again, he doesn't show up."

"You said it was tracking you?"

"Yes, most definitely." A little tremor wracked her. "It moved when I moved, stopped when I stopped, sped up when I did. I felt very threatened."

"That's when you called Gray?"

She nodded.

"Any chance it could have been your wolf?"

"No," she said flatly. "The forest is alive when Big Boy walks beside me. The forest was dead that day."

Dan was quiet for a moment, puzzled by her odd choice of adjectives. Slowly, she pulled her hands free.

"Julie, think back to the woods the day of the blizzard. Were the woods also quiet?"

"Yes, but I think that was because of the storm. The animals had all hunkered down."

"But how did the forest feel?"

"I was terrified," she whispered, looking up at him.

"Were you aware of something tracking you back then in the snow?"

"No. All I could hear were the snowflakes."

He nodded. "So on Saturday, Gray took how long to get to you?"

"Too long. It felt like forever, but was maybe fifteen, twenty minutes."

"What did you do?"

"I decided to keep walking, to shorten the distance between us."

"The animal in the brush?"

"It moved off."

"How does Lync factor into all of this?" asked Dan.

She locked eyes and frowned. "I'm not sure that he does. I rounded a bend and there he was: Mr. *GQ*. Smug. Arrogant. Cocky. I tried to walk on by, but he fell into step."

"Whoa. Whoa," said Dan, his hand in the air. "You are being hunted by God-knows-what and you come across another person on the trail and you just walk on by?"

"I tried to walk on by."

He just looked at her.

"In my personal experience, two-legged animals have always been more dangerous than four-legged ones. The threat ahead of me seemed far more dangerous than the threat behind me."

"You thought Lync was a danger?"

"I had been frightened by the animal in the brush, but I was terrified of Lync. I was in total flight or fight mode. I did both."

"What happened to the animal that had been tracking you?"

"I told you already. It had moved off."

"Before you encountered Lync?"

"Yes."

"What did Lync say to you?"

She turned away from him and took a shaky breath. "He asked me if I was afraid of the big bad wolf," she whispered. Dan closed his eyes. "Then he grabbed my arm and wouldn't let go."

She held up her right wrist, black with bruising, then rubbed her forehead as if to erase the memory.

"What happened next?"

"Gray entered the clearing and Lync released me. I had been pulling so hard against him that when he let go, I fell flat on my back. I got to my feet awkwardly and catapulted myself backwards into a tree trunk." She hung her head. "I'm sure I'm black and blue."

"Can I look?"

"At what?"

"At your back?"

Julie searched his eyes then nodded. She stood and turned around. "The muscles in my back are very tender. It hurts to move my arms. You'll have to lift my blouse yourself."

She felt his hands upon her hips. They slid under her top and ran along the small of her back. His touch was warm and calloused. He lifted her blouse slowly, tenderly running the pads of his fingers along the cuts, bruises and abrasions.

"Am I as bruised as I feel?" she asked.

"Yes," said Dan, his voice thick. He ran a thumb along her left shoulder blade and heard a soft groan.

"Hurts."

He stepped into her and wrapped his arms protectively around her torso, his head on her shoulder, his right hand between her breasts. His breathing was deep and slow, as if he were trying to regulate it. He hugged her to him as if he could will the bruises away, take away her pain. She rotated in his arms and as she did so, his right hand slid inside her bra, his fingers cupping her left breast. They both froze.

"I didn't do that on purpose," he husked.

"I know."

His thumb played gently across her breast.

"Are you going to exit?" she asked.

"I haven't decided," he said. "My hand is very happy where it is."

She reversed rotation and turned round to face him, doing her best to tug her shirt down to her hips, pain and all. When she met his eyes, her cheeks were flush.

"That was wonderful, Julie. Could we do it again?"

She smiled and shook her head. He lifted her chin and brushed his lips gently across hers, then he deepened the kiss and deepened it some more.

"You are vulnerable tonight," he said, his breathing heavy. "I won't take advantage. But I want to."

Dan drove the few short blocks to Julie's home in silence. Julie, in the meantime, scanned the border shrubbery and ink-black lawns for wolves. Her house was dark when the squad car pulled into the driveway. She approached the house door with her keys, opened it and hit the floodlights. The light relaxed her immediately.

"Thank you, Dan, I think."

He stood on her doorstep and smiled sadly. "I'm worried about you."

"I'm okay."

"No. No, you are not." He took a deep breath and exhaled forcefully. "I liked holding you in my arms tonight, Julie. I just wish it were under other circumstances."

"It can't be that way between us, Dan."

"Gray?"

She nodded. His eyes grew troubled, as he listened. "We have some things to work out, but we're working them out." She stood on tiptoes and kissed him lightly on the cheek. Just as she was about to pull back, he snaked an arm around her waist and pulled her to him tightly. He held her there for a long time until he felt her muscles soften.

"Good night Julie," he breathed, stepping back. He gave her a tender kiss on the lips and rubbed his cheek alongside hers. "I haven't figured all this out yet, but I will. And I'm going to do my best to protect you. I'm here. I'm here if you need me. I fall asleep at night hoping that you need me. And praying that you don't."

He walked back to the police car while she shut the front door and locked it. The dead bolt clicked hollow and empty.

She tossed her keys onto the coffee table and climbed the stairs in the dark. She froze in the doorway of her bedroom listening to a swoosh of skin on fabric.

"Gray?" she called into the darkness.

"It's me."

She crossed the room to find him in bed. He pulled her to him possessively, his touch both gentle and firm. She relaxed into the sanctuary that was his embrace and welcomed his hot hands as they touched her body.

"How did you get into the house?"

"I know where you keep your spare house key."

"How would you know that?"

"You are frequented by a very observant wolf."

"What other secrets do you know?"

"You cry during all the movie love scenes and you don't eat breakfast unless I cook it for you." He tugged her close. "What did Dan Keating worm out of you?" he said, tucking her hair back out of her face.

"Well, it's a long story."

"I've got all night," he said, bringing her hand toward his lips. He tucked his head into her neck and stiffened. "He has touched you." The tone of his voice stilled her. "I smell him on your skin."

"Dan wanted to see the bruises on my back."

"I don't like him touching you."

"Well, just for the record, he doesn't like you touching me either."

He grunted and pulled her to him, wrapping himself around her. His warmth melted the day's tension from her body and soothed her soul.

"Gray?"

"Yeah?"

"Am I your sack of potatoes yet?"

When he didn't answer, she turned around to face him. He searched her eyes for a long moment then moved to place a soft kiss on her left breast. Gently, she ran her fingers through his hair and cradled him to her.

He teased the nipple with his lips and Julie arched upward in response. Gray pulled back and propped himself up on an elbow, a soft smile playing at his lips. "Yeah, Julie, you are mine." He toyed with her curls. "Question is, are you willing to be mine forever?"

Her eyes flew open in surprise. "Are you proposing?"

"I'm trying to explain… sex."

"I think I'm aware of the fundamentals, Gray," she said dryly.

He laughed then grew serious. "Lycanthrope sex is based on different fundamentals."

"Like what?"

"Well, there is no such thing as casual sex." He kissed her nose. "If you and I make love, we'd bond with each other, or at least I would bond to you. Like geese do. It's a forever commitment, like a brand on the soul. It cannot be undone." He tucked a loose strand of hair back behind her ear. His face, so earnest, so serious, erased her smile.

"You don't want that?" she asked.

"This isn't about me," he said, his eyes searching hers. "This is about you. You'd never be free of me, even if you wanted to be."

"I don't understand."

"Lycanthropes play for keeps, Julie. Our union would be more permanent than marriage. And there is no escape clause. No divorce." He traced his fingers lightly down her neck. "We can't make love until you are ready to give me the rest of your life." He brought her hand to his lips and kissed it. "Would you like to think on this a little bit?"

"Yes. I think I should."

She awoke to find him holding her as always, his breath tickling her ear, his heat keeping her warm. She turned to face him and felt her body slide unencumbered beneath the sheets.

"Gray?" she said, coming fully awake. "Did you remove my nightgown last night?"

"Uh huh," he said, sliding a warm hand down the length of her body, pulling her close.

"And why?"

"I wasn't wearing any clothes, so I didn't think you should be wearing any either," he said with a devilish twinkle in his eye. She sat up and poked at his ribs.

He swatted her hands away as if she were a pesky gnat. She jabbed him again. He made a grab for her and missed. She jabbed him again. This time, he captured her hands then sat up to face her. "There are a few more things you need to know about lycanthropes, Ms. Hastings."

"Such as?"

"Such as they have powerful libidos. He hugged her to him with such power she was forced to expel the air from her lungs. "Once they claim their mate, they are passionate," he flipped her onto her back. "They are demanding." He wedged himself between her legs. "And they don't take 'no' for an answer."

"Oh!"

He bent to kiss her tenderly, smelling the faint musk of her arousal. He growled softly in her ear. "They become possessive, protective, and very, very needy when they have a mate."

"I thought all men were like that," she teased, trying to wiggle out from beneath him.

He held her firm. "Not by a long shot."

She continued to try and worm herself free.

"Julie. When lycanthropes become sexually active, they become very sexually active."

He shifted to sit on the edge of the bed and looked down at her appreciatively. Then, he swallowed and looked away.

"Gray?"

"Yeah?" His voice was deep.

"You've already bonded to me haven't you?"

He turned back to look at her, his eyes soft. "I've got to go to work, Spud." He exited the bedroom and came back as Big Boy. She wrapped a robe around herself and led him to the door. After nuzzling her hand, he bolted for the forest.

She stood there and watched him run.

What on God's green earth had she gotten herself into? She sat down on the edge of the sofa and stared into space. Absently, she listened to the morning sounds of her neighborhood, children's voices, car doors slamming, wind chimes. So normal. So reassuring. So routine.

She climbed the stairs slowly, showered and dressed. She looked in the mirror then hung her head.

Walk away. She felt guilty for thinking the thought, but it fluttered against her consciousness like a panicked moth. She gripped the sink tightly and took a few deep breaths.

Power through, she told herself.

Walk away, whispered her subconscious.

Power through.

31

Dan pulled into her driveway as she locked up to head off to work. He weaved a go-cup of coffee before her like a snake charmer. "For you," he said. "I thought I'd be your official escort and chauffeur."

"Wow," said Julie, brightening. "My very own star buck."

"You look like you could use a little java," he said, his face full of concern.

"I'm okay, Dan."

"You keep on practicing that one," he said. "I'll tell you when I believe it." She took the coffee from him and stood before him unsure of what to do next. Her hand started to shake. At first, it was just a little tremor, but it swiftly degenerated into a violent palsy. Dan placed both hands around hers trying to steady a cappuccino that was swiftly becoming a frappacino.

"My nerves are shot."

"I see that."

"Maybe coffee was not the best course of action."

"My apologies. I was all out of truth serum."

She looked up at him. "I haven't lied to you, Dan."

"But have you told me the whole truth?"

She had enough strength to continue to hold his eyes with her own, but not enough strength to speak. She shrugged helplessly. "Nothing else has any relevance."

"Can I be the judge of that?"

"No. It's personal."

Dan was not happy.

"I need to get to work," said Julie. "I have a surgery this morning."

"All right. I'll take you," said Dan. "But I will also pick you up at six o'clock. We can continue the conversation."

Julie shook her head and kept shaking it. She closed her eyes. She was beginning to feel a little boxed in. Dan was a crashing boulder of relentless pursuit. Gray was a quietly patient yet unmovable wall of stone. She found herself between a rock and a hard place and it was starting to make her extremely uncomfortable.

"Julie?"

She opened her eyes to look at him.

"I'm not asking."

The words ripped her heart apart like shrapnel. As Dan stood there, the light faded from her eyes. Julie was an ice sculpture in the front seat of his squad car and an automaton when she bid him goodbye.

Elliott called mid-day trying to schedule another gig for the band. She told him that she didn't want to sing for the band anymore. There was a lot of shouting after that and she ended up hanging up on him.

To top things off, she found Dan waiting for her in the parking lot after work. As she drew near, he opened the car door for her. She got in without a word. Resentment roiled in her.

"How was your day?" he asked politely. The undercurrent of tension was so thick that she felt as if she were drowning.

"Quiet. Yours?"

He gave her a significant look. "It will go better for me if you tell me what is scaring you so badly. In fact, it might go better for the next female hiker if I hear something from you besides one word answers."

"There is no need to bully me, Officer Keating," she said stiffly. "I really don't deserve it. There was nothing more I could have told you about my lost time in the blizzard. I omitted not one detail. I didn't see or hear anything. Ditto for the second woman. I didn't hear about either murder until days afterwards. You know this is true."

Her voice broke.

They drove the rest of the way to the station in silence, and Julie pivoted as far away from him as possible. When he parked the car, she was out the door and up the stairs far in advance of him.

"Sit," he said, gruffly.

She took a corner of the couch, unconsciously drawing her body up, pulling her legs back and away from him.

"Julie? What has upset you so badly?"

"I told you. It's personal."

"I need to hear about it." He leaned back, hoping she'd fill the space between them by relaxing and extending her body forward, but she sat rigidly frozen, physically withdrawn. Although the distance between them was three feet, it might as well have been three hundred miles.

"You are abusing your badge, Dan."

"Am I?" he asked. "Am I, Julie? Or are you hiding something?"

"Like what?"

"Like murder."

"Whose?" she asked, confusion flooding her face.

"Lync's."

Her jaw dropped open.

"We can't find him," said Dan.

"Is that unusual for someone who is accused of a crime? You expected him to be sitting on his front porch just waiting for your social call?"

He ignored her sarcasm. "Did Gray over-react when he confronted Lync? Hit him too hard by accident? Self-defense is a defendable position in a court of law."

Julie looked him straight in the eye. "Lync was alive when he walked out of the clearing."

"Was he injured?"

"Gray had wrenched his arm pretty good, but it was nothing life-threatening."

"What happened when Gray arrived?"

She frowned. "I've told you this already. I fell. I got up. I backed into a tree. By the time I had regained my feet, Lync was slinking away with his tail between his legs."

Dan cocked an eyebrow.

"It's a southern turn of phrase."

"What did Gray do?"

"He comforted me. I was upset."

"He took you home?"

"No. He took me to his cabin. Fed me some dinner."

"What time?"

"What time what?"

"What time did he feed you dinner?"

Julie shrugged. "Dinner time. I don't know. Evening."

"So," said Dan, "What did you do all afternoon?"

She just shook her head at him. "I washed the dirt off of myself. I was nauseous and light-headed. Gray insisted that I lay down. I did. I slept. When I awoke, Gray had dinner ready."

"Why didn't you call the police?"

"When?"

"After the incident on the mountain on Saturday?"

"And tell you what? That, gee, some man grabbed my wrist and wouldn't let it go? I've been beaten to nearly an inch of my life on multiple occasions and never breathed a word of it. After 20 years of silence, I'm supposed to suddenly run to the police and tell them that I've got a bruise?"

"Exactly my point."

Julie cocked her head. "Meaning what?" Her tone was a little hostile.

"Meaning that the bruised wrist is nothing to you, so why are you so shattered?"

She frowned. "I was hunted and accosted, isn't that enough?"

"No, Julie. No, it's not. You have survived much more than a bruised wrist in your life. I've seen the goddamned x-rays." He took a deep breath. "I've seen eyes like yours. Eyes change when they grapple with a horror that they can't process or accommodate or understand. What have you seen?" he asked.

She looked up at him, her eyes a tumultuous sea-green.

"What did you see?" he asked again.

"I saw Lync."

Dan reached for her hands. They were ice.

"Julie," he said softly. "I can only help you if you let me. I can only protect you if I know what you're up against."

She was silent a moment. "He grabbed my wrist. He grabbed it hard and squeezed. It happened so fast, I didn't have time to react. I didn't even drop the picnic basket. In fact, I clung onto the picnic basket." She shuddered violently. "It was his eyes. He looked at me as if…" She tried to form the thought, but it wouldn't come. It hovered on the edge of her consciousness just out of reach, just out of touch.

"As if?" Dan prodded.

"As if I was…" She shivered again. "I thought he…" She worked very hard to still her emotions. He watched her fight the terror. "Was going to…" She swallowed and turned away.

"Rape you?" he finished for her.

Her eyes flew to his. They were as rough and tumble as the surf. She shook her head vehemently. "No. No." She shuddered again. "I thought he was going to eat me. Alive." She swallowed.

Dan's stomach turned.

"He looked at me as if I were prey."

32

It was Gray's birthday. She pulled into the parking lot of his apartment complex and began to unload her packages and goodies.

Gray spoke of 'forever', yet hadn't even shared his birth date with her. This irked her a little. It was Ben Half Moon who had called to inform her and she couldn't hide the hurt she felt during their brief conversation.

"Gray's quiet," said Ben Half Moon, by way of explanation. "He doesn't like attention. I just thought you'd like to know so you could wish him well on that day."

She had thought a lot about Ben's comments over the course of her workweek, and each time, her stomach would pitch and roll because it wasn't the truth. Gray needed lots of attention. Gray needed love.

Unfortunately, his birthday clashed with her last scheduled singing gig with the Copper Pigs. She couldn't cancel, although the thought had crossed her mind. She was expecting the band to lay a pretty heavy guilt trip on her tonight as it was. Each of them was bringing in an extra three thousand dollars a month with her as lead singer. Her desire to quit had not gone over well.

Her strained relationship with Dan wasn't helping matters any either. The police were a family and she was distancing herself from one of their own. They made her feel like a traitor. She slid her key into Gray's lock and entered.

Glazed pecans from River Street Sweets went into a bowl on the coffee table in his living room. Gray loved this southern treat. A rich and heady Hungarian goulash went into a crock pot in the kitchen. She set the unit on low. She placed a loaf of homemade sourdough bread nearby on the counter with a crock of Irish butter. Her prized Kentucky Rum cake was set in an exquisite glass cake plate and a nice card adorned it.

There was a bread stuffed with ham and cheese and honey mustard for late-night snacking and a batch of oatmeal raisin cookies for a midnight munch. A berry cobbler went into the refrigerator for breakfast. Labels and bows were on every item.

She placed a vase of fresh flowers on his bureau and two gift videos on the TV. They were tied in a white ribbon with red hearts.

She had just finished her handiwork when her cell phone rang. "Hey!" she said, waiting for Elliott to answer the silence. Caller ID was a wonderful thing.

"Julie, I've made a horrible mistake," he said. "We're on at eight o'clock tonight, not nine."

"Okay," she said slowly.

"And it's not a casual local hangout. It's a glamour night tonight. We're at a hotel. I need to come get you in an hour."

"An hour?" Her head started to whirl, but she stilled the panic. "It's okay, Elliott. I just picked up the copper dress from the dry cleaners and I have my emergency heels in the car. I can be ready in time, but you'll have to pick me up at Gray's. It's his birthday today and I just dropped off his cake. I'll change here. Pick me up at 34 Keswick Lane, Apartment 405."

She hung up the phone, raced back to the car, grabbed her shoes and dry cleaning and flew back to Gray's apartment to shower and change, her heart hammering heavy in her ears.

Gray entered his own apartment to unexpected smells. There was a flood of scents – flowers, food, hot water, soap and Julie. He ushered his two guests into the living room and called out.

"Julie?"

"It's me, Gray," came the anxious reply. "I am so sorry to impose. I know that you have company coming this evening, but I stopped by to drop off some birthday surprises and while I was in the midst of it, Elliott called to say that he'd gotten confused and that I needed to be ready an hour earlier for pick up. He's coming here to get me. I didn't have time to go home and change. I hope that's okay."

"Of course," said Gray. "Where are you tonight?" He motioned for his guests to take seats in the living room, spied the pecans and opened the package, gesturing for them to partake.

"That's just it. Elliott told me it was the Rusty Nail in Cottonwood. It's not. It's some hotel gig in Rapid City."

"That's quite a switch." He picked up the two gift videos, read their titles and smiled. *Bull Durham*, his all-time favorite, and *P.S. I Love You*, a movie he'd never seen, but he appreciated the message.

"Don't I know it! Elliott is damn lucky I keep an emergency pair of heels in the car. I had just picked up my dry cleaning, so I'm in copper tonight."

Gray closed his eyes and groaned.

"I'll be fine," she said sternly, as if she had seen his face. "Why don't you pop into your kitchen and run inventory? I think you'll be pleased."

A few minutes later, Gray tapped lightly on the bathroom door. The water had long stopped running. "Julie, you'll need more than a towel when you exit the bathroom."

There was a moment of silence. "Why?"

He smiled. "My guests are already here."

"All right then," she said.

"Julie?"

"Yeah?"

"My guests are like me."

"Sioux?"

"Wolf." She cracked open the bathroom door. "With very keen ears." She blushed and he kissed her nose, then mouthed, "Follow my lead."

She applied some make-up, slipped down the hallway into the bedroom and donned her dress and heels. The copper dress shone brightly against her tanned body. The summer sun had bronzed her. This was, by far, the sexiest outfit she had in her closet. When she moved, the dress undulated like a field of ripe grain in the wind.

She stepped into the living room, her eyes hunting for Gray. He was standing, waiting, like a groom at the altar. She walked immediately to his side, grabbed the hand he offered her, pecked him sweetly on the lips, then turned for introductions.

Gray's strong arm lassoed her waist in a firm grip and he splayed a big hand possessively over her abdomen. His very body language said, 'mine.' He didn't need to make the verbal statement.

Two men stood to greet her, both were Nordic looking, both with flawless milk-white skin. They were every bit as big and wide as Gray and just as muscled. She gazed into their blue eyes, mesmerized by their handsome faces and beautiful bodies. They were light to Gray's darkness.

She had assumed that all werewolves would be dark-eyed and dark-skinned. Obviously, she had assumed wrong. The two strangers reminded her of snow and tundra and winter cold. She turned to Gray and just looked at him. He was deep, dark forest loam and autumn leaves. And absolutely frightening.

"Gentlemen, I'd like to introduce you to Ms. Julie Hastings." Gray nodded to the first man. "This is Hayden," said Gray. "He is the leader of the North American lycanthrope community."

A large man with platinum silver hair extended his hand. Her small hand was lost in his big palm as they shook in formal greeting.

"Finn is his second in command," said Gray.

The other man, a rusty blond, offered his hand in turn. She shook it as well, feeling the muscle and the strength in the firm squeeze he delivered.

The strangers watched her as she took a chair. Her dress sighed in a slippery glide of fabric and Gray's guests canted their heads as if listening to something only they could hear. She crossed her legs, her bare legs sliding against one another in another whisper of sound. Hayden and Finn were mesmerized by her every gesture.

She swallowed hard and looked to Gray in silent question. "You sound good, Julie," he explained. "There is a smooth and natural rhythm to the way you move. It's hypnotic, like ocean waves."

"You tell me this now?"

Hayden chuckled and reached for a handful of pecans. "How much have you told her?" he asked, chewing the sweet treats with unabashed enjoyment.

"A lot," said Julie.

"Not much," said Gray.

Hayden smiled and the devil danced within the ice blue fire of his eyes. "I see." He continued to watch Julie with focused attention, and she met his level gaze with one of her own. Hayden unsettled her, but she refused to be cowed. She put her hand on Gray's thigh and was pleased when he placed a hand on top of hers. It was impossible to feel fear with him by her side.

"What do you do for a living, Julie?" asked Finn.

"I'm a veterinarian."

"A healer?" asked Hayden. His eyes shifted to Gray. "You didn't tell me."

Gray did not respond.

"She has all the signs of a lycant, a powerful one."

Hayden looked at her in a way that made her squirm.

"Lycant?" Julie asked.

"Part wolf," said Finn.

"Why would you think such a thing?"

Hayden took a deep breath and hummed. The sound was a deep-throated rumble. "Only our sons carry the lycanthrope gene forward. Our daughters are human, but they are innate healers. They are born with a natural talent to cure the sick and mend broken bodies."

Julie processed that. "Okay. But what does this have to do with me?"

"You're a vet," said Finn.

"So, because I'm a vet, you think I'm part wolf?" she asked incredulously. She was trying to follow the logic and missing the direct-connect.

"There is a little more to it than that," said Gray softly. "Remember when I told you that you pull me to you?"

"Yes."

"It could be that you have that kind of pull on every lycanthrope, Julie. That's what Hayden meant by lycant. Lycanthropes are naturally attracted to the female of our kind, like bears to honey. No matter how weak the lineage. You see, the truly gifted healers can do more than fix broken bones. They can ease broken hearts too. They can literally pull the emotional poison from a person's soul."

"I can't do that," she said with a firm shake of the head.

"Lycants have other gifts too," said Finn. "Their body is music. It calms the beast in all of us."

"No truth there," said Julie. "I seem to introduce havoc into everybody's lives. Just ask the local police force."

No one said a word and the silence stretched long and tight between them. Julie could hear the soft ticking of Gray's kitchen clock, the faint sound of a small dog barking in the apartment below, a vacuum cleaner running down the hall.

"Do you know why I'm here?" It was Hayden again. Julie looked from Gray to Finn, but both of them sat very still.

"No," she answered, her voice soft and unsure.

"Gray has requested a 'kill permit,'" Hayden paused, watching her register his words. "Since we are so few in number, this type of decision requires very careful deliberation."

Julie was too stunned to respond.

"We understand that there have been a series of attacks?" said Finn.

Julie nodded, her mind numb.

"A wolf goes 'rogue' on occasion," said Hayden. "It happens when a man fails to knit the two sides of himself together as a whole. Eventually, one half ends up destroying the other by action or deed. Or the consequences of actions and deeds."

She nodded again, canting her nose toward Gray. The men went on to discuss the events of the last few months in great detail. She sat quietly and listened to the hum of their voices, her thoughts quite far away.

Gray ran his thumb across the back of her hand in a slow and rhythmic motion. Kill permit? She looked at the two men sitting across from her and swallowed. They could have just as easily been discussing the Sunday football game or ice fishing or…

"Julie?"

She looked up to find Gray gazing at her with gentle eyes. "Sorry," she said. "Have I missed something?"

"We're going to go wolf for a few days," said Gray softly. "See if we can track him. Lync. Are you okay with this?"

Julie nodded. She knew what he meant. "Of course," she said. "I trust you implicitly."

A smile tugged at the corner of his mouth. He didn't say "good" or "thanks" or "high noon." He simply nudged her nose and whispered, "I'm thinking that you just might have a little goose in you, Julie."

"A few minutes ago, you were thinking that I was part wolf."

"The two are not mutually exclusive."

She locked eyes with his just as Elliott knocked at the door. "My escort," she said, pulling back and standing up.

"Do we need to have a conversation about confidentiality?" asked Hayden.

"Of course not," said Julie and Gray simultaneously.

Julie nodded at the two men in farewell, her face grave, her eyes wary. She looked up at Gray.

"When?"

"We'll leave in the morning."

"Be right there, Elliott," she shouted.

"I have my cake, Julie," he said, nodding toward the kitchen. "But I want to eat it too. It's my birthday after all. Will you come back after you sing?"

"It will be late," she said, cautiously.

"And I will be waiting," said Gray.

Julie bolted out of Gray's apartment. Her heels clicked against the flooring like machine gun fire. Elliott followed behind her, his eyes following the swing of her hips and a lot of copper tassel. He couldn't keep up. She was wearing freaking FMPs, and he couldn't keep up.

"Why are we running?" Elliott asked.

"I thought we were in a hurry," said Julie, not breaking stride.

"I don't want you to break a stiletto. Or punch a hole through the floor. I'll put a bubble on the roof. Slow down, Jules."

She slowed then stopped, her shoulders set, her back to him. When he was abreast of her, she sighed. He bumped her gently with his shoulder. She bumped him gently in response.

"Who was all that muscle in Gray's apartment?"

She shrugged.

"Anything Fallston should worry about?"

"You are such a cop, Elliott."

"You didn't answer my question."

"No. You have nothing to worry about. Believe it or not, Gray is actually a good guy and he associates with very good people."

"Who are you trying to convince?" asked Elliott.

"You." She looked him dead on. "Someone. Anyone. Dan does not believe a word I say."

"Untrue," said Elliott. "He believes what you've told him."

"Really?" she asked. The relief was so evident, that Elliott smiled.

"He just wants to hear the parts you leave out."

She looked up at Elliott, her eyes a dark and serious green. "I told Cole," she said softly. "We talked it over. And he helped me, gave me some good advice. I'm better now. It really was a personal issue, not a police issue."

Elliott nodded and wrapped a brotherly arm around her shoulders. "I'll tell Dan to back off, but as for the Copper Pigs, you will have to fend for yourself. I expect them to gang up on you tonight. They won't let you quit."

"They cannot hog-tie me to a microphone, Elliott."

"That was one of the plans. There were a few others."

"Such as?"

"Well, we've got this holding pen back at the station."

"Oh, good grief. I don't want to hear anymore."

Elliott chuckled. "Julie?"

"Yeah?"

"I won't let you quit either."

"Could I maybe have a little break, then? A couple of weeks? I've had a rough go of it lately."

"I think we can manage a little sabbatical. The guys and I will use the time to learn a few new songs. Any requests?"

"*Please Release Me, Let me Go*?"

"Nah. We're not going to learn that one. How about *Stay*?"

She exhaled forcefully. "Okay. You win."

"Yippee."

They played until eleven. The tension that filled the air when Julie first arrived dissipated quickly, but then Elliott had boomed, "She's back on board, men" as soon as they had entered the room. She made her humble apologies and got bear-hugs in return.

"Damn good thing," said George. "But you weren't going to get away."

"We were hoping Elliott would sweet-talk you," said Ro-Bear. "If that failed, we were switching to Plan B."

"Yep, Plan B," said George.

"What was Plan B?" asked Julie.

"Well, Petey wanted to use the taser on you," said Ro-Bear, "but he got overruled."

"Taser!" exclaimed Julie.

"On low," said Petey, "Just a little jolt to bring you back to your senses."

"It was overruled. So that brought us to Plan C," said George.

"The holding pen back at the station?" asked Julie.

"Tsk. Tsk. Tsk. Someone has been divulging state secrets," said George. Everyone looked at Elliott.

"Whaaaat?" said Elliott. "I was just giving her a few options. Cooperation or coercion. She opted for cooperation. I had a solid plan, a successful plan."

Elliott handed her a cup of hot tea. She was surprised to smell the heady note of Gentleman Jack. "And I need this because?"

"Because the last song on the first set is *Hips Don't Lie* by Shakira."

"No!" Julie breathed.

"Paybacks are hell," said Elliott. "My band has been sweating bullets since you went all negatory on us. It's your turn to squirm, Ms. Hastings."

She squirmed all right. And she undulated and moved like she was alone, like no one was watching. And it wasn't the Gentleman Jack either. She had four men, four Copper Pigs that held on to her tightly. That did much to lift her spirits. And of course there was Cole and Rose. And there was Dan. And there was Gray. She also had a police force and a Sioux Nation. And Fallston.

The band closed with three encores. The last, *Rockin' to the Rhythm of the Rain*, was a Judds' number they had adapted, and she sucked the oxygen out of the room. When Ro-Bear hammered out the last beat, she did a sharp head-shake forward and locked eyes with a muscle-bound lycanthrope with platinum hair.

Hayden was in the room, off to one side, leaning against a wall, arms folded. She didn't move. Neither did he. The crowd was in an uproar all around them, but the two of them were like islands in the stream. It felt like an eternity before she took a breath, and it was Elliott's touch that made her resuscitate. She turned toward him, trying for normal.

His eyes searched hers and she smiled. Reassured, Elliott turned to pack up their gear, but Julie's eyes returned to the crowd.

Hayden was nowhere to be seen.

En route to Fallston, Elliott and Julie pulled into an all-night diner and ordered breakfast. Neither one of them had eaten anything that evening. The place was peopled with truckers who slurped their coffee in solitude. They looked rough in the fluorescent lighting, but then everyone did.

"I'm hungry enough to eat the business-end out of a skunk," said Elliott.

"Charming," said Julie, laughing. "I'm not quite so sure I could ever be so hungry."

"That saying goes back to the days of my great grandpa. Frontier times. I'm sure those years were rather lean."

She chuckled. Elliott excused himself to go to the men's room. Julie sat there in the vinyl booth toying with her paper placemat. It outlined a map of the United States. Absently, her finger traced the route from Virginia to Maryland, Pennsylvania, Ohio, Indiana, Illinois, Wisconsin, Minnesota and on into South Dakota.

She'd gone from lost to found in approximately 1,500 miles and 18 months.

Human, but daughter of a lycanthrope. She didn't remember her real father, just the beast that took his place. She gave a small shudder. A small part of her was angry with Gray for not having told her sooner, but then again, she had had a hard enough time grappling with his other-worldliness. How could he have expected her to handle her own?

Elliott slid back into the booth. "You okay, Jules? You look like you just lost your best friend."

"Nah," she said with a weak smile. "Just high noon that I acknowledged him. You know something, Elliott? I'm really glad you talked me back into the Copper Pigs."

"That's one of the best and worst things about a small town, Julie. Once you belong, there's no escape."

"No escape?" said Julie, on a sigh. She shook her head slowly. "Somehow that idea is not as scary-sounding as it once was."

Elliott pulled parallel to Julie's car, intending to wait while she turned the motor over. She stepped from the car, thanked him and shut the door. He wound down the window.

"I'll follow you home," he said.

"No need. I promised Gray I'd share a piece of birthday cake tonight."

"It's after midnight, Julie."

"He said he'd be waiting."

"All right, then," he said, with a frown. "I'll walk you up." He parked the car, joined her under the stars and stuck out an elbow. Julie crooked her arm around his. They walked across the parking lot in unison, their footfall in step, laughing quietly about the backstage banter and endless sass that flew between them all when they were not focused on a song.

He deposited her in front of Gray's door and she knocked softly.

"Thanks, Elliott."

He pursed his lips. "He will keep you tonight."

She took a deep and weighted breath, then nodded. "Probably."

"Are you sure about this?"

"Getting pretty close." She hugged Elliott fiercely, pecked him on the cheek and gave him a reassuring nod.

Julie watched him walk back down the empty corridor with a grave feeling of loss. It was impossible to please everyone. She'd go crazy trying. She knew that, yet she felt guilty and sad. The quiet scuff of Elliott's shoes against the carpet was so depressing. She knew he was pulling for Dan. A small part of her also wondered if Elliott was attracted to her himself.

Gray popped the door open and she stood there, rooted to the spot. He assessed her mood silently, then, without a word, he tugged her inside, shut the door and locked it. He attempted to wrap her in his arms, but she sidestepped him.

"Shower first," she said, placing a hand on his bare chest. "T-shirt second. Cake third."

"What's comes fourth?" said Gray. He wrapped his hand around the arm that held him at bay, tugged it to the side and pulled her close.

"We're going to have a serious talk about that."

She spent a good long time in the shower and she ran it hot attempting to wash away a world of worry. When she emerged, her skin was pink and her face was flushed. She wore an extra-large t-shirt and it swamped her petite frame.

She ate a piece of the birthday cake. Gray ate most of the rest of it. She watched him devour her baked good with a soft smile.

"You are packing carbohydrates like an athlete," she observed.

"I'll be on a long-distance run for the next few days," said Gray. "We lycanthropes require lots of calories. Especially the home-baked kind."

Julie snorted. "You are so spoiled."

"And loving every minute of it."

"Gray?" He heard the weight in that one word.

"Ruh roh."

"Don't you dare go Scooby Doo on me," she admonished. "I need some answers. What about all this lycant business?"

Gray shifted in his chair. "I'm not too involved in lycanthrope social mores, Julie. There has only been Lync and me these past few decades. South Dakota is definitely not mainstream and we, as Native Americans, are not the dominant culture. My instruction as to lycanthropy has been rudimentary and elementary at best."

"But you knew the term."

"Yes."

"Do you think that I'm a lycant?"

"Yes."

She sat back in her chair as the weight of that one word settled deep.

"Why?"

"You have a way about you, Julie. How often have I held you without taking advantage?" She went to answer, but he held up a hand. "Sure, it's part self-control, part love and respect, but even still, you are quite a temptation. In essence, you protect yourself with your peaceful vibrations."

She was quiet for a moment and Gray watched her as she toyed with her fork.

"If I left you, if I moved to another place…" She couldn't finish the question, but Gray gave her the answer anyway.

"Another lycanthrope would find you. He would calibrate to your tuning fork."

She nodded. Numb. She felt so numb. "Did I ever have a choice, Gray?"

"The truth?"

"Please."

"No, Julie. You never had a chance. Not from the moment I first set eyes upon you. But I'm a good man. I'm not one to force the issue. I gave you plenty of space and time, enough space and time to court you, woo you, and win you over."

She looked up at him, her face stricken.

"Come here to me, Spud." He opened his arms and she moved to sit on his lap. He wrapped her in his big, strong arms. "Doesn't this feel good?" She nodded into his chest. "Then you have nothing to fear, nothing to worry about. We're right for each other."

Julie sat quiet in his arms breathing in his scent, listening to his muffled heartbeat. She nuzzled his neck and felt him nuzzle hers in return. When she pulled away, she searched his eyes. They were dark and liquid, like molten chocolate.

"Are you going to make love to me tonight?"

"I want to. Yes," he said. "But I want to make sure that you understand what I'm asking of you."

"I'm listening."

"I'm talking about a life-long bond. Once committed to each other in this physical way, we would always belong to each other, Julie, in every regard. If we got married and then divorced, it wouldn't change a thing. I would need you like water."

"You've told me this."

"I haven't told you all of it."

"You might be able to pick up and move on, but I could not," he said. "Oh, I could probably contain myself for most of the month, but when the full moon came, I would track you down. I would find you too tempting to resist and you would be incapable of refusing me. I would ravish you whether you wanted me to or not."

"You said that you could never hurt me," she reminded him.

He tried to explain. "No. I won't. But you might get a bit... er... manhandled in the heat of the moment. He paused and looked at her." And, if you tried to fight me, I would win."

Julie was quiet a moment. "What if you tired of me?"

"I couldn't," he replied simply. "It doesn't work that way." He was staring at her with ancient eyes, sad and lonely. "You could turn into a one-eyed, two-toed, flying, purple people-eater and it wouldn't matter."

"That's true love, Gray."

"It is, Julie."

She felt the intensity of his emotion. She had wanted to wrap her soul around the warmth of that emotion, but his mood was dark.

"Is there more?"

"Most lycanthropes take their mates by force. These days, they call it date rape."

"Ah," she said, with a dry swallow. "And, do the same bonding rules apply?" She couldn't hide the nervous quiver in her voice.

"Yes, they do." He waited a moment as his words sunk in. "That is why most women avoid us in the extreme and they do this without even knowing why. Instinct, I guess. Most of us never share a bed with anyone under any circumstances, ever. Most of us never find willing mates. And, if we do take a mate by force, sooner or later the community usually finds a way to kill us or lock us away in retribution. For these reasons, we lead very solitary lives. That's why these days, we are so few."

"I see. So Lync was jealous of you because of me."

"Yes."

"This is why he found it so funny that I didn't know."

"Yes." He paused. "Outside of me, only he, as a lycanthrope, truly knew how vulnerable you were."

She snorted. "I've always been completely safe."

He smiled at her innocence and kissed her hand. "I have a worry."

"What is it?"

"Knowing what I know of your past, I am afraid that my passion would terrorize you."

She bobbed her head.

"I'm afraid that because of your past trauma, you'd run." He searched her eyes. "Julie, I'd have no choice but to follow. I worry that I'd haunt your dreams each and every month until they locked me away."

"I'm not afraid of you, Gray."

"I've held you, Julie. I've touched you. But, I'm going to be inside you." A lock of hair tumbled forward across his brow and she brushed it back. "And it's not enough for you to accept me," he said meaningfully. "You'd have to accept what I am, because we'd be making more of the same." He stared at her intently and she held his gaze. "How would you feel if I got you pregnant, Julie?"

"Would you want to get me pregnant, Gray?"

"Yes, and I would work very hard at it."

She smiled despite herself, but he didn't smile back.

"Would you welcome that child? Or, would you be repulsed by the thought of it?"

His words stung, and she frowned at the question. There was so much hurt in his voice that she stared at him confused and confounded.

"You need to know how you truly feel about everything."

"Gray, I've been frightened in spots, but repulsed? That's crazy talk. I'm not repulsed by you. Why would I be repulsed by a child you give me?" He pulled her to him and kissed her softly. She leaned into him and deepened the kiss.

He growled softly in her ear, his arms squeezing her just a little tighter. Suddenly, he lifted her and carried her into the bedroom, peeled back the covers and deposited her between the cool sheets.

"Do you trust me, Julie?"

He slipped into bed beside her and pulled her to him.

"I do."

"Do you accept me?"

"Yes."

"There is no going back."

"I understand."

He grabbed the hem of her t-shirt and lifted it to her shoulders then locked eyes with hers once more.

It was a question.

By way of answer, she pulled her arms out of the sleeves. He pulled the shirt up and over her head and she reached up to him, wrapping her arms around his shoulders, pulling him into her embrace. He bent to her in agonizing slowness, his eyes holding hers in silent communion. Then, he closed his eyes and kissed her.

Gone was the soft, tentative butterfly kisses to which she was accustomed. This kiss was hungry and deeply, gut-wrenchingly possessive. He took that kiss from her, wrestled it from her and he delighted in the taking. When he released her lips, there was triumph in his eyes and more. They flickered with fire and smoldered with intent.

"Passion?" she asked nervously.

"Uh huh," he growled.

"I think I like it," she said softly. "Could I have some more?"

33

Gray made love to her again in the pale light of dawn, his touch exquisitely slow and tender, and he cradled her to him when they were finished.

"You belong to me now, Julie."

"I know," she said, rubbing her cheek on his chest. "But, you belong to me too."

"Yes," he said, kissing her forehead. "That, Julie, is also true. When I return from the forest, I'll put a ring on your finger."

"Okay."

"I don't want there to be any misunderstandings between us."

She just looked at him and waited.

"I don't love you," he said softly. "Not in the traditional sense." She cocked her head, not quite sure she heard him correctly, but his eyes were soft and he wore a tender smile, so she listened patiently. "What I feel for you is so much more than that. You are my everything, my world. I will not die for you. No, Julie. I would survive anything to be at your side, to protect you, to keep you safe. My heart will beat as long as yours does. You will never be alone."

A fat tear ran down her cheek and he kissed it away.

"I know that you've been adjusting to the new me." He brushed her cheek and kissed her nose. "I'm so grateful that you could love this man and accept his wolf."

Another tear leaked out, and again, he kissed it away.

"I fell in love with Big Boy first," said Julie in a whisper. "The hard part was allowing myself to accept his big, scary human."

"Ah." He gave her an Eskimo kiss, then drew in a deep lungful of air and hung his head on her shoulder.

"What is it?"

"I want to make love to you again."

"Okay."

His head snapped up quickly.

"Okay?" He searched her eyes. "I'm trying so hard not to overwhelm you."

"Oh, you overwhelm me, Gray. Physically and emotionally. You completely overwhelm me. But, I like to feel your power and your strength. I like it. If you are holding back, there's no need."

He stilled completely, kissed her lips softly, then he took her at her word.

They left his apartment together in the morning light. She drove them to her house where he changed into wolf form and bolted out her kitchen door en route to the forest.

She folded his clothes neatly and tucked them into her bureau.

Her body was tender. She still felt his touch. Everywhere. It was like Gray was still with her in one sense, but without his physical presence, she was bereft. The weekend seemed to last an eternity.

Dan called to say they had finally found out some relevant information from an off-the-cuff remark made from one of Lync's co-workers. The investigating team had been interviewing anyone and everyone in the hopes of tracking Lync down.

"What kind of comment?" asked Julie.

"Turns out Lync was a big *Star Wars* fan," said Dan.

Julie groaned. "The man who answered my AAA call introduced himself as Luke Skywalker."

"I know. You told me." Dan was quiet a moment.

"Do you think the two are one and the same?" Julie asked.

"What do you think?" countered Dan.

"Yeah," said Julie. "When I first met Lync, he looked familiar to me, but I couldn't place him. Perhaps Lync was Luke."

"By the way, DNA results seem to confirm that the same person killed the tow truck driver and both women."

"Ah. So if Lync's a perfect match, you've got a conviction."

"No. I won't be able to convict Lync on DNA evidence," said Dan.

"Why on earth not?" asked Julie.

"The lab results are inconclusive."

"I thought you said that the lab results confirmed—"

"I said that the lab results *seemed* to confirm that the three murders were committed by the same person."

"Why would these results be contested?"

"Because in each instance, the lab has reported animal DNA in the mix."

Julie fell silent.

"Are you there?" asked Dan.

"Yeah," Julie husked.

"Are you all right?"

"Yeah," Julie said again. Her mouth had turned to cotton.

"The lab seemed to find animal DNA in every sample we've sent them lately, even Gray's."

If Dan was testing her, Julie didn't bite.

"Time to change labs, Dan."

"Yeah. In the meantime, as a member of the scientific community, do you have any ideas as to why the results would read as they do? I mean, how do mistakes like that happen?"

She was glad that Dan was not standing in front of her. He would have seen her pale. But, with his innate truth-detecting sonar, he probably had a good enough bead on her already.

"I haven't a clue." She paused. "But, if the mistake is consistent, it is probably due to one individual's error." She squeezed her eyes tightly, hoping she didn't get someone fired. "A new lab technician? Did the same techie perform all tests?"

"Yes. Way ahead of you on that one. Just wanted to see if we tracked in the same direction."

Julie responded with silence.

"I've put both your house and the veterinary office on a frequent police drive-by."

"Thank you, Dan."

"Sleep well, Julie. But please be sure to double-lock your doors."

By Sunday evening, the idea of staying at home alone one more night was well beyond her tolerance level. She was sick from worrying about Gray and Lync out there in the woods, sick from worrying about her safety. She jumped at every noise. Her only saving grace was that each time she looked out the window, there seemed to be a police car cruising on by. It helped her feel a little more secure.

She called Dan on his cell phone and left a message. "Hey, I appreciate all the police protection. Just wanted you to know that I'm off to the movies." She gave him the name of the theater and her estimated time of arrival back home. "Thanks, Dan," she said, hoping he didn't hear the emotion in her voice. "You are a very good cop."

She treated herself to an ice cream cone after the show and drove home with the windows down. Elliott pulled her over for doing 45 in a 30 mph zone.

"Haven't you got better things to do, Elliott?" she groused.

"Nope," he drawled. "You're on everyone's radar as of late."

"So, what are we going to do about this?"

"We are going to escort you safely home and come in for some coffee and cookies or whatever home-baked goodies you care to share."

She squinted her eyes at him suspiciously. "I made a pineapple upside-down cake this morning."

"Sounds wonderful."

"Let's race," said Julie, peevishly.

"Let's not," said Elliott, "Or I'll have to re-confiscate that confiscated car of yours."

"Indian-giver."

Elliott smiled, slow and lazy. "You keep that little pinto pony in a slow trot, hear? And I'll follow you back to the home ranch."

He tailed behind her. Nothing like a police escort. The streets were sleepy and vacant. Most of the houses had minimal lighting. The world was in bed. He pulled into her driveway behind her and killed the engine, the hot tick-tick of the engine filling the quiet night.

"Duty has such perks and bennies," said Elliott, emerging from the car. Julie reached the kitchen door before he did then backed right into his arms.

"Get your gun, Elliott. Do you have your gun?"

He pulled his weapon so quickly that she barely heard it clear leather.

"My kitchen door is open," said Julie, breathy and brittle.

Elliott looked at the door. The door frame was shredded. It looked as if something had simply eaten its way through the panel of wood.

"Elliott?"

"I'm calling for backup," said Elliott "Get back into your car. Lock the doors and stay there until I say so. Okay?"

"Elliott?"

"Get in the goddamned car, Julie."

She did as she was told. Her eyes searched the lawn shadows while she waited, and she listened with honed focus on the shrill pulse of the police sirens as they drew ever closer.

She called Gray on every number she had for him. Land, cell, and work. She left messages. She waited while policemen searched her yard and searched her house. She waited while the crime scene unit arrived and officially categorized the dust motes in her living quarters.

Then Dan showed up, rapped upon her window and walked on by. She was trying to be patient, but she'd had enough. She exited the car, and entered the house. Nothing seemed to have been stolen from what she could see. Everything was in order below. But then everyone was up top. She ascended the stairs to the second level and suddenly Elliott stepped in front of her, blocking her way.

"No, Julie," he said, his face full of worry.

"This is my home," she said, by way of response. "Please, Elliott. I've sat in the car long enough. I want to see what is going on!"

He was not happy about it, but he escorted her into the bedroom. Her eyes found Dan's, then the destruction around him. Her bedroom had been shredded. And not just mattress and stuffing. The furniture had been broken and splintered. The carpet and all her clothing were in tatters. The room was knee-deep in particulates. Someone had turned her bedroom, her private life, into confetti.

Julie made a soft little sound then turned on her heel. Dan snagged her around the waist before she hit the last step on the stairs as she descended.

"Julie," he said, turning her in his arms. "We need to have a very serious conversation about your safety."

She started to shake her head no, but Dan stilled her with a squeeze. "Did you take a look at your kitchen door?"

She wouldn't meet his eyes.

"We'll get to the bottom of this, I promise," he said. "In the interim, we need to keep you safe."

"I am not going to sleep at the station."

"Fine, but how about if you stay with Elliott or myself – myself preferably – while we sort this out?"

"I can't go home with either of you."

"I have a guest bedroom, Julie."

She made a soft sound, part-hum, part grunt. "I'd need a guarantee that I would get to sleep in it. Alone."

"If you want," he said slowly. "Have you called Gray?"

"Yes."

"And?"

"He isn't home."

"You can't reach him?"

"No."

"Then come home with me."

"No."

Both Julie and Dan turned at the sound. Gray muscled his way through the tattered threshold with purpose and urgency. She'd never seen him so commanding. He walked into her home as if he owned it and her as well.

"Are you hurt?" he asked, looking at Julie. His eyes were wild. Julie watched Dan's right hand drop to his gun.

"No," said Julie. "But my bedroom has been vandalized."

"Can I see?" asked Gray, reining in his emotion. He looked to Dan. Dan shook his head. "I don't think that's a good idea."

The two men locked eyes, and Gray drew a slow and deliberate breath, his pupils filling his irises with black. He turned to Julie and the look alone spoke volumes. "You need a place to stay." It wasn't a question, but she nodded anyway.

"What she needs is police protection," said Dan.

"Wrong, Officer Keating. She is mine to protect," said Gray, giving Dan a level stare.

"And since when is that?" asked Dan, his anger rising.

"Since she consented to be my wife."

The only word Dan could say in response was 'Julie' and his voice broke as he called her name.

34

Julie and Gray drove back to his apartment in silence. He reached for her twice, trying to hold her hand, but she pulled free on both occasions.

"We tracked Lync through the surrounding woodlands," said Gray. "He's very good under brush, savvy and clever in a way that belies his years." He sighed. "When I realized that he was tracking back to you, following my own path to your door, I was sick with worry."

"I had gone to the movies."

"Hayden and Finn will track him now. I am staying in town to watch over you."

Julie just shook her head, turned from him and looked out the window.

"Julie." His voice was deep. "You are angry with me."

"Yeah."

"Why?"

"You were brutal with Dan." Her voice choked. "You dropped an atomic bomb on him tonight, and all he was doing was trying to take care of me."

"He had other intentions. I could smell his adrenaline and desire from twenty feet away."

"Desire is not a crime."

"It is if you act on it."

"And who said that he would act on it? What on earth has gotten into you tonight?"

"Tonight? This is more than tonight. Dan fights dirty. He's personally requested that I leave you alone and on more than one occasion. I'm tired of the police harassment and the parking tickets. No, Julie. Tonight, I had to draw a line in the sand."

Julie felt her heart squeeze painfully. She was upset about what Gray had to say about Dan. She was upset with the way Gray had treated him. She folded her hands in her lap and studiously looked out the window trying very hard not to cry.

"I have committed myself to you," she said, her voice breaking with emotion. "And I am well aware of what that commitment means. You don't need to be all Neanderthal about it. In public. With people I care about."

Gray was quiet a moment. He debated whether he should try to justify himself again, but thought better of it. "Okay," he said simply. "I am sorry."

She turned to look at him.

"I am. I will do my best to see that it never happens again."

She continued to stare at him, her breathing heavy and agitated.

"I'm new at this too, Julie. And I haven't had much coaching. Now that we are bound, I'm doing the best that I can with what little I have to go on. My emotions are very strong where you are concerned."

"Well, you just can't be so possessive and territorial about things. We've bonded, right? There's no escape, right? What are you worried about?"

"I don't know, but I have a worry."

"Your first worry was unfounded. You do not terrorize me. What's the new concern? Let me dispel that too."

"That you will be taken from me and that I will be unable to protect you."

"Gray! Please stop! You are doing everything you can to protect me and so is the Fallston police force. If something goes wrong, you will find me. I have no doubt."

"No doubt, Julie?"

"Not a one, Gray. Okay?"

"Do you mean it?"

"Heart and soul."

"You would hang tough until I got there?"

"Of course!"

"I would get there."

"I know. Enough already."

Gray pulled into the parking lot of his condominium complex and Julie opened her door as Gray silenced the engine. She stepped into the night. He was by her side before she even had the car door closed.

They climbed the stairs to the fourth floor in silence. Gray opened his apartment and sniffed the air gingerly. Relieved, he ushered her into his home and bolted the door behind them.

"Bathroom?" he asked.

Julie nodded and moved off to take care of herself. Gray grabbed some candles and illuminated the bedroom in soft, flickering light. He was waiting for her when she entered. His chest and feet were bare. She was wrapped in nothing but a towel.

"No t-shirt for you tonight, Ms. Hastings," he told her. "In fact, I'd like to repossess my towel right now, if that's okay."

Julie unwrapped the terry cloth from her body and handed him the dampened fabric. He took the towel then devoured her naked form with his eyes. When he spoke, his voice was deep. "I want you so badly, it hurts." He swallowed painfully.

Julie took a deep breath and stepped toward him. "I'm not here to cause you pain, Gray. Just the opposite." She reached out and placed a hand upon his shoulder. "I'm the corn maiden, remember? You don't have to worry about taking me. I am already given."

He looked up at her, his eyes dark. "What do you need?" she asked.

"Forgiveness," he breathed.

"Okay." She paused. "But, here's the deal. No more cave man. I don't like it."

He nodded silently.

"I want your solemn promise."

"Promise."

Gray looked up at her quietly then opened his right hand. A black box sat in center of his palm.

"You weren't kidding about the ring, were you?"

"No."

Elliott stopped by the veterinary office at seven the next morning. Julie was just fixing herself a cup of coffee, so she fixed him one also. He squeaked when he moved, all that leather. There were so many attachments to his belt – cell phone, gun, nightstick, cuffs. She shook her head as she handed him a mug.

"You make a lot of noise for seven in the morning," she teased.

He was about to give her a flip rejoinder, but caught sight of the ring on her finger. "You weren't wearing that last night."

"No," she said, suddenly serious.

"Dan is devastated."

"I'm very sorry that Gray told him like that. And I'm very sorry to have hurt Dan. But, Elliott, I've told Dan for months that I wasn't right for him."

"He still had hope."

"I know."

"Why, Julie?"

"Why, what?"

"Why are you marrying Gray?"

"I love him, Elliott."

"But you love Dan, too."

She didn't deny it.

"So why are you marrying Gray?"

The silence stretched long between them. Julie didn't know how to explain. How do you tell someone that Gray was a lycanthrope and she was a lycant? You don't. That she didn't have a choice in the matter? Mostly true, but not the whole truth. That she was going to be a trouble magnet and that Gray was best able to protect her? Not likely to soothe a cop.

"I told you already."

Elliott gave her a sad smile. "Jules, I consider myself your friend. If you don't want to talk about it, just say so, but don't lie to me, okay?"

"I haven't lied, Elliott."

"But you're not telling the whole truth either, are you?"

She shook her head slowly.

"Do you want to talk about it?"

"I don't know where to begin, Elliott. I don't. And, trust me, you wouldn't believe half of it." Her somber face brightened in the pause. Just thinking about explaining her situation to someone made the whole thing seem ridiculous, ludicrous, and fairytale.

"I'll believe anything you tell me, Julie."

She stared at him a while. "Okay," she said. "I'm not sure I'm up to the telling of it just yet. It might take a while."

"Will I get to hear it before the wedding?"

"Probably not."

"Well, then, how can I change things?"

"I'm locked into the wedding, Elliott. Nothing can change that."

"How so?"

"I'm promised."

"Promises are broken all the time."

"Not these kind, Elliott."

"'Break-up', 'separation' and 'divorce' are real words, Julie."

"See. I told you that you wouldn't believe half of it."

The doorbell jingled.

"Time to prep for surgery," she said, standing. "And just for the record, I love you too, Elliott, my most fabulous Copper Pig. But I have a date with Gray Walker down at the courthouse this Friday."

Cole and Rose were seeing a lot of Gray. He dropped Julie off to work each morning and picked her up each evening. He called at lunch. He was hyper-vigilant about her safety even if the police no longer were.

Julie knew that the constant parade of squad cars by her home and the veterinary office was bound to become more and more infrequent. It was a lot of effort to expend for a threat that was becoming less real. It only stood to reason. Lync had not resurfaced.

Still, a small part of her wondered if the Fallston police force had simply washed their hands of her since she had officially become Gray's wife.

They didn't know what she knew.

Hayden had called Gray two weeks back to say that he and Finn had tracked Lync into Canada. Although the two men hadn't caught up with him, Julie took immense relief just in knowing that the man was no longer in the same country as she was. In fact, she took immense relief knowing that all three of them were no longer in the same country as she was.

She was safe, but the Fallston police force didn't know this.

"Everything okay on your end?" asked Cole over morning coffee. Although his tone was casual, his eyes were hard.

"Yes," Julie responded, giving him a firm and confident nod.

"You seem a little off-the-mark lately."

"I'm fine."

"You know, when I first got married, I followed my new wife around the house like a lost puppy. If she got up and left the living room to go into the kitchen, I traipsed after her. If she left the kitchen to go to the laundry room, I would hover in the doorway. She finally told me that I had to give her some private space. But, there for a while, I drove her nuts."

Julie shook her head in sympathy and took a sip of coffee.

"Just so that you know," whispered Cole. "This is what we call 'trading confidences.'" He paused. "It's your turn now."

Julie smiled despite herself and took another sip of coffee. When she set her mug down though, her face was somber. "Petey gave me a parking ticket on Saturday," said Julie, her voice suddenly tight with emotion. "The citation read 'parked too far from the curb'."

Cole took a deep breath and exhaled slowly. "How far were you from the curb?" he asked quietly.

"Six inches."

"Have you spoken to Dan?"

"I've called and left messages. He doesn't return them. I've stopped by the station. He won't see me."

"How about Elliott?"

"I've spoken to him. Tried to explain things. He's okay with me. Just sad. I think his friendship with Dan makes it difficult for him to do more than that. I've heard through the grapevine that the Copper Pigs are auditioning for a new lead singer." Her voice cracked. Then, she couldn't stop the tears. "I feel like I've lost half my heart."

Cole set his cup down and moved around the conference table to give her a fierce hug.

"They are shutting me out. It's like I've died. I'm dead to them."

"Don't say that, Julie," Cole whispered fiercely.

"But it's true. They hate me now."

"Oh, Julie," he whispered. "They are not that small."

"Then why am I such an outcast?"

"This will all work itself out. You'll see," he said. "My wife used to say that men are like bears. When they are wounded, they hide in their caves. She told me that no woman should ever follow a man into his cave, that the best course of action is to wait until they re-emerge. And when they re-emerge, they are usually in much better spirits. You just can't force-feed the healing process."

Julie shook her head. "Bears? I'm still wrestling with tigers!"

"You keep your eye on that tiger, Julie. He thinks you walk on water. The bears will come around."

"It just hurts so much."

"I had thought better of them." He paused and chucked her under the chin with his knuckles. "Half the animals I know behave better than their human counterparts."

Julie nodded in agreement.

"When I was a very young man – and this goes back a ways – I was out camping with my friends." The timbre of his voice locked her eyes to his, and his eyes were full of pain. He leaned heavily against the conference table. "We were doing crazy stuff, rock climbing without any safety equipment, jumping off cliffs into the river without knowing what lay beneath the water. There could have been rocks, trees stumps. Very typical teenage boy stupidity emboldened by bravado and peer pressure."

Cole looked at her and she could see in his mind's eye that he was back there reliving every moment.

"On a dare, I took an aluminum cook pot and a wooden spoon and walked up to a cave in the cliffs and banged on it loudly, shouting 'Anybody home?'" Cole swallowed. "There was." His eyes tightened. "A mountain lion had me on the ground before I had finished speaking. I was spun around and knocked down so forcefully, I broke the tibia in my left leg. My back was mauled. And my friends ran. And the mountain lion chased after them. I didn't find out until almost a week later that neither of them ever made it out of the forest alive." He swallowed the lump in his throat. "I guess I was the lucky one."

Julie respected the silence that fell between them. "How did you get help?" she whispered.

"Help found me," he said, his voice stretched tight with the force of his emotion. "It came in the form of the biggest wolf I'd ever seen. It approached me cautiously, willing me to trust it. I was frozen with fear and unable to move. I really thought that it would tear me apart. I was covered in blood."

Cole shook his head. "It sat beside me and pivoted its head between the cave and the mountain slope. I couldn't hear a thing. But the wolf was listening to my two best friends dying under the claws of a very angry she-lion. You see, she had little ones in the cave."

Cole cleared his throat, choking on the memory then nodded to himself. "They were my friends, you know."

Julie sat quietly. Not interrupting.

"I watched the wolf change. I watched him change into human form. He knew that the she-lion would come back for her young and that I could not move fast enough to escape her. So, he revealed himself to me to save my life. And he was someone I knew. Not a friend. Just an acquaintance. He picked me up and carted me to safety. It took three days hiking and he carried me the whole way."

"At night," said Cole, "he shifted into wolf form to keep me warm. I guess he knew that I wouldn't snuggle up to a naked man," he chuckled. "During the day, we talked. I was in a tremendous amount of pain, but he filled the day with stories." Cole looked at her. "If you don't mind, I'd like to compare stories someday."

Julie nodded silently.

He met her eyes. "Gray saved you on that mountain in the snowstorm, didn't he?"

"Yes," said Julie, her voice cotton-dry, "He smelled me on the wind."

Cole nodded.

"They are so lonely, you know."

"I know." She paused. "Gray gives so much. But he also takes all that I have."

Cole looked up at her in question.

"I'm already pregnant."

Gray showed up at the veterinary office with an edgy nervousness to his normally calm persona. She narrowed her eyes. She didn't have the energy for more movement than that. What she really wanted to do was go home and have a nice nap and a long cry or a nice cry and a long nap. She couldn't decide which.

"What's up?" she asked, suspiciously. "And what did you bring us for lunch? We're hungry." Julie had commandeered the 'royal we' since Gray had commandeered her body.

He laid out two Styrofoam take-away cartons and pushed one in her direction. The heady aroma of grilled meat filled the air.

"Beef brisket," said Gray. "Beef for boys."

"It might be a girl."

"Not if it eats enough beef."

She gave him a look. "Are there French fries?"

"I gave you a double order, extra crispy."

"Then by your rationale, I'll have twin boys who will be speaking French at birth."

"I have absolutely no problem with that." Gray cleared his throat. "I just found out that I have to go away for a youth counselor workshop next week. I was wondering if you would come with me."

"They didn't give you much notice," she said, chomping on a fry.

"I'm substituting for a colleague who broke a leg while cleaning his gutters."

"Huh?"

"He fell off a roof."

"How long is the conference?"

"A workweek plus travel days."

"Ah," said Julie. "On my end, Gray, I do believe that I've used up all my new employee goodwill with baseball, hospital visits and the Making Relatives ceremony. I can't go. I've already missed so much time."

"But I would like for you to go. It's New York City. You can't do that town without a girl. I have a girl now. It's very nice to say that."

"Big-time rain check. I can't. I have a job."

He closed his eyes and nodded. It looked as if the effort cost him the world. "You will just be so terribly lonely without me."

She smiled at his reverse argument. "Yes, I will," she acknowledged with a smile. "But I owe Cole. I seriously owe this man. I have missed so much time this year."

"I understand."

She reached across the table and took his hand. He squeezed back.

"I've always wanted to go to New York," she said. "Can you bring me back that Big Apple?"

"Sure."

"From all that I've read, you'll need to candy-coat it."

"I'll do my best."

Julie worked through her week with focus and intent. She helped Gray pack. She drove him to the airport. She spent her lunch hours reading about motherhood. And each evening, in Gray's absence, she drove to the building site after work to check on the progress of their home.

It was starting to look like a house now. The foundation and basement had gone in over the summer months. The subfloor was down. This week, while Gray was in New York, the workmen were framing out the rooms.

At night, when she called with the latest update, she could hear his frustration across the wire. When she tried to ease his homesickness, he just groused at her. And that was out of character for him. Her eyes had slid to the window. Waxing moon. And Gray was all alone in a big, BIG city.

Not good. Not good at all.

35

It was her turn to lock up. Rose and Cole had left at five. Julie had fed the boarders and tended to the sick and healing as part of her departure routine. Just as she'd grabbed her purse and keys, she heard footfall in the kennel.

It was just like Cole to return for supplies if he got roped in for a house call as a personal favor. And as usual, he was the only one to ever enter from the back.

But she thought he had mentioned something about a card game tonight. She crossed the reception area and pushed open the swing door that led back to the kennel.

"Cole?" she said quietly and stepped into the room.

Her air supply was truncated immediately. In a panic, she flailed against her assailant. He slammed her into the wall, head-on. She pushed backwards trying to reach for the fire alarm, but her eyesight clouded red from a busted eyebrow and she missed the handle. Her attacker wrenched her wrist and flung it through the glass wall of the medicine cabinet, slicing it open. He had rotated her and she used that momentum to continue the turn. She tried to kick him, almost catching him flush in the groin. Almost. He slammed her into the opposing wall, driving two exposed coat hook nails deep into the flesh of her shoulders.

When she screamed, he slapped her hard, splitting her lip against her teeth. The blow stunned her. He choked her next cry by pressing his forearm against her throat, pinning her to the wall.

The room was sprayed with blood. Her blood. Her entire body was screaming even if she could give it voice.

"Do as I say," said a hard voice in her ear. He eased the stranglehold he had upon her and pulled back.

"Lync?" The word sounded foreign to her. She rasped it out as if she'd been in a waterless desert for days on end.

"Do as I say."

He put a zip-tie on her wrists, then half-dragged, half-carried her to his car. Both her body and mind were sluggish and unresponsive. He had, in effect, beaten the fight out of her.

They drove through town and up into the hills to Gray's home site, as the bright, yellow light of an Indian summer faded into the soft golden light of early evening. And they were both a long time silent, Julie assessing the physical wounds to her person, Lync focusing on an exit strategy. His driving slowed, so did her breathing.

She was bleeding all over his seat and car carpet, but she took tremendous satisfaction in that. They'd catch him for sure.

"You are such a fighter, Julie," said Lync. "Gray must find that so exciting." His voice was whiskey soft.

"I've never fought Gray."

"Never?" He snorted.

"Not once."

"That's not normal."

"That is very normal. That's the way it's supposed to be," said Julie.

"Not for us."

"You're wrong, Lync. It can be that way for you, too. Gray courted me. When we made love the first time, it was because I wanted to."

"You wanted him?"

"I did."

"The shoe will be on the other foot tonight," he said tightly.

"Ah. So it's your force of will. Did you force the others too?"

"Yes."

"Why did you kill them? You were bonded to them afterwards. They belonged to you, right?"

"I don't want anyone to have that kind of power over me," he snarled.

"Power over you?" Julie was dumbfounded.

"You can't imagine the pull, the desire, the ache. I don't want that hanging over my head every day of my life."

Julie was speechless.

"Killing simplifies things," said Lync. "It does. It really does."

"Do you intend to kill me too?"

"Naturally."

"Why?" she asked. "I am bonded to Gray."

"You pull me more strongly than any woman I've ever met. You drive me crazy, Julie." He paused and pivoted his head in her direction. "I wasn't after Susan that day on the mountain. I was after you."

"And the other woman?"

"Another convenient distraction," he said grimly. "I was waiting for you."

"Did you kill the AAA driver?"

"I did." Lync chuckled darkly. "I was at the rest stop when he was given orders to go pick up your vehicle. I didn't get you then. Got you now."

Dan was right. He'd been right all along.

"I'm pregnant."

"Changes nothing."

"That's a double murder."

"Am I supposed to care about that at this point? They'll catch me sooner or later, but at least I'll die content." He smiled at her wickedly.

Julie looked at her right wrist. It was badly cut. She lifted it up and extracted a sliver of bloody glass with her teeth and spat it onto the carpet of Lync's SUV. A fresh rivulet of crimson coursed down her hand and between her fingers as she did so. But that wasn't the only serious injury. She could feel the blood trickling down her back, running down her spine. She smelled the sickly, iron-sweet nature of herself as it coursed out of her. And she worried.

"I carry a lycanthrope. I carry one of you, one that I welcome and accept with all of my being." She paused. "Lync... love, sex... doesn't have to be confrontational. It doesn't have to be life or death."

"It is for me."

"But, it doesn't have to be."

He struck out and slapped her. "Don't play shrink. I don't want or need a lecture."

Julie wiped the blood from her lips silently.

He watched her, and an odd silence fell between them. "You are not new to violence are you?"

"Violence is an old poison," she said, "I'm immune."

He grunted, impressed. "I didn't think Gray had it in him."

"He doesn't. My stepfather beat me." She paused. "Gray is the most patient and tender soul I've ever met."

"Gray is a killer."

"He damn near killed you, that's for sure." The fact that she wished that Gray had succeeded went unsaid, but not unheard.

Lync snorted. "I'll get him next time. Third time lucky."

Julie stiffened. "Third time?"

"First go round, I grabbed my hunting rifle and gave him a chest wound."

"You shot Gray? On purpose?"

"I was aiming for the heart and missed. Deflated a lung. He was back on his feet in two days. He's a healthy mother—"

Julie lifted her hands as if to stop his words.

"Fucker. So, yeah," Lync continued, "I heard gut wounds were the most painful. And I wanted to see him suffer. Next time, second time, I caught him flush. He was tracking a lost toddler in the woods. Had found him too. I get points for that, don't you think? I waited until the kid was saved."

Julie turned her head and stared out the window trying to compose herself as Lync pulled up to the construction site. Her unfinished house was backlit by a golden sun. She could smell the pungent tang of raw lumber as it wafted through the air vents.

How on the earth was she going to escape? She had to escape. She had to get away.

Lync got out of the car, shutting the door and walked around to her side. In a flash, she hit the lock button. The click was loud and ominous midst the quiet of the countryside and she watched Lync's face darken with rage. Her stomach tightened into a hard little knot. He held the keys and he fumbled with them, scrabbling at the door in an effort to reach her. Even when his key slid home the door wouldn't open. She held the lock button down. She felt the first flicker of hope wash over her.

How long could she hold out?

He stared at her through the glass, unfocused in his fury, then a slow smile spread over his face. He jiggled his keys at her, then popped the trunk with his toggle. The hatch door released with a sickening whoosh of air.

Wait. Wait. Wait, she told herself. *Wait until he is in the car before making a run for it.* She could individually open one door lock alone, without unlocking all doors. That would gain her a few seconds. She slid into the driver's seat. It was closest to the house.

But, she needed a weapon. Her eyes searched the construction site as she felt the car sag under Lync's weight as he entered the vehicle. Silently, she manually opened her door lock on the driver's door and placed her hand on the handle. She watched Lync advance through the hatchback area, then, as he straddled the back seat, she bolted.

She was surprised that she made it into the house, surprised she didn't hear the heavy footfall of pursuit. Then, with dawning awareness, she understood his game. He was going to hunt her.

The realization forced more tears from her eyes. She was on the first floor of their home. Their wonderful home. It smelled of pine and sawdust. She wiped her cheeks. She found a piece of re-bar and breathed a sigh of relief as her hand gripped the knobby steel rod. It wasn't much, but it was something. Her arms shook and her grip was bloody, but she squeezed that metal for all it was worth.

She walked through the open studs of the dividing walls of her home like a spirit, disembodied and disoriented. The pain overwhelmed her. Then she moved beyond it into a strange kind of numbness. She locked her jaws as her survival instinct kicked in.

Fight. Naturally, she would fight.

She heard the soft click of toenails behind her. He was coming for her as a wolf. She inhaled deeply, once, twice, just trying to still the rapid beating of her heart. She knew how to kill an attacking dog. And she had the appropriate weapon. She hefted the re-bar in her hand.

Lync approached her with his lips drawn back over his canines. Was he was smiling? He was smiling. Her stomach knotted. She acknowledged him with solemn eyes.

He padded though the trail of blood she had left across the plywood, leaving his red footprints across the blond sub-floor. She watched as he finger painted their home with red. And she waited for him to get close. He had to leap. It was then that she'd smash the re-bar into his forelegs and send him to the ground. Then, when he was down, she could crush his skull.

She squeezed the metal rod, rotating it in her palms with nervous energy as he approached. She wasn't a killer, but she'd kill if she had to. She thought of Gray. Those were his words.

They watched each other. Hunter and hunted. Then, they both stiffened when another set of toenails clicked softly across the plywood.

"Gray?" she mouthed, but no sound escaped her. Couldn't be. He wouldn't be back until Saturday.

Lync pivoted quickly, obviously considering the feet behind him more worthy of his attention. She watched her attacker as his black hairs bristled.

A huge white wolf walked into their line of sight. It was not Gray. It was not a wolf she'd seen before. But it was obvious that Lync recognized the animal confronting him, and he wasn't happy about it.

The two wolves circled each other silently, ignoring her completely. Slowly, she backed away. A ladder lay against the outside wall. It was propped against one of the first floor doorjambs. She gripped the rungs as the animals ripped into each other and half-slid, half-fell fifteen feet to the ground below.

Although she had knocked the breath out of herself with the fall, she tore away like the wind. The guttural cries, vicious snarling and horrific snapping of jaws were like liquid mercury upon her tired feet. She flew. She didn't feel the ground beneath her. She flew.

Dan Keating was making the rounds on Friday evening when he noticed Julie's car still parked in the veterinary parking lot. He glanced at his watch. Seven thirty. This was a little odd. Cole and company usually closed up at four p.m. on Fridays.

The part of him that still loved Julie wanted to make sure that she was okay. The cop in him insisted upon it. Either way, with all that had fallen between them, the man in him was uncomfortable about the thought of looking her in the eye.

He parked the squad car and stepped inside. A purse and car keys sat on the reception counter.

"Julie?" he called. His eyes drifted to the floor and he frowned. Blood. "Julie?" he called out again. When he received no answer, he unholstered his gun. He walked to the back, pistol in hand. As he pushed open the swinging door, his foot crunched on glass. The white walls were specked in red, smeared in red, but the room was empty. He stepped back carefully, trying to avoid walking over the trail of blood that led from the back to the reception area.

He followed it quickly, tracking it to the parking lot, tracking it to a spot, mid-gravel where it just disappeared.

He raced to his squad car and called for backup and issued an all points bulletin for Julie Walker, wounded, possible kidnap victim. He sent a squad car to check out her home then had the precinct check in with emergency in the off chance someone had taken her to the hospital.

He called Cole. Then he called Gray.

The big Sioux answered the call gruffly. Obviously, he had caller ID. Dan looked at his watch. No. It was pushing 11 p.m. on the East Coast. Chances were, he had caught the man in bed asleep or falling asleep. For a moment, Dan was at a loss for words.

"Gray, I need to ask you a question, and I need for you to answer it as best you can."

The phone was silent.

"If Lync had Julie, where would he take her?"

"What are you saying?" Gray was on his feet immediately. His voice, loud, panicked and commanding, probably carried throughout all of lower Manhattan.

"I don't think we have a lot of time, Gray," said Dan. "Where would he take her?"

"The mountain," said Gray, his eyes closed. "My building site."

"You need to come back."

"Is she hurt?"

Dan hesitated. "I don't know."

Gray opened his eyes to silence. "You lie to me," he whispered.

"You need to come back," Dan repeated, his voice as neutral as he could make it.

Gray booked himself on the next flight out. He packed within minutes. As he slipped into a waiting taxi, he called Ben Half Moon.

"Julie is in trouble and I'm in New York City. Dan Keating thinks Lync has her."

"I'll gather the men."

"I need you to check out the house she's renting—you know, it's the old Sweeting place. Check out the veterinary office and my building site too."

"Yes."

"If he takes her into hill country, you'll need trackers."

Two hours passed before he got another call. It was from Dan. Gray had just boarded the first leg of his flight when his cell phone chirped. Dan tried to explain the crime scene at the building site. Nothing was making much sense. The only thing that Gray could hold on to – the only thing that sunk in – was that Lync was dead and Julie was nowhere to be found.

36

Julie shot through the forest like an arrow, sure and swift. Her feet pounded the earth in heavy percussion, the briary undergrowth ripping at her ankles until they were red with blood. She didn't feel a thing as the thorns cut her skin. Her adrenaline nulled everything but the desire to escape.

Get away. Get away. Get away. The thought drummed to the rhythm of her heartbeat.

Within minutes, she heard footfall behind her, catching up. Catching up! She sobbed in desperation and ran all the faster. A painful stitch grew on her right side and she held her ribs tightly as she ran, bound as she was by the wrists.

He was behind her. She heard him. He was beside her, the foliage rustled to his footfall. He was in front of her. Of a sudden, she slammed into a huge wall of man who cradled her firmly.

"Stop," he said. "Just stop." He lifted her off the ground and held her immobile. "Lync is dead."

"You." It was all she could manage to say, she could scarcely draw a breath. Hayden loosened his hold, allowing her to pull back from him by a fraction. "You were the white wolf?"

"Me," he said, with a wry tug at the corner of his mouth. She wanted to believe in the smile, but his eyes had a predatory look that unsettled her.

"Could you untie me?"

"I could, but I won't."

"What do you mean?"

"I need some of your time," Hayden said carefully. "We will travel deeper into the Sacred Hills. There are caves there and I have gear stashed away. We can talk. I will tend to your wounds."

They both heard the approaching car. She wheeled about drawing a deep lungful of air, but he was fast and intuitive. A huge hand stifled her scream. His hold was iron and brutally tough. "Do you want me to gag you?" he asked quietly.

She shook her head side to side.

"Then you must cooperate."

He held her at arm's length and gave her an abrupt shake as the car passed. It was moving at a very fast clip.

"We will walk and we will walk quickly. You will go where I tell you and you will be absolutely silent at all times. Do I make myself clear?"

She nodded.

"Don't be stupid, Julie," he said, his eyes fixed on hers. "There is too much at stake for all concerned."

They hiked through the underbrush until the sun's rays grew thin and cool and blue. Finn joined them. He was white and blue-eyed in wolf form with just a hint of copper at the paws. She heard men calling for her at one point. Hayden had given her a stern look when the voices echoed off the hills. She returned his stare, her eyes full of reproach.

She had been breaking tree limbs and scuffing her heels from the outset doing her best to leave signs of their passage. As the sun set, she knew that the search would halt until dawn the next day. Humans, as good as they were at tracking, relied on their eyes. Her chest tightened. She hoped that they would search for her, but after marrying Gray and her wholesale disenfranchisement from the Fallston police force, she wasn't so sure.

Hayden led them to a small stream and bathed her bloody ankles. The cold water stung miserably as he cleaned the cuts and deep lacerations. He retrieved a knapsack from the hollow of a fallen tree trunk, took out a homemade salve and coated the cuts and abrasions, soothing them in an instant. He put a butterfly patch on her split eyebrow and rinsed her face of blood. Again, he applied salve.

"Let me see the wounds on your back," he said.

Despite her protests, Hayden unbuttoned her blouse to the mid-point. She dropped her head against his chest and sobbed. He slid the bloodied cloth from her shoulders and turned her roughly around. Her tears upset him.

He looked at the deep puncture wounds. "Are you up-to-date on tetanus?" he asked.

"Yes."

"Okay," he said, "Then, I'm going to clean the wounds, then pack them with a penicillin salve, but this is going to be quite uncomfortable for you. He took out a pocket knife and cut off a healthy portion of her skirt hem. He folded it into a thick wad. "Bite down on this. The wounds are deep and jagged."

She turned her head when he tried to insert the cloth into her mouth. "Have it your way," he said. He cleaned the first wound as if she were under anesthesia. She fought the pain for as long as she could before releasing one long, gut-wrenching scream of abject agony. Although she fainted, her voice carried down-mountain on a current of cold air.

Dan was refereeing between a cluster of by-the-book cops and group of hostile Indians about who was in charge of the search party when her cry reached them on the wind. It silenced them all and galvanized them into action.

Dan closed his eyes and locked his jaw. "No more discussion," he said. "We go." He pivoted his head to the Sioux Chief. "Ben, leave a tracker here at the house for Gray when he arrives. Knowing Gray, he'll catch up quick enough." Dan turned to the men. "If you see a wolf, shoot it on sight."

When Hayden finished tending to the wounds on her back, he woke her by bathing her face in ice-cold stream water. When she regained her senses, she showed him her right wrist. The wound still bled.

Hayden appraised the gash and lifted his eyes to meet hers. "I will need to cauterize this."

Finn, in wolf form, whined softly.

Julie knew what that meant and could scarcely draw a breath, just short little ones. She was hyperventilating. *Fish symbolize the ability to hide emotion*, she thought, rolling through the fetishes and their meanings. *Fox are adept at camouflage, they walk unnoticed. Frogs bring rain, abundance. They symbolize fertility.*

Hayden built a small fire and she watched as he heated a knife until it was red-hot and glowing. *Moles are protectors of growing crops. They rule the underworld. Moose are headstrong and unstoppable. Mountain lions are resourceful. Mice are masters of detail.*

Hayden approached her holding up the folded piece of skirt fabric and a hot knife. She shuddered, and opened her mouth for the gag.

There was a brief moment of searing, burning pain, followed by a sharp and throbbing ache. She bit down convulsively on the wad of fabric wedged between her teeth. Her pulse seemed to emanate from the very wound itself. Every heartbeat was magnified there. Thum-thum, thum-thum, thum-thum. It throbbed like a drum. Hayden wrapped her wrist, then pulled back.

She was drenched in her own blood, and under his scrutiny, she became acutely aware of her wretched personal state. She reeked of blood, all copper and metallic. She reeked of fear, so acrid and sour, but she also smelled of fight, all tangy and spicy.

Hayden observed her as if she were a zoo animal. She spat out the gag with difficulty. Having no saliva, the fabric clung to her lips and tongue before falling free.

"This is hardly a rescue," she said. "You may be the alpha wolf, but you are no white knight. I can't imagine why anyone would call you leader."

"You are in no position to antagonize, Julie Walker."

She turned her head to watch the white wolf that hovered in the background. She stared at him accusingly. "What part of this lycanthrope culture am I missing, Hayden? Gray tells me that he is, above all things, human. I believe him. You and Finn and Lync are something altogether different." She watched the white wolf flinch at her words, then she turned her eyes to Hayden. "Explain this to me."

Hayden grew uncomfortable. "He knew love."

"Who did?"

"Gray. Despite being forcefully sucked into a lycanthrope union, Gray's mother loved him."

"And your mother?"

"She despised me. I was the product of a rape. Chances are, Lync was too."

"And Finn?"

Her question was greeted with silence.

She frowned. "So you lycanthropes just keep perpetuating the same mistakes, right?"

"We have needs."

"Everybody has needs. Don't even go there. You get as good as you give."

That night, they camped in a cave. Hayden had stashed food, blankets, kindling and logs for a fire in a dark, inner recess. They ate beef jerky and drank bottled water.

Finn served as border patrol.

She was inordinately thirsty. In fact, she was much more thirsty than hungry, but she forced herself to eat. She was dead on her feet and although she was silent, her body just screamed in pain.

She looked at Hayden as she ate. He watched her as well. He was big, like Gray, and just as strong. He was less patient and even more demanding. "What are your intentions?" she asked firmly. The question took every ounce of strength she possessed.

"I haven't decided yet," he said slowly. The intensity of his stare made her drop her eyes. "I would like to know about your courtship," said Hayden. "Every detail."

She told him.

"You slept together platonically?" he asked incredulously.

"Yes."

"Naked?"

"At times. Usually during his full moon moments, he would feel the need to feel me."

Hayden was silent for so long that she finally had to ask, "What is so unusual about that? He was being patient."

He waved away her words as if swatting a gnat. "Gray waited for you to accept him?" he asked, his face non-believing.

"Of course," she replied. "He warned me about the bonding commitment and his demands on me. He wanted to make sure I'd be okay with his overwhelming self. Being a lycanthrope, you must surely know how demanding you all are."

"I took my wife."

"And? How is that working out?"

"She died several years ago."

"Suicide?"

She saw his muscles bunch in readiness. He was going to hit her. Instead, he rolled out a thick blanket and started to bank the fire. "Come here, Julie."

"Absolutely not. I'll freeze to death before I share your blanket. I know all about buffalo robes."

He smiled. "I'm not giving you the freeze-to-death option." They stared at each other. "I will not touch you tonight."

"You won't touch me ever."

"Enough," he said, his voice angry. "Come here."

"No."

Sure. He was banking the coals, but she was on fire. "You can force me. Yes, you can," she said heatedly, "But there is no honor in that. You will betray your friendship to my husband and you will dishonor everything that is sacred in my marriage. I have willingly bonded with your kind. I grappled with this, Hayden. When I said 'yes' to Gray, I knew what I was doing. I chose to bond with Gray, and I choose to carry his child."

Hayden was livid. "So be it," he said. He grabbed her wrists ruthlessly and staked her to the ground against the far wall. "You sleep well. I offer you my warmth. If you choose the cold, that is your choice."

She was never more grateful for a hard, cold unfeeling piece of earth. She welcomed its unyielding surface with a train-wrecked soul. His rough treatment re-opened the cut on her wrist. She laid her cheek upon it and pressed down as hard as she could to staunch the flow of blood.

She fell asleep in a little pool of red.

Hayden roused her early. He frowned when he saw her blood-caked face but quickly put two and two together. He re-dressed the cut, wrapping it more tightly and washed her face. He was silent as he did this. Focused. A muscle jumped sporadically near his jaw line. He didn't apologize, but she hadn't expected him to.

Then, they were on the move again. They walked quickly and with a purpose. She was weak, but she trudged on without complaint, never faltering. She walked by his side, but she looked at her feet or looked away. It was all she possessed by way of passive aggression, tied as she was, and silenced by his command.

At one point, Hayden sent Finn back down-mountain. His job was to distract and defray the attention of those in pursuit. Julie was injured and moved too slowly. The search party would be gaining on them.

"What do you know about wolves?" asked Hayden as they marched.

"What do you want me to know?"

"Have you no respect, woman?"

"Not until it is earned."

Hayden moved so quickly that Julie had scarcely a moment before his hand grabbed her shirt and her feet left the ground.

"The alpha wolf takes any woman he pleases from the pack."

"Gray and I aren't pack."

Hayden snorted. "All lycanthropes belong to me." He shook her roughly then set her back down.

She shuddered under his hostile stare. "You are taking me away? From my husband?"

"Gray, of course, will fight for you," Hayden acknowledged.

Julie nodded dumbly.

"I'll kill him."

She shook her head in defiance. "No. You won't."

"Trust me, Julie. I will. You could save his life by simply accepting me as your mate."

"Trust me, Hayden. When Gray gets through with you, they won't be able to identify you by dental records."

"You think he can defeat me?"

"I know he can."

Hayden chuckled, but his eyes were dark. "You are willing to risk him? You are so sure?" He paused. "What if you are wrong?"

Julie said nothing.

"I'll make you a deal. Sleep with me, and when the battle comes, I promise not to kill him. I'll let him live."

"No."

"No what?"

"No sleeping with you."

He locked eyes with hers. It was a dominance contest. He tried to cow her with his power. He tried to cow her with his might. She held his gaze unblinkingly.

"Have you any idea what it takes to defeat the alpha male?"

Julie's eyes opened wide in surprise. "If there is a way to defeat you, I'll find it," she avowed.

Hayden nodded slowly, sincerely afraid that she just might do that very thing.

Gray arrived at his building site looking more like a natural disaster than a human being. Tom Running Deer sat in wait for him, hunched, worried and frustrated at not being able to lift a hand. Gray stepped from his SUV like a disembodied spirit.

"What do you know, Tom?" asked Gray, his voice tight.

He grimaced and met Gray's gaze full-on. "Someone has taken her, Gray. We don't know who, but she is suffering by his hand. We all heard her scream. There were wolf prints all over your sub-floor in what we assume to be her blood. Dan has issued an order to kill any wolf on sight."

Gray changed on the spot. He just dropped to all fours and went wolf. Tom Running Deer had never seen such a thing, as close as the two of them were.

"The police will shoot any wolf on sight, Gray," Tom repeated. "Dan's orders. And, you will have to run right through them."

Gray growled ferociously in response and bolted for the hills. Dan Keating was the least of his worries.

Hayden snared a pheasant mid-morning and roasted it over an open fire for lunch. Julie ate ravenously, holding her belly with both arms when she had finished, knowing well where the food was going.

Hayden handed her the last drumstick. "Eat," he commanded. Although full, she took it and ate it anyway. She didn't say thank you.

"I will untie you tonight," he said, watching her stiffen with surprise, "If you share my blanket."

"No," she said quietly.

"You are putting undue strain and stress on your body and upon your child."

"We are very strong," she said, hugging her abdomen.

His cheek twitched. "As you wish."

He set a ruthless pace and walked her until dusk. That night, he staked her hands again to the earth. She dug her fingers in and held on tight. She held on for all that she was worth.

The next day, Julie found it hard to get to her feet. Fortunately, Hayden seemed reluctant to start out again. He watched her collect herself, her motions slow and deliberate as she tried to compartmentalize the pain.

"You are tough, Julie Walker."

She just stared at him. "Would Gray have chosen otherwise?"

He turned his head away. "Do you know why I am the alpha male?"

She shook her head to the negative.

"I am the son of a lycanthrope, but my mother was the daughter of a lycanthrope. I possess two lycanthrope genes."

He assessed her silently. "Your true father passed on a lycanthrope gene to you. I smell it in you. Gray found you irresistible, no doubt, and Lync couldn't resist at all. You are a doctor, a healer. Makes sense, no?"

She stared at him blank-faced and he watched her carefully. "You are rather quick to accept what I am telling you." He paused. "Why?"

"Gray told me as much."

He was watching her carefully. "Oh, you trust him, for sure. But, I doubt you would willingly accept such a pronouncement if you didn't have some kind of inkling of your own."

Julie said not a word.

"I want to know," demanded Hayden.

In her mind's eye, Julie was re-living the incident while interning at her local zoo. She struggled to find her voice. "How closely are we linked to true wolves? Do they recognize us by scent?"

He assessed her silently for a moment. We. She'd used the word 'we'. He nodded slowly. "You would never need to fear a wolf in the wild. They always protect our kind."

She nodded absently and looked at her left hand as if it belonged to someone else. "I thought they would rip me to shreds, but they didn't."

"Tell me."

She did. He was quiet a long time after she finished speaking.

"I may be wrong, Julie." She looked at him warily. "Perhaps you have more than one lycanthrope gene in you."

His words unsettled her for a reason she couldn't explain. He approached her and crouched down on his haunches in front of her. She was instantly on her guard.

"I am torn, Julie," he said. "We are a dying race. If you and I were to have children we could strengthen the bloodline."

She shot to her feet. "Listen to me, Hayden. Please." Her chest heaved with her emotion. "Gray told me that most of your kind take their mates by force. What if that was not the case? What if the men were taught from early on to court their mates?"

He listened silently.

"Lycanthropes would start to rebound population-wise with the establishment of healthy relationships. Taught by example."

"Share my blanket tonight."

"I'm pregnant, Hayden."

"I just want to hold you."

"No."

He walked her all day long. Then, once again, come nightfall, he staked her hands into the hard earth. Julie closed her eyes, trying to get comfortable. She failed. A wave of emotion washed over her as she thought of the baby within her.

"Be tough for me, little man," she told him silently and curled into a fetal position. She tried to calm her upset by keeping her mind busy. *Buffalos symbolize endurance. Beavers are builders. Bears symbolize power and strength.*

Her eyes flew open. Bear. She was going to name her son Bear. The rightness of it filled her chest with a warmth that expanded through her whole being. Bear Walker. And he would be strong and he would be powerful. He, too, would possess two lycanthrope genes. She smiled into the darkness. And she was going to raise him right.

Gray could smell her on the forest floor. She smelled of blood and terror, but there was that tangy essence too, faint though it was. She was a sweet and spicy accent to the earthy undertones that filled his nostrils. Ah, she was a survivor. He smelled her fight.

Mine, he thought. He tracked her as a man possessed and his bead was sure and swift.

Too swift.

Finn met him halfway up the mountain slope. Gray could tell from the white wolf's body language that he was uncomfortable with his role as interceptor. It was obvious, eye-to-eye, that they both respected each other. There was no growling, no hostile positioning, no war between them. It was nothing personal. Finn did as Finn was told. Gray could only respond in kind.

They fought like warriors. Finn fought because Hayden commanded it. Gray fought for his mate. They both fought to kill.

Gray's chocolate eyes turned obsidian black as he lunged for Finn's jugular with purpose and intent. The white wolf tried to dodge the attack but failed. He had underestimated Gray, underestimated the power of his devotion.

Gray savaged him ruthlessly. Finn feigned defeat, but Gray only clamped down tighter on his jugular. There would be no games today. Finn, surprised that his ruse had gained him nothing, flailed helplessly, scrabbling the barren soil for a toe hold, for some kind of purchase with which to push back. His paws connected with a boulder and he shoved. He shoved with every ounce of strength within him.

He flipped Gray, then jumped on him to keep him down, but Gray quickly wriggled free. The two of them were up and on their paws as if they had springs and attacked each other with a ferociousness that silenced the entire forest. They were a rolling tangle of white and black fur.

A rifle shot stilled them both.

The next morning, Julie awoke to find Hayden watching her. She bolted upright only to be tugged earthward again by her bindings. She fell heavily, ungracefully. He approached her slowly and unsheathed his knife.

"I will free your hands, if you promise to stay with me without trying to escape."

She nodded.

"Your word?"

"Yes."

He cut the plastic zip-tie that held her with a pocketknife and she cradled her raw wrists to her chest. The synthetic rope was crusted black with dried blood and her lower arms were awash in purple bruises.

"I would like for you to consider a proposal."

She waited.

"If something happens to Gray, you will marry me."

She stiffened and a silence fell between them. "Hayden," she said, her voice flat. "I want to be perfectly clear. If something happens to Gray, I'll kill you myself. I'll hunt you to the ends of this earth. You will never ever be able to sleep again with both eyes closed. Even if it means that I die too, I'll get you. And I'll be sure that you die first."

"Such talk! I could snap your neck right now, Julie Walker."

It was her turn to chuckle. "And I would torment you for the rest of your life."

Hayden paled.

"Gray tells me that I can calm the spirit with the music within me," she paused. "But, it is within my power to wreak havoc as well. I'll make your life a living hell."

"I would rather keep my inner peace," said Hayden cautiously.

"And I," said Julie, "would like to keep my marriage vows."

They marched most of the rest of the day in silence. Hayden was suddenly on his best behavior, as jailors go. He herded her over the rough spots of their forced march with a hand on her elbow. He was attentive to her every need. Water? Bathroom break? Rest pause?

"You would like for me to free you?" said Hayden.

"Of course," she snapped.

"One night. I'm not asking for sex. Give me one night to hold you and I will release you, next morning."

"I'm not giving you anything."

"A kiss, then Julie, one sweet, chaste kiss and I will release you."

She stared into his ice blue eyes. They were like mirrors, so perfect in their reflection. And what was reflected was her heartfelt conviction. For days on end, Hayden had accepted her forceful repetition of 'no' while continuously bargaining for 'yes'. Was that it? To defeat him all she had to do was keep saying 'no'?

"I'm sorry, Hayden, not even a kiss, chaste or no." She paused. "Why don't you act like the leader you are supposed to be and return me to my husband, earning the respect and honor of the lycanthrope and the Sioux nations both? How about showing a little of your mettle as a man instead of preying upon someone weaker than you?"

Hayden's jaw fell slack.

"You were amazed at my relationship with Gray. Lync was amazed at my relationship with Gray." She eyed him with disdain. "Neither one of you get it. Sometimes by giving, you get a lot more back in return. And as for giving, I will give you nothing, Hayden. You haven't earned my trust or my respect. And listen to me good. I am not putting my husband at risk by saying so because he is a better man than you. If there were to be a contest of strength, he's got you beat. To capitulate at this point would be to deny him, and I won't do that. Ever!"

Hayden's nostrils flared. "What has Gray told you?"

"What has Gray told me about what?"

"You know something!"

"I don't know anything about anything anymore." Hot, angry tears leaked from her eyes and cascaded down her cheeks.

Hayden took a deep breath, trying to control his temper. "Gray told you about the rights, didn't he?"

"What rights?" asked Julie, genuinely nonplussed.

"The rights of refusal."

Julie shook her head numbly.

"I am within my rights to choose any woman within my pack."

"I want to hear about the refusal part."

He glared at her. "I could opt to fight your mate in a contest of strength, or I could opt to challenge you, as his woman, in an attempt to win you."

Julie choked on a sob. "You call this," she held up her bruised and bloody wrists, "trying to win me over?" She fairly screeched the question at him and her body quaked with borderline hysteria.

"I didn't say court you, Julie. I'm not talking about seduction."

"Well, what are you talking about then?"

"I am talking about winning."

Julie shook her head stupidly. "Win how?"

"It's a test to see how much a woman trusts the one to whom she's bound. You believe Gray will save you."

"Of course."

"I've tried to get you to bargain for your release. Five times over you've refused me. So, by law, I must let you go if—"

"If what?"

"If Gray has not told you how to defeat me in advance. If he has forewarned you, then you are mine."

"How will you know if I am telling the truth?"

"Your eyes will tell me everything I need to know."

"And what if you willfully disbelieve the truth?"

Hayden released such a deep and angry growl that Julie bolted backwards. He caught her before she had taken the second step.

"Did Gray speak to you about the rights of refusal?"

She met his eyes with every ounce of strength she had left within her.

"He did not."

Hayden released the death grip he had on her wrist. He had reopened the wound. Blood flowed freely again. It pooled in the palm of her hand as she cradled it to her chest.

"Then I am compelled to let you go."

Julie was dumbfounded. "After after all this, you are just going to let me go?"

"Not after all this, Julie." Hayden's hand swept down the mountainside and the trek they had just climbed. "It's because of all this."

She wasn't about to argue with him. He was angry and frustrated. Not a good combination for human or wolf. She looked away, and as she did so, a gentle calm washed over her. It came in the form of a wind that carried her scent down the mountain.

Find me, Gray, she thought, her eyes following the breeze as it moved through the trees and on down the slope. *Find me.*

She stood there a long time, almost frozen in time, her focus so intent that she forgot about Hayden. She didn't realize he was so close until he touched her.

She nearly jumped out of her own skin.

"I had hoped to steal you, Julie." Hayden ran two rough and calloused hands along her upper arms. "I'm not proud of that, especially where Gray is concerned, but you must understand the power of my desire. It's genetic. With your chemistry, I'm like a moth to a flame."

She just stared at him.

"I don't know you Hayden, but I do know Gray. He was very pulled to me also, but he never ever attempted to steal me. In the beginning, I hurt him often with my fear and my distrust." Her voice broke. "He worked patiently to win my love and my loyalty."

"He succeeded."

"Yes. He could have taken my body at any point. Date-rape, as they say. But he would have never won my soul that way."

She looked at him warily. He was distracted, looking skyward.

"The moon will be full tomorrow. I don't think I'll be in a mood for just conversation at that time." She followed his eyes.

"Your bloodline makes you special, Julie. What I want, what I wanted," he corrected, "I wanted for all the right reasons, please understand."

"But that doesn't make it right," she finished.

He gave her a tight nod of acknowledgement.

"You are truly letting me go?"

He saw the disbelief in her face, the uncertainty and nodded again.

"I could carry you off, but I'd never win more than your loathing. That's not what I want… especially now that I know you. Your words have given me much to think about."

A wave of dizziness washed over her. "Hayden, I'm not feeling very well."

The physical demands were taking their toll and the chance of freedom made her positively light-headed.

"If you mean what you say, could we start back? Now?"

"Give me a moment," he said, and walked away. She stared after him in confusion, trying to focus her thoughts. Although the forest was quiet, all she could hear was ringing in her ears.

She nearly jumped a foot when a huge white wolf emerged from the underbrush and trotted toward her. He dipped his head and started to move slowly down the trail they had just climbed. She followed numbly, her footfall heavy and slow.

He returned to her periodically, checking on her progress. When she fell too far behind, he'd find her, tug her to the forest floor, and sit beside her while she rested.

"You know," she said, "you are much nicer as a wolf than as a human being. I don't like you as a man at all."

He whined sadly.

"Truth hurts, huh?"

Hayden lay flat and rested his head on his front paws.

"Gray has always been so protective of me. Both as wolf and man." A tear slid down her dirt-streaked face. She swallowed a sob. "Hayden, you lycanthropes are tough to take. You are so very demanding, but from this mate's perspective, I feel that your needs are less intrusive when I know that the arms that wrestle me to bed are the same ones that hold me warm and safe and sacred."

She struggled to her feet. They assessed each other. "Could you court a woman, Hayden? Do you have it in you? There is strength and power in gentleness."

She started down the path on unsteady legs. They were making good time, she thought, all things considered. It was early afternoon and her return route downhill was considerably faster than the uphill climb had been. She tried to work out the mathematical puzzle as if in grade school. If an airplane left Paris at 3 p.m. traveling at 375 mph and an airplane left New York at 5 p.m. traveling at 425 mph at what point in the 3,000 mile expanse of the Atlantic would they cross? As in grade school, the answer eluded her.

"Hayden?"

She called out for him and was startled at how quickly he appeared by her side. "I've not thanked you for saving me from Lync. Obviously, for a while there, I wasn't quite sure which of you would have been the greater evil." He gave a soft whine and looked away. "I just wanted to say thanks for saving me and also thanks for returning me."

"I'm not exactly sure what I'm going to tell the police about all this," she said thoughtfully. "I certainly can't give them your name." He whipped his head around to look at her. "I could say that Lync was attacked by a wolf. I could tell them that I was rescued by some reclusive mountain man who then decided he liked my company too much to give me up then changed his mind after three days of my non-stop chatter. What do you think? Plausible?"

Hayden shook his head dubiously.

"I'll tell them you called yourself Holden Caulfield. You know, he was that messed-up character in *Catcher in the Rye*?"

Hayden growled softly.

"He was a total loser," she said. "But he gets it together in the end."

The wolf stopped and watched her pass.

"Do you know the story?"

He nipped her derriere as she walked by. It was just a light nibble, but she screamed, long, loud and piercing, releasing days of pent-up fear. The silence afterwards was deafening. She had paled and was rooted to the spot, her heart pounding violently within her chest. Hayden eyed her cautiously.

Before she could breathe a word, they heard voices. Lots of them. At the most, the search party was a quarter mile away. She looked off into the foliage, then back down at the animal at her feet.

"Why don't you go now?" she whispered.

He ran a tight circle and then stopped quickly, his blue eyes dancing. He bolted into the bracken in front of her. She tried to track his frantic rustling, but lost him somewhere midst the trees. He re-emerged on two legs behind her. His sudden presence and his nakedness turned her hands to ice. She screamed again as he closed the gap between them.

"Goodbye, Julie," he said softly. "I just wanted to say goodbye." Then he turned and dropped back into the forest in a whoosh of pine branches.

She stood there a moment dazed and confused, then sunk to the forest floor. She could hear the shouts of the search party as they approached, but she was shaking so violently that she didn't have the strength to call out. Someone would find her.

Someone did.

37

Big Boy emerged from the dark underbrush of the forest like a silent shadow. He was soaked in blood, but it was not his own. Escaping after Finn had been shot had been a narrow thing requiring a long and difficult detour. His muscles screamed and his lungs burned. But, truth be told, he hadn't quit racing since the phone call in New York.

He saw Julie sitting silently midst the pine needles and approached slowly, crouching beside her, nuzzling her hand, begging forgiveness for not being there when she had needed him.

"He didn't touch me," she whispered staring off into the woods, "Though he wanted to. I fought a war of words, Gray. It was my only weapon of strength, but I won." She paused. "You never told me about his entitlement to any female in the pack."

He pulled back, his eyes a jet and lifeless black. He was haunted.

She wiped away a few angry tears. "I know you couldn't tell me certain things, but I could have been better prepared. Your son, Bear, is strong within me, but he is very hungry and totally exhausted."

She kissed his furry head and sagged against him, sobbing brokenly. "He has such fight, our son. Even in the womb, he gave me his strength. You should be proud."

Gray sat up on his haunches and pressed his chest against her, his head over her shoulder. They were neck to neck. Then he made a sound she didn't think a human or wolf was capable of making. It was part wail, part howl, part song.

Hayden listened to the cry from a distance, his heart also in his throat. He lifted his head and howled in response, his ache and loneliness crashing though the forest like a wounded animal.

She rested in the silence that ensued, but the shouts of the searchers were getting closer. "Go or change," she whispered. "I worry about the guns they carry."

Big Boy barked softly and moved away from her. When he returned he was a blood-spattered Gray.

The rangers air-lifted her out of the state park and gave her top-rate emergency care. It must have been the blood. Her clothing was soaked in it. She could see the shock on the faces of the search party when they looked at her. She must have appeared even worse than she felt. When they all started to converge on her and Gray in the clearing, she just closed her eyes and held on to him silently. The horror on their pale faces was too much to bear.

It was Dan who made the call for the chopper. She could hear the tight anxiety in his voice when he spoke. She shuddered and moaned softly, squeezing Gray ever so tightly.

"I won't leave you," said Gray. "I'll be with you the whole time. I won't leave your side."

He didn't.

When she awoke in the hospital bed, Gray sat beside her.

"You know," she said, when her eyes opened. "We've got to stop meeting like this."

Gray placed his chin on the mattress and touched his nose to hers.

"The baby is fine, right?" she asked.

He nodded.

"Good. I've named him."

"Yes."

"I hope you don't take any issues with that. I was staked to the ground in a cave for three days. He's my bear. He's granite tough, I promise you."

"Bear Walker. Done."

"It's a good name."

"Yes." He watched her carefully.

"What?" she asked.

"Do you still want me?"

The shock on her face was real. "And why wouldn't I?"

"Because I've dragged you into a nightmare of epic proportions for one thing."

She shrugged. "My choice, remember? And if I remember correctly, we're already quite committed to each other. And for a lifetime, right?"

"Yes."

"So your point is?"

"You've suffered a lot. I will want to hold you, Julie."

"Gray," she said, reaching toward him. "I hope you would like to do more than that. The moon is full. Get me out of here. Take me home. I'm your wife."

Hospital discharge required a police interview. Lync was dead. Julie herself had been kidnapped and held hostage. Gray was found naked when the search party arrived in the clearing. There were a lot of questions. Dan entered her hospital room somber and concerned. He carried a box of doughnuts and institutional coffee in Styrofoam cups. She smiled at the sight of him. It was an automatic response. Then, she closed her heart and closed her eyes. It hurt to look at him.

"Hey," he said softly to her. Dan nodded curtly in Gray's direction, noticing how tenderly the big Sioux held her hand. Gray's body was as close to the mattress as possible without physically being on it himself.

"I gotta ask you a few questions," Dan said quietly.

"Can Gray stay?" she asked.

"I'm afraid not."

There was a moment of awkward silence before Gray got to his feet and kissed her on the forehead.

Dan slipped into Gray's chair, set the coffee and doughnuts on Julie's meal tray and swung it between the two of them. "Dig in," he said softly. "The sugar will do you a world of good. I understand he didn't feed you much up on that mountain."

Julie just stared at the doughnuts in front of her.

"Petey gave me a parking ticket," she said, giving Dan a hostile stare.

"I apologize for that."

Julie nodded.

"You wouldn't see me or take my calls."

"It was bad of me, I know. But I hurt too much to talk to you, Julie."

"I was never anything but honest with you on all fronts, Dan."

"That's true. My fault for not listening. I'm very sorry," he said. "Sorrier still that you didn't think the force would protect you."

Julie grunted. "And you know this because?"

"Because I've spoken with Cole."

He nudged a doughnut in her direction. "Please."

She tucked into the Krispy Kreme, thinking hard. "I'm not sure I'm comfortable with Cole's breach of confidence."

"You were kidnapped. He was trying to help."

She took a sip of java. "Crappy coffee."

"Cole taught me how to make it." That earned him a smile.

"How are you doing?" he asked, his voice sobering.

"Fair to middling," she responded, staring at her doughnut.

"Can we talk?"

"A little bit."

"I need an official statement."

"I know. I will give you an official statement." It wasn't going to be a lie if she phrased it like that. Official statements are edited truths after all. She took a deep breath.

"Any time you are ready."

"I don't know where to start," she said with a weary sigh.

"What happened Friday afternoon at the veterinary office? You were closing, yes?"

"I was," she said. "I was closing. I got delayed by a walk-in emergency."

She paused and her face clouded.

"I'm sorry, Dan," she said. "What was the question again?"

"What happened at the veterinary office?"

"Ah." She shook her head as if to clear it. "Well, I had a late walk-in patient. When I had finished, I heard a noise in the back room."

"Lync?"

"Uh huh." She frowned, contemplating. "You know, Dan, I did something really, really stupid. I went to investigate." She closed her eyes, then opened them and stared off into space. "Have you ever watched those horror flicks where the buxom blonde comes home, notices a forced entry, flicks the light switch and the house stays dark. What does she do? She goes in anyway. Mind, you are watching this whole scene thinking, 'Run, run!' Does she run? No. Does she die? Of course she does."

"You didn't die."

"No, but I had a very blonde moment."

Dan smiled despite himself.

"He grabbed me from behind." She paused, thinking. "I fought him as best I could, but he was inordinately strong. I know strength. My stepfather used his against me all the time, but this was unreal. He was savagely brutal." A single tear ran down her cheek. She wiped it away brusquely and looked at him full in the face. "The more I struggled, the more violent he became. I thought he was going to rip me apart or break me in two." She swallowed. "I stopped fighting." She swallowed again. "I just stopped. He had my wrists tied in a flash. He half-carried, half-dragged me to his car and he did this so fast my head spun."

"Where did he take you?"

"Directly to Gray's home site."

"Were you conscious? Did he talk to you?"

"Yes and yes," she said. "He told me that he intended to kill me like the other women."

"He admitted to the killings?"

"Yes."

"They were both mauled by a wolf, Julie."

"Yes, his pet wolf."

Dan sat back in his chair.

"His pet wolf was waiting at the building site when we got there."

Dan leaned forward in his chair watching her carefully. There had been wolf tracks across the plywood sub-floor at Gray's home site, but no footprints. Truth be told, there were two sets of wolf tracks across the plywood. Lync's naked body was found in the middle of them. His clothes were found discarded haphazardly on the walkway into the house.

"Did Lync admit to the rapes as well?"

"Yes," she said, her voice catching. "He told me that he had needed to kill them so that he wouldn't be hungry for them anymore."

"Those were his words?"

"I'm paraphrasing. He said... I can't remember what he said, but he felt that he had to kill them afterwards, so he could be free of them. Their pull."

Dan scribbled a little more on his note pad and blew out a lungful of air. He looked up at her with steely eyes. "I remember you telling me of your encounter with Lync on the mountain. You said that you thought he was going to eat you alive."

"Yes."

"What happened at the building site?" She was silent for so long that he didn't think she had heard him ask the question.

"Julie?"

She turned to him absently.

"What happened at the building site?"

She shook her head again as if dispelling something ugly and disquieting. In actuality, she was rehearsing her story, making sure she got it straight in her own mind before verbalizing it. Dan was sharp. She had to be very careful now.

"He kicked his wolf. He kicked it viciously," she said. "I wasn't sure why the animal got the brunt of his ire instead of me, but I was glad it wasn't me."

"The animal accepted the beating?"

"At first," she said, "Then, it started to growl. At Lync. When it attacked, I ran. I ran into the forest. I ran hard, Dan. I ran so hard. But in the woods, I collided with a stranger, a man I've never seen. Come to find out, he had been in the brush when Lync and I had arrived and had watched the whole scene. He told me so."

"Why didn't he help you?"

She lifted her eyes to his meaningfully. "My thoughts exactly. I knew immediately that I wasn't being rescued."

"Who was he, Julie?"

"I have no idea. He called himself Holden Caulfield, as in *Catcher in the Rye*. Do you remember the story?"

"Vaguely. Was he African-American, Caucasian, Native American? How old? How tall? Any discerning features?

"He was... I don't know what he was. He was not Caucasian," she lied. "A young man. Brown eyes, black hair. Wiry build."

"Could you give us a composite sketch?"

"I think so. I could try. He was an itinerant wanderer, I guess. I don't know. Maybe he lived permanently in the Black Hills? I don't know. But he didn't untie me and he didn't release me. He took me deeper into the forest. He had gear tucked away in each of the caves we slept in."

"What were his intentions?"

"I asked him that very question. And he was very non-committal. He said that he wasn't sure. It was obvious that he was grappling with issues. His conscience? Who's to say?"

"I know that you were not assaulted."

She nodded.

"Did he threaten you?"

"Every minute," she said, and shivered. Her hand began to tremble so noticeably that she set her doughnut down. "I had no choice but to cooperate. But I worked on him with my words. I think I made him see reason." She shrugged. "I'm sure I did, because he did release me."

"You were in pretty bad shape when we found you."

"At night, he staked me to the ground. Sometimes, he tended to my wounds, sometimes his rough treatment opened them."

Dan pursed his lips with a frown on his face. "Can we go back to Lync for a moment?"

Julie nodded.

"He was naked when we found him." Dan paused. "It is highly unusual for a man to undress before assaulting a woman."

"Personally, I found that very frightening." She swallowed and remembered Hayden stepping into the clearing right before she was found. The sheer raw manliness of him was deeply unsettling. "Do you remember me telling you about that day on the mountain when I ran into Lync?"

He nodded.

"I didn't think he had assaulted anyone. He was neat as a pin. Obviously, he had undressed before her attack too. Stashed his clothes."

Dan clicked his pen a few times.

"Gray was naked when we found you on the mountain."

"I don't remember that part."

Dan was silent a moment.

He was silent a good, long moment. "Did you know that Cole is my god-father?"

"No." She was genuinely surprised.

He gently placed a dog-eared, battered, and broken-spined book onto the hospital table between them. She knew the cover. A tiger stretched out comfortably within the confines of a lifeboat. She lifted her eyes to meet his.

He knew.

They stared at each other silently. Then, she closed her eyes.

"Cole tells me you met the tiger in the jungle the week you were so upset."

"That was months ago, Dan Keating," she said, her voice flat and dead calm. "It's too late."

"It's never too late. Julie. You have choices."

"Not anymore. I'm locked in, and I am locked in of my own choosing. It's the best for all concerned."

Dan digested that.

"Will Holden Caulfield resurface anytime soon?"

"I don't know."

"Do you think that he might?"

She shrugged. "Hopefully not. I do believe that I convinced him to walk the straight and narrow."

"If he does resurface, do you think that your tiger will be able to handle him?"

"My tiger?" she asked, feigning innocence.

"Gray."

They locked eyes again.

"Gray is not my tiger, Dan," she said, flipping the book over. "Gray is my wolf."

For information about *Touched by the Moon*, the sequel to *Touching the Moon*, check the publisher's website:
www.aakenbaaken.com

CPSIA information can be obtained at www.ICGtesting.com
Printed in the USA
BVOW011307061212

307109BV00010B/3/P